ZOE MAY lives in south-east London and works as a copywriter. Zoe has dreamt of being a novelist since she was a teenager. She moved to London in her early twenties and worked in journalism and copywriting before writing her debut novel, *Perfect Match*. Having experienced the London dating scene first hand, Zoe could not resist writing a novel about dating, since it seems to supply endless amounts of weird and wonderful material! As well as writing, Zoe enjoys going to the theatre, walking her dog, painting and, of course, reading.

Zoe loves to hear from readers, you can contact her on Twitter at: @zoe_writes

Also by Zoe May

Perfect Match
How Not to Date a Prince

When Polly Met Olly

ZOE MAY

ONE PLACE. MANY STORIES

HQ
An imprint of HarperCollins*Publishers* Ltd
1 London Bridge Street
London SE1 9GF

This edition 2019

First published in Great Britain by
HQ, an imprint of HarperCollins*Publishers* Ltd 2019

Copyright © Zoe May 2019

Zoe May asserts the moral right to be
identified as the author of this work.
A catalogue record for this book is
available from the British Library.

ISBN: eBook: 978-0-00-832161-1
Paperback: 978-0-00-833076-7

MIX
Paper from
responsible sources
FSC™ C007454

This book is produced from independently certified FSC™ paper
to ensure responsible forest management.

For more information visit: www.harpercollins.co.uk/green

Typeset by Palimpsest Book Production Ltd, Falkirk, Stirlingshire
Printed and bound in Great Britain by
CPI Group (UK) Ltd, Melksham, SN12 6TR

Chapter 1

Surely, I'm not qualified to be a matchmaker?!

You'd think getting a job at a dating agency might actually require you to have found love, or at least be good at dating, but apparently not. I've been single for three years and I haven't had a date for six months, yet I'm pretty sure I'm nailing this interview.

'So, what kind of message would you send Erica?' Derek asks, handing me a print-out showing a dating profile of a pretty, tanned brunette. Derek is the boss of To the Moon & Back dating agency, although with his nicotine-stained teeth, lurid purple shirt stretching over his giant pot belly and cramped city office, he's not exactly what I imagine when I think of Cupid.

What kind of message *would* I sent Erica? When Derek says 'you', he doesn't mean me, as in Polly Wood. He means me pretending to be 34-year-old bachelor Andy Graham, because that's what my job as a matchmaker would involve. While Andy, and the rest of the busy singletons on the agency's books, are out earning the big bucks, too busy to trawl internet dating sites looking for love, I'll be sitting here with Derek, firing off messages on their behalf in the hope of clinching dates. It's a little morally questionable I suppose, since the women will be chatting to me beforehand, and will no doubt become enamoured with my witty repartee and effortless charm, but to be honest, I haven't really given the moral side of it much thought. According to Derek, it's what all dating agencies do, and anyway, ethics somehow stop being so important when you really need cash.

I try to put myself in the mindset of Andy, while thinking up a message for Erica. I only know about him from reading a form he's supposedly filled in, which Derek gave me to study five minutes earlier. According to the form, Andy is an ex-army officer turned property surveyor. He grew up in a small town in Ohio where his family still reside. His younger brother, aged 31, has already settled down with a wife and three kids, and reading in between the lines, I get the impression that Andy feels he's beginning to lag behind. He works long hours, reads Second World War history books in his spare time, enjoys visiting aviation museums and likes to play tennis at the weekends. Oh, and he has a penchant for Thai food.

I take a look at Erica's profile. She's 32, lives in the Upper East Side and works as a fashion buyer. Her interests are listed as: 'yoga, fine dining, dinner parties (hosting and attending!), dancing, cocktails with the girls, travelling, tennis, and festivals'. Erica sounds cool. She sounds fun. She seems like a girl about town. And to be perfectly honest, she strikes me as a bit too cool for Andy. I can't imagine her wanting to visit aviation museums or discuss Second World War history. But for all I know, Andy could have stunningly handsome looks that somehow make up for his yawn-inducing interests. But from what I do know so far, he and Erica hardly seem like a great match. I glance up at Derek, scanning his face for any sign that this might be a trick question, but he simply looks back, keen with anticipation. He doesn't seem like he's testing me; he clearly thinks Erica is in Andy's league, although as far as I can see, the only thing they have in common is tennis.

'So, what do you think?' Derek presses me.

'Erm, I'd keep the opener light. From Erica's profile, you can tell she's a breezy, happy kind of person. I'd try to mirror that tone,' I tell him, biding time while I attempt to think of a witty opener.

'Good tactic,' Derek agrees with an encouraging nod.

'Thanks,' I reply as I desperately try to come up with an attention-grabbing message. Something that will capture Erica's attention among the deluge of 'hey, how r u? x' type openers she probably receives all the time. But what can I write? What could Andy possibly say that would grab Erica's attention when their only mutual interest is tennis?! Then suddenly, it hits me. I smile to myself.

'I'd probably go with something along the lines of "I'm glad to see you're a tennis player, because I'm going to court you",' I tell Derek.

He snorts with laughter. 'Good one! Cheeky! I think Erica would like that.'

I grin, feeling a flush of pride. 'Thank you.'

'Great line! Very good!' Derek laughs.

'Thanks. I mean, why play singles when you can play doubles?' I add, cringing internally. I think I might be taking the tennis puns too far now. Fortunately, Derek laughs again, clearly not adverse to a good sports-themed chat-up line.

'Indeed!' he says.

A couple of cars honk loudly outside and for a second, I'm taken out of this surreal alternative reality of pretending to be Andy messaging Erica and it hits me that the real me has probably got this job. In fact, I know I have. I'm 99.99 per cent sure. I can tell by the way Derek is regarding me like a proud father. I can tell in the easy, relaxed way we've been chatting the entire interview. We seem to have really hit it off, which is a little disconcerting seeing as I'm, you know, a respectable (okay, at least semi-respectable) person and he's a middle-aged owner of a slightly shady dating agency. Maybe it's because I'm British, having grown up in Cornwall before moving to the States when I was 18. Derek said he used to date a Brit, recounting how they went on holiday to Cornwall one summer. He even described it as 'heavenly'. Or, perhaps we click because we went to the same university. Derek's barely looked at my CV but he glanced at it for a second as I came in and when he saw that I went to Wittingon Liberal Arts College, that was it. He was gone. Even though our degrees were thirty years apart, he was treating me like an old chum, reminiscing about his times at the college bar, where he insisted with a chortle and a wink that he'd had 'many a wild night'.

He went a bit misty-eyed talking about those days, which isn't that surprising really. I only left three years ago and sometimes even I get misty-eyed thinking about it. Probably because everything has gone a bit awry since. I moved to the States for university convinced I'd make it big here, but now I'm beginning to think there's a reason my dad, who grew up in New York, left to marry an English woman and live in Cornwall. Because while my student days were idyllic, it turns out real life in Manhattan is nothing like the dream world of a liberal arts university. The chaotic streets of New York bear no resemblance to the tree-lined pathways of the campus; people in the city don't spend hours having picnics and reading poetry; and a degree in photography, although widely revered among my college peers and considered of utmost importance by my professor, seems to hold little to no currency in the real world. I've found that out the hard way, which is why I'm here, trying to clinch this job, which despite being a bit shady, is surprisingly well paid. Well, by my standards anyway. It pays twice as much as my last job as a barmaid and I'm pretty sure I won't have to wash pint glasses or deal with annoying drunks. Although you never know.

Derek studied an equally impractical course – media studies and communication skills – and from a quick Google search this morning, it doesn't seem like he's managed to put it to much real-world use either, unless he was a very communicative boss in his former career as an adult entertainment company director. Or in his stint as a used car salesman. Yep, it's fair to say that neither of us would quite make the list of our college's star alumni. Despite Derek's questionable background, his latest venture, To the Moon & Back, seems to be doing surprisingly well. The company won Dating Agency of the Year at the prestigious US Dating Awards a few years ago. And it's received a ton of rave reviews online with former clients claiming that thanks to the agency, they finally met the love of their life after years of struggling to find a partner. It was even profiled by *The New Yorker*, which described it as an, 'innovative and ambitious dating service with a friendly personal approach'.

The website of To the Moon & Back is incredibly slick too, which is why I was a little surprised when I rocked up to find that in person it consists of nothing more than a client lounge and a cramped back office. With a central address on Wall Street, I thought it was going to be as swanky as its zip code, but it's tiny. Located at the top floor of a financial advisory firm, it's nothing like the salubrious offices below. The client lounge, which Derek showed me through earlier, is like a kooky cocktail bar, with a huge sofa laden with sparkly cushions and throws, two comfy armchairs, an ornate coffee table, low-hanging gold lamps and sumptuous curtains. Leading on from the lounge is this pokey office, which features Derek's worn-looking old desk, a dated Mac computer, a filing cabinet, a shrivelled pot plant in the corner and an incongruous and oddly distracting waving Chinese cat ornament which sits proudly next to Derek's monitor. Derek told me he's been running the whole operation himself since he launched the business two years ago, but apparently, he now needs extra help looking after his client list of 'successful single bachelors' and fighting off competition from rival agency, Elite Love Match, which Derek claims are 'scum, a bunch of charlatans, the worst dating agency in New York'.

Derek's stomach growls and he reaches into his desk drawer, pulling out a pack of Oreos.

'Fancy a biscuit?' He thrusts the pack towards me.

'Sure!' I reach for one, smiling gratefully.

Derek sips his coffee and takes a bite.

'So...' he ventures through a mouthful of crumbs. 'Where would you suggest taking Erica for a first date?'

'Oh!' I feel my face light up. Now *this* is my forte. I may not be a natural when it comes to love, but I do know New York's fine dining scene inside out.

Not because I frequent such establishments, just because I know them. I read about them. I follow every major food critic in the city on Twitter and I have an encyclopaedic knowledge of Manhattan's high-end dining scene. I suppose it's to me what Second World War history is to Andy Graham. These places represent the glittery side of New York. The side of the people who've made it. The holy grail, if you will. And yes, I'm more likely to order in from Domino's than actually go to such places, but I like knowing that they're there. Just in case.

'How about Zuma?' I suggest. Zuma is a new Japanese fusion restaurant in Midtown. It was opened a couple of months ago by a Michelin star chef and it's been getting rave reviews.

'Interesting, why Zuma?' Derek asks.

'Well, the food's meant to be great, but it's also classy and cool. It's not just your run of the mill bar or café, it's the kind of place you take someone to impress them and I think Erica would feel complimented by the choice. It sets a good standard for a first date. Oh, and it's not far from the Upper East Side so it's convenient for Erica too.'

'Very convenient! Especially if she and Andy hit it off,' Derek adds, raising an eyebrow suggestively.

'Yes,' I laugh awkwardly.

'Zuma is a great choice,' Derek says. 'Have you been?'

'No.' I admit. 'I've just heard about it.'

I'm about to ask Derek if there'll be any opportunities to go to such places within the job role. The online ad mentioned 'networking with clients' and you never know, such networking might take place in fancy bars and restaurants, particularly if the clients are as successful as Derek makes out. But as I open my mouth to speak, a buzzer sounds, a shrill bleep chiming through the office.

'Sorry Polly, I'd better answer that.' Derek gets up and crosses the room.

'Hello?' he answers, pressing the button on the intercom. 'Brandon! Sure, come on up!'

I glance over my shoulder to see Derek buzzing his visitor up.

'Brandon's one of my clients. Great guy,' Derek tells me, with a warm smile. 'He's a super successful lawyer, a real high-flyer but not so successful in the love department.'

'Oh…' I utter regretfully.

'Yeah, well, I'm working on it.' Derek sighs.

'Right.' He claps his hands together. 'I'm going to have to wrap things up I'm afraid,' he says, pulling a face, as if calling time on the interview is going to come as a major blow to me. 'But it's been excellent meeting you, Polly.'

'It's been excellent meeting you too!' I enthuse, a little too brightly.

Derek smiles at me with that broad paternal smile and I smile politely back. I put on my jacket and we head out of the office.

'"I'm going to court you!"' Derek chuckles as he leads me back through the client lounge. 'I think you'd be a natural at this job, you know.'

'Really?' I ask with slight trepidation as we pause at the exit.

'Yes, really.'

Derek reaches over to shake my hand. 'Thanks for coming in. I'll be in touch very soon,' he says, with a conspiratorial wink. A wink that tells me, without a shadow of a doubt, that the job is mine. Any sliver of doubt I had has now been wiped out. It's in the bag and for the first time in my life, I feel both relief and dread at the same time. My dream has always been to be a photographer, not a matchmaker, but money is money.

I pump his hand, thanking him, before heading out the door.

As I walk down the narrow office corridor with its ugly hexagon-printed carpet, I try to imagine pacing down it daily. Every morning and every evening. On my way to and from that tiny office with Derek and his waving Chinese cat. Could this be my domain? My new life? My new routine? Could I look at this ugly hexagon pattern every day? This building and this job are hardly where I imagined I'd end up.

'Excuse me.' A male voice interrupts my thoughts and I look up to see a man, an incredibly handsome man, who must be in his early thirties. He's tall, with dark hair and striking blueish green eyes.

'Sorry!' I move out of the way to let him pass. He's wearing a smart grey suit and carrying a briefcase; he looks every inch the corporate city worker. He must be here to visit the financial advisory firm downstairs. 'Umm, that's To the Moon & Back,' I inform him, gesturing down the hallway. 'You know, the dating agency.'

'Yes.' The man smiles. 'I know…' He eyes me with a bemused look. Then suddenly, it dawns on me.

'Oh! Are you Brandon?' I ask, fully expecting him to say no. He is definitely not how I imagined Brandon. Or any other of To the Moon & Back's clients, for that matter. In fact, when I pictured them, I envisioned different incarnations of Derek: balding, overweight and middle aged.

'Yes… and you are?'

Yes? I try not to gawp. Brandon?! How is this guy Brandon? How is he single?

'I'm Polly. Polly Wood. I just had a job interview with Derek,' I tell him, with an awkward laugh.

'Right. Nice to meet you, Polly,' he says, with that bemused, sparkly-eyed look.

'Nice to meet you too!' I reply.

He smiles, causing the skin around his eyes to crinkle and dimples to appear in his cheeks. He has the most perfect smile. In fact, everything about him is perfect. He's around six-foot tall but not too towering. He's slim and lean-looking, and even though he's wearing a suit, I can tell he's muscular without having the ripped build of a gym addict. He looks clean-cut with his corporate suit and short brown hair, but he doesn't look boring. His eyes tell you that there's more going on and a light dusting of stubble along his jawline makes him look sexy rather than slick.

'Well, good luck! I hope you get it,' he says, and for a second, our eyes lock and a charge of intensity passes between us.

He hopes I get the job? So he can see me again? I can't quite figure out whether he's just being polite and glib or if he actually wants me to get the job so that our paths might cross. Because I, for one, would definitely like that.

'Brandon!' Derek bursts through the door, arms outstretched as though greeting an old friend.

'Derek!' Brandon turns towards him with equal enthusiasm.

'See you around, Polly,' he says, smiling over his shoulder before heading down the corridor.

'See you,' I echo as I walk away.

Chapter 2

The first thing I see when I arrive home is my flatmate with what appears to be a giant spider stuck to his cheek. He plucks at one of the legs before letting out a shrill scream.

'Ouch!'

'Gabe! What are you doing?' I close the front door and cross the flat to where he's standing peering at his reflection in the mantlepiece mirror. A garland of fairly lights is strung around it, illuminating his face, and as I get closer, I realise that what I thought was a spider is in fact a humungous false eyelash that Gabriel appears to have glued to his cheek.

'Oh my God,' he groans. 'I got these cheap lashes, ninety-nine cents a pair. Total bargain! But now I see why. These things come with industrial glue. My finger slipped at I tried to apply the damn thing. It fell on my cheek and now it won't come off!' Gabe yanks at the lash, causing his skin to pull. 'Ouch!' He winces in pain.

'Stop pulling it!'

'But it won't come off!' he whines. 'I can't go to work like this. I'm freaking out!'

'Honestly!' I tut, hanging my jacket by the door, before walking over.

Gabe looks me up and down. 'Why are you dressed like a secretary?'

I glance down at my outfit. I donned a black shift dress and a suit jacket that have been gathering dust at the back of my wardrobe for my interview at To the Moon & Back. It's not exactly my usual attire.

'I had a job interview,' I tell him. Derek only invited me for an interview a few days ago and mine and Gabriel's paths haven't crossed since. He works for a HR firm in the city and often stays over at his boyfriend's place, which is closer to his office.

'A job interview?' Gabe raises an eyebrow and scans my outfit once more. 'For a proper job?'

'Umm… kind of.'

'Kind of?' Gabe tugs at the eyelash stuck to his cheek and winces.

'Yeah.' I reach across and gently pull the eyelash, but it won't budge. It's well and truly stuck. 'Wait, I've got an idea.'

I head to my bedroom to retrieve some nail varnish remover that's hopefully strong enough to cut through the glue. Gabe doesn't normally wear false lashes, but on Friday night's it's part of his work uniform. While he spends most of the week in his office job, he unleashes on Friday nights, going from Gabriel, HR consultant, to Gabriella, drag queen. Gabe performs at The Eagle, a gay bar downtown. I think it's how he lets off steam – he shakes off his corporate shackles by swapping fusty suits for over-the-top dresses, trading boring meetings for belting out pop songs. Gabe always says he's going to quit, but I can't see him doing so any time soon. He loves The Eagle, even if he doesn't want to admit it. No one really wants to admit they love The Eagle. It's most definitely not the place to be seen with its sticky floors, fluorescent lights, and over-the-top camp entertainment. And yet even though people don't exactly brag about going there, it's always packed and everyone seems to have a good time.

It's actually where Gabe and I first met. I used to work behind the bar. As far as bar jobs go, it was a good one to have since most of the guys were fun as opposed to sleazy. Gabe used to perform there nearly every night, back when he was trying to make it as a singer. We instantly clicked over our mutual love of Blondie, Madonna, Amaretto sours and purple eyeshadow, as well as having both moved from small towns to the city in pursuit of our dreams. Gabe wanted to be the new Prince, while I wanted to be the next Mario Testino, even though we were just working in a crummy gay bar. We decided to abandon the crappy house shares we'd been living in and get a flat together. That was a couple of years ago now. After a while, Gabe quit singing there every night and got a job in HR, while I stuck to bar work, trying to get photography jobs on the side. I had a stroke of luck a few months ago when I managed to clinch a freelance job with a marketing agency which involved taking staff photos for the company website. It paid so well that I decided to chuck in my bar job and try to make it as a full-time photographer. Except I think I had beginner's luck, because ever since, work's dried up. I've emailed my portfolio to hundreds of companies, but no one's been interested, and I've been struggling to find work that pays a living wage. My money's running out, which is why I ended up trawling through job adverts online, looking for a regular job. My mum keeps telling me I should come back home to Cornwall. She works as a receptionist at the local GP and apparently, there's a job opening at a nearby surgery, but I can't face moving back home, with my tail between my legs, to take a job my mum's sorted out for me, even if it is sweet of her to suggest it. It's too much like failing.

Unlike me, Gabe's been doing well for himself. In fact, with his HR job, he could probably afford a slightly better flat than the grotty two bed we share in Brooklyn, but he sticks around. We get on well and I think he prefers to spend his extra money on nice clothes and good nights out rather than rent. I find my nail varnish remover on top of my chest of drawers, grab a bag of cotton wool pads and head back to Gabe, who is still peering into the mirror while tugging at the eyelash.

'You're making it worse!' I tell him, observing the red patch that's appeared on his skin. He pulls a glum face as I wet the cotton wool and begin dabbing at his cheek.

'Be gentle!' he insists, eyeing the bottle of nail varnish remover with caution. 'Christ, do you think that's going to work? I don't think that stuff's meant to go near your eyes.' He squirms.

'Then stay still!'

'Fine!' He sighs, squeezing his eyes closed as I dab the cotton wool against the giant eyelash in an attempt to dissolve the glue.

'So, tell me about this job then,' Gabe says.

I fill him in on the job interview, describing Derek and the strange set-up at To the Moon & Back while I remove the eyelash. As I recount the interview, I realise I've hardly been thinking about it at all. The interview itself has been totally eclipsed in my mind by meeting Brandon in the hallway. I can still feel the excitement of how he made me feel – the frisson of attraction I felt when looking into his gorgeous aquamarine eyes. I still can't get my head around how someone like him would need a dating agency. He intrigues me more than the job, but I don't bother mentioning him to Gabe. At least not for now. I fill him in on my conversation with Derek instead.

'Ha, got it!' I declare eventually, pulling the eyelash free.

'You did it!' Gabe grins, reaching up to touch his cheek. 'Thanks babe!'

'No worries!

Gabe grabs a wet wipe from the pack on the coffee table and dabs at the red patch on his cheek as I settle down on the sofa. 'So, you… A matchmaker?'

'Yep!' I reply brightly. Gabe, of all people, knows how woefully unqualified I am for this job.

'But don't you have to have, like, good dating skills?' Gabe asks, raising an eyebrow.

'I have good dating skills!' I huff. I may not have been on a date for a while, but that's not because I'm bad at dating. I can date. I may not be in a relationship, but I can date just fine! I simply took a break from dating to concentrate on my photography work – clearly that hasn't worked out so well.

'You haven't been on a date for *ages*,' Gabe reminds me.

'I'm aware of that, thanks! I've had other stuff to do. Anyway, my job isn't to get myself dates, it's to arrange dates for other people. They might be infinitely cooler than me, it could be easy!'

'Oh yeah.' Gabe nods. 'Good point.'

I poke him, laughing. I think back to Andy Graham. Okay, maybe he isn't infinitely cooler than me, but I can't imagine it would be much of a challenge to get someone like Brandon a date. I think back to his gorgeous smile; no, it definitely wouldn't be difficult.

Gabe peers into a handheld mirror and dabs a concealer stick over the red patch on his skin. I reach for a glass of Coke with ice that he's left on the coffee table and take a sip. It's laced with vodka.

'So, you'll just be messaging poor unsuspecting single people all day, trying to charm them on behalf of the agency's clients?' Gabe asks.

'Exactly.' I nod.

'So basically, you just have to be really good at making conversation?'

'Yeah, I guess!'

'Hmm...' Gabe muses. 'Remember that guy you fancied – you know, that hot Greek guy, Darius or something, that we met in Soho. The one with all the necklaces...'

'Demetrius,' I correct him, thinking back to the man in question – an extremely sexy, tall, dark guy I met while sipping a mojito at a street party last summer. He was wearing a ton of hippy necklaces and had that cool, boho, traveller look.

'Yeah, him. Didn't you send him a peach and aubergine emoji with a question mark and a winky face when you were drunk?'

'Shut up!' I hiss, feeling a fresh flush of shame even though it was months ago. Demetrius and I struck up a great conversation in person, but then I ruined it a few days later with my appalling texts. Naturally, I never heard from him again.

'Trust you to remember that,' I grumble, taking another sip of the drink before placing the glass back down.

'As if I'd forget. That was classic.' Gabe laughs as he powders over the concealer on his cheek.

'Hmmph.'

'What about that guy you called Mike for four dates then it turned out his name was Matt,' Gabe sniggers.

'That was his fault! He should have corrected me!' I insist, recalling the man in question: an overly polite British guy who sheepishly admitted on our fourth or fifth date that his name was, in fact, Matt. I'd even cried out 'Mike' in bed by that point. I shudder at the memory.

'That was brilliant.' Gabe sighs. 'Oh, and remember that guy you saw in the hall who asked if you needed someone to "service your pipes" and you thought it was an innuendo.' Gabe chuckles.

I roll my eyes, recalling the cringe-worthy incident in question. It may have been years ago, but I'm still mortified by the memory. A few days after Gabe and I first moved into our flat, this really attractive guy started talking to me in the hallway. When he asked if I needed anyone to 'service my pipes', I thought he was just being really flirty and forward. I didn't realise that he was literally a plumber. It was only when we were in the flat and I was offering him a glass of wine, and he pulled out a toolbox from his bag that I realised that he really did want to service my pipes. I tried to style it out and ended up with a $150 bill for pipe servicing. Literal pipe servicing, that is. The incident was so embarrassing that two years later, I still scan the hallway every day before I leave the flat just to check he's not there.

Gabe giggles at the memory as he begins applying winged eyeliner.

'Okay, I think we've established that dating chat isn't quite my forte,' I admit. 'But for your information, I'm pretty sure I got the job, so there!'

'Seriously?' Gabe scoffs.

'Yeah!' I tell him about the way Derek responded to me in the interview while Gabe perfects his eyeliner flicks. 'Honestly, I think the job's in the bag!'

I expect Gabe to be happy for me, but he seems a bit off. He screws his eyeliner closed and places it back in his make-up bag. 'Don't you think the job's a bit…' He pauses, searching for the right word. 'Wrong?'

'Wrong?' I echo.

'Yeah.' Gabe shrugs as he rummages in his make-up bag again, before pulling out a lipstick. 'Don't you think it's a bit messed up? To message women pretending to be someone else? What if they start to like your banter? What if they like cheeky emojis or being called Delia instead of Diana?!' Gabe jokes.

'Ha! I don't think it's a big deal. It's just messaging, right? Everyone seems different over messages to how they are in real life. They probably won't even notice.'

'I don't know,' Gabe muses as he pulls off the lid of his chosen lipstick – a bright pink shade he used to wear all the time called Back to the Fuchsia. 'I think I might feel a bit cheated if I'd been talking to someone for a while and it turned out they'd just hired someone to write their messages.'

'Well, it's not like I'm going to message them about their deepest darkest secrets, I'm just setting up a date,' I insist.

'I suppose,' Gabe reasons as he applies the lipstick, but I can tell he's not on board.

'Look, I need the money,' I remind him. Gabe knows better than anyone how much I've been struggling lately. I've been living off horrible ready meals and barely going out thanks to the crummy pay of my intermittent freelance photography jobs. I even had to borrow a hundred dollars from him to cover last month's rent.

'I guess,' Gabe says. 'But can't you get a different job? Like a normal office job. Admin or something?'

'Admin?'

'Yeah.'

'You need qualifications for those jobs. Or experience,' I point out. I've seen ads for admin jobs online and even the dullest-sounding positions still require a degree, a secretarial qualification or relevant experience.

'Hmm… you have qualifications though,' Gabe says, a little hesitantly.

'I have a photography degree, Gabe. They don't want arts degrees. Trust me, I applied to a few and heard nothing,' I tell him. After all, it's not like getting a job as a matchmaker for To the Moon & Back was my first choice of role.

'Well, it just seems a bit morally dubious, that's all.' Gabe perfects his pout, before popping the lipstick back into his make-up bag.

'Well, no job is perfect, is it?'

'I suppose.' Gabe sighs. 'So are you going to take the job then?'

'I don't know.' I shrug. 'I haven't officially been offered it yet. But I probably would take it. It's not like I have any other options right now.'

'Hmm…' Gabe murmurs. 'Well, why don't you come out tonight? Have a night out, let your hair down, and then sleep on it. You might feel totally differently in the morning.'

It's clear that Gabe really doesn't want me to take the job. He isn't a fan of online dating. He met his boyfriend Adam in the coffee shop near his office. He's all about real life over online. Perhaps it's because one of his friends got catfished once; he sent the guy nudes and then found them on some creepy website.

'I shouldn't… I don't have any money,' I say.

'Come on.' Gabe shoots me a look. 'You know you're going to get free drinks at The Eagle.'

'I guess,' I murmur. That's another great thing about The Eagle. Since I used to work there, I always get free drinks from my old work mates whenever I go. I should probably just have a quiet night, stay home and consider my options. I even agreed to take on an unpaid freelance job tomorrow for an Instagrammer who's releasing a cookbook and I'm meant to be at her flat bright and early in the morning to photograph the recipes. But a night out at The Eagle is kind of tempting. It would be fun to just dance and let my hair down, especially after all the job-hunting I've been doing over the past few weeks.

'Come on! We'll have fun!' Gabe insists brightly.

'Okay, fine!' I relent, reaching for the vodka and Coke.

Chapter 3

When I set out to be a photographer, I didn't think I'd end up photographing turnips, yet here I am, in a swanky kitchen in Chelsea taking what feels like the one-hundred-and-seventy-fifth shot of a turnip resting on a bed of wilted spinach, pomero and chopped dates.

'Darling!' Alicia Carter, famous health food Instagrammer, bursts through the doorway carrying another bowl of salad. She places it down on the table. 'This is one of my favourites. Absolutely delicious!'

'Great!' I insist weakly, eyeing the latest salad bowl. I could really do with some toast and a cup of coffee. After a late night at The Eagle, that's precisely what the doctor ordered – not another bowl of salad to photograph.

'Can you make sure it's in sharp focus? Try to capture the colours,' Alicia advises me.

'Yep, definitely!' I insist. 'Just need five more minutes on this one.' I glance towards the turnip.

'No problem! Take your time!' Alicia says, clapping her hands together before turning on her heel.

She's preparing the salads in the kitchen next door with all her cool, health-conscious friends. All morning, I've been overhearing them discussing the importance of balancing macro and micro nutrients and debating the merits of hot yoga versus hatha. They're all tanned, athletic and glowing and not one of them has even acknowledged me. I'm clearly not worthy of attention, like the cleaner who's minding her own business as she dusts and tidies the house. I know it probably shouldn't bother me, but it does. Manners go a long way, particularly when you're not even being paid. I agreed to take on this job photographing recipes for Alicia's new cookbook, because I thought it might open doors. After all, Alicia does have nearly a million followers on Instagram and her cookbook, based solely on raw vegan recipes that aim to help readers 'rediscover the fruits of the earth and enjoy an invigorating plant-based diet', is probably going to be huge. But then, as Gabe reminded me this morning, while I lugged my camera, tripod, lights and screens out of the flat, that's what I said about my last job when I got paid peanuts for taking wedding photos for an actress who promised me she'd put me in touch with all her friends. She didn't. It was a similar story with the job before that. I keep hoping that one of these jobs is going to kickstart my career, but it doesn't seem to be working out like that. I've just been lumbering from one rubbish job to the next. I peer down my lens at the salad, adjusting the focus until it's in perfect definition.

Having taken a dozen or so pictures, I scroll through the images on the back of my camera. They're okay, but there's still too much shadow on the left-hand side of this goddamn turnip. I adjust the bowl and take five or six more pictures until I get one I like. I examine the picture. The turnip glistens, its purple to beige skin capturing the light, almost glowing. If a turnip could be described as beautiful, then this is one beautiful turnip. I smile, feeling a twinge of professional pride. And then a second later, I kick myself. A swell of pride over taking a good picture of a frigging turnip?! Oh, come on. The day I start revelling in taking pictures of vegetables for pretentious cookbooks is the day I declare my true photography dreams officially over. I always imagined I'd be some cool portrait photographer, taking pictures of singers, artists, filmmakers and intellectuals, the movers and shakers of my generation, not vegetables! I like to get an intimate rapport with my subjects, getting to know them, so that they don't just look beautiful and striking in shots, but unmasked too. Like when Mario Testino shot Kate Moss or when Sam Shaw shot Marylin Monroe. They don't just look stunning in the photographs, they look vulnerable, off-guard and real. But here I am, taking intimate off-guard shots of a turnip instead.

'Polly!' Alicia bursts back into the room, looking flustered. 'I'm so sorry, but I completely forgot about the pumpkin seeds.' She reaches into a bag of seeds she's holding and scatters some over the salad.

'Can you take a few more pics? With seeds.'

'Okay.'

'Yeah, it's just this one, the last and about half a dozen more. I'll bring them back out from the kitchen,' she says.

'Half a dozen more?' I gawp. I don't think she has any idea how long it took to capture each salad at just the right angle with just the right focus and light. I have almost two hundred pictures on my camera for those half a dozen salads, and now I need to take them all again, with bloody pumpkin seeds?!

'Is that okay?' Alicia asks brightly as she scatters a few more seeds over the turnip.

'Yes, of course!' I insist, trying hard to conceal my frustration.

'Fab! I'll go and get them

I let out a sigh once she's left the room. All of my efforts for the past hour have been reduced to nothing because of the stupid pumpkin seeds. I want to go home, but now I'm going to be stuck here, taking more photos of salads. *Think of the credit*, I tell myself. Having my name in Alicia's book is going to be great. Surely, I'll get more jobs. Better jobs. Paid jobs. I pick up my camera and start snapping away.

Alicia starts bringing in the salads, placing them on a table nearby. I take a few more shots of the turnip salad, before swapping it for the bowl of chopped fennel, cucumber, radishes and lettuce that Alicia's placed on the table.

'Try to get a shot of that one quickly, the lettuce is going to go limp any second. I can tell.' Alicia eyes it warily.

'Will do.' I position it in front of the lights. Alicia scatters some pumpkin seeds over it and I snap away.

Alicia brings in a few more salads as I try to get the perfect shot.

'Polly, hun...' Alicia says.

'Yep?'

'We're just heading to Diabolos,' she says. Diabolo's?! Diabolo's is the coolest restaurant in New York and I can't believe Alicia's going there. She's cool and everything but this is Diabolo's! It's the place to be seen. It's A-list central.

'Oh, nice!' I look up from behind my camera, to see her placing two more bowls of salad on the nearby table.

Alicia flaps her hand anxiously towards the salad. 'Get a good shot. That lettuce is going to turn. Bad batch! Trust me.'

'Of course, will do.' I look back down the lens and snap away.

'So... are you coming?' Alicia asks.

The salad is in perfect focus and I take a few more pictures, not wanting to ruin the shot. But my ears have pricked up. Am I coming?! Just when I thought I was having a terrible day, it's about to get a hundred times better! Even though this job has been frustrating and unpaid, Alicia's making it up to me by taking me out for dinner at Diabolo's! No wonder her friends haven't acknowledged me all day. They've just been busy preparing the salads, and they probably knew they'd have a chance to get to know me over dinner. Am I coming? Of course I'm coming!

'I'd love to!' I pull away from my camera, confident I've got the shot I need, a massive grin on my face, only to see Alicia and one of her friends looking back at me, confused.

'Oh…' Alicia grimaces. 'Sorry Polly, I was just talking to Seb.'

Seb, a skinny guy with a mound of dreadlocks piled on top of his head, smiles awkwardly.

'Of course! Haha, sorry!' I feel my cheeks burn crimson. How embarrassing. How completely embarrassing.

'We would invite you, but we booked a table months ago. It's so hard to get bookings there!' Alicia rolls her eyes. 'And you're coming, aren't you, Seb?'

'Well, I was going to, but it's cool, Polly can go in my place,' Seb suggests.

Alicia frowns and casts him a sideways look but he just smiles encouragingly. I think he means well, but as if I'm going to be a tag-along like that!

'No, it's okay! Sorry, I just overheard you and err, you know…'

'Don't worry about it!' Alicia insists. 'Look, we have to run, but you'll be okay here, won't you?'

I glance over the salads. There are still five left to photograph. 'You're leaving now?'

'Yes! Our table's booked for lunch and we have to get across town. Don't want to be late.'

Seb winces, smiling apologetically.

'Of course not!'

'So, shall I just let myself out when I'm done?' I ask.

'Yes! Martina will clear everything up.' Alicia glances towards the cleaner, who is busy rearranging some books on the coffee table. She smiles over politely. 'She'll let you out. Oh, and feel free to tuck into the salads after you're done, if you want?' Alicia suggests.

I look down at the lettuce, which is beginning to wilt, going brown at the edges, as predicted.

'Great, thanks!' I enthuse.

'Thanks so much, Polly.' Alicia comes over and envelops me in a hug. 'Can't wait to see the pics!' she adds, before bouncing out of the room. Seb follows, giving me a limp wave.

I wave back and let out a sigh the second they're out of earshot. 'Idiot, absolute idiot,' I curse myself.

'Don't worry about it,' Martina says, giving me a sympathetic smile. 'One of my clients went to that restaurant last week. Apparently, it's completely overrated.'

'Really?'

'Yeah. You're not missing out on much.' She gives me a mischievous wink and I smile back.

My phone buzzes. It's an email from Derek.

From: derek@tothemoonandback.com

To: Polly.wood@gmail.com

Dear Polly,

Thank you for coming in yesterday. It was great to meet you.

I was very impressed by your interview and would like to offer you the position as matchmaker at To the Moon & Back.

I hope to hear from you soon.

Kind regards,

Derek

I write a reply. Part of me has been resisting taking the job at To the Moon & Back, but who am I trying to kid? I keep hoping that doors will open in the photography world, but the only door that's opening is Derek's.

From: Polly.wood@gmail.com

To: derek@tothemoonandback.com

Dear Derek,

Thanks for your email. It was great meeting you too and I'm delighted to be offered the job as matchmaker.

When would you like me to start?

Best wishes,

Polly

28

Chapter 4

So, it turns out Andy Graham – the 34-year-old bachelor who enjoys Second World War history books and visiting aviation museums – isn't just a fictional character invented for interview purposes. He's a real bonafide client of To the Moon & Back, and my first assignment at the agency is to create a dating profile for him and bag a date.

Sitting in front of my computer, I try my best not to be distracted by the waving cat ornament a few feet from my desk, as I peruse Andy's Facebook page looking for his most winning pictures, so I can upload them to his dating profile. I click through shots of him playing tennis and dining in restaurants with friends, as well as a couple of highly questionable selfies that he appears to have taken with a webcam that feature terrible lighting, awful angles and a double (okay, more like triple) chin. It's not that Andy's really ugly, but he's not attractive either. He's somehow totally non-descript. He's just *there*. With his sandy blond hair, slightly bulbous nose, smallish blue eyes behind glasses and pudgy cheeks, he's hardly a head-turner. But on the other hand, he's tall (six foot) and he appears to have quite a lean, toned physique. I guess he just lacks the wow-factor.

'So, found any good pics?' Derek asks, pulling me out of my reverie.

He takes a sip from his third black coffee of the day. What I've learnt so far about Derek's morning routine is that it involves drinking three cups of incredibly strong instant coffee in quick succession and munching on at least half a dozen Oreos. I'm still sipping the cooling dregs of my first cup of coffee while he's practically downing his third. The coffee he's been making using the kettle in the client lounge is so black that it pretty much has the consistency and taste of tar, but I'm still grateful for it. Having become far too nocturnal during my freelance days, a strong black coffee is exactly what the doctor ordered. As well as getting wired on caffeine, Derek likes to lovingly spritz his collection of plants with water. The cluster of spider plants and cacti in the corner of the office next to some filing cabinets add a pop of colour to the otherwise dull and unin-spiring room. The walls are a drab grey shade. I think they might once have been white, but over the years, the paint has taken on a dirty, muted hue. All the office furniture is old and battered-looking, including my desk, which wasn't here when I came for my interview last week. Derek must have picked it up second-hand somewhere. Having spritzed his Venus flytrap a few more times for good measure, Derek comes over to take a look at my computer screen.

'There's this one.' I quickly click away from the photo open on my screen – a shot of Andy wearing a Guns N' Roses T-shirt with what looks like a food stain, gazing blankly into his webcam. Definitely not the best dating profile shot. I click back to one of him and a friend dining at an Asian restaurant, in which he looks highly excited by the prospect of eating noodles. For some reason, the picture is slightly overexposed in black and white, which makes Andy's features look a bit sharper than they do in the other shots.

'This one's alright,' I say.

'Not bad.' Derek nods, taking another sip of his coffee. He heads back to his desk and sits down. 'Try to use at least five. One full body shot. A few others clearly showing his face. No friends in any of them; we don't want to confuse women over which one's him. Oh, and teeth. Make sure you include a photo of him smiling so people can see he has decent teeth. Some women are very particular about that,' Derek muses. 'Wait, he does have good teeth, doesn't he?'

'I think so!' I zoom in on the picture open on my screen. Andy's smiling while holding a pair of chopsticks, a slither of salmon clamped between them. His teeth look normal and I feel a wave of relief. At least dodgy teeth aren't something I'm going to have to worry about when scoring him a date.

'Great!' Derek replies. 'His consultation was a few weeks ago and I couldn't remember. I was going to say, if his teeth aren't great, then maybe don't use a toothy smiling shot. You don't want to put people off. We had one client, he had teeth like Austin Powers, and his shots were all big smiley pics... We couldn't get him a date for months.' Derek rolls his eyes at the memory.

'So, what did you do?' I ask.

'We brought him in, took some pics of him in the lounge smiling with his mouth shut. Within a week, we scored him a date!' Derek tells me with glee.

'Oh, great!' I enthuse.

'Well, kind of...' Derek grimaces. 'When his date saw him in person, she ran a mile. In the end, he got his teeth fixed. Found someone eventually.'

'He got his teeth fixed?' I balk.

'Yeah, a full set of veneers,' Derek explains, sitting back down at his desk.

'Eek. That must have been expensive.'

'Sometimes you've just got to do what you've got to do.' Derek shrugs. 'You can't expect someone to fall for you warts and all. Life isn't a fairy tale. People are more superficial than that, especially in New York. Sometimes you have to up the effort. Lose some weight, beautify yourself. Packaging is important. You've got to make yourself as appealing as possible in this competitive dating world. I thank God I met my wife before online dating took off. I have no doubt she would have swiped left on me!' Derek jokes.

I laugh. Derek is funny – in fact so far, he's surprisingly easy company – but I can't help feeling just a little bit deflated at his words. Does finding someone really have so much to do with great 'packaging'? Are New Yorkers really that superficial? My heart sinks a bit at the prospect as I save Andy's picture onto my desktop and click onto Match.com where I'm already halfway through setting up his profile. I feel a bit guilty now as I look at Andy's picture. Here I am, judging him for his pudgy cheeks and non-descript looks. I'm probably not much better than the woman who ran a mile at the sight of her date's Austin Powers teeth. Maybe Derek's right and dating success does come down to looks, in which case, I could probably stand to lose a few pounds and tone up a bit. I upload Andy's photo and set about choosing another. I opt for a shot of him playing tennis. It shows off his tall and fairly athletic physique. As I scroll for a third, my thoughts wander to Brandon.

'So, if dating is all about packaging, then how come people like Brandon are single?' I ask.

Derek looks over, a mischievous twinkle in his eye. 'Like the look of Brandon, do you?'

I laugh nervously. 'He's objectively good-looking. I mean, he looks like a model,' I point out in what I hope is a matter-of-fact business-like tone.

'I'm just teasing!' Derek jokes. 'Yes, he is good-looking. And he's a great catch all-round. He's a partner at Statten & Jones – one of the most highly respected law firms in the city, he's donated a lot of money to charity. He played semi-professional soccer in his early twenties and studied at Harvard on a sports scholarship.

He even designed an app, which he sold to Google when he was twenty-eight. He's an absolute genius. And he's set up for life.'

'Wow…' I murmur, in awe. 'He designed an app in his spare time?'

'Yep! While making partner at his firm. He's an exceptional guy,' Derek tells me proudly, as though Brandon is his firstborn child.

I suddenly feel incredibly mediocre, realising there are people like Brandon in the world who can design lucrative apps in their spare time, while I'm sat at home guzzling pizza and watching *Keeping Up with the Kardashians*. Maybe I need to step up my game. I make a mental note to brainstorm app ideas when I get home.

'He's quite something,' Derek adds with a twinkle in his eye. Derek seems so fond of Brandon that I'm almost beginning to wonder whether we both have a crush on him.

'Mm-hmm, he sounds it,' I agree. 'So seriously, how is someone like him single? He's the full package!' I blurt out, before blushing a little.

Derek smiles knowingly.

'I mean objectively-speaking, from a matchmaker's point of view, I need to understand this stuff.' I clear my throat.

'Of course.' Derek winks. He leans back in his chair and gazes ponderously into the middle distance, steepling his hands over his pot belly. 'You see, the thing about Brandon is he's very picky. Very, very picky. I've told him he should be more flexible in his criteria, but he wants what he wants and he simply won't settle for anything less.'

'Oh right,' I reply, a little taken aback. 'And, erm, what does he want?' I ask in as light and breezy a tone as I can muster.

Derek raises an eyebrow sardonically, knowing full well that I'm into Brandon. 'He has very specific criteria, I'm afraid,' Derek tells me. 'He likes blonde girls with blue eyes. Tall – preferably over five foot eight. Slim. Toned.'

'Really?' I grumble, realising that with my brown hair, untoned body and five foot six height, I'm not even remotely his type.

Derek nods. 'Yep, he's very specific. Has a thing about waist to hip ratio too and torso to leg ratio. It's all got to be in proportion for Brandon,' Derek tells me, his voice tense. I get the feeling Brandon's been giving him grief over prospective dates for a while.

'Hip to waist ratio?' I gawp.

'Yep, you asked why he's single!' Derek takes a bite of another Oreo.

'What about personality? Does he have specific criteria for that too or is it all about the "packaging"?' I ask.

'Nope, he has specific criteria for that too,' Derek sighs. 'She must have been to an Ivy League university. He wants a high flyer. Someone corporate – a businesswoman, a PR boss, a consultant, that kind of thing. She has to be independent, preferably a homeowner. Sporty too. Oh, and she needs to enjoy travelling. Brandon's a bit of a jet-setter.'

'Jesus!' I say, without thinking.

'I know, right?' Derek rolls his eyes and pops the last piece of his Oreo into his mouth.

'How does she have the time to be a sporty traveller while she's a high-flying businesswoman?'

Derek shrugs, causing his pot belly to wobble slightly. 'Don't ask me.'

I laugh. It's clear that Derek's not exactly an expert on juggling work commitments and fitness.

I can't help feeling a little disheartened. I got a distinctly flirty vibe when Brandon and I first met in the hallway last week, and I'd secretly hoped that that maybe – just maybe – I stood a chance. I don't usually date guys like Brandon, but I thought I might somehow get my very own Hollywood-style romance. I can't pretend I haven't entertained girlish daydreams over the past few days in which he whisks me off my feet like a knight in shining armour and we end up having a sickeningly cheesy happy ever after. Ha. As if. It turns out I'm not slim enough for Brandon, or Ivy-League-educated enough, or fancy and corporate enough. Hmmphh. I dread to think what he'd make of my flat-share in Brooklyn with Gabe or my employment history of being a barmaid at The Eagle. Brandon would never want a girl like me.

'The thing about Brandon is he can get pretty much anyone,' Derek comments, interrupting my self-pitying thoughts. 'And I think it's gone to his head. He thinks that because he can have everyone, he can impose all these criteria and still get what he wants but we're only matchmakers, we're not miracle workers. Yes, Brandon's a catch, but there's only so much we can do.' Derek shakes his head exasperatedly.

'Hmm…' I narrow my eyes. Yes, Brandon's criteria are specific and annoying and extremely demanding, but there are surely a ton of women in New York who fit the bill. Even walking to the office this morning, I saw at least half a dozen petite blonde women marching through Wall Street in corporate suits who looked like Brandon's type and would probably be thrilled to date him. So, where's Derek going wrong?

'How about I try to find him someone?' I suggest.

Derek shoots me a sceptical look, as though I'm going to put myself forward or something.

'For the record, I don't mean me!' I point out, and it's true. Now that I know Brandon's nit-picking criteria, I'm not remotely interested in pursuing him. I know he'd never date me; I'm more interested in him as a professional challenge. Brandon is an absolute catch and I'm sure Derek must be underselling him in some way if he can't find him a good match.

'But you've got Andy to look after and I've assigned you a few others,' Derek reminds me. He's already emailed me a list of clients.

'I know, but I'd love to at least have a look at his dating profiles, just out of professional curiosity! Maybe I could give some feed-back from a woman's perspective.'

'Okay,' Derek relents. 'I suppose that can't hurt. I'll email his details over in a bit.'

'Great!' I enthuse as Derek reaches into his desk drawer for another Oreo. He presents the pack to me, but I decline, thinking of my apparently undateable figure.

I turn my attention back to Andy's photos. I crop a picture of him busting some moves on the dancefloor at a family wedding. It's a bit blurred and I suspect the person who took it might have had a bit to drink, but at least it makes him look fun. Then I add another picture of him posing next to a model aircraft at an aviation museum which I'd previously dismissed as looking too nerdy. Once I've uploaded a couple of pictures, I begin crafting as witty and cool a bio as I can possibly muster, chanelling the personality of Andy. I'm midway through writing a self-depre-cating joke about being a history buff when I realise that Derek's swivelling his chair towards my desk. He plonks a brochure down next to my keyboard. It's slick, in black, pink and gold shades, and emblazoned with the words, 'Elite Love Match: Meet Your Match.'

'What's this?' I ask, even though I know Elite Love Match is the agency Derek referred to in my interview as 'the worst dating agency in New York'.

'I need to give you an assignment,' Derek says in a serious tone.

'An assignment?' I ask with trepidation. I flick my eyes towards Andy's profile and think of all the other clients whose love lives I'm meant to be sorting out. Haven't I got enough assignments?

'Yes. I need you to be a mystery shopper. You need to pose as a potential client at Elite Love Match.'

'What?' I balk.

'I need the inside scoop on what this operation is really like and obviously I can't go there myself – the owner, Olly Corrigan, knows me. But you're new. You're totally fresh to the New York dating agency scene, he won't have a clue who you are.'

'You want me to be a spy?' I raise an eyebrow.

'A mystery shopper. A researcher, you know!' Derek shrugs, causing a few of the Oreo crumbs that have landed on his belly to fall to the floor.

A mystery shopper? I thought I was here to be a matchmaker and now Derek wants me to go on an undercover operation. Could this job get any weirder?

'Look, you just need to go along and act as though you want to sign up and then tell me what you thought of it. It's nothing shady!' Derek insists with an uneasy laugh.

'I guess…'

'Who knows, you might actually sign up!' Derek suggests, clearly in a desperate attempt to make me feel like what I'm doing isn't totally weird and underhand.

'Sure!' I give him a pointed look. New York dating agencies don't come cheap. As if I'm going to sign up to one on the salary he's paying me.

'Okay, maybe not,' Derek relents. 'But could you at least just check it out? Since they came on the scene last year, they've been cleaning up. Tons of people who've had consultations with us have ended up signing with them. I can't have that. I need to know what the founder Olly Corrigan has that we don't. And the only way I can truly know is to get a first-hand insight into what they offer. It could really affect business if people keep choosing them over us.'

'I don't know, Derek…' I'm still not particularly comfortable with the idea.

'The thing is, Polly, my wife, hurt her knee recently. She fell off a ladder while doing gardening and really messed it up. The medical bills are huge. I won't be able to pay if Olly keeps taking all my business,' Derek tells me glumly.

'Really?'

'Yes, really,' Derek sighs. 'I'm in a really tricky situation here. I know you don't particularly want to go snooping around at our competitors, but I need to know what they've got that we haven't. I need to help my wife.' Derek fixes me with such a pleading, desperate look that I can't help but feel sorry for him.

'Okay, okay, I'll help. Is your wife okay?' I ask. 'It sounds bad.'

'She's okay. She can walk, most days, but she can't over-exert herself. Some days it plays up and she ends up in a lot of pain,' Derek says sadly, brushing some Oreo crumbs off his belly.

'Oh God, okay, I'll do it, but I should warn you, I'm not a very good liar,' I tell him. 'We'll have to create a whole backstory for me if this is going to be convincing. I'm an amateur photographer living in Brooklyn. They're not going to believe that someone like me could afford a membership.'

'True.' Derek nods. 'You do photography though, don't you? Can't you just tell him you're a successful photographer?' Derek's eyes are wide and hopeful, and I can tell he's quite proud of this suggestion, even though it stings a little. If only I were a successful photographer. If only that wasn't a lie.

'I guess,' I murmur. 'But it's a bit risky. He might want to see my website or he might start asking after my clients. I reckon I could get found out. Maybe it's better to say I have one of those jobs that are so boring that no one ever asks any follow-up questions.'

'Like what?' Derek muses.

'I don't know… Like an administrator? Or an accountant or something,' I suggest.

'Yes! But perhaps not an accountant. It is a business after all, you don't want Olly Corrigan asking you to do his books!' Derek comments.

I giggle. 'Oh God, no!'

'How about a chartered surveyor?' Derek suggests.

A chartered surveyor? That does sound pretty boring.

'Definitely! Polly Wood, chartered surveyor. Perfect.'

'Great!' Derek laughs, a little mischievously. 'I suppose you can keep your real name and your other interests the same. They don't know you. No need to lie about those,' Derek reasons. 'They say the best lies are a blend of reality and fiction.'

'I guess. May as well keep that part of it authentic.'

'Exactly.' Derek smiles confidently. I smile back, and a momentary silence passes between us. 'So, do you want to call them and arrange a consultation?'

'Oh, right now?' I glance at my computer screen, which shows Andy's profile, which according to Match, is only 40 per cent complete.

'No time like the present!' Derek insists.

'Right! Okay!' I glance around my desk until my eyes land on a dusty old phone that looks like something from the Seventies. 'So, shall I just book in for as soon as possible?'

'Yep,' Derek replies as though it's self-evident. He swivels his chair back over to his desk. Having roped me into being his spy he's already tuning out of the conversation. I open the brochure to see a picture of the owner Olly Corrigan and *oh my God* is he attractive. He's not what I expected at all. I'd thought he was going to be like Derek or something, but he couldn't be more different. He's probably only five years younger, but he's in great shape. He's standing in front of a sign for the agency, wearing a crisp white shirt. His arms are folded across his chest and the sleeves of his shirt are rolled up to reveal detailed tattoo sleeves with intricate butterflies and flowers. He's wearing a pair of trendy tortoiseshell glasses, worlds away from the hideous aviator-style specs Derek rocks. His eyes are gorgeous – deep brown and kind-looking – and somehow the crows' feet around them only add to his handsomeness. He smiles subtly at the camera with both his eyes and his mouth.

I opened the brochure to find the agency's phone number, but I have a quick read of the message underneath Olly's picture.

Olly Corrigan

Founder
New York born and bred, NYU-educated entrepreneur.
'If I can't find you love, no one can.'

I raise an eyebrow. Cocky. Underneath is the address and phone number of the agency. I can feel Derek's eyes on me, so I pick up the receiver.

'Is there a dial-out code or anything?' I ask.

'Nope. You're good to go,' Derek replies.

'Okay!' I dial the number, feeling a little self-conscious with Derek listening in. After three rings, a polite receptionist answers with a crisp, clear upbeat voice. I tell her my name is Polly Wood and I'd like to book in for a consultation. I'm slightly worried she might ask me about my job since I'm still not totally down with faking being a chartered surveyor yet. I need to at least read up on it a bit. Fortunately, the conversation is pretty painless and all she does is take down my name and number and book me into the diary. I'm just about to breathe a sigh of relief and hang up, when she makes an unexpected request.

'I'll need to take the one-hundred-dollar consultation holding deposit, an additional fifty dollars will be payable on the day. Have you got your card ready?'

'Errr…' I mutter. 'One second!'

I place the phone down on the desk. Derek looks over curiously. I dash over to him.

'She wants money! A holding deposit!' I tell him in a hushed voice.

'Give it to her then,' Derek suggests with a shrug.

'But…!' I feel my cheeks burning. I don't want to admit to Derek that my bank account is so depleted that if I pay this woman a hundred dollars, I'll have approximately twenty dollars left for the rest of the week, including travel, food and everything.

'I'll transfer it to you now, but you can't give her my card details, can you?' Derek says. 'She knows who I am.'

'I guess not. Okay…' I grumble, skulking off back to my desk.

I grab my handbag and reluctantly retrieve my wallet. Derek had better pay me back because if he doesn't, I'm screwed.

I pick up the phone. 'Sorry about that,' I say. 'I couldn't find my wallet for a second there.' The lie rolls effortlessly off my tongue and I find myself wondering whether this whole phoney mystery shopper thing will really be that hard.

'No problem,' the receptionist replies, flawlessly polite, before asking for my card details.

She takes them down.

'Excellent, thank you,' she says eventually. 'We'll see you on Wednesday!'

'Fab!' I enthuse, but I can barely believe that people are willing to spend $150 just for a consultation when I can barely afford to upgrade to Tinder Plus.

I say goodbye and hang up.

I look over at Derek, still a little flustered. 'Well, there's your first bit of insider info. It's $150 just for a consultation,' I tell him.

'That's okay. It's worth it for the research.'

'Hmm…' I muse. 'Derek, I'm not a $150 consultation kind of girl. They'll surely sense something's up?'

'Nah!' Derek rejects the idea, still looking at his screen.

I feel a twinge of anxiety bubbling in the pit of my stomach. I have a feeling something is going to go wrong and I'm going to make a complete fool of myself in front of the utterly gorgeous Olly Corrigan.

'I just transferred the money to you,' Derek says, and for a second, I have no idea how he did it without my card until I remember that he has my bank details to pay my wages.

'Great, thanks.' I feel a small wave of relief. At least that's something. Although I'm still not looking forward to my consultation on Wednesday.

Chapter 5

What does a chartered surveyor wear? Pretty much standard office clothing according to Google. And certainly nothing particularly trendy, which is why I've teamed an old black skirt I haven't worn since graduation with a white shirt and a pair of frumpy court shoes.

'What do you think?' I emerge from the office loo, having just changed. 'Do I look like a chartered surveyor?'

Derek scrutinises my outfit. 'Yeah, I think so.'

Thankfully, To the Moon & Back has a laid-back dress code and over the past week, Derek hasn't seemed to mind me wearing my regular clothes, which tend to consist of leggings, smock dresses, jeans and checked shirts. I love a good checked shirt. Gabe used to make fun of me for having what he refers to as a 'lumberjack aesthetic' since my standard outfit of choice consists of ripped jeans teamed with a plaid shirt, tied at the waist in a vague nod towards femininity. I think it looks cool, but Gabe teases me that I belong on a logging farm rather than the streets of Manhattan. I don't care though, it's been my style for years and I'm comfortable with it. Unlike how I feel now, in my stiff office get-up. Nope, right now, I most certainly do not feel comfortable. Not only does the outfit feel unnatural to me, but it's also a bit tight. I haven't worn the skirt for three years, when I was at least a dress size slimmer. It's so tight that the zip only goes three quarters of the way up. I've managed to loop a hair tie through the clasp fastening at the top to make it stay up, which is fortunately covered by the hem of the white shirt. It's not ideal, but it should do. With my black tights and hair pulled back into a bun, I feel dowdier than I've felt in a very long time.

'You look great,' Derek comments, not entirely convincingly. 'You definitely look the part.'

'Are you sure?'

'Yep. You look like a chartered surveyor,' Derek insists.

I laugh. 'That's what every girl wants to hear.'

Derek grins. 'I aim to please.'

I smile and pick up my handbag from the desk. I've already checked my make-up (I tried to go for a toned-down professional look), so there's nothing really keeping me here. I've powdered my nose, re-read the Wikipedia page on chartered surveying at least fifty-seven times and made Derek scrutinise me from head-to-toe, which isn't something I'd ever imagine requesting. I pull my handbag onto my shoulder.

'I guess I'll be off then,' I announce.

'Go get 'em!' Derek says, punching the air.

'Haha,' I laugh weakly. 'Right, see you later.' I edge towards the office door. My hands are already clammy, and I haven't even set off yet. I'm simply convinced Elite Love Match will sniff me out as a fraud, a spy, a mystery shopper. I'm sure it's going to be awkward as hell, maybe worse than awkward, probably downright humiliating. There's a reason I gave up drama classes at the earliest available opportunity at school. I am not a good actress. I'm a behind-the-camera person, not the kind of person who wants to take centre stage. Derek would probably do a better job at this if he just shoved a wig and a dress on.

'You'll be fine, Polly! You've got this,' Derek insists.

'Haha, sure. Okay, bye!'

'See you later.'

I wave over my shoulder as I slip out of the office and cross the client lounge, which never ceases to tickle me with its kookiness. With the late afternoon golden sun streaming through the half-closed red curtains and glinting off the mirrored wall-hangings, it feels almost like a tarot reader's cave. I smile to myself, momentarily forgetting my nervousness as I leave the office.

Elite Love Match is only a five-minute walk from To the Moon & Back since both agencies are based close to the busy city professionals they wish to attract. It's a bit like the rehab centres dotted around Wall Street that offer 'stress detoxes' and counselling for strung out office workers, who need a quick fix of stress relief that they can fit in during lunch or before their evening gym class. A guy in a black suit charges towards me, his eyes fixed to the ground, a look of busy intensity on his face. He doesn't appear to clock me and makes no effort to move so I dodge out of his way to let him pass.

'Rude!' I mutter under my breath as he charges ahead, although as I walk on, I'm not sure if he was being rude or if he was just so harangued that he didn't even register another human being. I feel sad at the thought. There's a reason I've always dreamed about being a photographer. I want to be free. My own boss. I don't want to be the kind of person who's chained to a desk with corporate pressures left right and centre. I could never spend my entire working life in a stressful office job, cashing in pay checks month by month. No, I want to be independent, to work in a cool studio and roam around the city, taking pictures of people at unique interesting locations. Capturing beautiful images and being creative rather than just grinding away making money. Maybe I won't earn as much as these corporate types, but at you can't put a price on living a more relaxed, stress-free life.

Suddenly, I stop in the street and look around. I was so lost in thought that I stopped registering the block numbers. I glance at the nearest road sign and realise I'm three blocks away from

Elite Love Match. Right. I keep walking. I must push thoughts of Polly the wannabe photographer out of my mind and get into the mindset of Polly, chartered surveyor and corporate drone. I straighten my back and walk purposefully towards Elite Love Match. When I arrive at the right block, it's hard to miss with the huge slick lettering emblazoned across the front of the building by the entrance. I pause outside and look upwards, taking in the five- or six-storey expanse of the building's gleaming exterior. I step closer to the revolving doors and try to subtly peer through the glass in an attempt to figure out if there are other companies based here. Surely this entire office block isn't just for Elite Love Match?! How could that be possible when the company's only been around for a year? Sure, their brochure was impressive, but I hadn't imagined their premises would be this different to Derek's set-up with his tiny office and client lounge. If I was nervous before, I feel even more jittery now. This company is legit. It's properly legit. They'll probably sniff out an imposter like me in a second.

A man talking into a mobile phone comes through the revolving doors and casts a curious glance in my direction, probably wondering what I'm doing lingering outside. I take a deep breath and try to steel myself. What's the worst that can happen? The worst-case scenario is that they sense I'm lying about my job, they think I'm weird and I end up being awkwardly shunted out of the building. But, never mind. What's a casual dose of humiliation? All in a day's work, I guess. I hitch my handbag a little higher on my shoulder and head through the revolving doors, plastering a smile onto my face as I cross the wide marble-floored reception. I can feel the immaculately presented receptionist looking me up and down and I walk up to the desk.

'Hi, I'm Polly Wood,' I tell her. 'I have a consultation.'

'Hi Polly.' The receptionist, who looks like she belongs in a commercial, gives me a pearly smile. She glances back at the screen of her computer, no doubt verifying my name in the diary.

'I'll just call to let them know you're here. Please take a seat,' she says, gesturing towards a sofa by the reception desk.

'Great!' I reply as she picks up her phone receiver.

I head over to the sofa and sit delicately down, making sure the dodgy zip on my skirt doesn't come undone as I do so. It's not the most comfortable sofa. It's modern and boxy, a fancy Scandi design – certainly not the kind of sofa you'd veg out on. As the receptionist makes a quick call, I ponder the sofa, wondering whether they make such seating deliberately uncomfortable so that office workers don't get too relaxed and laid-back.

'They're sending someone down for you now,' she says.

'Excellent!' I enthuse, with a bright smile that I hope conceals my nerves.

A silence passes between us. I look over at a tall plant by the desk with long wide leaves and try to think of something to say, but my mind has gone blank. I glance back at the receptionist. She's smiling at me. I smile back. She keeps smiling. The air conditioning fan whirrs overhead.

'Do you work nearby?' she asks, breaking the painful silence.

'Oh, sort of. My office is on Staten Island,' I tell her. Derek and I already decided that it would be sensible if we base my chartered surveying office in a boring and unfashionable part of town where no one is likely to have spent much time.

'Right.' The receptionist nods.

Fortunately, we're interrupted by a man striding towards me with his tattooed arm outstretched. As well as researching chartered surveyor stuff this morning, I also did my homework on Olly Corrigan. According to his Wikipedia page, he's forty-three years old and half-Italian, with his mother moving to New York from Genoa in the Sixties. Both his father and brother are well-respected financiers, but Olly seems to have broken the family mould, having studied music at NYU and had a series of odd jobs, before turning to the world of business in his late twenties. And according to his Instagram account, he's *obsessed* with fashion. In every single photo he's dressed in cool, carefully put together, trendy outfits. He even tags all the designer labels he's wearing in each post.

He smiles widely as he approaches. He looks just like his Instagram pictures, clearly handsome enough not to need Photoshop. His smile is broad and charming, and he has the most perfect dazzling white teeth. His eyes are crinkly and twinkle behind his tortoiseshell glasses. He has one of those smiles that's contagious, like someone with a really infectious laugh that you just can't help but join in with, and I find myself beaming broadly back at him despite my nerves.

I stand up to shake his outstretched hand as he gets nearer.

'Polly,' he says, giving me a firm handshake and fixing me with his beguiling eyes. 'Great to meet you, I'm Olly.'

'Hi Olly' I reply, trying to ignore the fluttering feeling in my stomach as our eyes lock on each other. 'Great to meet you too.'

'Let's head up to my office,' he suggests, gesturing back across the hallway.

'Sure,' I reply.

His office? I didn't actually expect to have a one-to-one with Olly Corrington himself. I thought my consultation would be with one of his staff. Derek's going to love this! A first-hand consultation with the boss. Except now the pressure's even more intense to convince him I'm a regular singleton looking for a date and not just a total imposter.

The receptionist looks over at us, a quizzical expression on her face.

'Are you okay, Gina?' Olly asks.

'Oh...' She frowns, looking flummoxed. 'Yes, I just assumed you'd be sending down Celia or John,' she says.

'They're busy,' Olly tells her.

'Oh right' she replies, still looking a little perplexed as we head towards the lift. I glance at Olly as we walk. He's a few paces ahead of me, which gives me the perfect chance to check him out. He's just as polished as his Instagram photos led me to believe he would be. He's wearing a burgundy shirt with an abstract print at the rear, the sleeves turned up to show off his tattoos. He's teamed it with dark jeans that look incredibly expensive – slim fit and artfully distressed with the hems tucked into a pair of chunky black boots. The overall impression is of one of wealth, style and unabashed ostentatiousness. Olly is clearly the kind of man who wants to be noticed. He turns to me as we arrive at the lift and I smile innocently, as if I haven't just been giving him an appreciative once-over.

'The office is on the sixth floor, I'm afraid,' he says, reaching for the button.

'No problem!'

The lift doors open and we step inside. I know we'll have small talk in the lift and I brace myself for him to ask me a similar question to Gina, about how far I've had to come to get here. As he presses the button for the sixth floor, I gear myself up to lie about being a chartered surveyor on Staten Island.

'So…' Olly says. 'Have you used a dating agency before?'

'Oh!' I comment, a little shocked but mostly just hugely relieved to not have to lie just yet. 'Actually no, never.'

'Ah, I see.' He nods. 'So how did you hear about us?'

Oh, you know, I just Google-stalked you because you're my boss' number one competitor, I think.

'I read about you in *Time* magazine,' I tell him, which is technically true. I did read a gushing article in *Time* magazine last night hailing Olly as a 'New York matchmaking God'. The interviewer sounded smitten, describing him as 'the best thing to happen to Manhattan's dating scene for years'.

'Ah yes, they gave us some good coverage,' Olly recalls, flashing me with another dazzling smile.

With his sparkly crinkly eyes and natural charisma, I can see why the interviewer at *Time* would have fallen for his charm. He's incredibly handsome. Even though he's much older than the kind of guy I'd usually find attractive, he has the type of face that ages well. His bone structure is strong and his features are incredibly symmetrical. The thing is, he knows it. I can just tell by the way he's smiling at me, holding eye contact, expecting me to turn to mush. And maybe under normal circumstances, I would, but I feel mentally detached. I'm not my usual relaxed self, I'm in undercover spy mode and instead of getting too swept up in the charm of a good-looking guy, I'm trying to stay focused on making observations and mental notes instead.

The lift arrives at the sixth floor, the doors parting to reveal an open-plan office with a dozen or so trendy-looking staff sitting behind the giant screens of state-of-the-art Mac computers. Their eyes flick up at me and Olly as we pass and I can feel them watching us as we make our way towards Olly's private office, which is enclosed in polished glass walls emblazoned with the Elite Love Match logo.

'After you,' he says, holding open the door for me.

'Thanks,' I reply, smiling shyly as I slip past him.

His office is slick and impressive, with a wide desk, flanked by two wide leather desk chairs. It's immaculately tidy and clutter-free, a giant Mac computer taking centre stage next to a stainless-steel desk lamp.

'Please, take a seat.' Olly gestures towards the seat opposite his desk. 'Can I get you anything? Water, tea, coffee?'

'Oh, water would be great,' I reply as I sit delicately down, willing the zip on my skirt to stay in place.

'Still or sparkling?' he asks as he sits down opposite.

'Sparkling, please.'

'No problem.'

Olly picks up his phone, presses a speed-dial button and makes a call to someone I assume is his assistant, asking her to bring two sparkling waters.

'So…' he says as he hangs up, fixing his deep brown eyes on me. 'What's brought you to Elite Love Match today?'

He leans back in his chair and regards me with a gentle patient expression. I can't quite tell if he's putting on an attentive 'listening face' as part of his sales routine or if he really is genuinely interested.

'Well, I've been single for a while now and I just don't seem to have any luck with men,' I tell him and so far, I'm being 100 per cent honest. Why lie? This bit is all true, I do have terrible luck with guys.

'What do you mean you don't have any luck,' Olly asks, tilting his head to the side.

'Umm…' I cross and re-cross my legs and glance at the stack of business cards in a neat metal holder on his desk, next to a matching desk tidy. It feels weird to be having such an intimate conversation in such a corporate environment. I think back to the last few guys I've dated. I met one guy through my barmaid job at The Eagle – a trainee architect called James. He was probably the only straight man in the bar one Friday night and we immediately caught each other's eye. He was gorgeous and at first, everything seemed to be going brilliantly. We had a couple of amazing dates, sharing everything from our favourite books and films to childhood memories and our hopes and dreams. Then after our third date, which culminated with us sleeping together, he stopped texting and that was that. I never heard from him again. He ghosted me. It took me months to stop worrying that I was terrible in bed and just accept that he was an asshole. And then before him, there was Mike (the guy I called Matt the entire time we were dating). He was sweet but unlike James, we just didn't connect. Conversation was always awkward and clunky, no matter how much time we spent together. I kept hoping we might relax into each other's company, but it never quite happened.

Sometimes, late at night, Olly's question about why I don't have any luck with men has stalked my mind, replaying over and over as I try to get to the bottom of it. *Why don't I have any luck*

50

with them? Is it possible for a person to be consistently unlucky in love, never quite meeting the right person just because fate hasn't been on their side, or is there something about me that's causing these dating disasters? The only theory I've come up with is that on some level, I just haven't felt ready for a serious relationship even though everyone else seems to want to be in one.

My relationship role models are my parents and they met when my mum was 30 and my dad was 33. My mum used to tell me when I was a kid that she was so glad she 'got to know herself before getting to know someone else'. She was perpetually single until she met my dad, but she'd done a ton of stuff, like charity work, studying and travelling around the world. My dad had travelled a lot too and even though he'd had girlfriends, he'd never been able to stick at a relationship, until he found my mum and decided she was the one, leading him to settle down in Cornwall. I think part of the reason I've pretty much always been single is because I took my mum's advice on board – I wanted to make sure I got to know myself before finding someone else. I've always thrown myself into non-love-related activities. I was a bit of a swot at school because back then I was focused on getting good grades so I could get into a US university. Then at university, I threw myself into my photography studies. I focused on having a good social life and I made the most of all the extra-curricular activities on offer. I knew I was paying way more in tuition than I'd be paying for university in the UK so I wanted to make sure I got the most out of it. With all that going on, I didn't have much time for love. And then when I graduated and moved to New York, I became focused on trying to become a professional photographer and getting ahead. All my life, love has taken the back seat. It's felt less important than achieving my goals and getting to know myself. Except, I feel like I know myself prettywell these days and annoyingly, I still can't seem to find love. But I guess you can't force these things.

'I suppose I haven't met anyone for a while who I have a

genuine spark with, you know, where it just feels effortless. The kind of spark that you just can't ignore, when you're just drawn to someone and neither of you can stop thinking about each other,' I tell him, looking into his eyes and feeling that fluttery feeling in my stomach again. 'I suppose I just want that.'

Olly nods understandingly. Without realising it, I've somehow opened up to him more than I've opened up to anyone for weeks. I've been so focused on trying to be a photographer that I've barely admitted to myself that I want to fall in love, let alone to friends or family or anyone else close to me. Whenever I talk about my love life to Gabe, he just takes the piss. And I don't really blame him, because my love life has always been a bit of a joke. It's been awful dates and cringe-worthy encounters one after the other. Even I've been trying to see the funny side, but I suppose deep down, it's sort of stopped being that funny. It would be nice to fall in love and be happy, rather than making snarky and sarcastic jokes about my rubbish dating history the whole time.

'Real romance…' Olly muses. His eyes have gone all misty and soft. 'It can be rare these days.'

'Yes.' I glance down at my lap.

'So, you're looking for something serious then?' He clears his throat, leans forward and reaches into a desk tidy for a form.

'Yes,' I reply.

'Great.' He plucks a pen from his stationery holder and ticks a box on the form. His soft, sensitive manner seems to have evaporated.

'And what kind of man are you looking for? Let's start with physical preferences.' He glances up from the form.

'Oh, right. Yes. Well, umm, tall, but not too tall. Maybe five foot nine?'

Olly nods and makes a note.

'Attractive,' I add.

'Of course,' Olly says. 'You're an attractive girl so we'd naturally match you with someone equally attractive.' He flashes me his dashing smile.

'Sounds great!' I comment, holding his gaze for what feels like a little too long. *Is he always flirty with clients?* I find myself wondering. Derek certainly can't add flirting to his approach, I'm pretty sure it wouldn't go down nearly as well.

'So what kind of looks do you tend to go for?' Olly asks.

'Dark hair, brown eyes, strong features, a nice smile,' I tell him, gazing into his eyes, until I realise that I'm pretty much describing what's in front of me.

Shit! I look away, feeling my cheeks burn up. How utterly embarrassing! Olly smiles knowingly.

'Younger, though,' I blurt out, before mentally cursing myself. *Nice one, Polly.*

Olly raises an eyebrow. 'Oh, you like younger men?'

Shit. I meant younger than him, except I only meant to think it, I didn't mean to actually say it out loud.

'Young,' I mean. 'Around my age.'

'Gotcha.' Olly makes a note on the form while my cheeks flare. 'Anything else? What kind of body type?'

'Erm... Slim, in good shape, but not too muscular. I don't want someone who spends their life taking selfies at the gym,' I tell him.

Olly laughs as he makes another note. I glance at his upper body. Good shape, but not too muscular. Damn it, I've done it again. I've simply described Olly.

Fortunately, his assistant comes in carrying a tray with two tall glasses of sparkling water, breaking the tension. She's wearing skinny leather trousers with impossibly glamourous high heels – the kind of thing I wouldn't even wear on a night out, let alone to work. She places the glasses elegantly on two slate black coasters on the desk.

'Thanks.' I look up and she smiles politely before leaving the room.

Olly thanks her before picking up his glass and taking a sip.

'Right, so what about weight? Would you say he's around 165 to 170 pounds?' Olly asks.

I laugh, fully believing that he's joking but he simply looks back at me with a perplexed expression. He's actually serious! He wants me to specify my ideal partner's precise weight.

'Umm, yes, I guess so. 165 to 170 pounds would do fine,' I reply, trying not to smirk.

'Right. Five foot nine. 165 to 170 pounds.' Olly makes a note.

I take a sip of my water, as I try to suppress how weird and clinical this feels.

'So, what about his lifestyle? Would you be happy to date a smoker or a drinker?' Olly continues, with a business-like, almost bored expression on his face.

'A social drinker would be fine. I think a tee-totaller might be a little bit boring and obviously, I'd rather not date an alcoholic.' I laugh, but Olly doesn't join in, he just makes another jotting. It's like the charged flirty vibe between us has been completely sucked from the room.

'Smoker?' Olly asks.

'Umm, no thanks. Non-smoker.'

'What about dietary preferences? Healthy? Meat-eater? Vegetarian? Vegan?'

'Erm… healthy?' I suggest. 'I don't really care what he eats, as long as he doesn't expect me to cook for him!'

Olly allows himself a tiny smile. 'Okay, shall I check the "no preferences" box?' he asks.

'Yes, I suppose so.'

'Right.' Olly makes another dutiful note.

'Income. What level of income would you prefer your partner to have?' Olly asks.

'Income?' I echo.

'Yes…?' Olly regards me with a slightly impatient look. 'What kind of income bracket would you prefer?'

'Erm...' I fidget with a loose thread on the hem of my skirt. All these questions are so formulaic and impersonal. It's the same vibe as when my parents dragged me to a home and garden store one bank holiday weekend when I lived back home because they wanted to get a new kitchen. The sales assistant went though all kinds of boring questions about their kitchen design criteria, from the width and height of the kitchen units to the positioning of electrical sockets. I feel like I'm going through a similar process now. Next, Olly will be offering me a deal on appliances.

'I don't know. Anything really, I'm not that bothered about money.'

'Right...' Olly frowns and gives me a strange quizzical look that I can't quite figure out.

'You see, usually, clients have a very specific idea about the kind of partner they're looking for,' Olly explains, gesticulating with his pen. 'They've spent a long time dating and they've figured out which qualities and lifestyle choices don't work for them in a partner, and then they come to us hoping that we can help them find that special someone that fits the bill.' He frowns, eyeing me intensely. 'It's not often that we have inquiries from people who seem as flexible about their requirements as you.'

'Oh...' I can feel myself sweating. I look away from him, avoiding his penetrating gaze. Is he beginning to sense something's up? Does he realise that I'm not quite for real?

'You're a professional, working as a chartered surveyor. I would have imagined you were looking for someone from a similarly professional background, or is that not the case?' Olly asks, propping his tattooed elbows on the desk and leaning forward, regarding me with that cutting stare. He's totally sussed me out, realised I'm a phoney or a time-waster, and now he's making me squirm.

'Absolutely. You're right. It would be better to date a fellow professional,' I insist in a firm tone that I hope conveys a sense of conviction. 'A professional like myself.'

'Mm-hmm...' Olly seems completely unconvinced. 'Would you be looking for someone with a similar income to yourself, or higher?'

Oh God. I Googled pretty much every aspect of being a chartered surveyor, from which university course I completed to recent building developments I could have worked on. But it didn't occur to me to look up how much I might earn. I have absolutely no idea how much chartered surveyors make. It's the kind of personal question I never expected would come up. I mean, I'd presume they earn a decent wage, but it could be one of those professions like being a lawyer where you can make a ton from commission. I simply don't know.

'So, what are your thoughts?' Olly presses me. His look is a bit deadpan now and I feel like he's running out of patience.

'Umm...' I decide to take a stab in the dark. 'Yes, similar income. $100–120,000 a year,' I tell him, with confidence. If I just muster enough confidence, then maybe I can style this out?

'Right.' Olly makes another note on the form. 'That's an impressive salary for someone so young,' he says, eyeing me with that quizzical look again, but now it's just really beginning to annoy me. Who's he to say that a 25-year-old like myself couldn't be on $120,000? Maybe I'm just really ambitious and hard-working. Hmmph.

'Thank you,' I comment, with a blasé smile.

'Okay!' Olly responds with a quirk of his eyebrow. I look at his arms as he picks up the form and continues asking me questions about my perfect man, covering everything from my preferences over his living arrangements (house share, renter, home owner, etc.) to his religious beliefs. I answer the questions with false assertiveness, trying to emulate someone who knows what they're looking for, while taking in the detailed butterflies emblazoned on his arms. The artwork is really impressive, and I find myself wondering when he got his tattoos done – was it back when he was young? Or perhaps he had them done more recently to compliment his striking fashion choices and trendy image.

By the time Olly finally reaches the end of the form, I feel completely depleted. Talking about love has never felt more unromantic.

Olly makes another note. God knows what he's jotting down now, and who even cares? I just want to go. This whole situation is making me feel uncomfortable. Olly may be ridiculously hot, but everything just feels a bit superficial and contrived, from the slick glass-panelled office, minimalist décor and watchful staff outside with their high heels and trendy haircuts, to this soulless checklist-based consultation.

'Right.' Olly looks up from the form and even he isn't doing anything for me anymore. The playful flirty look that was in his eyes when we first met has gone, replaced by a dead, emotionless stare. 'Given your criteria, I feel very confident we can find the right man for you... Polly.'

He adds my name after a second's pause, as though he nearly forgot to, but then decided to make his standard sales spiel sound a bit more personal. I nod and force myself to get back into character.

'Great, and how long do you think it will take?'

Even as I ask the question, I hate myself a little bit. It's like asking how long my new custom designed made-to-measure kitchen would take to be installed. Can you really set a timescale on how long it will take to find the man of your dreams? Surely love doesn't quite work like that?

'Good question.' Olly nods, as if that's something he's been expecting me to ask. 'Our average turnaround time for clients is three to four months, but with you I expect it might be shorter.'

Turnaround time? Did he really just say that? Is my love life a corporate assignment?

'Why do you think it'll be shorter?' I ask.

Olly's eyes suddenly become animated again and I can detect

a flicker of emotion, although I can't quite figure out what it means.

'Yes, attractive women like yourself are usually less of a challenge when it comes to finding a partner,' Olly says in a flat, matter-of-fact tone that doesn't quite disguise the flicker of flirtation in his eyes.

Is he attracted to me? Does *he* find me attractive or is he just assessing my attractiveness in the cool, clinical way he would do if he was ticking a box to denote it on a form? I'm pretty sure it's the former. I think, and in a way hope, that he personally finds me pretty, and instinctively, I reach up and touch my hair, tucking it behind my ear. Olly isn't my usual type – he's too corporate, too self-consciously cool, and he's significantly older than me – but he does have a remarkable face and it's impossible not to be just a little bit drawn to him. But even though I'm attracted to him, I can't ignore his offputtingly clinical approach to love. I can't tell if it's just the way he goes about running a dating agency or whether he really does have such a heartless attitude to dating and relationships.

'And, erm… how much does the service cost?' I ask.

'Right, well, we have various packages…' Olly starts running through different price plans, all of which are ludicrously expensive. Each plan has a monthly retainer that costs more than my rent alone, but instead of balking, I nod pensively as though I'm weighing up the options, as though splashing thousands on a dating service is no biggie. No biggie whatsoever.

'How does that sound?' Olly asks, watching my face for a reaction.

'Ummm… it sounds reasonable,' I lie. In actual fact, it sounds extortionate. Even compared to Derek's operation. Derek's charges are still pretty high, but they're not quite so jaw-droppingly expensive as Elite Love Match's.

'So, if I decide to speak to other agencies in the city, what would you say is the reason I should pick you over them?' I ask, feigning an equally business-like persona. This question should be useful for Derek and I concentrate closely as Olly answers.

'You're single and there's a reason for that,' Olly notes, taking me by surprise. 'You obviously have standards. We respect those standards. Other agencies might try to talk you into lowering your standards but we're not like that. We're confident that we can find you the partner of your dreams, someone who fits all your criteria.' Olly smiles confidently, and I find myself smiling back, even though on the inside, I'm withering.

He's just like the kitchen salesman back home, from the confident way he promises to fulfil a vision to his charming sycophantic smile. But unlike the kitchen salesman, who's slightly smarmy, overly confident sales pitch was just a bit annoying, Olly's approach is kind of depressing. It's one thing selling kitchens, it's a whole other ballpark to sell love. Olly reduces relationships to criteria. To him, falling in love takes place over billable timescales. He probably considers dates to be deliverables. My heart feels like it's shrivelling up inside my chest.

'So, how does that sound?' Olly asks again, in a confident upbeat tone.

'It sounds great!' I lie. 'With the criteria and timescales, it couldn't be more efficient!' I plaster a smile across my face.

'Exactly!' Olly beams back.

'Fabulous! Well, I'll sleep on it – I'm not one to make decisions on the cuff,' I tell Olly and as I expected, he nods understandingly.

'Absolutely,' he says.

Of course, he respects my need to weigh up the investment decision that is finding a partner. He probably thinks I'm going to go home and do a cost-benefit analysis or use a pivot table to analyse my options.

'Well, thanks a lot for today. I'll be in touch!' I insist, getting up to go.

Olly copies, rising to his feet.

'So…' he ventures. 'How about I give you a call in a few days and you can let me know your thoughts?'

'Absolutely!' I enthuse as I slip my arms into my jacket. 'Sounds great!'

'Great!' Olly echoes with a smile.

He opens his office door and ushers me out, offering to walk me to the lift. As we pass through the office, I glance around at the staff. There must be at least twenty of them and they all look incredibly cool and well-dressed. They couldn't be more different to the way Derek and I look at work, with me in my lumberjack gear and Derek in his aviator-style glasses with his shirt covered in a near-constant dusting of Oreo crumbs.

'I never realised dating agencies had so many staff,' I comment.

'Oh.' Olly glances over his shoulder at his fashionable team as he presses the button for the lift. 'They don't all work for Elite Love Match,' he tells me.

'Who do they work for?'

'I own a PR agency. I handle quite a lot of the Elite Love Match work, with the help of my assistant and a couple of others. That lot—' he gestures over at his team '—they handle PR.'

'I see.' I nod. 'That must be great having both of your businesses under one roof,' I say, making glib chit chat while we wait for the lift to arrive.

Meanwhile, I make a mental note to pass on this useful nugget of information to Derek. I wonder whether he realises that Elite Love Match is a relatively small operation – not much bigger than To the Moon & Back.

'Well, it was great meeting you.' Olly pumps my hand and gives me his dashing smile, which I'm getting the feeling is a pretty well-used tool in his arsenal of charming moves.

'You too.'

'I'd love to work with you and I'm confident I can find you the man of your dreams,' Olly says, eyeing me with a look of sparkling intensity.

The man of my dreams. The words linger in the air between us. Olly's hand is still clasping mine. We're holding each other's gaze and I feel suddenly, acutely aware of his palm against mine. Neither of us can quite look away, and I can't help wondering what he's thinking. Is the soft tender look in his eyes part of his sales pitch or is it something else? I gaze into his eyes, trying to figure it out, when all of a sudden, the lift doors start beeping as they close.

'Oh, damn it.' Olly steps forward and blocks the doors from closing, letting me inside.

'Sorry about that, Polly,' he says, with an apologetic and almost sheepish smile, as I get in the lift. 'I hope to hear from you soon.'

'Of course. Speak soon,' I utter, still reeling. What happened just then? I smile politely and Olly smiles back – not his dashing salesman smile this time, but a softer, almost wistful one – as the lift doors close.

Chapter 6

I don't know whether I'm coming or going as I leave Elite Love Match. Literally. I walk down the street for a good five minutes, before realising I'm going in totally the wrong direction. I turn around, but I must have drifted down a side street or two because I'm on a block I don't recognise at all and certainly didn't walk down on my way. Urghh. I stand still and force myself to get a grip. The truth is, I feel a bit lost. I retrieve my phone from my handbag to consult Google Maps. I don't know where I am or, for that matter, how I feel. I don't think I've ever had such a rollercoaster of emotions towards one person in such a short encounter, from attraction to flirting to mild disdain and then back to attraction and dare I say it, tenderness. There was something in Olly's eyes when he shook my hand as he said goodbye and swore he'd find me the man of my dreams, and I can't quite put my finger on it. Was he being suggestive, hinting that perhaps *he* could be the man of my dreams, or was he just messing with me? Was he trying to get my attention so I'd sign up to the agency? I don't know if he was being sincere or whether he's just a staggeringly good salesman, using his seductive charm to reel me in.

I'm still thinking of his crinkly-eyed smile when my phone buzzes. It's a text from Derek.

How did it go? I've had to run. My wife's knee's playing up. Take the rest of the afternoon off if you like and we'll catch up tomorrow. Derek.

I glance at my watch. It's 4 p.m. and I'm due to finish work at 5.30 p.m. An hour and a half off – not bad. It's probably a good thing that I don't have to go back to the office in my dazed state. I draft a quick reply.

Hi Derek, it went pretty well. I'll fill you in tomorrow. Hope your wife's okay. See you, Polly.

I hit send and drop my phone back into my bag, feeling relieved that I don't need to be anywhere. At least now, I can just let my mind wander.

I head into a nearby café, order a coffee and perch at the window, people-watching for a while as I replay the meeting with Olly in my mind, trying to figure out how I feel about him. Part of me is wildly attracted to him and yet another part finds him and everything his agency stands for incredibly depressing. I want to see him again and yet I feel repelled by the idea that I might not fit into the height bracket or income criteria that someone like him would demand me to have. I sip my coffee and try to focus on how the meeting went from a mystery shopper point of view instead. There was definitely a moment when Olly seemed to doubt me, but I think I managed to recover from it. I think he felt I was legit in the end, or at least, he stopped caring either way.

I watch as office workers begin to pass the café, heading home, and it occurs to me that Gabe might be able to leave work early and hang out. With me working on freelance jobs all over the place or being broke and cooped up in the flat, it's been a while since we went to a bar or grabbed dinner. I send him a text in the hope that he doesn't have plans with Adam. He replies as I'm finishing off my coffee, saying he'll be done with work in twenty minutes and do I want to come and meet him. I've never met Gabe at his office before, even though I've walked past it a few times. I tell him I'll be there and then leave the café, navigating my way a few blocks to the skyscraper where he works.

Gabe's waiting for me outside as I arrive. He stands next to a corporate water feature – a fountain made from bricks – which is both tranquil and urban. He hasn't notice me yet and looks tired and bored.

'Hey!' I greet him as I approach.

He turns to look at me, his distracted bored expression replaced by an animated smile. We hug.

'Wow, so this is your fancy bank, eh?' I comment as I look upwards, taking in the vast gleaming structure.

'Yep. This is it!' Gabe follows my gaze, looking markedly less bothered. 'That's where I sell my soul for a paycheck.'

I laugh.

'Come on.' Gabe tugs gently on my arm. 'Let's get away from here.'

'Long day?' I ask as we walk away from his building.

'Something like that,' Gabe sighs. 'Every day is a long day.'

I glance over my shoulder as we walk away, taking another look at Gabe's workplace. It's so tall and imposing with its huge globally recognised logo emblazoned across the front. Other office workers are beginning to trickle out, looking neat and professional, like Gabe, in their suits. It's strange to think that this is the world Gabe's inhabited for the past year and a half. It couldn't be any more different to our kooky flat in Brooklyn or The Eagle on a Friday night. His life definitely has two sides to it.

'Let's get a drink,' Gabe says as we head towards a cluster of restaurants and bars nearby.

'Good plan!' I agree.

'How about here?' Gabe says, pausing outside a glass-fronted high-end chain bar. Its tall, rustic, wooden benches contrast with stainless-steel, low-hanging lamps. Everyone is perching on stools, the women drinking cocktails and prosecco and the men sipping pints from slender glasses. It looks totally stiff and uptight.

I wrinkly my nose. 'Urghh. That's so not us, Gabe.'

Gabe laughs. 'There isn't anywhere like The Eagle around here, Polly. I know you don't frequent these parts often but this—' he gestures towards the pretentious bar '—is all we have.'

'Nooo.' I groan. 'I refuse to believe it. Surely not everyone in the city wants to drink in such wanky establishments.'

'It's not that wanky,' Gabe insists. 'I go there with Adam quite a lot.'

I link arms with him and steer him away. 'Come on, there must be somewhere nicer.'

'By nicer you mean a dive bar, don't you?' Gabe teases.

'Exactly.' I smile smugly.

We keep walking, passing other pretentious bars, which appear to be exact replicas of the first and I'm beginning to wonder whether Gabe was right, maybe city workers really do all drink in poncey establishments where they're forced to perch and drink from tall slender glasses and have weird uptight fun, when suddenly, I spot what appears to be a dive bar from the chain Milano's tucked away down a side road.

'Is that Milano's?' I squint at the sign in wonder, as though it might just be a mirage.

'Oh, not Milano's,' Gabe grumbles. 'What if someone sees me?'

'It'll be fun!' I insist. 'Anyway, just tell them I dragged you there.'

'Urghh… fine,' Gabe sighs, rolling his eyes.

'Come on!' I give his arm a gentle tug. He groans as we head down the side road.

Milano's is the opposite of Wall Street's sleek pretentious bars. Every surface behind the bar is covered with flags, beer mats and stickers for everything from workers' unions to biker associations. The place seems to have a total aversion to leaving any inch of wall uncovered. In the seating area, the walls are plastered with blurry pictures taken of punters over the years, photographed by other drinkers who weren't able to keep a steady hand. Everyone's smiling in the pictures and looks relaxed, if a little wasted. The Rolling Stones are playing on a jukebox and a TV flickers on the wall in the background. A few solitary drinkers perch at the bar nursing pints, occasionally chatting to one another. They look like they're probably regulars. Gabe raises an eyebrow and I can tell it's not quite his kind of establishment.

'Oh, come on. Drinks on me!' I suggest.

'Fine,' Gabe sighs as I order two pints. The barmaid sings along to the song on the jukebox as she pours each one. She's totally unselfconscious and I'm already liking the laid-back vibe of the bar. I pay her, tipping generously even though I can't really afford to. I hand Gabe a pint and we head to one of the tables in the corner. We take off our coats and sit down.

'So, how's office life?' Gabe asks as he sips his pint.

'Weird,' I admit, filling him in on my meeting with Olly. I whinged to him last night about having to be a mystery shopper while I selected my terrible outfit. Naturally, Gabe didn't approve. He already thinks my job is a bit dodgy and the fact that I was being asked to go and spy on a rival business was just another level of shadiness that he wasn't on board with.

I tell him about Olly, from his impressive offices and effortless charm to his weirdly clinical approach to dating.

'It felt so prescriptive and formulaic, he had a checklist for everything – height, income, diet – and then he ticked a load of boxes for the criteria that apply to my ideal man,' I tell Gabe, taking a sip of my pint. 'It was just so heartless and unromantic.'

Gabe shrugs. 'Relationships aren't all fireworks. Sometimes those kinds of things do matter.'

I wrinkle my nose. 'When you met Adam, you weren't like, "And how much do you earn? Would you describe yourself as a social drinker or regular drinker? And are you a night owl or an early bird?" No! You just felt a connection. You had a spark!'

'Well, yeah…' Gabe's eyes go momentarily wistful and I expect he's thinking back to how he and Adam met – they bumped into each other in Starbucks. Literally bumped into each other. Gabe was looking down at his phone and accidentally walked straight into Adam, who was also distracted, causing Adam's green matcha latte to spill all over Gabe's shirt. After Adam flirtatiously helped him clean himself up in the bathroom, they ended up having lunch together and swapping numbers. Gabe was so excited when he got back that evening. He didn't just have a spark with Adam, he had fireworks. I'd seen him have crushes on guys before, but I'd never seen him quite as into anyone as he was with Adam.

'You just followed your heart. You didn't reduce Adam to a set of criteria,' I say.

'No,' Gabe admits, taking a sip of his drink, 'but criteria are important, and the reason Adam and I work is because he does tick a lot of boxes too. If he'd just been gorgeous, but didn't happen to have a good job, a similar lifestyle and whatever else, then perhaps we wouldn't have lasted as long as we have. These check boxes are important when it comes to long-term relationships and not just flings. That's your problem, Polly, you just want the cute exhilarating moment when your eyes lock with someone across a crowded room. You want electricity and excitement. But attraction fades. You need someone who's actually compatible or otherwise things will keep fizzling out after a few weeks.' Gabe finishes his drink. 'Want another?' he suggests.

I look down at my glass, which is two thirds empty. 'Sure.'

Gabe gets up and heads over to the bar, leaving me to mull over his words. Although he's being a bit unfair when he says my relationships only last weeks (one lasted three months!), he is kind of right. I do tend to focus on romantic sparks, probably at the expense of compatibility. I like the magic of fancying someone, when you first meet someone new and they just seem like the best person in the world. I love flirting, going on dates and building up to the first kiss. I adore the thrill of getting intimate with someone I'm really drawn to – the chemistry of not being

67

able to keep your hands off each other. I love it when everything's sparkly and new. In fact, Gabe's right, I'm a honeymoon-phase addict. I'm pretty good at finding people I fancy, but things always do go downhill when I realise that the person I found utterly gorgeous and charming actually has intolerable flaws. Like my last sort-of boyfriend, Aaron. We were together for two months, the sex was amazing and we'd have these awesome cosy nights cooking for each other and going for walks holding hands through the city. It was so romantic until one day, we were walking hand-in-hand through Central Park when a cute little dog ran up to us. I was about to kneel down to pet him when Aaron kicked him away, like he was a pest. I couldn't believe it! All this time, I'd been dating a guy who thought it was acceptable to kick dogs. I never saw him again after that.

Then there was Luke – an Australian chef – who seemed like a great catch. He was tall, attractive and smart, and we got along great until he made a few passing comments that just didn't sit right. He got sick and ended up needing his appendix removed. He forked out for a senior surgeon. I assumed it was for the extra expertise, but he admitted that he 'felt more comfortable in the hands of a man'. I told him to go find the hands of a man because this *woman* was done.

Actually, maybe Gabe's right. Maybe successful relationships do only work if you've got a mental checklist of criteria and instead of being blinded by butterflies in your stomach and raw physical attraction, you start off by assessing your partner's compatibility, rather than focusing on how pretty the city looks at night as you stroll hand-in-hand trying to pretend life is like a Hollywood movie.

'What's up?' Gabe arrives back at the table holding a tray with a few more drinks and a couple of shots.

'I was just thinking about what you said.' I sigh as I pick up a drink, muttering thanks. 'I suck at relationships.'

'Well, your track record isn't the *best*,' Gabe agrees, as he places the tray down on the table. 'But who am I to judge? After all, you're the matchmaker, not me!' He winks as he sits down.

'Me, a matchmaker,' I tut. 'It's like you trying to be a…' I look at Gabe's skinny effete frame. 'A bodybuilder.'

Gabe smiles. 'Bit harsh, but true. Or you, trying to be a chartered surveyor!' Gabe jokes. 'By the way, did Olly buy it?'

'I'm not sure,' I admit as I reach for a shot.

We clink our shot glasses together and then down them in one, before wincing.

'Yuck!' I comment.

'Bleughh!' Gabe pulls a face.

His phone buzzes and he picks it up off the table.

'Sanjay,' he explains, opening a message. Sanjay was our boss, although he feels more like a pal, from The Eagle. Gabe sends a few messages while I sip my drink, trying to get rid of the taste of the shot.

'Sanjay's with Jim, shall I invite them?' Gabe suggests. Jim's another one of our old workmates.

'Yeah, why not?' I shrug as I take another sip of my drink.

I haven't seen Sanjay and Jim for a couple of months and it would be good to catch up. Jim works behind the bar. He's been working at The Eagle for years, while freelancing as a web designer. He likes to go on about coding and programming languages but he's a sweet mild-mannered guy with old-school gentlemanly values. Whenever we used to work together, he'd always serve the rowdy customers, sparing me the aggro when he could. Sanjay's less mild-mannered. In fact, he's incredibly boisterous, but he's fun. He opened The Eagle. He owns a string of bars across New York and even though they're not the classiest of establishments, he's still super flash. He wears a Rolex and has an apartment overlooking Central Park, and even though he's incredibly ostentatious, he's not stuck up at all. He's one of the funniest warmest people I know.

Gabe and I catch up on a bit of gossip, sipping our drinks,

while we wait for Jim and Sanjay to arrive. The bar starts filling up with an after-work crowd and someone turns the music up. The atmosphere is actually pretty good for 7 p.m. on a Wednesday night and I can tell by the way Gabe is looking curiously around the bar – taking in the well-dressed punters that have also chosen this place over the pretentious bars down the road – that he's beginning to reassess his view of Milano's. It beats those poncey city bars hands down, and I can practically see him making a mental note to come here again.

'What's up party people!?' Sanjay bellows as he approaches our table. A few other drinkers turn to look as he barrels over, embracing us in big hugs. Jim trails behind a little sheepishly.

It turns out Sanjay is in such high spirits because he's just snapped up a disused bar in a property auction and has big plans to renovate it and make a fortune.

'Let's celebrate! Drinks are on me!' he announces, before heading to the bar to get a round.

Jim fills us in on some news from The Eagle.

'A new guy came in for a singing audition today,' he says, causing Gabe's ears to prick up.

'A new guy?' Gabe asks.

'Yeah. He's a George Michael lookalike. Spitting image. And he sounds the same too.'

'What?! But we do drag queens at The Eagle, not lookalikes,' Gabe huffs, clearly not impressed with the idea of having the spotlight on someone else.

'I don't think that's set in stone!' Jim says. 'It's just kind of happened that way that it tends to be drag queens that perform. Sanjay doesn't seem opposed to having lookalikes, or cover artists as they prefer to be known.'

'Cover artists?!' Gabe sneers, knocking back the last of his drink. 'What is The Eagle? A cruise ship?'

Jim shrugs, looking a little awkward. Unlike me, he doesn't quite understand how protective Gabe gets about The Eagle. Gabe loves singing there. It's his only creative outlet these days and I think he sees it as *his* place with *his* fans. He's already sidelined his singing ambitions enough, the last thing he needs is to get sidelined at The Eagle too.

Fortunately, Sanjay arrives back at the table with our drinks. He's carrying a tray loaded, and I mean loaded, with drinks.

'Oh my God!' I gawp at the shots – a rainbow array of tinted spirits that make me feel nauseous just looking at them.

Gabe reaches for a yellow-coloured shot before Sanjay's even managed to place the tray down on the table.

'Congratulations, mate!' he says, toasting Sanjay with the shot glass, before knocking it back.

Sanjay tells us all about his plans for his new bar, while we all down shots. It feels like we're back at The Eagle, at one of the lock-ins we'd have after work, where we'd sit up until the early hours of the morning chatting rubbish and setting the world to rights. I'm feeling happy and fuzzy inside, not just from the company but from the booze too.

Jim goes off on a tangent about coding and I momentarily tune out and glance around the bar. For a second, I think I spot Olly standing with a couple of friends further along the bar, but it can't be him. It must just be someone with a similar outfit of skinny jeans and a burgundy shirt. Someone who also has tattoo sleeves. Surely, it's not him? I crane my neck, trying to get a better look, when suddenly the man turns and I can barely believe it. It *is* Olly. Handsome, dapper, flash Olly is in this crummy dive bar, which is probably the last place I imagined someone like him would frequent. He's the kind of guy I'd assume would be swanning off to some exclusive private members' club or would have reservations at one of the new Michelin-star fusion restaurants that keep opening in Soho. But instead, he's here. In Milano's, ordering – I watch the barman handing him a drink – a pint of ale!

'What are you looking at, Polly?' Gabe nudges me and follows my gaze towards the bar. 'Who's that?' he asks as his eyes land upon Olly.

'That's Olly. The owner of that dating agency I visited,' I tell him, in a hushed voice, even though there's no chance Olly's going to overhear me in this crowded noisy bar.

I cower in my seat, self-conscious about being spotted.

'That's Olly?' Gabe asks, peering over.

'Shhh!' I hiss. 'Stop staring!'

'He's seriously hot!' Gabe comments, leering at him.

'Stop staring, Gabe!'

'Who's hot?' Sanjay pipes up, glancing around.

'No one!' I hiss.

'Who?' Sanjay presses.

'Yeah, who?' Jim asks, looking across the bar.

'Guys stop!' I insist, but it's no use. Gabe points drunkenly across the bar.

'That guy!' he says.

Sanjay and Jim immediately look over, clocking Olly in a second. He's by far the hottest guy in the bar and he naturally stands out compared to all the other boring-looking drinkers in their dull office clothes.

'That's Olly Corrigan!' Sanjay pipes up. 'He was featured in *Time* magazine last month. I remember because I spent a solid half hour drooling over the article and wondering if he might be gay.'

Gay?! It hadn't even occurred to me that Olly could be gay but it might explain a few things – his incredible fashion sense, for one thing.

'What did you conclude?' I ask with a slight sense of trepidation.

'Straight,' Sanjay sighs. 'Googled him in the end and found some old article about his ex-wife. Apparently, they used to run a PR company together.

'Oh, right,' I say, thinking back to Olly's grand offices. Did he and his ex-wife build an empire together? Is she still in the picture?

Sanjay knocks back the last of his drink. ''Nother round?' he suggests.

'Guys, can we go somewhere else?' I ask, eager to get away from Olly. The last thing I need is for him to spot me knocking back shots with my friends from the gay bar. It hardly fits my boring chartered surveyor image.

'What? I thought you loved it in here?' Gabe pipes up.

'I do!' I hiss. 'But I can't relax with him in here.' I signal towards Olly, who now appears locked in conversation with two equally trendy and out-of-place companions.

Gabe rolls his eyes. 'Alright,' he sighs, turning to Sanjay and Jim. 'She's been undercover. He's not meant to know who she is. Long story.'

Sanjay raises an eyebrow; he looks perplexed. Jim just regards us blankly, I think he assumes we've had too much to drink. Sanjay suggests that we get a cab and go to one of his bars, which we all know will mean free drinks all night. Gabe jumps at the chance and we gather our stuff to go. We're all a little pissed as we drunkenly weave through the crowded bar. One of mine and Gabe's favourite songs – 'Atomic' by Blondie – is playing and Gabe gets side-tracked, bursting into song, clasping my hand and pirouetting with me in the middle of the bar. For a second, I forget about Olly and, drunk on the music (and the booze), I let Gabe spin me around, ducking under his outstretched arm like a clumsy ballroom dancer. We used to dance like that at The Eagle all the time. The floors would be sticky with spilt drink and my trainers would peel off the ground as Gabe would twirl me around, his sparkly drag frocks sparkling under the flittering light of the mirror balls. The song ends and we collapse into each other's arms, laughing.

We link arms and stagger across the bar – the shots having caught up with us – giggling away, when all of a sudden, I look over and see Olly eyeing me with a curious, unreadable look.

'Oh shit,' I mutter under my breath.

'What?' Gabe asks, before spotting Olly, who is now only three or four metres away. Somehow, we've ended up drunkenly dancing towards him. I force a polite smile.

'Hello Polly,' Olly says in an oddly distant voice, his eyes roaming from me to Gabe.

'Hi, how are you?' I ask, nervously, even though it was only a few hours ago that we said goodbye.

'Good, and yourself?' he asks the question with a raised eyebrow as though passing judgement on my inebriated state.

'Great. Just having a few after work drinks,' I say, with an awkward laugh.

'Yep, after work drinks,' Gabe chimes in. I shoot him a look and see his pupils are dilated to the point that his brown eyes appear almost black – the way they look whenever he gets drunk. The shots have clearly gone to both of our heads.

'And are you a chartered surveyor too?' Olly asks Gabe, with a sceptical tone.

Sanjay is standing by watching the encounter with a completely bemused expression on his face. *Please, please don't say anything. Please don't blow our cover,* I silently urge him.

'Oh yes. I'm a chartered surveyor. Yep!' Gabe insists.

I slip my arm under his, clamping him to my side in an attempt to lead him away from Olly.

'We should go,' I mutter.

'So you work together then?' Olly asks.

What is up with him? Why can't he just say hi and bye? What's with all the questions?

'Oh yes. Long day at the office. Just been chartering those surveys,' Gabe comments, his lips twitching as Sanjay catches his eye.

I glare at him. *Chartering those surveys?!* What the hell?!

'Yep, long day!' I mutter, pulling Gabe away before this gets any worse.

'Right.' Olly frowns. 'I thought you worked on Staten Island. That's quite far to have come for after work drinks?' he says, raising an eyebrow.

'Yes, well, we just love Milano's! Anyway, got to go, bye!' I pull Gabe away, who has now crumpled into laughter, and shuffle out of the bar, praying that I never see Olly Corrington again.

'Wait!' Olly says. He reaches forward and places his hand on my arm, before stepping forward into our path.

Gabe giggles at my side but Olly ignores him, choosing instead to fix me with an oddly intense sobering look. His eyes are questioning, perplexed and vulnerable. There's an openness in them now that we're not in his office and he's not trying to sell me something. Up close, his face is even more attractive than it looked from across his desk earlier. The crows' feet around his eyes make him look sensitive and mature, almost thoughtful. His hand is still resting on my forearm and I'm acutely aware of his touch. I glance down at his fingers and he quickly lets his hands drop.

'Who are you, Polly?' he asks, his eyes boring into me. They're so penetrating that I can't bring myself to lie. I'm not Polly Wood, a chartered surveyor from Staten Island, that's obvious to both of us, and yet I can't tell him the truth: that I'm working for To the Moon & Back. I can't betray Derek like that.

'Umm…' I squirm, breaking eye contact and glancing down.

'You're not a chartered surveyor, are you?'

I can't bring myself to look at him. I know I don't have my wits about me right now to keep the act up.

'Why did you lie when you came to see me today?' Olly asks.

I look back up and his eyes look darker, almost hurt. I want to answer but I'm not sure how to explain it. It's clearly bothering him that I lied, and that makes me wonder whether that moment we had when we said goodbye at the lift was, in fact, genuine. If Olly wasn't just a little bit interested in me, why would he care whether or not I'd lied?

'Come on, babe.' Gabe tugs on my arm and pulls me away.

'Let's go!' Sanjay says, and before I know it, I'm being swept out of the bar. Gabe probably thinks he's doing me a favour, saving me from an awkward situation with Olly, and in a way, he is, yet I can't help feeling really guilty.

I look over my shoulder to see Olly watching me, with that perplexed and uneasy expression.

'I'm sorry…' I utter, as Gabe pulls me through the door.

Chapter 7

You probably wouldn't think it would be possible to edit a picture of a turnip for two hours but somehow, I've managed it. Alicia has decided she wants to use the turnip shot on the cover of her cookbook and apparently, it's essential that I edit it to absolute perfection. And by absolute perfection, I mean follow a checklist of criteria outlining pixels, sizing, colour saturation, scale, brightness, and well, the list goes on. I know I took on this job for free for the experience and to get my work out there, but I didn't anticipate it would involve quite so much effort.

I'm at work and I'm meant to be messaging women on Match. com on behalf of Andy Graham, but Alicia's demanding the image now and I can't let her down. Apparently, the publisher has only just told her the book's going to print and she needs it straight away. I've tilted the screen a little so that Derek can't see that I'm working on a turnip when I should be turning Andy's love life around. I'll make it up later by working into the evening, even though I really should be going home to have an early night after staying out far too late with Gabe, Sanjay and Jim.

As I tweak the colour saturation on the image, my mind starts to wander in its unfocused hungover state. The turnip takes me back to when I was a kid and my parents used to try to have Sunday afternoon family gardening sessions. It was their thing. They met through a volunteering project to turn a derelict plot of grass into an uplifting garden at a children's hospital. My dad had just arrived in the UK and had got a job teaching at a school in Cornwall. He was trying to make new friends so took part in the gardening project, which my mum had organised. She's loved gardening since she was a kid and apparently, she first took a shine to my dad while teaching him how to prune a rose bush. She was tickled by this New York guy who didn't have a clue about horticulture and they bonded immediately, chatting away while clearing weeds and planting flowers. Ever since, gardening has been their thing and our garden back home looks like it belongs on the Chelsea Flower Show.

I tried to get involved when I was a kid. My mum even gave me my own flower bed to look after during our family gardening sessions, but all the pansies I planted rapidly shrivelled up and died, only to be replaced by weeds. Despite my mum's attempts to make me green-fingered, gardening just never appealed. I wasn't naturally a country girl. For as long as I can remember, I've wanted to live in New York. Ever since I was little and my dad told me stories about my late grandmother, who was a semi-famous artist and a social butterfly who'd spend all her time at parties, mingling with creatives and leading a wild and exciting life while living in a little Manhattan studio apartment. She was a bit wayward and apparently couldn't even remember the name of my dad's father – an English violinist who disappeared after a short fling. Even though she sounded a bit wild, I idolised the exciting vision of city life, while my dad had flat out rejected it. His childhood had been a bit chaotic and even though he loved my grandmother, despite her slightly unconventional ways, he fantasised about going to England and swapping Manhattan for a calmer life – a dream he eventually fulfilled.

I never got to meet my grandmother and I think my dad told me about her as a cautionary tale, but I took it the opposite way. I began lusting after the vivid, wild, busy New York life he'd left behind, and I set about trying to learn everything I could about the place. I watched movies set there, read books, looked at thousands of pictures and covered my bedroom walls with posters. While my friends had boybands emblazoned on their bedroom walls, I had a huge poster above my bed of the Statue of Liberty, and I used to gaze up at it at night and swear that I'd go there. I made a firm promise with myself that one day I'd live in New York. I even got a biro one time and drew a small stick figure that was meant to be me right in the statue's crown. I'd heard that you could go inside and climb right up there. To my 12-year-old self, reaching the crown represented the ultimate New York experience, the pinnacle of my dreams. I don't think my dad was overly happy about my wish to move back to the States – I think he'd have preferred me to embrace the country lifestyle – but he and my mum eventually accepted that America was where I wanted to live, just like my dad had wanted to make it to England.

I have an urge to pick up the phone and call home, but I glance at the time display in the corner of my monitor, it's 2.30 p.m. there. My parents will be at work.

'What's up?' Derek looks over.

'Oh, nothing,' I insist, quickly clicking away from the turnip picture.

'Really? You looked miles away.'

'Oh, really!?' I laugh, feeling a tiny bit homesick, although it's probably just the effects of last night's booze and a lack of sleep.

'Hmm…' Derek frowns. 'Let me finish this and then we'll head out to breakfast. Have you eaten yet?'

'Um, no, I haven't actually,' I admit. I couldn't face food this morning.

'Well, let's have a staff breakfast! It'll be my first ever To the

Moon & Back team outing!' He smiles goofily, and I can't help laughing.

'Okay, cool, sounds good!'

'Great, give me a second,' Derek says as he finishes off filing some accounts he's been grumbling about.

I tilt my screen, making sure that Derek can't see and quickly adjust the saturation on the turnip shot, cropping it to the exact dimensions Alicia's asked for, before double-checking the list to make sure I've addressed all the other edits and then email it over, with a sense of relief. I click back onto Match, hoping that some messages might have arrived for Andy, but his inbox is empty.

'Are you ready?' Derek asks brightly as he pushes his chair back from his desk.

A recommended match pops up on my screen of a stunning girl called Katarina, who's probably way out of Andy's league. 'Yeah, sure.'

I quickly save Katarina's profile to Andy's favourites before grabbing my handbag.

'I know a great pancake place, fancy it?' Derek asks as I pull on my coat.

'Sure,' I reply, smiling.

I follow Derek out of the office. It's funny. At my interview, I thought he was going to be a massive creep, but I was wrong about him. He dresses like a bit of a creep, that's for sure, with his tacky shirts and aviator-style glasses and he certainly doesn't have the most wholesome of pasts, having produced movies such as *Forrest Hump* and *Indiana Bones and the Temple of Poon*, but he's sweet. He's got a good heart and he seems like someone who's turned their life around. He may have been sleazy once, but he's married now, and he treats me with a vibe that's paternal rather than pervy. He's not the porn boss pest I feared he might be, instead he's simply the owner of a struggling dating agency trying to make money to cover his wife's medical bills. He's the kind of boss who takes his new member of staff out for pancakes because they're looking a bit down. He winds his scarf around his neck before locking the office up.

Derek waxes lyrical about the pancake café as we walk down the block and cut down a few side streets. It's a cold day and there's a light spattering of snow. The icy flakes land on my cheeks, waking me up. Just as the cool air begins to pinch, we arrive outside a corny Fifties-style diner with a pleasingly tacky retro vibe.

'Brilliant!' I comment as I take it in.

Derek smiles. 'They do all-you-can-drink coffee here too,' he tells me, as he holds open the door.

We sit at a table by the window and a waitress, who's even wearing a Fifties-style apron and name tag, hands us some laminated menus.

Breakfast has never sounded so delicious. As I read the menu, I can't decide between a stack of pancakes with grilled banana and blueberries and a classic stack with lemon and sugar. All the choices sound incredible. They certainly beat my usual breakfasts of black coffee and rice cakes.

The waitress comes back over with two coffees and takes our order. I order the stacked pancakes with banana and blueberries. Derek opts for the same.

'So…' Derek takes a sip of coffee. 'Tell me about your consultation with Elite Love Match. Let's debrief. How did it go?'

'It was okay,' I reply, even though I can't stop picturing the expression on Olly's face last night – the quizzical hurt look in his eyes when he asked me who I really was. It was such an awkward, uncomfortable moment. I take a sip of coffee and try to forget about it. I certainly won't be telling Derek about that part of our encounter.

'So, what was the office like? Fancy? As fancy as they make it out to be in the brochure?' Derek asks, with a hint of trepidation.

I nod, feeling a little bad for him. 'It was really fancy.'

'How fancy are we talking?' Derek asks.

I fill him in on what the building was like, from the slick reception area to the spacious open plan office with Olly's private office attached. I feel a bit bad describing to Derek just how swanky Elite Love Match was but he did ask me to go there so I could give him an honest report on what it was like. Nevertheless, he looks a bit deflated.

Fortunately, the waitress arrives with our pancakes, which are so hot and fresh that they're steaming. My stomach rumbles. The pancakes look plump and fluffy, the golden syrup glistens and the banana slices and blueberries look bright and fresh. This is probably the most colourful, delicious-looking meal I've eaten in months – not just photographed or seen on a picture I'm editing on my computer screen. It's been ages since I went to a café or a restaurant for a proper sit-down meal. I simply haven't been able to justify the expense when all my money's been going on photography supplies and getting by.

I reach for the sugar bowl and dust some sugar over my food. I feel ravenous. Derek's plate is piled high with fluffy pancakes and looks equally delicious. We both tuck in, making the odd enthusiastic comment about the food in between mouthfuls.

'So, Olly has a slick swanky office,' Derek says eventually, pausing from demolishing his pancake stack to reach for his coffee.

'Yeah, it's slick but it's completely lacking in…' I pause, brandishing my fork around as I search for the right word. 'Soul,' I land upon. 'His whole business is completely lacking in soul.'

Derek raises an eyebrow. 'What do you mean?'

'It's formulaic. And kind of intimidating.' I think back to sitting opposite Olly and the serious way he quizzed me about my criteria and income, like some kind of job interview. 'It wasn't welcoming,' I tell Derek. 'To the Moon & Back is better. It may be smaller, but it's friendly and cosy. It feels more genuine.'

Derek nods as he chews on a mouthful of pancake, but he

doesn't seem particularly convinced. I get the feeling he just thinks I'm trying to make him feel better when that really isn't the case. The more I think about it, the more I can totally see why high-flying people like Brandon would choose Derek's dating agency over somewhere like Elite Love Match. It seemed a mystery to me at first that they'd opt for Derek's strange tarot lounge set up, but if Elite Love Match is the competition, it makes total sense. I'd do exactly the same. I try to explain what I mean.

'You have a personal approach. To the Moon & Back is a friendly dating agency, that's your USP over *Olly* Corrigan,' I explain.

Derek still looks unconvinced. 'Friendliness? That's our USP?' He picks up a small jug of maple syrup and drizzles some more over his pancakes.

'Yes! The personal touch. Trust me, you don't need flashy offices.'

'Hmm…' Derek sets down the jug and cuts a corner off one of his plump-looking pancakes. 'And what did you make of Olly? Was he as charming as the press always make out?'

'Erm…' I look down at my pancakes and carefully cut a bite as I try to answer in a way that doesn't totally give away how completely intense, charged, flirty and magnetic my encounters with Olly were. Even now, a day later, I'm still struggling to find the right words to describe him.

'He's alright.' I shrug. 'He doesn't have anything that we don't have,' I tell Derek, even though I'm not entirely sure that's true. Olly is a ridiculously charming businessman after all. He's probably in some swanky corporate meeting right now while Derek and I are sitting here gorging on pancakes.

'Just alright?' Derek asks, seemingly unconvinced.

'Yeah, just alright,' I lie again, taking a sip of my coffee.

'Hmm…' Derek murmurs. 'But everyone seems to love him. The press has been singing his praises non-stop from the second his agency's doors opened.'

'Well, he probably just charmed them. He has that slick charm, I guess, but he's not very warm,' I tell Derek.

'Okay…' Derek muses. 'So, you think we should be warm?'

'Exactly. While he's being all cold and slick, we'll be warm. We'll be the friendly personal agency to his corporate love machine,' I say.

Derek laughs. 'Alright then. I'll revamp the website today and add some stuff about being a personal, approachable agency. Maybe we can pick up some of the clients who didn't want to sign with Olly,' Derek says pensively, as though he's thinking aloud.

'Sounds like a plan,' I comment, popping the last bite of my pancake into my mouth.

'Okay. Good work, Polly,' Derek says, before signalling over his shoulder for the bill.

Chapter 8

It's funny how your life can change in such a short space of time. Only a week ago, I was taking photos of turnips in Alicia's dining room, wondering how I was going to pay my rent, and now I'm a matchmaker with a paycheck! I feel pretty good and even better to be taking photos in Central Park with my friends.

Scarlett and Amy are two friends from university who also moved to New York after graduation. Amy studied fashion and works as a designer's assistant, while Scarlett, who is fluent in five languages, has developed a specialism in travel photography. She's managed to get a ton of contacts at travel magazines around the world and she's constantly jetting off to weird and wonderful locations, snapping the most amazing exotic scenery for editorial features.

We wander through the park, taking photos of the scenery and catching up. It feels good to be in the zone again – twisting my lens and snapping my surroundings. As much as I'm enjoying my new job as a matchmaker, nothing beats that deep focused feeling I experience when I'm trying to get a good shot – that sense of pure concentration and fulfilment when you're just in the zone and doing exactly what it is that you're meant to be doing.

Scarlett's got a trip coming up to visit a coastal village in

Morocco that's meant to be the hottest new travel destination. She's super excited about it and describes the scenery of 'rugged stone beaches, rickety old shipping boats, seagulls and white fortress walls' that she can't wait to photograph. Meanwhile, Amy starts whingeing about her demanding diva boss who's being incredibly picky about the design of pieces for her autumn/winter collection. The way Amy describes her reminds me of Alicia with her ridiculous demands for the turnip picture. I ended up staying at the office until 8 p.m. the other night making up for the time I'd spent working on them in the morning when I was meant to be matchmaking. Fortunately, Alicia seemed happy with the pictures in the end, but I'm really glad that job's over.

'Have you got any more photography jobs coming up?' Scarlett asks, glancing over as she adjusts the lens on her camera before taking a picture of a robin that's perched on a bench in the park.

'Umm, no. Not yet.' I laugh a little awkwardly. Scarlett has really excelled since university. Somehow, she's totally found her feet in the photography world, while I'm still floundering. She's not arrogant or smug about it. She knows I'm a decent photographer and I know she wants me to do well, that's why she's always asking about my jobs and encouraging me to keep going.

'I'm a bit busy at the moment with the dating agency stuff. I'll probably try to do some more photography jobs on the side once I'm settled in,' I tell her, forcing an upbeat smile that probably comes across a lot more positive than how I feel.

The thing is, as much as I'm grateful for having found a job, I am a bit worried about photography. Even though matchmaking is entertaining, I'm worried that I might get sucked into it and abandon my true ambitions to become a full-time photographer. So many people who do arts courses seem to go down that route. Wannabe actors who've studied drama for three years move to New York and then end up being extroverted waiters at fancy restaurants. Or aspiring writers do courses in creative writing

86

and then end up writing newsletters for boring companies. I don't want that to happen to me. I want to stay true to my original photography dreams; I don't want to give up. It's just like when I decided, aged 12, that I was going to live in New York. I believed I'd made it and even though sometimes, it seemed farfetched, I stuck to my guns and kept on believing, and then I made it happen. I want to achieve the same thing with my photography ambitions. Although becoming a proper photographer seems like an impossible dream sometimes, I have to keep believing in it if it's ever going to happen. A few months ago, I even stuck a poster on my bedroom wall of a Mario Testino portrait of Marilyn Monroe. Like the Statue of Liberty poster I had on my bedroom wall when I was a kid, I wanted to have the Mario Testino poster there as an intention-setting tool – a daily reminder to keep chasing my hopes and my dreams.

'Don't get too sucked into that place though,' Scarlett warns, lowering her camera from taking pictures of the robin. 'It sounds funny and everything but you're a photographer, not a match-maker.'

'I know,' I reply. 'I'm not going to give up, I just need a bit of money to tide me over for a bit. I couldn't keep scraping away like I had been doing, eating cheap dumplings in Chinatown for dinner because I couldn't afford a proper meal.'

'You were eating at the Dumpling Dictator's?' Amy asks, raising an eyebrow.

The Dumpling Dictator is a legend in Manhattan. She's been running a dumpling takeaway in Chinatown for twenty years but refuses to learn more than about twelve words of English. Her menu consists of six things, two of which she doesn't serve and two of which are tea and coffee. She gets queues around the block for her dumplings, which come with two different fillings – pork or vegetables. If you don't make your decision within about twenty seconds of getting to the front of the queue, you're kicked out of the takeaway. The local press picked up on her antics and dubbed her the 'Dumpling Dictator'. Her behaviour would be enough to turn most customers away, but people keep coming back, probably because she serves five dumplings for a dollar-fifty and that's a deal you can't beat.

'Oh yeah, me and the Dumpling Dictator are like this.' I hold up two fingers intertwined. Amy laughs.

An alarm beeps on Scarlett's phone. She takes it out of her bag and looks at the screen.

'Oh, that talk with Anthony Bollaris is on in half an hour, we'd better go,' she says, looking at both me and Amy.

'Cool.' Amy hitches her bag up her shoulder.

Anthony Bollaris is a multimedia artist who everyone but me seems to love. He's doing a talk at the Met this afternoon ahead of an upcoming exhibition that's been advertised across the city.

'You guys go, I'm just going to stay here and take some pictures,' I tell them.

Scarlett makes a weak attempt to get me to come, but when she sees that I do genuinely just want to hang out in the park alone and take photos, she lets it go and I hug them both goodbye before wandering down the winding paths by myself, taking snaps of interesting things I see. I try to get into the zone: the pure state of focus, concentration and fulfilment I usually get when taking pictures, but even though I'm enjoying myself, I feel a bit distracted. I walk around for a bit, snapping away, before settling down on a bench.

I flick through the photos I've taken. Some have turned out okay, but it's not been my best session. A lot of them are quite amateurish – a pseudo-meaningful snap of a man sitting alone on a park bench and a close-up shot of a pretty flower. They're the kind of photos I used to take as a teenager. I sigh. For some reason, I'm just not feeling it today. I linger on the park bench, not sure what to do next. I glance at my watch, it's 3.30 p.m. I decide to call my parents and see what they're up to.

I get out my phone and call the landline, which rings five or six times. I'm about to hang up when my mum answers.

'Hello.'

'Hey Mum, it's me!'

'Polly, hello love,' she answers. I smile to myself. No one else calls me love and it's good to hear.

'I was just washing the dishes, had to dry my hands. What are you up to? Is everything okay?' she asks. I picture her standing in the kitchen, the phone pressed between her cheek and shoulder as she dries her hands on a tea towel.

'Yeah, everything's fine,' I say, gazing blankly across the park.

'You don't sound fine, what's up?' My mum asks, a note of panic in her voice. Ever since I moved to the US, she's always been slightly on edge about my well-being. For the first few months I lived in the States, she made me text her every day, as if a liberal arts college was a crime-infested ghetto. I had to tactfully suggest, after two months of fretful daily communication, that maybe we could go a day or two without talking. She was reluctant at first, but she got used to the idea. Now we chat a little bit in a family group chat during the week (my dad likes to send pictures of the garden) and we usually catch up on the phone at the weekends. Except last weekend, we missed calling each other. I was preoccupied with my photoshoot for Alicia and somehow, neither of us got around to calling. I mentioned starting a new job by text, but I didn't go into too much detail. I'm not sure how my mum would feel about me flirting with women on the internet for a living.

'How's the new job? Is everything okay?'

'Yeah, yeah… It's fine, don't worry,' I insist.

'Really? Are you sure? Because if it's not working out, the vacancy at the surgery is still available. They were saying yesterday that he needs someone to start ASAP and I thought of you. It would be a nice steady job. Something to get you started. You could stay at home for a bit, save up. Your dad and I would love to have you around.'

'I know mum, maybe, but I want to give things more of a chance here first,' I say, feeling a little guilty.

'Yes, I know.' My mum sighs. Like my dad, she's not a city person and she doesn't really understand how I could choose a busy, crowded, bustling metropolis like New York over the beautiful, peaceful, natural scenery of Cornwall. She doesn't get that I like the adventure, the people, the unpredictability. Even though it's not always easy in New York, your luck can change in a second and suddenly life can be spectacular. Whereas in Cornwall, gazing over the rolling fields, the days would just blur into one another and I'd always feel as though life was just passing me by.

'So, what's up? Talk to me,' my mum says.

'Oh, nothing's up. I've just lost my photography mojo today,' I tell her.

'It'll come back love. Is everything else alright?' she asks. My mum has something of a sixth sense when it comes to knowing if something's up with me. If I'm totally honest, although I'm finding working as a matchmaker kind of interesting, the weird clinical attitudes the agencies have to romance has got to me a bit. I think on some level, it is bothering me. It's nothing like the love between my parents back home.

'Mum,' I venture, 'You know when you met Dad, how did you know he was right for you?'

'Umm…' My mum goes quite for a moment, thinking. 'I didn't at first. I wasn't looking for a boyfriend, I was just getting on with my gardening projects and work, then your dad came along. I thought he was handsome and interesting, but I didn't think he'd stick around. He was just this funny bloke from New York. I thought he'd spend a few months here, get bored and be on the next plane back home, but then a few months turned into a year and before I realised it, we'd fallen for each other and he wasn't going anywhere. Sometimes love comes along when you least expect it, I suppose.'

I smile to myself. 'So you didn't have, like, a mental checklist you went through then?'

'A mental checklist?' My mum echoes.

'Yeah, you know, earns such-and-such amount, early riser or night owl, six-foot-two.'

My mum snorts with laughter. 'No! Of course not! What are you talking about?'

I tell her about my consultation at Elite Love Match.

My mum howls hysterically. 'You New Yorkers are crazy. You're not ordering a robot with special hi-tech features, you're talking about human beings. You can't control love.'

'That's what I thought!' I add. It feels good to hear my mum, who's been married for twenty-five years, confirm my suspicion that the way Olly Corrigan does love is not realistic.

My mum's laughter finally dies down. 'Honestly love, people who look for a relationship with a mental checklist are going to be single forever. It just doesn't work like that.'

'Yeah, I thought it seemed a bit much.'

'It really is. It's very extreme. I can't wait to tell the girls at Bridge about that,' my mum says. 'They'll love that.'

We chat for a bit longer before she hands me over to my dad, who asks about my news before telling me about a gong meditation class he's started going to at the village hall and an 'incredible' new jam seller at the farmers' market. He ends up having to dash to catch the market, which is held on Saturday mornings because he wants to get there 'before all the good stuff goes'.

I say goodbye and send them my love before hanging up, feeling more relieved than I expected to know that love isn't just a checklist.

Chapter 9

The rest of the weekend is fairly uneventful. I catch up on sleep since I still haven't quite got used to going from my irregular freelance routine to my regular nine-to-five employment. Gabe and I hang out in the flat on Sunday evening. Adam's flown to Chicago for a business trip and so unlike most Sundays, which Gabe and Adam reserve for doing coupley things, he ends up in the flat with nothing better to do than relax with me. So, we snuggle up under a duvet on the sofa, order pizza and binge-watch horror movies – the perfect antidote to all the romance that's become the theme of my life. By Monday morning, I feel sufficiently recharged and by the time I arrive at the office, clutching two coffees fresh from Starbucks for myself and Derek, I feel almost excited to be back at work and walking through Derek's bizarre client lounge. I feel pumped – ready to fire off messages to unsuspecting women and lock down dates.

'Morning Derek.' I breeze into the office, where Derek is already sitting at his desk, a look of concentration etched onto his face as he eyes his monitor.

'Morning Polly,' he says, glancing over with a friendly smile.

'Got you a coffee.' I head over to his desk and place a latte down.

'Thanks!' Derek smiles, looking genuinely touched. 'That was sweet of you,' he says. 'Did you, err, put any sugar in it?'

'Oh, no, sorry.'

'No problem.' Derek pulls open his office drawer and takes out a box of sugar cubes. He pulls off the lid of the coffee cup and gently drops a few in while asking me about my weekend.

'It was alright. I took some pictures, relaxed,' I tell him as I take off my coat.

'Ah yes, I almost forgot you were a photographer. How's that going?' Derek asks.

'S'ok.' I shrug as I drape my coat on the back of my desk chair. I don't really have the energy to talk about my photography dreams to Derek. The two worlds of To the Moon & Back and photography aren't exactly aligned.

'How's your wife doing?' I ask.

'Her knee's been playing up a bit. She's been experiencing some pain. She's got an appointment with a doctor, so we'll see how it goes,' Derek says.

'Ah, okay.'

'Thanks for asking though,' Derek says, frowning at his monitor. I get the feeling he also doesn't really want to talk too much about his personal life at work.

'I've revamped the website,' he tells me. 'Gave it a warmer friendlier feel, like you suggested.'

'Really?' I walk over to Derek's desk to get a closer look. The homepage is displayed on the screen, and the agency now has the tagline, 'A personalised dating service tailored to your individual needs'.

'Nice!' I scan the text on the homepage, which Derek has also peppered with the words 'friendly', 'bespoke', 'warm', even 'gentle'.

'We'll see how it goes, eh?' Derek says with a cheerful grin.

'Fingers crossed!' I smile back, holding up my crossed fingers as I head back to my desk.

I sit down and log onto Match. I'm really hoping Andy Graham has finally received a message. I sent a ton on Friday and I'm praying that at least one person has got back to him. It's been a whole week now and I haven't even managed to strike up a conversation with anyone, let alone set up a date. For my first client, it's not exactly going brilliantly.

'Yes!' I blurt out as I see a little '1' hovering over Andy's inbox. One message! Fantastic!

Derek glances over, questioningly.

'Just a message, for Andy,' I explain.

Derek nods and gets back to tweaking the website.

I open Andy's inbox to find a message from the stunning blonde woman whose profile I favourited last week.

Katarina:

Hello Andy,

  I love your profile!

  I think we might have quite a lot in common. It would be great to chat! Have you been on Match long?

  Don't be a stranger.

  Xxx

  Katarina

A lot in common? I raise an eyebrow, before clicking onto her page. She says she lives in Midtown and describes herself as a 'professional model and actress'. She looks impossibly glamourous and half her pictures are high-end editorial shots or photos of her larking about backstage at New York Fashion Week. She lists her interests as 'fashion, fine art, dancing and keeping fit'. What part of that is in any way in line with Andy's passion for aviation museums or Second World War history? They hardly seem like a good match to me.

94

'How's it going?' Derek asks, looking over expectantly.

'Oh, err, great! Yeah, excellent!' I lie, still trying to get my head around Katarina's message.

'Chatting to someone?' Derek says, spotting the message open on my screen.

'Erm…' I hesitate, not sure whether I should reply. Katarina seems a bit (okay, a lot) out of Andy's league and I don't particularly want to set him up for failure. 'Might be. Sort of,' I reply vaguely.

'Excellent. Andy could do with a date.'

'Sure.' I laugh awkwardly.

A silence passes between us.

'So, are you going to message the lucky lady?' Derek asks, with a cheerful optimistic look on his face.

'Of course!' I insist, smiling brightly as I open up a reply window. I can feel Derek's eyes on me as I start typing. I know I should probably try to find someone a bit more suitable, but I really need to look busy. I need Derek to believe I'm a decent matchmaker, or at least trying to be one. I start typing the first things that come to mind.

Andy:
Hi Katarina,
   Wow, thanks. You profile isn't too bad either!
   In fact, you look beautiful!
   I've only just joined Match – new to this whole thing. What about yourself?
   Xxx
   Andy

It's a pretty boring message but I can feel Derek's eyes on me, so I hit send. I glance over at Derek, who nods and smiles proudly, as though pleased with my efforts. I smile back and quickly click out of the messages. As much as I'd love to believe that someone

95

like Katarina would be a perfect match for Andy, it's hardly likely. He wants a proper relationship – a serious connection – and I need to find someone truly compatible, not some gorgeous model whose life is going to be worlds away from his.

I need to find a sweet girl, someone who shares Andy's nerdy interests. I start scrolling through profiles and go through the recommended matches of the day. After clicking through a few profiles of women who look a bit too cool, feisty or outgoing for Andy, I finally land upon someone who seems like she could be just right: a cute cardigan-wearing 27-year-old librarian called Heather with curly brown hair who describes herself as a Ravenclaw and lists history and visiting museums among a long list of hobbies that also includes board games, cosplay, Eighties electronica, steam punk and politics. Jackpot!

I'm scrolling through her profile, drinking it in, unable to believe what a great fit she is for Andy when suddenly another message pings through from Katarina.

Katarina:

Hey Andy,

> *Beautiful? Thank you! That's so sweet.*
>
> *I've been on here for a few months now, thought I'd check it out. Not having much luck so far though. Hopefully that might change!* ☺
>
> *What are you up to?*
>
> *Xxx*

Huh? Not having much luck? I'd imagine someone like Katarina would be inundated with messages.

'Going well, is it?' Derek asks, looking over again.

'Oh yeah, of course. It's going really well!' I insist brightly, even though I'm pinning all my hopes on things working out with Heather at this point.

'Excellent, you're doing a great job,' Derek says. 'Oh, and before

I forget... there's something else I was hoping you could help with?'

'Not more spy work?' I grumble.

Derek smirks. 'No, not more spy work. We're having a party. A big Valentine's Day singles mixer,' Derek enthuses. 'We do it every year and this year I want it to be bigger and better than ever before. We'll show everyone, including that cad Olly Corrigan, what we're made of. I want it to be a love fest – a night to remember! Something to put us on the map as the friendliest, warmest, most approachable dating agency in New York!'

'Right!' I comment, noting how Derek's really taking this personal approach stuff to heart. 'Sounds fun.'

'Oh, it will be,' Derek insists. 'This is going to be the biggest and best Valentine's party ever. Picture love heart balloons, heart-shaped confetti, champagne, fancy cocktails, smooth music, low lighting, chandeliers.' Derek's eyes glaze over with a look of wonder, clearly lost in the fantasy.

'Uh-huh.' I nod. 'It's sounds amazing. But, umm, where do I come in?'

'Oh yeah.' Derek snaps out of his reverie. 'I need you to scout venues. I've made a shortlist, but I need you to go visit them, chat to the owners, see what kind of deal you can get us.'

'Okay! Sounds fun,' I reply, grateful for the excuse to get away from my desk. 'Hang on a minute,' I add as a thought hits me. 'I thought you said the business was struggling. Can we really afford the party to end all parties?'

'No, we can't,' Derek admits, 'but if we can get sponsors, they can help. Leave that side of it to me.' Derek taps his nose conspiratorially.

'Okay, so I just go and see if the venues are nice then? No funny business?' I ask, feeling sceptical after last week's assignment.

'Honestly, that's it!' Derek throws his hands up in mock

surrender. 'I promise. Just check out the venues and report back. That's all.'

'Okay cool,' I reply as another message from Katarina pings into Andy Graham's inbox.

'Sounds like things are going well for Andy?' Derek observes.

'Oh yeah! Great!'

'Brilliant. Well I'll email over a few venue ideas in a minute and you can decide which one you want to go to first.'

'When shall I go?' I ask.

'See if they can book you in for tomorrow?' Derek suggests. 'I'm just emailing over some venue details now.'

'Okay, cool. Will do,' I reply brightly, as I click out of Katarina's message and scroll through Heather's pictures. She has a kind face. She looks like the sort of girl who, if she was your friend, would never forget your birthday and would always be there for you if you were having a crisis. But it's not just her looks, her interests couldn't be more ideal for Andy. If his name was put into the sorting hat, I'm sure he'd end up in Ravenclaw too. I can practically picture them nestled together on the sofa on cold evenings with their books, or enjoying a museum together on a Sunday afternoon, chatting about the exhibits in hushed tones. They'd be such an adorable couple! I draft her a message, writing and rewriting it multiple times to make sure it piques her interest without feeling too keen. I drop in a few references to history and Hogwarts that I'm pretty sure she'll appreciate and hit send.

I fire off another half a dozen messages to other potential matches just to be on the safe side in case Heather doesn't reply. It is a Monday morning and it's not exactly the peak time for people to check their internet dating profiles. Or at least, that's the reason I'm telling myself no one's replying. I log out of Andy's account and decide to focus on another of the agency's clients instead – a 43-year-old divorcee called Steve, who should be an easier sell. He's a hedge fund manager with a love of fine art and marathons. He's in great shape and has a yuppy look about him

– a light tan, chinos, designer sweaters and a neat salt and pepper beard. He's not exactly my type. I don't dig his preppy look, his smile seems a bit smug and I don't buy the interest in art. He strikes me as the kind of bloke who sees art on a similar level to buying sports cars – status symbols to impress his friends. But nevertheless, a lot of women are into rich guys and I suspect it won't be too hard to find him a date. Sure enough, after messaging three or four women that meet his criteria (blonde, slim, under 30 *eye roll*, and university-educated), one replies, and we message back and forth happily. Apparently, she's on an early lunch break. My stomach starts to rumble after a bit, so, channelling Steve, I tell her I have to call a client overseas and I'll message back later. Always best to leave them wanting more, I reckon.

I tell Derek I'm off for lunch and head down to the café on the street below. Derek tends to spend lunch at his desk, but I like to have a walk around the block and watch the world go by for a bit. On my second or third day working here, I found a small unpretentious café that does cheap sandwiches and has seats by the window that offer the perfect people-watching vantage point. I buy a falafel wrap and claim my spot. Someone's left a newspaper behind and I flick through it, munching on my wrap and pausing now and then to gaze idly out of the window, taking in the sharply-dressed office workers, charging down the street to grab a lunchtime snack, and the tourists, whose meandering strides and wide-eyed expressions are a dead giveaway that they're clearly not from New York. Everyone's going about their business and even though I'm only separated from them by a pane of glass and a few feet, no one glances in my direction and for a few moments, I get entranced, just watching. All of a sudden, a familiar figure catches my eye. It's Brandon, looking even more handsome than I remember. My heart beats a little faster. He's just so ridiculously good-looking, with his piercing blueish green eyes, chiselled features and dark hair. Not to mention his tall, lean physique. He glows. And it's not just me that notices. A few other women on the street do a double take as they walk past him, clearly impressed by what they see, but Brandon seems oblivious. He just charges ahead, the edges of his long coat buffeted by the breeze. I crane my neck to try to see where he's heading, desperately hoping he might be stopping in at To the Moon & Back, and to my delight, he does. He slips through the revolving doors of our building, disappearing inside. Oh my God. Just when I thought today was going to be a mind-numbingly boring day, Brandon is stopping by! I hop off my chair, grab my sandwich wrapper and empty coffee cup, shove them in a nearby bin and hurry out the door of the café, eager to catch up with him.

I dash across the road and head back into the building. Brandon must already have reached the office as there's no sign of him in reception, so I walk over to the lifts and jam my finger on the button. Not only do I want to flirt and chat to Brandon, but I want to see if I can grill him on his criteria and somehow persuade him to alter his demands so that maybe they don't stay restricted to corporate, Ivy-League-educated, sporty high-flyers and start to encompass arty photography wannabes who prefer pizza to Pilates instead. It's a long shot, but you never know!

The lift arrives, and I head inside, pressing the button for the top floor. The lift shoots up the shaft and I quickly apply a slick of tinted lip balm before the doors open. I hurry down the corridor and push open the office door, to find Brandon sitting in the client lounge, one leg folded over the other, and an arm spread across the back of the sofa. He looks over as I burst into the room, a suave relaxed expression on his face as though he was expecting me. He's so cool and composed that it's almost jarring.

'Hey, hi! How are you?' I smile, tucking my hair behind my ear as I cross the room towards him.

'Hi Polly! Good to see you,' Brandon stands up and extends

his hand towards me. We shake hands formally as though we're business associates, which in a way, I suppose we are. Shaking his hand and being so close to him, I'm immediately struck by another wave of attraction. Not only does he have the most insanely striking eyes and model-esque bone structure, but he's so tall and manly. He has the kind of build that makes you feel feminine and dainty. His imposing muscular frame is so different from my own, so mesmerising and appealing that I immediately feel my body react, a surge of attraction that feels like it's causing every cell to suddenly awaken, as though springing to attention after an extended slumber.

I smile innocently as we let go of each other's hands. Brandon beams back, his look friendly and professional and I feel embarrassed – almost guilty – for the ridiculously charged feelings I'm experiencing. He's just a professional single man and I'm a pervy matchmaker. How totally cringeworthy.

'I'm glad to see you got the job!' Brandon enthuses, and I can't help feeling touched that a busy man like himself remembers our encounter in the corridor after my interview. Could it be that I made as much of an impression on him as he did on me?

'Yep, bonafide matchmaker! Haha! At your service!' I tell him, doing a little salute, before wondering why the hell I'm doing a salute.

Brandon grins. I clear my throat.

'So, erm, are you here to see Derek?' I ask, trying to sound business-like.

'Yep.' Brandon rolls his eyes. 'That was the idea anyway, but he's on the phone to someone and so he asked me to wait.'

'Oh, really?' I frown. Derek told Brandon to wait? Brandon is his star client. He adores Brandon. 'That's odd.'

Brandon shrugs. 'He said he was on the phone to someone asking if they could sponsor a party or something. It's okay. I'm on lunch, I can wait.'

'Ah, right. Makes sense. Well, maybe I can help you,' I suggest, sitting down in the armchair opposite the couch and gesturing for Brandon to sit back down.

'Maybe you can,' he comments, a flicker in his eye. I can't tell if he's amused or if he's being flirtatious, but either way I'm getting that flushed cells-springing-to-life feeling and I catch myself tucking my hair pointlessly behind my ear again as I hold his gaze. His piercing eyes bore into me as I think to myself, *maybe I can, Brandon, maybe I can help you. In many ways.*

'So, erm…' He gives me an expectant look.

'So, uhhh, yes!' I smile, forcing the images that have flooded into my head to disperse. 'Dating! So, how's it been going then? Are you having any issues? Anything I can help with?' I babble.

'Well, yes.' Brandon glances away, his brow furrowed. 'It hasn't been going particularly well, if I'm being perfectly honest.'

'Really?' I cock my head to the side. 'But why?'

'Well, we weren't having much luck on the traditional dating sites and the last few dates were a bit of a bust, so Derek said that maybe we should try a different strategy. He suggested that apps might work better. He said he's set me up with a Tinder profile, but he hasn't given me an update. So, I was just coming over to have a chat and see how it's all going.'

'Surely you'd know if he set you up with a profile?' I ask. 'Surely you'd feel the breeze.'

'Huh?' Brandon looks confused.

'The breeze as every woman in New York swiped right,' I explain.

Brandon laughs, a little more loudly than I'd expected. So loudly in fact that Derek pops his head around the door to see what's going on. He still has a phone cupped to his ear but seems satisfied that I'm keeping Brandon occupied.

'You're funny, Polly,' Brandon says, still smiling.

'Thanks!' I reply. I want to add, 'There's more where that came from, Brandon, if you'd only change your bloody dating criteria' but I manage to stay schtum.

'But seriously, it would be good to have a date. I do pay a fair amount of money for my retainer and it's been a while since Derek's arranged anything.'

'Absolutely. Maybe I can arrange something for you? Perhaps your love life needs a fresh pair of eyes.'

'Perhaps.' Brandon nods. 'What would you suggest doing differently?'

'Well, I mean… I'm sure I can get you a date. Derek seems to like my dating message openers.'

'I can imagine they're pretty good,' Brandon says.

I smile proudly. 'Brandon, with your looks and my witty repartee, a date is in the bag, I promise.'

Brandon grins. 'You promise? I like your confidence,' he says, looking me straight in the eyes in a way that makes my legs turn to jelly. I'm thankful I'm sitting down. I smile back at him, but I can't help feeling a little frustrated. If he thinks I'm so funny and likes my confidence, why can't he date someone like, I don't know, me?

'So…' I lean forward a little. 'Is your criteria totally fixed?'

'What do you mean?'

'The whole Ivy League, sporty, slim blonde thing? Maybe you could be a bit more flexible. I mean, what if there was someone just a little different who could end up being a great match for you? You wouldn't want to overlook them, would you?' I ask, in as light and breezy a tone as I can muster. I sit up straighter, adopting my most professional posture.

'Sorry, Polly,' Brandon comments in a cuttingly impersonal way that makes my stomach do a little anxious flip. 'But I've dated before and through a process of what I guess you could call trial and error, I've realised that it's 99 per cent not going to work if my partner doesn't have those qualities.'

'Right.' My heart sinks. Great. So much for talking Brandon round. Clearly, he would never – in a million years – date someone like me. My hair is too brown. I went to the wrong university, I don't like sports and I'm two dress sizes larger than what he goes for. Let's face it; I'm not Brandon's type and apparently, there's no changing that. But then suddenly, a thought occurs to me.

'What about a peroxide blonde?' I suggest. After all, I could always dye my hair.

'Nope. Natural. I love fair hair.'

I nod. 'Fair hair. Great. Well, errr…' I glance across the room, suddenly aware of a shredder in the corner that I'd never noticed before and the fan whirring overhead. It's like all the romance and sparkle I had injected into my interactions with Brandon has suddenly been sucked out of the room. He's not remotely interested in me and he never will be. The reason he remembered my name the other day wasn't because he fancied me, it was just because he's a polite, considerate man, nothing more. And he's not been charming and cute with me because he wants to get into my knickers, it's simply because he's trying to be nice to the new recruit at his dating agency. He's probably one of those people that just effortlessly charms everyone they meet. A bit like Olly. No wonder he's risen to the top so quickly; I bet all his colleagues love him. He probably remembers the names of everyone's kids and organizes the office Christmas social. I gulp, pushing away my melancholy as I sit a little straighter. Brandon is a professional man who wants a professional and efficient dating service, and I need to stop messing around and give him that.

'I'll find you someone, Brandon. I'll see what Derek's been up to with your profiles and have a think about why it's not been working. Leave it with me. I'll get you a date,' I assure him.

Brandon smiles. 'Thanks Polly.' His eyes glimmer and I realise that's just how his eyes are, it's not a flirty look, it's just him. He's just a glimmering shimmering man. He's beguiling. I dread to think of all the women, including myself, who must have dreamed of having a chance with him only to have their hopes shattered.

The office door swings open and Derek comes in, looking

pleased with himself. I can already see that the phone call's gone well and some party sponsorship must be in the bag. He glances between me and Brandon.

'Sorry about that,' he says to Brandon. Brandon stands up and they clasp palms in a friendly handshake. 'Urgent business, really couldn't wait.'

'No problem,' Brandon insists, smiling warmly.

'So how is everything, Brandon? Let's sit down and discuss your dating strategy,' Derek suggests, gesturing for Brandon to take a seat, but he stays standing.

'Actually, I think it's sorted now.' Brandon glances towards me. 'Polly's suggested she has a shot at matching me up with someone and she seems pretty confident she can get results.'

'Absolutely!' I enthuse, even though I'm wincing a little at the corporate turn of phrase 'get results' when talking about romance. What is it with these men? Women are not results. Love is not a deliverable. Perhaps there are cracks in Brandon's shiny veneer, I wonder, as I smile happily back.

'Right! Well, sure! Why not? I'm sure Polly will do a great job.' Derek gives me one of his paternal smiles and I can tell I'm clearly in his good books after helping him with Elite Love Match and now this.

'Great, well, I'd better head back to the office,' Brandon comments, picking up his coat which is draped over the armrest of the sofa. He pulls it on.

'Got to watch out for that breeze,' he says, giving me a wink as he says goodbye.

Chapter 10

I didn't think it would be impossible to find an Ivy-League-educated, slim, sporty high-flyer but I'm beginning to wonder if this ideal woman Brandon seems to want is just a cliché or if every woman who fits that bill has already been snapped up. Every time I think I've found someone, something goes wrong. For example, I enthusiastically swiped right on a blonde woman with a profile picture of her playing Beach Ball on holiday. We got chatting and she seemed great – funny, keen and friendly – but then it turned out she hadn't been to university and owned her own handmade accessories business, selling her designs online and at markets. I was pretty sure that wouldn't fit Brandon's criteria so I let the conversation fade out and unmatched. Then there was a profile of another woman who was the perfect dress size, had studied at Harvard and worked as a PR executive. So far, so good. But she had brown hair and I remembered what Brandon had said. He wasn't into brunettes. Only natural blondes, he couldn't even handle dyed blondes. I keep swiping, swiping left on so many pretty, lovely-looking girls simply because they're the wrong dress size or went to the wrong university. The more I swipe, the more I'm beginning to get frustrated with Brandon. He may be the quintessential catch, but I can see why he's single if he has such strict exacting standards. I'm reminded of the way Olly made me feel when asking for my criteria, reducing my ideal match to a check list of qualities.

Just as I'm having that thought, Gabe twists his key in the front door.

'Hey.' I glance over my shoulder.

'Sup?' he replies as he closes the front door and he comes in, wearing his suit and tie.

'Just swiping,' I reply, as I swipe left on a red head.

'For yourself or for those creepy blokes you're trying to get dates?' Gabe asks as he takes off his blazer and hangs it over a chair.

'The creepy blokes,' I tell him.

He flops down onto the sofa next to me. His tie is a little askew and his pupils look dilated.

'Drunk?' I ask.

'No, just had a few after work,' Gabe says.

'I thought you hated your colleagues?' I ask.

Gabe's always going on about what bores his colleagues are. He calls them 'the corporate machines' because when he first started working at his company, he couldn't get his head around how their lives literally only comprised of sleeping, working and winding down from work. He couldn't believe how dull and limited their aspirations were, when he wanted more from life than just climbing the corporate ladder. While his colleagues would hang out after work discussing office politics, Gabe would usually do a runner. For Gabe, the job was just a way of making a bit of money so he could have some financial security before eventually going back to singing. Except he's been there for three years now.

'Needed a drink.' Gabe shrugs.

'Bad day?' I ask, swiping left on a pretty 30-year-old who unfortunately happens to be a DJ.

'Not really,' Gabe sighs. 'Just the usual crap and felt like letting off some steam.'

'Oh okay,' I murmur as I swipe left on another brunette.

Gabe peers over my shoulder. 'Do you really need to do that in your personal time? Shouldn't you leave work at work.'

'Yeah, I guess,' I admit. 'It just gets a bit addictive, though. You just keep swiping, trying to find the right person. It starts feeling like a computer game or something after a while. Like Angry Birds.'

'Trying to get to the next level,' Gabe adds as he loosens his tie.

'Exactly, except I can't seem to progress from level one.'

'Your job!' he tuts, as he pulls the tie free from his neck. He tosses it onto the coffee table.

'How's it going then anyway? Have you found a date for that Andy guy?' Gabe asks, remembering one of our conversations last week when I was whinging about how tough it was to get anyone to engage with Andy.

'No, still looking. I'll get there eventually,' I insist.

Gabe raises an eyebrow. 'For someone who can't seem to get off level one, you're pretty confident.'

'I'll get there in the end. Anyway, I'm not trying to get him a date at the moment. I'm trying to find someone for this guy called Brandon.'

'Brandon?'

'Yeah, he's amazing, properly gorgeous,' I tell Gabe, before filling him in on Brandon's incredible professional and philanthropic achievements. 'Such a catch. Look.'

I click onto Brandon's profile and brandish my phone at Gabe.

'Fuck me!' he says, flicking through the pictures wide-eyed. 'He's gorgeous.'

'I know, right?'

'I thought all the guys at the agency would be total geeks, to be honest.'

'Nope. I thought so too but it's not like that at all. There are loads who are totally hot and really successful. You kind of have to be successful to use the service in the first place. Dating agencies don't come cheap.'

'I guess,' Gabe muses. 'But I thought they'd be, like, rich and ugly. Nerdy financiers or something. I wasn't expecting absolute hotties like this.' Gabe drinks Brandon's pictures in, swiping between them.

'Neither did I,' I admit, thinking back to how cringe-worthily flirty and flustered I got around Brandon earlier.

'Can't you date him?' Gabe suggests. 'I'd be all over that in a second.' He hands my phone back to me, which is open on a particularly dashing shot of Brandon wearing a suit in front of a swanky city office. It's a professional-looking editorial shot, taken from one of the magazine articles about his app, and he looks model-handsome.

'He's incredibly fussy though. Incredibly.' I explain about all of Brandon's criteria.

'Take it that doesn't include men then?' Gabe sighs.

''Fraid not.'

'Damn,' Gabe mutters.

'I'm glad I'm not the only one who fancies him,' I comment.

'What do you mean?' Gabe wrinkles his nose.

'Every time I see him, I get all hot under the collar and start flirting. It's not even remotely professional, I just can't help it. It's like he has this intense masculine energy that just brings out some primal instinct in me and I start practically throwing myself at him.'

'Really?'

'Yeah, I just want to rip his clothes off,' I admit sheepishly. 'It's a bit embarrassing.'

Gabe sniggers. 'Well, it has been a while, hasn't it?'

'What do you mean?'

'It's been a while, since you got laid.'

I glance down. 'Yeah, I guess so,' I admit, placing my phone face down on the coffee table. Even the photo of Brandon is having an effect.

'How long's it been?' Gabe asks.

'I don't know. A while.'

'Like how long?'

'Umm…' I rack my brains, but I can't even readily recall the last guy I slept with it's been so long. 'I don't know, but I'm fine,' I insist, picking up my phone again and reflexively swiping left. 'You know, just a little twitchy.'

Gabe eyes me cynically. 'You're horny, babe.'

'I'm not! I'm fine!'

'Girl, you're so horny you probably get aroused when you touch up a photo.'

I giggle in spite of myself. 'Shut up!'

'You're so horny you probably go to Starbucks just to hear someone cry out your name,' Gabe teases.

'You're such a dick, Gabe!'

'You probably wink at the ticket machine in the subway when you press the button for a single,' Gabe sniggers.

I roll my eyes. 'Come on, I'm not *that* bad.'

'Seriously, babe.' Gabe gives me a pointed look.

'Okay, fine,' I sigh. 'So it's been a while.'

'Yeah, maybe it has, but now you're surrounded by single men. You're in the perfect job. What are you waiting for?' Gabe asks, looking genuinely baffled.

'I'm a matchmaker! And FYI, I'm trying to be a professional one! The last thing I should be doing is shagging the clients.'

'I guess,' Gabe reasons. 'Shame though, with a fine piece of ass like that.' He glances towards my phone.

'Yeah, it is a shame,' I sigh, as if my professionalism is the only thing stopping me from getting with Brandon, and the fact that I don't meet any of his ridiculous criteria has nothing to do with it.

Chapter 11

Derek's top choice of venue for the party couldn't be any more perfect. I didn't expect him to suggest such an incredible place, but the venue he's sent me to visit is ideal. In fact, it's somewhere I've always wanted to go. It's a restaurant called The Grill at Bryant Park – one of my favourite spots in New York. The park is tucked behind New York Public Library and it's always a hive of activity. Every night, something interesting's happening at Bryant Park, from band performances to outdoor cinema events to yoga classes. There's also a carousel for kids and stone tables patterned with chessboards where people catch up over a game. When I first moved to the city, I used to come to Bryant Pak just to sit and think and soak up the vibrant energy of the place. The Grill sits on the edge of the park – a huge conservatory-style restaurant covered in winding ivy – it seems just as exciting. If it's not bustling with diners, there'll be a glamourous private party taking place.

I walk over, feeling excited as I cross the path towards the restaurant and head inside. I've wanted to go to The Grill for ages and now here I am, visiting to check it out as a party venue! The owner greets me warmly and shows me around. Its tall glass conservatory walls and roof give it a feeling of expansiveness. It feels almost like an extension of Bryant Park, with the trees in the park visible on one side and the New York Public Library on the other. Lit by warm lighting, it's like a cosy cocoon within the park, and the inside outside look is heightened by a few tree trunks growing indoors that pierce the conservatory ceiling as well as plants and foliage decorations dotted throughout the venue.

'We usually decorate the venue with fairy lights and chandeliers for events like yours, to give a feeling of cosiness,' the owner says.

'That sounds wonderful,' I enthuse. I know exactly what he means because I've seen those parties going on in The Grill. They're hard to miss from Bryant Park and they always look incredible, but standing inside the conservatory, I can truly picture how good the venue will look. With Derek's plans to adorn the place with heart-shaped balloons and sprinkle love heart confetti everywhere, it's going to be gorgeous. It'll be a beautiful cocoon within the bustling city, sending out the perfect message to clients – that we're a friendly intimate agency, a cosy place of where they can feel relaxed and at ease, while also making new connections across New York.

'We book up fast so let us know if you're interested as soon as you can,' the owner advises.

I want to tell him there and then that I'm interested. I know Derek and I won't be able to beat The Grill. It will be impossible to find a venue as perfect – but I tell him that I need to discuss it with my boss and promise to let him know soon.

I try to call Derek the moment I leave but his phone's engaged; he's probably talking to sponsors or new prospective clients. I barely concentrate while visiting the other two venues on his list, which are just your typical nice modern bars. They're lovely, but they have nothing on The Grill. I head back to the office, walking the mile-long route. As I'm walking, I pass an independent book-store that has a kooky café inside doubling up as a hipster meeting spot. It's the sort of café that serves chai seed smoothies and soy lattes to bearded freelancers who can afford to hang out there all day buying this and that while they tinker about on their laptops. It's the kind of place I'd actually quite like to frequent, but unfortunately my budget hasn't allowed it recently. I peer through the window, checking out the artsy books on display, when my eyes suddenly land on a black chalkboard sign.

Exclusive book launch of RAW! by Alicia Carter, Instagram sensation & raw food chef, 7 p.m. on Friday.

Alicia? A book launch? For a moment, I think the store must have made a mistake and Alicia is probably just holding one of her meet and greets or something, but the sign definitely says 'book launch'. It stipulates the name of the book and everything. When Alicia said the book was going to print, I had no idea things would be moving *this* quickly.

I head into the shop and walk up to the nearest member of staff – a skinny guy with glasses.

'Hi, I just saw the sign for the book launch with Alicia Carter,' I say.

'Yeah.' He smiles politely. 'It's next week,' he tells me.

'Right, yep. And erm, do you have a guest list?' I ask.

He thinks for a moment. 'I don't know. Actually yeah, I think there is one. It's pretty exclusive.'

'Okay...' I murmur.

'Obviously, I can't reveal the names on the guest list,' he comments. 'It's an invite-only launch.'

'Of course not,' I agree, wondering where the hell my invite has got to. I was the photographer for the cookbook after all.

'So, if the book launch is invite-only and so exclusive, why are you advertising it?' I ask.

'Just building up hype ahead of when the book comes out. Plus, a lot of the people who come here have been invited,' he tells me, with a slightly patronising look.

'Right, okay. Thanks,' I grumble, before skulking out of the shop.

113

I walk a few paces down the busy street trying to take in what has just happened. Alicia is having an exclusive book launch and she hasn't even invited me. Me! The photographer! How could this be happening? I pull my phone from my handbag and scroll through my messages and emails. I can't see any from her. I search her name in my inbox, my junk, my spam, even my bin in case I accidentally deleted it, but there's nothing. I open my messenger app and fire off a message asking about the party. I keep an eye on my phone for a few minutes, watching out to see if the ticks at the side of the message turn blue, showing that it's been read, but they remain grey. Urghh. I can't believe it! Surely it can't be that I spent a whole day taking pictures of turnips, not to mention the hours I spent meticulously editing those pictures, and I'm *still* not deemed exclusive enough to attend the book launch. I sigh loudly as I chuck my phone into my handbag. I walk down the street, trying to hold my head high, even though my heart is sinking. Glum-looking suited city workers and steely women in court shoes and neat shift dresses pass me by. With setbacks like this, I can't help feeling I'm never going to make it as a photographer, but I know I'm never going to be like these office workers either. I don't have a clue what kind of future awaits me, but I don't want to follow Gabe's path – forcing myself to do a job I hate, being a square peg in a round hole. I feel so lost.

I check my phone once more a few blocks further. The ticks have gone blue now, meaning Alicia's read the message, but she hasn't replied. I try to tell myself that she's busy, but she was never too busy to respond to my messages when we were working on the photo edits. And I know from spending time in her company that she never looks up from her phone for more than a few minutes at a time. I can't shake the feeling that I'm being snubbed. Derek's sent me a few messages asking how the viewings are going. My stomach's starting to rumble so I nip into a café to grab some lunch and give Derek a quick call.

I order a coffee and a bowl of soup and sit at a table in the corner. I give Derek a quick call to report back on how fantastic The Grill is. He seems thrilled that I like it. I tell him I'm grabbing lunch and will be back at the office soon. Derek's excitement over the venue lifts my spirits somewhat. After all, I may not be going to Alicia's event, but at least I have an incredible Valentine's party in one of the coolest venues in New York to look forward to. Alicia still hasn't replied, but it doesn't really matter. I click onto Brandon's Tinder profile on my phone in an attempt to distract myself with some swiping. I might not have been invited to the launch of a book I took the photos for and my photography career may not be panning out remotely as I wanted it to, but at least I have a job. I'm a matchmaker, and I'm going to matchmake.

I start swiping: brunette (left swipe), personal trainer (left swipe), girl who describes herself as a 'homebody' (left swipe), curvy girl (left swipe) etc. I'm beginning to get cramp in my thumb from all the swiping when I finally land upon a profile that might have potential. The profile shot is of a slim pretty blonde in a bikini lying on the deck of a yacht. She has a broad open smile and blue sparkly eyes and looks like a catalogue model. So much so that I'm tempted to write the profile off as a fake or some kind of bot and I nearly swipe left, but something stops me. Hope, I guess. She's called Eve and from this photo alone, she's ticking so many of Brandon's boxes. She looks slim and toned. Check. Her sandy luminous blonde hair is swept into a wispy ponytail that blows over her shoulder in the breeze – so long that it tickles her elbow. Check. And the yacht she's posing on looks like it's near a Mediterranean coastline. Clearly a fan of travelling. Check. I scroll onto the next photo. It's a completely different vibe to the first. She's snuggled on the sofa in a plush-looking lounge reading a book. She's wearing an oversized jumper with long sleeves, reading glasses and her hair is tied in a side plait. She looks sweet and I can't help wondering if the fancy-looking apartment in the background is her flat. Could it be that she's a homeowner? Because that would be yet another tick.

The rest of the images appear to give a complete 360-degree view of Eve's life. There's a shot of her rocking corporate chic in a pencil skirt and a blouse, with a boxy handbag dangling from her arm, standing outside an office block on Wall Street. Her hair's slicked back in a tight bun at the back of her head and she's wearing glasses again. Even in a severe corporate suit, she looks stunning. The shot reminds me of the one Brandon uses on his profile – the magazine shoot image of him taken in front of his firm, looking every inch the high-flying lawyer. Eve's just like the female Brandon. This is too good to be true. I check out her profile information. She's 32. Studied economics at Columbia and works as a Senior Manager at leading bank, J. C. Fisher. No way. Her bio reads, 'Eligible man required in role as boyfriend for leading singleton. Please swipe right to apply. Unfortunately, we regret that we cannot offer personal feedback to unsuccessful applicants.' I smile. Witty too. Surely, she has to be a catfish or something.

I swipe right anyway. It feels strange to make a right-swiping gesture when my thumb is so used to swiping the other way. I feel a prickle of nervousness, but then 'It's a Match' pops up.

'Yes!' I yelp without thinking, letting out a little squeal. A stern-looking woman reading the *The Wall Street Journal* on the table opposite glances over, unimpressed, and I clear my throat, burying my head back to my phone.

It's a match! I've matched with Eve and she seems absolutely incredible. But before I get too carried away, I decide to conduct a little Google search to see if she's legit. I type her name, university and workplace into the search bar, fully expecting nothing to come up. She definitely seems too good to be true. Google delivers a stream of results, the first of which is a professional profile for a blonde called 'Eve Samuels' who went to Columbia and works at J. C. Fisher, just like her dating profile claims. The profile shot is a black and white company headshot in which Eve's wearing a white shirt and black blazer, glasses and no make-up. She looks less glamourous than she does in her Tinder pictures, but she's still naturally beautiful, with bright engaging eyes and long thick hair. I click on her profile and scan her employment history. She secured an internship at an investment bank straight out of university, was awarded an entry level job there after six weeks and then progressively climbed the ranks, before taking on the role of Senior Manager a year ago. Impressive. I feel my own ego shrinking slightly as I take it in. Eve's such a success story. Her steady rise to the top of the corporate ladder is intimidating. It's an existence I can't even begin to contemplate. I could never do what she's done; that corporate determination just isn't in me.

I take a sip of coffee and shrug off the thought. This isn't about me. This is about Brandon and I may well have just stumbled across the jackpot. Now I just need to think up a decent opening message. A few come to mind.

Hey Eve, beautiful, smart, successful – what's the catch?

Not overly original. I could compliment her pictures, but she probably gets that all the time. Or I could ask her where she's sailing in the yacht shot. None are particularly inspiring ideas for opening gambits but the quality of the opening message probably doesn't matter quite so much when I have Brandon's looks on my side. I'm about to hit send when suddenly, a message pops up from Eve. She beat me to it!

Eve: *I just saw the best upsexy ever.*

Huh? I frown at the message. What's she on about? Maybe she is a bot after all. I type a reply.

Brandon: What's upsexy?
Eve: Oh, Brandon! *Winking emoji* I'm doing okay, how are you?

I snort with laughter, causing the paper-reading woman to shoot me another reproving glance, but this time I just don't care. I've matched with Eve! She's perfect and she's funny.

Brandon: You got me! Great line btw, although to be perfectly honest, you had me at 'It's a Match'.

I hit send. It's a bit of a cheesy message, but it'll do.

Eve: Really? Surely a guy like you has all the matches.

Wow, she's gorgeous, funny and she's flirting. I debate how to respond. Of course, someone as hot as Brandon would have a ton of matches, if he wasn't so damn fussy. But I can't go telling Eve that, actually, she's the first girl that meets his ridiculously exacting criteria. I type another message.

Brandon: None as pretty as you.
Eve: *blushing*
Brandon: But really, you're beautiful, well-educated, successful and funny. What's the catch?! I thought at first you must be a bot or a catfish.

I wait a few moments, taking a few sips of coffee and gazing across the café at the people working on laptops, having a catch up, or simply texting. A few minutes pass, and Eve hasn't replied. I start worrying that maybe I've come across as too keen and put her off. Or maybe she was offended that I suggested she might be a bot. Oh no, just when I thought I'd struck gold, I've probably screwed it up. I sigh and then my phone buzzes. It's her!

Eve: A bot! Hahaha. You know how to flatter a girl. But if I'm totally honest, I thought the same about you – you're gorgeous, smart, successful and funny yourself. So, I'm going to fire that question right back at you. What's the catch?!

I smile to myself. This could actually be for real. Eve is clearly not a bot. I ponder over her question, thinking back to Brandon. Does he have a catch? There's definitely no catch when it comes to the looks department. I know that for sure. And there's no catch professionally. I've already checked Brandon out online and found dozens of articles in which interviewers try to deduce the secret to his staggering success. If anything, Brandon's Tinder profile undersells him when it comes to his professional life. And he's certainly well-educated. And funny. And cool and charismatic. Before I know it, I'm daydreaming about us sitting on the sofa in Derek's chintzy client lounge, with one thing leading to another. Maybe Gabe's right. Maybe I do need to get laid. I glance over at the barista. Perhaps I *should* order a coffee just to hear someone cry out my name, like Gabe jokes.

No. I must focus on the task at hand. I reread Eve's message. What's the catch? The only catch I can think of is Brandon's annoying fussiness, but I can't say that, can I? I need to write something quickly, I'm taking way too long to reply.

Brandon: Hmmm. I'm stumped! Maybe we're both just perfect, or else we're both just very advanced bots?
Eve: Maybe. I'll show you my source code if you show me yours ☺

I snigger, while typing a response.

Brandon: Stop it. You're making my floppy disc hard.
Eve: That's okay. Although maybe you could upgrade to a hard drive. A very hard drive.

I giggle. I love Eve. I'm almost beginning to fancy her myself.

Brandon: hkjdf9723[;Pakdsjfhp89-0jhksadgfy
Brandon: Sorry, is it hot in here or did my system just crash?
Eve: lol! I don't know about you, but I'm pretty sure my CPU's malfunctioning because I'm feeling a spark.

My phone buzzes, but this time it isn't Eve. It's Derek, asking when I'll be getting back to the office. He's clearly beginning to suspect that I'm bunking off. I'd better head back. I take a final sip of my coffee, even though I really don't want to leave. I'm enjoying my banter with Eve, but I have to admit, I'm a bit surprised she has time for back and forth chit chat like this. It's 3 p.m. – peak office hours – and yet she's chatting to guys on Tinder. It's a bit strange, but maybe she's just one of those people who's got so high in their career that they no longer need to do much work. Unlike me. I'm going to have to pick this chat up again later.

Brandon: I'm going to have to log off before my system crashes completely. Catch up later?
Eve: Haha. Smooth. Speak later. X
Brandon: Perfect. X

I drop my phone in my bag and head out of the café, feeling pleased with myself.

Chapter 12

I know Gabe's right and I should probably leave work at work, but I can't seem to stop messaging Eve. She's so funny and cute and cool. Brandon's going to absolutely love her.

We've moved off the topic of bots to general chit chat about our days, which I'm having to wing a bit seeing as I have absolutely no idea what Brandon's been up to. I've been referring vaguely to a 'work project' to make it sound like Brandon's keeping busy but it's a bit difficult pretending to be a high-flying lawyer when I don't know a thing about law. Eve even asked whether the project has been impacted by some stock market fluctuations. I didn't have a clue what she was on about, so I told her everything was going well, but mentioned that we were having an internal office issue to make the story a bit more convincing. Really, I was just injecting my own frustrations over Alicia and not being invited to the book launch into the narrative.

> **Brandon:** *A colleague has been overseeing a project and was meant to involve me, but they've been ostracising key members of the team.*

I type, thinking of Alicia, while hoping I sound convincingly corporate. Eve quickly fires a message back.

Eve: Urghh. I hate that. Responsibility needs to be shared equally between all stakeholders in project work. If people don't feel valued, they can't add value.

I raise an eyebrow. What's she on about?

Brandon: I suppose. It's just this individual has demanded a lot from me and now doesn't seem to be acknowledging my help.

I send the message, feeling a strange sense of relief to be offloading, even if I am doing it through the alias of Brandon, and pretending I'm a lawyer in a difficult office situation rather than a struggling photographer sitting on her couch.

Eve: If the person is really out of line, maybe you should escalate the issue to their line manager? Perhaps they need to be reminded of the company's ethos or policies.

Oh God. I wish! Eve and I are from completely different worlds. Alicia doesn't have a line manager, I can't escalate things. That's not remotely how it works. Our whole arrangement was meant to be based on good faith, there's no company ethos or policies in place. I really need to wrap this conversation up before it gets any weirder.

Brandon: Yeah, maybe. Thanks for the advice. It's been annoying, but I'll try to just let it go.
Eve: No, don't let it go! That'll only make it worse. If you let someone walk all over you once, they'll only crush you harder the next time. That's what I've realised. J. C. Fisher is ruthless. If I don't come across as strong, people will destroy me.

122

I read Eve's message, my interest piqued.

> **Eve:** *It's down to you to set the standard for how you expect to be treated. Once you set a high benchmark, people will rise to it. It's been the biggest learning of my professional life, and personal life too.*

Interesting. Eve seems to have dropped the corporate jargon. She's speaking English again and not just regular English, meaningful English.

> **Brandon:** *You're right. I think I need to raise the standard. It just got me down a bit.*
> **Eve:** *It sounds like it, but don't let it get you down. 'No one makes you feel inferior without your consent'. That's one of my favourite quotes. It's by Eleanor Roosevelt. If you let this person make you feel bad, you're giving them power over you. Try to shrug it off and move forward instead. Assert your worth and let go. That's a way better power move than feeling down about it or angry. I used to get like that all the time, then I heard that quote and it struck a chord with me.*

Wow. Suddenly I'm not Brandon at all; I'm me, Polly Wood, and I'm feeling really quite moved. Eve's right. I haven't been setting the standard for how I should be treated high enough. I've been showing everyone the utmost respect, bending over backwards to fulfil their demands and pandering to their whims in the hope they'll be appreciative and kind back, but it hasn't been working out like that. My clients have just been taking advantage of me instead. In my desperation to grow my photography portfolio, I've got into the habit of accepting crummy jobs for little or no pay, I've worked all hours and I've not stood up for myself. In a weird way, I've allowed myself to be taken advantage of. I'm letting people make me feel bad about myself and inferior, when I shouldn't be giving them that power at all.

My phone pings.

Eve: Trust me, I learnt all this the hard way!

I take in the message, finding it hard to imagine someone as beautiful and smart and confident as Eve being pushed around but I believe her. I can tell she's speaking from the heart and if she managed to assert herself and change, then I can too.

Eve: Eek you've gone quiet...

Oh no! She's right. I have gone totally quiet. I've been lost in thought. I need to stop allowing myself to be Polly, getting lost in my own personal thoughts and feelings, and instead get back into the mindset of Brandon. Cool, confident, charismatic Brandon.

Brandon: I was just thinking about what you said. You seem so accomplished. Hard to imagine you being pushed around...

I scroll through Eve's photos while I wait for a reply, focusing on the image of her dressed in a severe skirt suit with her hair scraped back, looking every inch the accomplished business-woman.

Eve: Aww, thanks Brandon. I'm doing okay now, but it took trial and error to get there, believe me.

'What are you doing?' Gabe comes into the kitchen and looks over my shoulder. I quickly click out of the messages to Eve.
'Nothing.'
Gabe raises an eyebrow. He reaches for a bag of bagels and

the chopping board. 'You looked all pensive and weird. Who are you messaging? Is it that Brandon dude?'

'Pah!' I let out a snort. As if I'd be messaging Brandon. 'Not quite. I'm messaging a woman pretending to be Brandon though.'

'Oh God,' Gabe groans as he takes a knife and starts slicing through a bagel. 'You're messaging a poor unsuspecting woman pretending to be Brandon...' He shakes his head.

'Oh, come on, you make it sound like I'm doing something terrible,' I huff.

Gabe slips the slices into the toaster and turns around to face me, leaning against the worktop.

'You know I don't approve,' he reminds me. 'I hope you're not sexting her, because that would be really wrong!'

'No! I'm not sexting!' I insist, making a mental note to try to keep the conversation platonic. Gabe's right, sexting would feel kind of wrong. I probably already went too far earlier with the comments about my hard drive.

'Good! Why do you look so thoughtful then?'

I shrug. 'I don't know. She just got me thinking, I guess. She's an interesting person,' I tell him.

'Let's see?'

'Fine.'

Gabe plonks himself down in the seat next to me and peers over at my phone as I click back into Eve's Tinder profile and scroll through the photos.

'Wow, she's gorgeous!' he says. 'Are you sure she's real? Her profile looks a bit fake.'

The toaster pings and Gabe gets up.

'Yeah, I wasn't sure at first, but I found her on Google. I found a work profile about her. She seems real.'

'Ha!' Gabe scoffs as he plucks the bagel slices from the toaster and places them on a plate. 'Why do people always think work profiles are legit? You can create fake information about your career just as easily as you can fake a Tinder profile.' Gabe gets some spread out of the fridge. 'People always think professional profiles are somehow factual or something, but they're totally not. Trust me, we get applicants all the time who have these amazing online CVs and websites – they look so impressive, but then you find out they've been lying about everything.'

'I suppose,' I grumble, feeling suddenly deflated. Gabe's right. I did assume that Eve was legit simply because her work profile looked good, but what if she's a balding middle-aged man sitting in his parent's basement who just faked it? What if we're both catfishing each other?

'Hmm…' Gabe murmurs as he assembles his bagel. 'She could very well be real, I'm just giving you a heads up. I don't want to see you get too excited only to get totally let down.'

'Yeah, I know,' I sigh. Deep down I know Gabe isn't deliberately trying to be a spoilsport. 'I was just so excited about completing level one.'

'You thought she was the one, right?'

I nod.

'Babe, she might still be. I'm just trying to be Cupid's rational sidekick.'

I laugh, when my phone buzzes.

Eve: Are you busy? Hope I didn't get too preachy.

'Is it her?'

'Yeah,' I reply, as I start typing a message.

Brandon: Don't be silly. Beauty, brains and wisdom, what more could I want?! ;)

'What are you saying?' Gabe asks, before plonking down on the sofa and taking a bite of his bagel.

'Oh, nothing.'

'Tell me!' he insists through a mouthful of food.

'No!'

Gabe swallows. 'You're flirting, aren't you?' he teases.

'Maybe. Yes. It is kind of my job,' I remind him.

'Oh man,' Gabe laughs.

A message pings through from Eve.

Eve: *Hmmm, I don't know. How about a date?*

Oh my God! Eve wants a date. I get up and head to my bedroom.

'Where are you going?' Gabe asks.

'I need to message Eve privately. You're distracting me.'

'Poor girl,' Gabe sighs. 'If she is a girl,' he adds.

I roll my eyes indulgently. 'Yeah, well if she is a girl, she gets a date with Brandon. Nothing poor about it.'

'Hmmph. True,' Gabe murmurs, before taking another bite of his bagel. I smile over my shoulder before shutting my bedroom door.

Chapter 13

'Derek, Derek!' I burst through the office door, desperate to tell Derek about my progress with Eve.

'Morning!' Derek looks up from the breakfast sandwich he's demolishing at his desk and shoots me a bemused look. 'Everything okay?'

'Everything's way better than okay!'

Derek wipes a streak of ketchup from his chin. 'What happened?'

'I got Brandon a date!' I enthuse.

'Really?' Derek looks sceptical. 'Does she meet the criteria?'

'Yep, and then some. She's an absolute dream woman, Derek!' As I take off my coat and fire up my computer, I fill Derek in.

'She sounds perfect.'

'She is! She's so smart and wise. She seems really thoughtful and humble. She's clearly a really reflective person,' I say, thinking back to the things she said last night about setting your own worth. I thought about that a lot as I was falling asleep. Alicia may not have bothered to invite me to the launch of the cookbook, but that doesn't mean I can't attend. She can't exactly turn me away. Alicia can try to keep me down and put me in my place, but it's up to me whether or not I allow it and I'm putting my foot down. Like Eve said, I set the standard for how I'm treated.

'You sound quite taken with her yourself!' Derek comments with a wink.

'Ha! She's not quite my type Derek, but she's definitely a catch.'

'Let me see her,' Derek says.

I rummage in my handbag for my phone and open her profile, before presenting my screen proudly to him.

Derek peers at the photos. 'Oh wow, she's a stunner, isn't she? Brandon's going to love her!' he enthuses as he swipes through Eve's photos. 'Shame Brandon's in Switzerland or he'd be dying to take her out.'

'He's in Switzerland?' I gawp.

'Yeah, work trip. You'll have to keep Eve entertained for a few more days,' Derek tells me.

'Really?' I grumble. I know it's my job to message women and while I don't think it's as wrong as Gabe makes out, there are limits. I was beginning to feel a bit guilty last night when things got deep with Eve. There she is, probably thinking she's having a moment with Brandon and it's actually some random girl. We kept on chatting for a bit before bed and once I suggested a date and she agreed, I was hoping that would be it. I thought Brandon could take over from this point onwards.

'When's he getting back?' I ask.

'Friday, I think,' Derek says, taking another bite of his sandwich.

'Oh, right,' I sigh as I log onto Match.

The intercom buzzes, causing me to jump. 'Who's that?'

'Ahh!' Derek's eyes light up. 'That'll be my new potential client, Elliot Brown. He got in touch the other day. I've got three consultations booked in today thanks to our new and improved website. It seems like people are responding to the new approach.'

'Really?'

'Yep. You were right in your critique of the market. Elliot said he'd visited a few other dating agencies but was drawn to our friendly vibe. You know, I always thought I needed to be bigger and better and swankier to succeed, but I think that might actually be Olly Corrigan's downfall.'

'Ha!'

Derek buzzes Elliot up.

'Right, I'll be next door,' he says as he gathers his client consultation forms.

'Good luck, Derek. You've got this!' I fist bump the air.

'Derek laughs and does a wink and a shooting motion at me as he heads into the client lounge, closing the door behind him.

Life's been so full on over the past few days, with Alicia and Eve, that I've barely thought about Olly Corrigan. Not that there's much to think about. So I was kind of attracted to him and we had an awkward moment in Milano's – it doesn't really matter now. He obviously knew I was a phoney and probably thought I was really weird for being such a time-waster, but who cares? All that matters is that Derek's business is doing better. I may not have been the most convincing mystery shopper but I did achieve my objective. I helped Derek get an edge over the competition. I should probably put Olly out of my mind, but instead, I find myself Googling him and within seconds, I'm scrolling through his Instagram pictures. Most of his photos are overly posed snaps of him hanging out in galleries or restaurants, or leaning against graffitied walls or urban doorways while wearing the latest high-end fashion. They tend to have completely meaningless captions like, 'Happy Saturday everyone. Have a great one' or 'Can tomorrow be Sunday again?' In some of them, he's even gone so far as to caption them with the cringeworthy hashtag '#whatOllywore' and then a list of items with the labels tagged. I can't help rolling my eyes. He clearly thinks he's some kind of influencer.

But he's hot, there's no denying that. He's got a naturally handsome face and that smile… And with his tattoos and tanned skin, he does cut a striking figure. He's definitely the kind of guy who stands out in the crowd and in a city like New York, that's not an easy feat. But his dress sense is a bit questionable. He's in his forties and yet he's wearing bomber jackets and sneakers like he thinks he's some kind of cool kid. He definitely dresses younger than his years and while there's nothing wrong with that, if he were a woman, he'd probably be called 'mutton dressed as lamb'. I click on a few more pictures – there's one of him sitting cross-legged on a yoga mat in a pink T-shirt and camouflage jogging bottoms with a caption professing his love for Hatha. Could he be any more of a city boy metrosexual? His latest photo, posted last night, is of him sitting in a bar, dressed in a stylish black shirt holding a glass of champagne, with the caption, 'A stumbling block for the pessimist is a stepping stone to the optimist'. Interesting. I copy and paste the quote and I'm about to Google it, when a message pings through on Match, distracting me. It's from Heather – the cute Harry Potter fan who I thought would be a great match for Andy – saying how interesting and cool he sounds!

As I write a reply, I can't help feeling pleased with myself. I feel like a proper matchmaker. Maybe this is a good job for me after all! I log into my work emails and find the files of the latest clients Derek's assigned me and pass the morning setting up profiles for them, while intermittently messaging Heather, who seems sweet, normal and genuinely interested in Andy. Crisp winter sunshine streams in through the window and I can hear Derek's laughter from next door as he cracks jokes with the new client. He seems to be really embracing the new personal approach of the agency. Maybe it'll be To the Moon & Back that wins Dating Agency of the Year in the next New York Dating Awards and not Elite Love Match. Maybe the underdog will strike back. I send a few more messages to Heather but my growling stomach starts to distract me. I was in such a rush to get to the office this morning to tell Derek all about matching with Eve that as usual, I forgot to eat and now my stomach is rumbling. I decide to head out for an early lunch and grab some client files to read while I'm out since I really should be working. I shove them in my bag, put my coat on and slip through the client lounge. Derek's sitting opposite a guy with dark hair and an unusual spiky fringe, who looks like he's in his early thirties. They both turn to look.

'Just heading out for a snack,' I say as I scurry past.

Derek smiles. 'See you,' he says, before returning his attention to Elliot.

It's a fresh winters day. The air is cool but the sky is bright, with a sharp blue winter's sunshine. It makes a nice change from the overcast rainy weather the city's been having in recent weeks and I decide to make the most of it, walking a few blocks instead of dashing into the café opposite work like I usually do. I amble along for a bit until I spot a cute rustic-looking café that I haven't seen before with a blackboard outside advertising a range of delicious-sounding specials. I head inside and check out the canteen displaying dozens of freshly made salads and sandwiches. I decide to take an early lunch, ordering a sandwich and a coffee, before perching at a table by the window. The food is delicious, and I demolish it pretty quickly, before grabbing a newspaper that someone's left behind on a nearby table to have a read while I drink my coffee. I decide to send a quick message to Eve.

Brandon: *Hey, how's your day going? Bad news – got a massive work project and I won't be able to meet until the weekend. We'll have to wait a few more days. Luckily, I've heard good things come to those who wait x*

Flirty message sent, I turn my attention to the paper. I'm deep into an article about a shark attack off the coast of Malaysia when a familiar voice distracts me.

'Latte, extra shot. Cheers buddy.'

I look over my shoulder to see none other than Olly Corrigan.

'So, how's uni going? Did you get that coursework in?' he asks the barista.

Shit. I quickly turn away. I should have realised that I'd wandered into his part of town. His office is just around the corner. This must be his local, he's clearly on friendly terms with the staff. I shrink into my seat. As long as I don't turn around again, hopefully he won't notice me. The last thing I need is another awkward conversation with him. I'll just keep my head down and read the paper. Or pretend to read the paper, because the truth is that I can't stop eavesdropping. As it turns out, the barista is a psychology student and Olly seems to have some kind of specialist knowledge in psychology because now they're discussing dream theory – of all things – as the coffee machine churns away.

Olly seems so locked in conversation, comparing the theories of Jung and Freud with the barista, that I dare to steal a glance at him over my shoulder. Fortunately, he doesn't spot me. He's standing at the counter clutching a takeaway coffee in one hand and gesticulating with the other as he explains why he thinks Freud's interpretation of dreams as expressions of unfulfilled desires is wrong. He's clearly really passionate about it, advocating that Jung had a 'much stronger, more grounded approach'. He's dressed in his usual outlandish clothes. He's wearing a polo shirt with a print of pineapples that makes an eye-popping contrast with his tattoos and he's got on the same tortoiseshell glasses that he was rocking last time we met. I quickly turn back to the paper, worried he'll sense me looking.

Luckily, he seems too wrapped up in his conversation. Even I'm feeling quite engaged, it's actually pretty interesting, and it's funny to think that just an hour or so ago, I was rolling my eyes at Olly's Instagram account and his 'whatOllywore' hashtag, writing him off as a vapid poser and now here he is, having a fairly intense conversation about dream theory with the barista at his local coffee shop. This Olly is smart, friendly, reflective and nice. He's nothing like the persona he presents online, or the cold cynical businessman he seemed to be when we met.

Olly says goodbye to the barista, wishing him good luck with his dissertation. I turn slightly away, cowering into myself to avoid being spotted as he leaves. I lift the paper to conceal my face as though I'm completely engrossed. I peer around the edge of the pages as he pulls open the door of the café to leave. He doesn't appear to have noticed me and I let out a sigh of relief when all of a sudden, he lets the door swing closed and tuts to himself, as though he's forgotten something. I cower behind the paper as he comes over to the napkin stand, which is only a few feet away from me, where sachets of sugar, salt, and sweetener are displayed. Bloody hell! He's so near. I should have anticipated this! I lift the paper higher, holding it as wide open as I can so that it conceals me fully, while hoping I just look like someone who really adores the news. I can just about glimpse Olly's legs as he approaches – a pair of red checked patterned trousers with turned up hems. Talk about clashing prints. I cower behind the paper, practically holding my breath while he lingers at the napkin stand.

'Excuse me, can I grab a stirrer?' Olly says.

What the… Why is he talking to me? I peek around the side of my newspaper and realise that he's trying to reach a pot of stirrers someone's left by the window just beyond my plate. For goodness' sake!

'Polly?' Olly says, recognising me instantly even though only a fraction of my face is protruding from behind the newspaper. Great. Just great.

'Hi!' I smile uncomfortably, before dumping the paper on the table, giving up. I reach for the pot of stirrers and present it to him. 'Here you go,' I say glumly.

Olly raises an eyebrow, looking taken aback. He freezes for a moment, before slowly reaching for a stirrer. He's holding both his mobile phone, three sachets of sweetener, and his coffee cup in his other hand, and has his sandwich clamped under his arm. His phone's flashing with unread messages.

'You're a long way from Staten Island, once again,' he says dryly. I meet his gaze, taking in those rich brown eyes, full of intelligence and depth. They're both handsome and beguiling. He takes a stirrer and I immediately place the pot back down, before hopping off my stool.

'Erm yeah, you know. Projects all over the place. Lots of building work. Everywhere,' I babble, avoiding eye contact.

'Uh-huh...' Olly says, eyeing me strangely.

I grab my bag, desperate to get away. Why's he standing there staring at me? Can't he see he's making me uncomfortable.

'To the Moon & Back?' Olly says suddenly.

'What?' I look up and realise he's looking down at some client files from the agency that I printed out on Derek's letterhead paper – the ones I shoved in my bag before I left the office. The papers are sticking out of my bag and the To the Moon & Back's logo is clearly visible.

'Oh, err...' I can feel my cheeks flushing red. My mind races. The papers are clearly internal office documents, I can't just pretend I'm a client of To the Moon & Back. Olly's not stupid. The game is up. It's clear I work there.

'I have to go, sorry!' I gabble, avoiding eye contact as I dash past him and hurry out the door. My heart is pounding as I practically run down the street to get as far away from Olly as possible. Great. Just great. Now he knows I'm a super shady spy who went poking around his business. He must thing I'm so dodgy. And the annoying thing is that I really don't want him to think I'm dodgy because he's gorgeous. He's so bloody gorgeous.

I turn a few corners, feeling confident I've gotten away from him and then check my phone. There's a message from Eve, responding to the one I sent from Brandon about how they'll have to wait until the weekend for a date.

Eve: I've also heard that absence makes the heart grow fonder. So, I hope you'll be pretty fond of me by the weekend. X

I force Olly out of my mind and send a quick reply.

Brandon: *Ha. I already am. X*

Chapter 14

I'm in a surprisingly good mood on my way to Alicia's party, especially considering I haven't been invited. Perhaps it's because I've had a great week at work. I've finally managed to bag Andy a date with Heather. He was absolutely thrilled and has taken over messaging her now. I gave him the login details to his Match profile and he messaged me last night to say that he feels he's made a 'really promising connection'. And then, of course, there's Brandon and Eve. Brandon's been busy working with his client in Switzerland so I've continued to message Eve and honestly, if he doesn't want her, I'd be almost tempted to date her myself. She's funny, sweet, smart and philosophical. We've discussed everything from the meaning of life to our favourite films (I had to consult Brandon's client file to see what they were). Derek's really pleased with my match-making skills. Things have picked up. He's managed to get a sponsor for the party and he's signed up a couple of new clients by emphasising the personal approach To the Moon & Back takes in comparison to our rivals. I feel like I've got into my stride at the agency, even if things outside work still aren't going particularly well. Not only has Alicia still not invited me to the book launch, but she's also completely ignored me.

From a few blocks away, I can already see a hubbub of activity at the bookshop. It glows with a warm yellow light that spills onto the street. A few guests gather around a couple of tables on the pavement outside, enjoying a drink. I'm hit by a sudden wave of nervousness as I approach. I feel small and awkward attending a party I'm not officially meant to be attending, but then I remember what Eve said: 'No one makes you feel inferior without your consent' and I straighten my back and walk taller, as I head into the bookshop. There's no reason why I shouldn't be here. I took those photos in exchange for getting my name out there and networking, so I should network. Plus, I really want to see the book, I want to take photos of the launch for social media and make the most of it.

A few people glance over at me as I head into the venue. They're a typical hipster crowd, a couple of guys with long beards and skinny jeans and slim bohemian girls in cute dresses. I feel a little less trendy. Being broke has had an affect on my wardrobe and my outfit is nothing special. I'm wearing an old vintage shirt I found in a charity shop and a pair of black skin-nies. Electronic music is playing in the background and people are standing around chatting while sipping from glasses of champagne and fancy-looking cocktails. Probably some of Alicia's concoctions containing your five a day. On a table at the back of the bookstore is a giant pyramid of cookbooks with a crisp rendition of my turnip picture on the cover. I feel a swell of pride. It looks amazing! I rush up to the table and pick up a copy of the book. The photo looks incredible! Far better than I imagined. I'd thought the turnip shot was a bit of an odd choice for the front cover, but it looks great! It gives a rustic feel to what is otherwise quite a modern-looking book. The title *RAW!* is emblazoned across the front in a bold font. I can't stop smiling to myself as I hold the book. I look over my shoulder for someone to share the moment with when suddenly, I spot Alicia.

She's standing in the corner of the store, laughing loudly, sipping champagne while chatting to an older man with a distinctive grey quiff and large thick-framed glasses. Sensing my gaze, she turns to look my way. The moment her eyes land on me, the amusement falls off her face. She says something to the man, excusing herself, before striding towards me in her pointy Louboutin's.

'Polly,' she says uneasily, giving me a questioning look.

'Hi Alicia. How are you? The cookbook's looking great.' I gesture towards the table.

'Thanks!' Alicia laughs awkwardly.

'Great picture resolution,' I comment.

Alicia smiles uncomfortably. A second's painful silence passes between us.

'So, erm, what happened? Did my invite get lost in the post?' I ask with a nervous giggle.

'Oh…' She squirms. 'I asked my assistant to send you an invite. She must have forgotten to.'

'Uh-huh. I mean, I thought I would be invited seeing as I took the photos. There are quite a lot of people here.' I gesture around the room.

Alicia nods awkwardly.

'I messaged you a few times. Did you not get them?'

'Erm…' Alicia's mumbles, glancing nervously away, as though looking for some kind of conversational get-out. Normally when I'm watching someone squirm, I'd back off, but I keep thinking of my conversation with Eve. She wouldn't take this rubbish. She would assert her worth. She'd set the standard for the behaviour she will and will not accept from others.

'Did your assistant forget to reply to those messages as well?' I ask, raising an eyebrow.

Alicia's cheeks flush. She takes a hungry sip of her champagne and avoids my gaze. Even though making people uncomfortable has never been my bag, I have to admit, I'm enjoying this. It feels incredibly strange to stand up for myself, but also pretty good.

'I've been really busy, Polly,' Alicia tells me.

I can't help rolling my eyes. 'So have I, Alicia. I started a new job last week, but I still found the time to edit all your photos and reply to your emails. I've been so excited about this book. I worked hard because I wanted to see your vision become a reality and to be part of this, so it's just been a bit hurtful to have ended up feeling left out. Especially since it doesn't seem like you or your assistant were too busy to invite everyone else. Is it just that I'm not enough of an influencer to get an invite?' I ask.

'It's not that, it's just… Sorry, Polly,' Alicia grumbles, looking suitably sheepish.

The apology is welcome, but it still doesn't feel like quite enough. I'm not at all happy with the way she's handled this but I'm not going to push it, especially not in the middle of a party.

'Looks like the pictures came out well at least,' I comment, flicking through the copy of the cookbook I'm holding. The photos do look great, they're printed in high definition on good quality gloss paper and they jump off the page. The lighting is perfect, the detail's sharp, and the way the images are arranged with the text looks really classy and professional. It's impressive.

'Yes, they did.' Alicia smiles uneasily again and glances awkwardly around the room. I get that I made her feel uncomfortable before, but can't she just relax now? I'm admiring the photos, I'm not attacking her.

I flick through the book back to the first few pages, where the copyright information is listed. I do a quick scan, looking out for my name. I spot Alicia's name – of course – it's in huge letters, with her company information alongside the address of the publisher, but I can't see mine.

'Oh, where's my credit?' I ask in a tremulous voice as I nervously flick through the next few pages.

Alicia reaches for the book and tries to take it from me. 'Let's go and get a drink,' she suggests, looking nervously towards the bar.

I eye her warily. My heart beating a little faster. 'Alicia, where's my credit?'

'Erm…' She takes the book and scans the first few pages. 'It should be there,' she croaks, flicking back and forth through the first few pages.

'Should be there? *Should?*' I balk.

'Yeah!' Alicia insists as she flicks through the pages again. 'Is it not? How odd.'

My stomach lurches. I thought not being invited to the launch party was bad enough, but has Alicia deliberately not included my credit? Is this why I wasn't invited?

'Are you serious, Alicia? Did your assistant forget to add that too?' I ask, my stomach fizzing with anxiety.

'I don't know… Umm, I'm not sure… I don't know what happened…' Alicia mumbles, looking away.

'I did those photos in good faith, Alicia. For free. You promised you'd give me a credit. That was our deal!' I cry out, exasperated. A few other guests look around.

Alicia takes a step closer to me. 'Can you keep your voice down, Polly?' she hisses.

'No!' I step away from her, my frustration bubbling over. 'Do you not want your guests to realise that you stole my images? Do you know how hard it is being a freelance photographer trying to make a name for yourself? Scraping by, living in a crappy apartment, surviving on cheap dumplings from Chinatown while taking on photography jobs for free just to build a portfolio?'

Alicia regards me blankly; of course, she can't relate. She's a rich girl who's had everything handed to her on a plate.

'Do you know how hard it is to try to build yourself up from nothing?' I ask. Something hot falls down my cheek and suddenly I realise I'm crying. I flick the tear away, how utterly embarrassing.

'I did those photos just for the credit – just for the credit! – and you couldn't even give me that.'

Alicia's face flushes pink. She glances awkwardly at her guests who I realise are all now watching us. She looks completely mortified. Speechless.

I flip the cooking book over in my hands and check out the label. It's a staggering $39.99, which is practically my entire food budget for a week. 'Wow,' I utter.

A large tough-looking man dressed in black comes over and grips my elbow. 'Can I see your invite, miss?' he asks.

I look at Alicia, astonished. She must have summoned him over while I was checking out the price sticker on the back of the book. She glances away.

'I took the photos for this book,' I tell the security guard.

'I'm sorry, this is a private party,' he tells me. I look him up and down, noting his heavy frame and the bulging muscles under his tight black shirt. Only someone like Alicia would hire security for a book launch.

The fizzing anxious feeling in my stomach is growing stronger and I'm aware of other guests watching me. So much for asserting myself and not letting other people make me feel inferior, I've never felt so inferior in my life.

'It's okay, I'm leaving.' I place the cookbook back on the pile and avoid eye contact with Alicia, the security guard, and all the other guests as I hurry out of the bookshop. My eyes are flooding with hot angry tears and I can't face the humiliation of everyone seeing me break down. I step outside onto the street, where a few people, oblivious to the drama inside, are enjoying a cigarette. Finally, I blink, and the tears pour down my cheeks. I let them flow as I hurry away from the party, feeling two inches tall.

I'm never going to make it. Ever. It doesn't matter how hard I try. Or how many nights I stay up late editing pictures, or how many unpaid, crummy jobs I do, nothing ever seems to work out. I'm just a lost cause. My photography dreams are a non-starter. My university sold me a dream that was never going to materialise. I'm a failure. The tears flow down my cheeks as I walk back to the subway. I'm aware that a few passers-by are looking at me, but I don't care. I'm nothing to them. I'm just another crazy New Yorker with a drama that is of no consequence to their lives at all. Why should they be bothered about me? My tears are nothing to anyone.

'Polly?' I hear a man's voice say.

I look over – my eyes bleary – to see none other than Brandon stepping out of a cab. For once, he's not wearing a suit. He's dressed down in jeans and a thick cable knit sweater and a long dark coat. He looks every inch the wholesome catalogue model. I wipe my eyes with the back of my hands, flicking the tears away. Great. Just great. Not only have I just had one of the most awful and humiliating moments of my life, but now I have to run into the top client of To the Moon & Back, not to mention one of the hottest men I've ever seen, while being an absolute emotional wreck. Can this night get any worse?

I force a weak smile. 'Hi Brandon.'

'What's happened?' Brandon asks, his face etched with concern. 'I was just driving past and I saw you and…' He takes a step out of the cab, leaving the door open. The engine rumbles.

'It's fine. Honestly, don't worry.'

Brandon comes closer, giving me a kind tender, look. His eyes are filled with what looks like genuine concern, although I don't trust my own judgement anymore. I thought Alicia was genuinely going to give me a photography credit and I was wrong about that. What do I know?

'Talk to me, Polly,' Brandon says, placing his hand on my shoulder. The touch is so foreign that it makes me flinch. It's been ages since I had any kind of physical contact beyond hand-shaking.

'Sorry,' Brandon says, letting his hand fall away. He looks embarrassed, as though he's been inappropriate.

'It's okay.' I meet his eyes, and the expression in them really does look like kindness. 'I've had a rough night and I didn't expect to see you, that's all,' I tell him.

'I know. I can see you've had a bad time. Want to talk about it?' Brandon asks.

I glance towards the cab. The engine's still running, the door wide open.

'Don't you need to be somewhere?' I ask.

'Not really.' Brandon shrugs. 'I was just heading home from the airport but I'm not in any rush. Come on.' He gestures towards the back seat of the cab. 'Sit down for a minute and you can tell me what's happened.'

I hesitate. If this were any other man, I probably wouldn't just hop into the back of a cab with them, but it's Brandon. Gorgeous, sexy, charming Brandon.

'Really?' I search his eyes, questioning why he'd want me to pour my heart out to him after a long flight, but all I see is kindness and empathy. Perhaps he's just a really nice person, perhaps he actually cares.

'Of course.' Brandon gestures towards the backseat.

'Okay.' I smile, before taking a step forward and clambering into the cab.

144

Chapter 15

'So, what's up?' Brandon asks as we drive away. He looks genuinely interested, and yet I'm aware of the fact that he's just flown all the way back from Switzerland and my cookbook issues are probably the last thing he needs to hear about.

'Are you sure you want to hear it? Don't you need to be getting home?' I ask before sniffling. My nose is still dripping from my crying fit.

Brandon shrugs. 'It's okay.' He asks his driver for some tissues and he retrieves a small pack from the glove compartment.

'Here.' Brandon hands them to me and I take them. I tear the packet open and blow my nose, a little self-consciously since blowing my nose is the last thing I want to do in front of Brandon. He looks so handsome. The amber streetlights are glowing through the cab window accentuating the shadows and contours of his chiselled cheekbones and straight nose. He seems almost statuesque in the sepia light and I can't help cringing at the thought of how I must look right now, with mascara tears streaking my cheeks.

'Thanks.' I finish blowing my nose and place the bundled-up tissue on my lap.

'It's okay. So, what happened?'

'If you really want to know I can tell you, but what about your cab? Aren't you heading home?' I ask.

'No, it's fine. We can cruise around.'

'Really?' The idea of just cruising around in a cab is a foreign concept to me. Being in a cab is pretty much a foreign concept in itself. The last time I used one was a novelty when I first moved to New York but since then, I've just taken the subway everywhere. Cabs are too pricey and the idea of casually *cruising* around in one is so strange to me. But I guess the fare is probably spare change to Brandon, even if we cruise around all evening.

'It's totally fine,' Brandon insists. He really doesn't look bothered at all.

'Okay.' I smile, before telling him everything. From how I first found Alicia on Instagram to what just happened at the party, including a scene-by-scene account of everything from Alicia's face when she saw me to the security guard gripping my arm. It feels nice to offload. Brandon's a good listener and makes sympathetic noises in all the right places. And it's strangely relaxing to just cruise through the city in no rush for anything, observing life beyond the window, close and yet distant.

'That's awful,' Brandon sympathises.

'I know.' I glance down, feeling glum.

'What she's done is completely illegal. She's stolen your copyright,' Brandon says.

'I know. It sucks.'

'Yeah, it does suck.' Brandon sighs, looking genuinely sad for me. 'But the good news is, I can help you.'

I frown, wondering what he means. Does he have another pack of tissues stashed away or something?

'How?'

Brandon's face breaks into a smile. 'I'm a lawyer, Polly. I don't specialise in copyright law, but this is a simple, clear-cut case. I'll send her a copyright infringement notice tomorrow morning.

She'll have to recall all the books printed and reprint them with your copyright.'

'Seriously?' I gawp. I knew Brandon was a lawyer, but he specialises in tax. It had never occurred to me that he could flex some legal muscle.

'Definitely,' Brandon answers affirmatively, as though it's nothing, even though what he's offering is huge. Huge! Brandon works at one of the leading law firms in Wall Street. God knows how much his fees would cost. Probably thousands. Alicia would never in a million years expect someone like me to be able to afford the services of a firm like Statten & Jones. She won't know what's hit her.

'Really? That would be absolutely incredible,' I croak. I can barely believe Brandon would do something so completely self-less. It's such a helpful gesture, and I feel myself welling up again. I dab my eyes with my tissue and let out a pathetic little sob.

'Polly, really. I want to help. What she's done to you is wrong and you don't deserve to be treated like this. I can see you've been trying hard and you've been up against it. If there's anything I can do to help, of course I will.'

I dab my eyes again. 'Thanks Brandon. That means a lot. It really does.'

'I can see that.' Brandon smiles kindly and places his hand on my knee, giving it a squeeze. I don't feel the electric impulse of attraction that I've felt from his touch before, but it still feels good to be comforted by Brandon. He's more than just sexy, he's kind too. He's the full package: successful, competent and compassionate.

'It's like you're just waving a magic legal wand and making everything better,' I joke.

Brandon laughs. 'The fairy godmother of the legal world. I'll take it.' He grins. 'Anyway, it's the least I can do seeing as I hear you've found me a date. I'll be your fairy godmother seeing as you've been my Cupid.'

I smile. 'Derek told you about Eve?'

'Yeah, he emailed me last night. He said you'd managed to find me the perfect match,' Brandon enthuses. He looks so optimistic and it's incredibly bittersweet. I'm so glad I've managed to find him someone as cool as Eve, but his happy, eager expression is just another reminder that I'm not remotely on his romantic radar. If I thought Brandon might have started warming to me – my plight perhaps igniting an alpha need to protect, a spark of sorts – then I was clearly wrong.

'I have indeed. She's awesome.'

'Tell me about her.'

'Of course. I'll show you her too.' I rummage in my bag for my phone, find Eve's Tinder profile and present it to Brandon. I watch his face as he scrolls through her pictures with a strange curious feeling, that's part excited anticipation and part dread. I want him to be impressed with my matchmaking skills and I want to feel the professional pride of having finally found someone for one of the agency's pickiest clients, but I also don't want to lose him. If Eve really is his type, then there's absolutely no hope for me. Brandon's silent as he clicks through her pictures, his face unreadable.

'What do you think?' I ask.

'She's beautiful,' Brandon says, in a sincere tone. 'Really beautiful.'

I smile, but it's a little forced. My heart has sunk a bit too.

'Is she real? She looks too good to be true.' Brandon pauses on the photo of Eve on the sofa, looking cute with her side plait and oversized woolly jumper. In his cable knit, with their model good looks, they'd really go well together. It's impossible to deny. 'She went to Columbia. Works at J. C. Fisher. She seems really impressive,' Brandon notes. There's hesitation in his voice and I can tell he's feeling sceptical.

'I think she's genuine. Obviously, you can't be 100 per cent sure until you actually meet the person in the flesh but I found her online,' I tell him, trying to ignore the cynical words of Gabe replaying in my mind that professional profiles can be faked just as easily as dating profiles.

Brandon nods pensively. 'And you've been chatting to her?'

'Oh yeah! Loads. She's awesome. Seriously, she's way more than just a pretty face. She's got a lot to say for herself. She's so smart, so sensitive. She's witty and philosophical. I've loved chatting to her. I'm going to miss her!'

Brandon laughs. 'So, what's she into?'

I tell him about Eve's interests and the kinds of things we've chatted about, and I get so enthusiastic as I recount our chats that I momentarily completely forget about Alicia. I'm back in that little bubble, texting Eve on the way to work or in bed in the evenings or sitting in the office with Derek. It's a bit tragic but I've felt more of a connection to Eve while posing as Brandon than I've felt to most of the guys I've ever chatted to on dating apps while being myself.

'She sounds great, Polly,' Brandon says, his voice warmer. 'It sounds like you guys have done a lot of talking.'

'Oh...' I shift a little in the seat. He's right. We did do a lot of talking. A lot more than I probably should have engaged in. I'm meant to just make a bit of chit chat, just enough to set up a date, before the client takes over but I definitely went overboard. Way overboard.

I giggle awkwardly. 'Yeah, I did get a little carried away. Sorry.'

'Don't worry!' Brandon insists. 'But you might have to send me a copy of the conversation in case she refers to something. Do you guys have in-jokes yet?'

'A few!' I admit, thinking back to mine and Eve's conversation about floppy discs and hard drives.

'Oh God!' Brandon laughs. 'Well, if she and I don't hit it off, maybe you guys can give things a shot,' Brandon jokes.

'Honestly, if I was going to question my sexuality for anyone, it would probably be Eve,' I admit.

'Wow! If you're as taken with her as this after a few days texting, how am I going to cope after a date?'

I laugh. 'You'll probably want to marry her.'

'You'd better buy a hat then.'

I laugh again. And it occurs to me that Brandon has completely turned my mood around. I've gone from crying in the rain to laughing, my problems wiped away.

'Thanks for tonight Brandon. You've really helped me,' I insist.

He smiles kindly. 'Well, fingers crossed, I think you might have really helped me,' he says, taking one more glance at Eve's profile before handing my phone back. 'I'll get the letter drawn up tomorrow. Email me Alicia's details. We'll take her down,' Brandon says with a wink.

'Excellent!' I reply, resisting the urge to do an evil laugh.

'Now, are you sure you're feeling better? Are you feeling ready to head home or do you want to drive around a bit longer?' Brandon asks, cupping his hand over his mouth to stifle a yawn. Our conversation was probably the final straw, pushing him over the edge, from just about handling his jet lag, to needing his bed.

'Yeah, I'm fine now, Brandon. Genuinely. Thanks so much. Just drop me off at the nearest subway and I'll head home. Thank you. I really owe you.'

Brandon laughs. 'Don't be silly. Where do you live?'

'Brooklyn,' I reply awkwardly. 'But honestly, you don't need to drop me home.'

'I'm not leaving you at the subway,' Brandon comments, as though 'subway' is a dirty word.

Brandon leans forward to the driver. 'Can you head to Brooklyn?' he asks.

'Oh no, you don't have to.'

'Polly, please,' Brandon stresses, giving me a sincere look. 'I know you Brits get awkward about this stuff but stop worrying.'

'Haha, okay,' I relent.

'Cool,' Brandon says. He gives me a tender smile as the driver weaves through the city traffic and takes me home.

Chapter 16

The moment I wake up the next morning and turn on my phone an email pings through from Brandon, sent at 6.45 a.m.

> From: brandon.fox@stattenjones.com
> To: polly@tothemoonandback.com
> Hi Polly,
>   I looked into our copyright law files and found the standard notice we send. It's been issued to Alicia (see attached). This should sort things out.
>   Hope you're feeling better,
>   Brandon

I open the attached file to find a tersely written legal notice informing Alicia of copyright infringement and the legal consequences. I lie in bed, rereading the letter a few times as a smile creeps onto my lips. What a wake-up call Alicia must have had. Literally and metaphorically. Maybe now she'll realise that she can't just push everyone around and take advantage of them. I bash out a reply to Brandon.

From: polly@tothemoonandback.com
To: brandon.fox@stattenjones.com
Hi Brandon,

Thanks so much. Talk about taking swift action! I really *really* appreciate this!

Good luck on your date tonight with Eve ☺

Polly

I get out of bed and take a long soothing shower. As I lather soap over my body and massage shampoo into my scalp, I can practically feel the frustration and sadness of last night flood down the plug hole. Sending legal notices is in no way how I wanted things to end up with Alicia, but I can't just let her take advantage of my free labour and steal my work. It feels good to have someone like Brandon in my corner, standing up for me. I condition my hair and try to get into a good mood for the day ahead. I'm meeting up with Scarlett to go for a walk, take photos of street art and have a catch-up. It should be fun. I hop out of the shower, feeling revived and upbeat as I dry my body off and get dressed. It feels weird to be getting ready without being in a hurry to get to the office. It feels even weirder to be slinging my camera strap over my shoulder, having not touched it for days.

I head into the living room to find Gabe is lounging on the sofa watching *America's Next Top Model*. He's still in last night's make-up, his false eyelashes casting shadows over his cheeks as he looks up, blinking sleepily. He must have come home after I went to bed last night and by the looks of it, he crashed out on the sofa. He's draped in a green woolly throw, but the strap of a pastel blue satin dress is visible, looping over his shoulder. His wig's on the coffee table and his hair is slicked back.

'Hey babe,' he croaks, with a lazy smile.

'Hey.' I perch at the end of the sofa. 'Late night?'

'Yep. Wild night. We did Eighties classics. I did a rendition of 'Total Eclipse of the Heart' by Bonnie Tyler. Everyone went wild.

It was so much fun,' Gabe tells me, his eyes sparkling. His eyes always sparkle like that when he talks about singing. He never gets the same infectious enthusiasm when he talks about work. He never gets any real enthusiasm when he talks about work, actually.

'Classic song,' I comment. I've heard Gabe's Bonnie Tyler renditions and they're amazing. Gabe has the kind of strong, pitch-perfect, emotional voice that can carry her powerful dramatic ballads. I still remember how the hairs on my arms stood on end the first time I heard him sing 'Total Eclipse of the Heart'.

'Yeah, it's a classic,' Gabe says, reaching over to the coffee table to grab a glass of Coke. He winces as he takes a sip and I instantly know there's vodka in it. I used to be more onboard with Gabe doing his drag queen show every Friday night, but seeing him now, hungover and drinking last night's booze as a morning refreshment, just makes my heart feel a bit heavy.

'It totally is a classic, but don't you ever feel like you're too good for The Eagle?' I ask, a little nervously. I probably shouldn't say anything, but perhaps because of Brandon's intervention in my life, I feel more emboldened than usual to speak up. Gabe might not want to hear what I really think, but maybe it could help him.

'What do you mean?' Gabe flinches, the comment clearly taking him by surprise.

'You're an amazing singer Gabe, and yet the only people who are hearing you sing are a bunch of drunks down at The Eagle,' I blurt out. It comes out a little harsher than I had intended.

Gabe sits up a bit, causing the throw to fall around his waist, revealing the sequined bodice of his dress.

'What's that meant to mean?' he asks, giving me a hard look. He takes another sip of his vodka and Coke.

'I just think you're wasted on The Eagle, that's all,' I tell him.

Gabe rolls his eyes dramatically, causing the shadows of his lashes to slide over his face.

154

'I just think that we set the standard of our worth. It's something I've been thinking about a lot this week, and do you really think you're setting a high enough standard for your singing career?'

'Are you serious?' Gabe scoffs, with a mean laugh.

My stomach does a little flip. Maybe I shouldn't have said anything.

'Yeah,' I insist in a slightly high-pitched awkward voice. 'I mean why not get some gigs at better places? You could get spotted by a record label or something,' I suggest.

'It's funny, because a few months ago The Eagle was good enough for you, too,' Gabe reminds me, raising an eyebrow before taking another sip of his drink.

'Not really. I quit, remember?'

'Yeah, to go and work for a dating agency.' Gabe rolls his eyes.

I fiddle with my camera on my lap, twisting the lens. 'So? I'm still trying to get my photography career off the ground. I haven't given up on it,' I insist.

'Wow, Polly,' Gabe sighs, looking exasperated. 'I'm lying here tired from a gig and you're telling me I've given up on singing?'

I squirm in my seat. 'No. Not given up. I just think you could aim higher, that's all.'

Gabe scoffs. 'And I think you could get a bit more realistic. Did you ever consider that you might not be the next Mario Testino? Or that I might not want to be the male Lady Gaga? Maybe I just enjoy singing? Maybe that's good enough for me?'

'Okay, fine!' I insist. 'Sorry I said anything.'

'No really. When was the last time you just took pictures because you enjoyed it?' Gabe presses me, fixing me with a serious, cutting look.

I pause, considering his question. I took photos last weekend in Central Park, but I was too busy feeling homesick, and worrying about what love really means, to really get into it. And I definitely didn't enjoy taking photos of turnips for Alicia. And it's not like

I enjoyed many of the rubbish freelance jobs I did before that. Maybe Gabe's right. Maybe I have stopped taking genuine pleasure in my photography work.

'I do enjoy it sometimes. I'm heading out to take photos now,' I point out, lifting my camera from my lap to draw his attention to it.

'Do you? Do you really? Because all you ever seem to do is complain about photography.' Gave regards me with a cynical expression. 'Yet here I am actually enjoying what I do and you're judging me for it,' he huffs.

'I'm not judging you, I'm just—'

'Leave it, Polly!' Gabe gets up from the sofa. 'My head's pounding okay?' he sighs.

'Well, drinking vodka and Coke probably isn't helping,' I note.

Gabe shoots me a look. 'I'm taking a shower,' he grumbles.

'Okay, fine,' I reply. 'See you later,' I add, but Gabe ignores me, casting a withering glance over his shoulder as he slopes off to the bathroom, closing the door behind him.

I get up and hoist my camera strap onto my shoulder, feeling odd. I didn't mean to upset Gabe, I was genuinely only trying to help. I didn't expect him to take my feedback that badly. I consider calling him back, banging on the bathroom door, but I don't want to annoy him even more. We often have silly arguments like this and they're usually forgotten fast. It's a side effect of having such a close and open friendship. And anyway, on some level, he's got a point. His cutting barb about Mario Testino may have been a little harsh, but I have become so focused on trying to make it as a photographer I've lost the joy I used to take from it. It's been a while since I just snapped away, lost in that bubble of concentration and pure pleasure, when you're just so wrapped up in what you're doing that time loses meaning. I think the last time I felt like that was when I did my final project at university – a street photography project – taking candid portraits of familiar local faces in the town, from a train conductor to a busker who played guitar on the sidewalk. Capturing a sense of people's spirit in those shots was what made me want to be a portrait photographer. It was all I thought about for weeks. Real life just disintegrated into the background while I spent hours upon hours walking around, chatting to random people, getting a rapport with them to the point that they'd open up and allow me to take their picture. It was heaven. I was addicted to getting the perfect shot. These days, all I do is grumpily take photos to support my clients' projects, to further their visions and goals, while my own goals and enjoyment recede into the background.

I grab my coat and my wallet, and I head out the front door, determined to enjoy photography for the sake of photography today. Gabe's right. I need to enjoy myself. I need to get back in the zone.

Chapter 17

I didn't realise how obsessed I've become with focus, lighting, depth of field and framing until I suggested to Scarlett that we just take random snaps – fun, cute shots of each other larking about in front of the cool arty murals of Brooklyn. We didn't compete to take the most striking or professional shot; instead, we just had a laugh, just what Gabe pointed out I hadn't been doing lately. We spread our arms wide in front of some painted fairy wings and we pretending to pick apples from a giant mural of a tree. We just snapped away. And funnily enough, without trying so hard, the pictures turned out better. They weren't as technically well composed but they had more energy. They were more eye-catching – our spontaneity shining through.

It was a brilliant day, and it totally helped me take my mind off the Alicia situation. However, by Saturday night, I kept finding myself thinking about Brandon and wondering how his date was going with Eve. It was a bittersweet feeling, wanting him and Eve to hit it off, for both his sake and Eve's, while feeling a little sad that someone as kind and good-looking and brilliant as him would be even further from my reach if they ended up getting on. If I'm totally honest, I know Brandon probably only offered to help with Alicia because he saw me crying my eyes out on the street and felt sorry for me, but a small part of me has secretly wondered if perhaps he might have a romantic soft spot for me. Perhaps I'll be the woman that breaks the mould. The untoned brunette photographer who happens to steal his heart. Surely stranger things have happened?

Back at the office on Monday morning, I refresh my inbox, half hoping that an email from Brandon might ping through telling me the date was a total bust. But there's nothing. Not one update about the date.

'I was just thinking, shall I call Brandon?' I ask Derek as I glance at the clock: it's 9.45 a.m. 'I want to know how his date went with Eve.'

'No, not at this time on a Monday morning,' Derek objects, through a mouthful of Oreos. 'No way.'

'Okay,' I sigh.

Derek gives me an indulgent look.

'Drop him an email if you really want to know, but he'll be busy now. And it is a bit keen,' Derek points out with a smile.

'Yeah, I'll do that.'

I open my emails and bash out a quick message to Brandon asking how his date went. I can't resist adding, 'Heard anything from Alicia?' at the end of it either. I can't imagine how Alicia must have reacted to a terse copyright notice from one of the biggest law firms in the city. The thought of it actually makes me a little nervous. I remember reading about a famous CEO who had a large plush white fur rug in front of her office desk so that the moment anyone entered her space, they had to adapt to the surroundings. They had to be neat, controlled and respectful so that they didn't tarnish the expensive rug. The CEO shaped the way people behaved around her, just through that subtle gesture of furnishings. Alicia's like that too. With her expensively bohemian clothes, exacting standards and impatient attitude, she just creates a vibe. She doesn't necessarily force people to behave differently towards her; they just do. Around her, I succumbed to her pickiness, I acquiesced to her impatient attitude and became quick and efficient. I didn't even think about it, it was simply how I knew I was meant to behave. I didn't want to burst the Alicia bubble or rock the boat. Legal notices are never welcomed by anyone but particularly not by controlling, highly-strung people like Alicia. Even though I know she deserved it, it makes me squirm to think of how she would have responded. Of course, her online presence has given nothing away. She posted a blog last night on 'Five reasons bananas are a superfood', although it was probably pre-scheduled.

To my surprise, Brandon replies pretty much instantly.

From: *brandondfox@stattenjones.com*
To: *polly@tothemoonandback.com*
Hi Polly!

Sorry I didn't get in touch yesterday, but I had a valid reason. I'll drop by at the office later and fill you in on everything. All good news!
Brandon

A valid reason? Was he sick? I read the message out to Derek and ask him what he thinks.

'That's Brandon for you.' Derek shrugs. 'When something's important, he prefers to chat in person. He's old school like that.'

'Okay,' I murmur, thinking back to Friday night. I recall Brandon's attentive expression as I poured my heart out. He was properly listening, taking everything in. It's not like he had one eye on his phone like most people these days. Derek's right, he is pretty old school.

Derek sighs loudly and reaches for the trusty pack of Oreos in his desk drawer. I've come to realise that if he eats more than three or four, something's usually bothering him.

'What's up?' I ask.

'Urghh,' Derek grunts while taking a bite. He hands me the pack and I reach for one. There are worse ways to deal with life's stresses.

'You know that guy we had in last week? The one with the strange haircut?' Derek says.

'Elliot Brown?' I ask, recalling the guy with the spiky fringe who came in last week for a consultation.

'Yeah, Elliot.' Derek scratches his head. 'Well, he seemed really keen. He said he couldn't wait to meet the woman of his dreams. He seemed so eager to sign up, he even wanted a full tour of the place.'

'A tour?' I wrinkle my nose.

'Yeah, he wanted to see the office, so I showed him. I told him we were a small agency and it wasn't much, but he seemed really impressed. He said he was going to sign up and that he'd be in touch the next day, but I haven't heard a word. Not one word.'

'He ghosted you?' I grimace.

'Yeah. Something like that,' Derek grumbles.

'That's rude,' I comment. 'When was it he came in?'

'Last Tuesday,' Derek reminds me.

'Hmmpph, so he's had a week to get in contact… Plenty of time.'

'Exactly. He could have at least got in touch and told me he was busy or still considering it, but he's just gone quiet. Radio silence,' Derek huffs, pulling another Oreo from the pack. He presents the pack to me, but I decline.

'Erm… I guess you win some, you lose some,' I reason.

'Yeah. I guess.' Derek replies glumly. 'You're right. It's just frustrating. I was excited to sign up a new client. But I suppose I just have to put him out of my mind.'

'Exactly!' I resist the urge to smile as I turn back to my computer, Derek sounds exactly like a disappointed dater. I log onto Match. I need to reply to messages for Steve – the art-collecting hedge fund manager. I chat to matches until the intercom buzzes at around midday. Derek's on the phone to a balloon supplier for the party so I answer it.

'Hello, To the Moon & Back,' I chirp in my most sing-song receptionist voice.

'Polly, it's Brandon,' Brandon says, and I immediately buzz him up, my finger a blur as it shoots to the entry button. I'm dying to hear about his date with Eve.

'Brandon's here,' I whisper to Derek, who's looking over curiously. He nods, and I slip next door into the client lounge and plump up the pillows, arranging them nicely on the sofa.

'Polly!' Brandon pushes the door open and gives me the broadest, most charming, spectacular smile he's ever given me, and that's saying something. Every smile I've ever seen from Brandon has been a red-carpet worthy 100-watt showstopper – he's just that gorgeous and charismatic – but this is like that and then some. Perhaps it's because his eyes are sparkling too, the skin crinkling around them.

He strides towards me and envelops me in a warm hug. He smells delicious and even when he pulls away, he's still beaming, radiating joy.

He clutches my shoulders. 'You – Polly Wood – are a miracle worker!' he states.

'Really?' I grin.

'Yes!' he insists, letting his hands drop from my shoulders. 'I can't believe it! I really can't,' he gushes with an air of disbelief as he settles into the armchair.

'So, I take it you and Eve hit it off then?' I ask, smiling brightly while I try to quell the tiny sinking feeling of disappointment; Brandon truly will never be mine.

'We sure did!' Brandon grins. 'She's perfect, Polly. I know I shouldn't get too ahead of myself but wow…' He shakes his head in disbelief as though he can't believe his luck. 'Where did you find her?'

'Tinder!' I remind him.

'I know, but all this time I've been looking for a woman like Eve. Really, for years. In a city as big as New York and out of all the millions of people here, I haven't managed to find anyone like her, even remotely like her,' Brandon enthuses, beaming.

'I'm so glad! So, she was the same as her photos then? Not a catfish?'

'Definitely not a catfish!' Brandon insists, shaking his head in disbelief, as though he can't quite believe his luck.

'Was she as interesting in person too?' I ask.

'Oh yes. She ticks all the boxes. Intelligent, successful, independent. She's fantastic!'

I smile, the disappointment falling away. It's not like I seriously thought Brandon would go for me, it was just a daydream. Here he is, radiating hope and enthusiasm and excitement and it's impossible not to feel anything other than happiness for him. It's catching. I have the strange urge to message Eve and have a girly chat with her to see what she makes of Brandon, but of course, that's impossible.

'Wait, are you bringing her to the Valentine's party?' I ask, brightening up.

'What party?' Brandon asks. I give him the low down.

'Sounds great, Polly, but why would I bring Eve to a singles mixer? Plus, I don't really want her to know that I used a dating agency.'

'Hmm… I guess. But there'll be a lot of people there. Just think of it as a party, rather than a singles thing. No one needs to know you were one of our clients. You can just say you wanted to go as a favour to your friend – me!' I clap my hands against my chest.

Brandon raises an eyebrow. 'A favour? I guess I do owe you one. You did find Eve,' Brandon muses. 'And we're getting commission from the damages Alicia's paying up.'

My ears prick up. 'The what?'

'Oh yeah. My copyright guy got stuck into your case. She's

agreed to pay $5,000 to you for violating your copyright. All further use of the images will be credited. We've got it all in writing. Sorry, it's not higher but the figure was based on the first print run, which wasn't particularly large.'

'$5,000?' I gawp.

'Yeah, like I said, not a lot but she only had a thousand copies printed and they've all been recalled now.'

'Not a lot?' I balk. Five thousand dollars may not be much to Brandon, but it's huge to me. It would be such a big help, yet I can't quite feel happy about it. Even though Alicia has treated me terribly, I can't help feeling a little bad. She's may flaunt a privileged lifestyle online, but I'm not sure how I feel taking that much money from her, even if it is a legal payment.

'Do you think she can afford it?' I ask timidly.

Brandon guffaws. 'Of course, she can afford it. She's from the Carter family. They're loaded. This is spare change to them! We deal with them all the time. They're always up to stuff like this – screwing people over. They get into plenty of legal trouble. You'd think they'd have learnt by now.'

'Really?' I gawp, feeling my heart sink at the thought of how much I've been taken advantage of. Clearly Alicia could have afforded to pay me for my work.

'Yeah. Not a nice bunch, I'm afraid. I'd have warned you not to get involved with them if I'd known you back then,' Brandon says.

'Wow, okay…' I murmur.

'Honestly, don't feel bad. It really is nothing to them. But hopefully it's some help,' Brandon says kindly.

'It's a massive help. It's an incredible help,' I tell him. My eyes begin tearing up and I look away, blinking the emotion back. Not only does it feel like justice has been served but the money is a big deal. It might be nothing to Alicia, but it means so much to me. Five thousand dollars will give me breathing space. It'll help me get up to date with my rent, pay Gabe back some of the

164

money he's been lending me here and there. Maybe, I'll put some of it towards getting a proper photography website set up, who knows? The point is, this payment will give me time and possibilities – the precise things I've been lacking recently. But I don't want to make a big deal of it. Making money is nothing to Brandon. Just like messaging someone on Tinder for him is nothing to me.

I still feel on the brink of tears when fortunately, Derek bursts through the office door and I'm saved the embarrassment of getting weepy and sentimental. As usual, Derek greets Brandon like his first-born child, and then sits down on the sofa next to him.

'So, tell me about Saturday then? I hear Polly found you someone special?' Derek asks.

'Very special,' Brandon replies and his eyes get that twinkly look about them again. He starts telling Derek about the date, from the moment he first saw Eve ('such a stunning, beautiful woman') to the food they shared (oysters followed by duck at one of Chelsea's fancy eateries).

'And, did you have a kiss goodbye?' Derek asks.

'What are you like, Derek?' I tut.

'Oh, come on! Don't pretend you don't want to know, Polly,' Derek retorts.

A mischievous smile plays on Brandon's lips. 'Let's just say, we had a kiss goodbye this morning,' he says.

'This morning!?' I balk.

'Eve came back with me on Saturday and she didn't leave until this morning. When I said we hit it off, I meant it,' Brandon tells us with a smug gleeful grin.

'Wow, Brandon!' I'm impressed. I mean, I know he's Brandon Fox, one of the hottest, most eligible bachelors in New York but seriously? He not only managed to have an amazing date with Eve but an amazing weekend too. That's some pretty impressive work.

Derek nudges Brandon like a jock would having found out his mate got lucky after prom. I roll my eyes.

'Right, that's my cue to leave,' I say, getting up.

'Good to see you, Polly,' Brandon says.

'You too.' I thank him again for his help with Alicia and then go next door, leaving him and Derek to catch up.

I smile to myself as I sit down at my desk. I still can't believe Brandon's just casually managed to get me $5,000 from Alicia. Especially considering I didn't even get paid for the photos in the first place. I send a quick text to Scarlett to tell her. I know she'll be thrilled for me, considering how much she disapproves of all my unpaid photography work. After taking a few moments to calm down and take what's just happened in, I turn my attention back to Match.com.

Through the office door, I can hear Derek saying goodbye to Brandon. He comes back in, waving over his shoulder.

'Polly!' he says as he closes the office door behind him. He catches my eye and there's a twinkle of pride in his expression.

'To say I'm impressed would be an understatement!' he gushes.

'Huh?'

Derek sits down in his office chair and swivels around to face me. 'I've been trying to find someone for Brandon for months and you've managed it in a week!'

'Oh, well, I guess I got lucky,' I say with a modest smile.

'No, it's more than just luck! You totally understood Brandon. You kept Eve interested. You set up the date. I've never seen Brandon so happy. I'm really impressed, Polly, genuinely,' Derek says. His enthusiasm is infectious and even though he's busy complimenting me, I can't help noting how genuinely happy he seems to be for Brandon. Derek may not own the swankiest dating agency in New York, but he certainly does take a personal approach. You can tell that he cares about his clients; he's totally invested in Brandon's love life.

'Thanks, Derek. Brandon does seem to really like Eve,' I say.

'Like?! I've never seen him get like this over anyone.'

I grin. 'Maybe I should buy a hat,' I joke.

'Fingers crossed, eh?' Derek winks. 'Oh, that reminds me. Could you go and buy some cupcakes from Angel's Bakery? I heard they're great and I really want to try them out. I'm thinking of getting them to supply us for the party.

'Sure!' I reply, feeling excited about the prospect of going to Angel's. Its cupcakes are legendary in the city, but I've never got around to going.

'Go somewhere nice for lunch while you're at it as well, on me,' Derek says.

I protest, telling him that it's not necessary but he insists.

'Okay, well, thanks Derek!'

'No worries.' He reaches into his trouser pocket and pulls out his wallet.

'Oh, and here's the company card,' he says, handing it to me. 'I'll text you the pin.'

'Thanks, Derek,' I murmur as I take the card and slip it in my wallet, before Googling Angel's Bakery and looking up the address. 'Oh, Angel's is on 54th street. Isn't that just around the corner from Elite Love Match?'

'Yeah.' Derek shrugs.

'I keep running into Olly. It's looking really suspicious,' I warn Derek, although I omit telling him flat-out that Olly already knows who I am.

'It doesn't matter,' Derek says. 'I'm sure Olly has bigger fish to fry.'

'I guess, but what if he thinks I'm still creeping around there.'

A smirk plays on Derek's lips. 'Well, wear sunglasses or something. Be incognito.'

I roll my eyes. 'Seriously? What next? A wig?!'

'You never know, it might suit you!' Derek jokes.

I laugh, shaking my head.

'Stop worrying!' He urges me. 'Just nip into Angel's Bakery, grab some cupcakes and then get something to eat. Enjoy yourself!'

'Okay.' I nod. Derek's right. I'll just dash in and out, I probably won't even see Olly.

'Just have a nice lunch. Treat yourself after your success with Brandon.' Derek says.

'Thanks Derek,' I say as I gather my things. 'That's a really sweet gesture.'

'No worries. Go to a nice restaurant.' Derek smiles. 'Enjoy it.'

'I will.' I smile back, grabbing my coat to go.

Chapter 18

I feel a bit bad splashing out on a fancy lunch, even if Derek said I could treat myself. I can't help thinking of his wife and her knee surgery so I head to an upmarket sandwich shop rather than a restaurant. It's the kind of place that has all organic ingredients and serves delicious sandwiches on fresh ciabatta bread. Far nicer than the cheap sandwiches I usually have for lunch, but not too pricey. Not exactly breaking the bank.

I opt for a grilled aubergine and hummus sandwich and people-watch office workers darting about on their lunchbreak while I tuck in. The sandwich is so tasty but I'm a little on edge. I can't help keeping an eye out for Olly, even though with his out-there dress sense, I'm sure I'd spot him immediately in a crowd. Derek's right though, I probably shouldn't feel nervous about running into him. Like Derek said, Olly probably has much bigger fish to fry. I am no doubt completely irrelevant to him. He probably can't even remember my name and has written me off as some time-wasting weirdo, yet I feel kind of stalkerish continually hanging about in the area where Olly works. As though I'm creeping on him or have some strange obsession. It wouldn't surprise me if he assumed I'm some desperate fan girl who developed some kind of infatuation after following him on

Instagram. It probably wouldn't be the first time that kind of thing's happened to Olly.

I finish my lunch and leave the café, then head down the road to Angel's Bakery, where I admire the rainbow displays of delicious-looking cupcakes. It even smells of sugar inside and I select half a dozen gorgeous cupcakes so Derek can try some of the flavours (it'll make a nice change from Oreos), before paying with the company credit card. With the lunch time rush dying down, the street is pretty quiet now. Olly's probably busy with client consultations or securing press coverage or whatever. I relax a little bit and do a spot of window shopping. After all, Derek did say I should enjoy myself, and my lunch didn't take long.

I nip into a few shops – a retro sweet shop where I buy a jar of lemon sherbets to have at home with Gabe, and a shop that sells hats and scarves where I try on a ridiculously expensive silk scarf that makes me look way older than my years. I wander over to a jewellery shop a few doors down from Elite Love Match, where I pause to admire the window display of glittering rings, necklaces and bracelets, which glint in the winter sunshine. I'm probably getting a bit too close to Olly's office, but I just want to have a quick look at the jewellery. I'm checking out a beautiful emerald and diamond ring, sparkling in the sunlight, when suddenly, a man comes through the revolving doors of Elite Love Match and I stiffen, ducking my head in case it's Olly. But it's not. The person is shorter and as he steps out onto the street, I look over my shoulder and spot an unmistakable spiky black fringe. It's none other than Elliot Brown, the guy who had a consultation with Derek at To the Moon & Back last week. The guy who didn't get in touch after claiming he was going to sign up with us. He must have decided to sign with Elite Love Match instead. Urghh. He catches me looking his way and instantly, a look of recognition flashes across his face. Great, now I have to speak to him.

'Hi Elliot!' I step towards him, extending my hand. 'I'm Polly.

I work at To the Moon & Back. We met the other day when you came in for a consultation.'

He limply shakes my hand. 'Ah yes.' He smiles, but it's a forced uncomfortable smile – one that doesn't quite reach his eyes. He clearly thinks I'm about to go into pushy sales mode or something.

'I just thought I'd say hi,' I mutter, regretting talking to him at all. So what that he never got back in touch? Just because Derek was upset about it, doesn't mean I should be haranguing random people in the street. I'm about to excuse myself and scurry off when I spot a lanyard dangling around his neck, with the Elite Love Match logo, Elliot's photo and the job title 'Business Development Manager'.

'What's that?!' I point to it, aghast. 'You work for Elite Love Match?'

He immediately whips his coat closed, covering his name badge. 'Errr… sorry, I err…' He looks over my shoulder, clearly desperate to get away from me. 'Got to go. Meeting. Sorry, bye.'

He smiles awkwardly and scurries past me, hurrying away.

'Wait, but…' I mutter after him as he dashes away, but he doesn't turn back. I watch him disappear down the street, until he's indecipherable among the other passers-by. My mind is churning. If Elliot works for Elite Love Match, what the hell was he doing at To the Moon & Back? It doesn't make any sense. Did Olly send him to spy on us too? Is snooping just common practice in the dating agency world? I should probably be heading back to work, but I can't seem to move. I feel rooted to the spot, gripped by irritation. I want to know what's going on. I turn on my heel and find myself charging into Elite Love Match, pushing through the gleaming door.

Thankfully the receptionist is a different one to Gina, who was working last time I visited. She looks momentarily startled, but quickly corrects her expression, plastering on a bland smile.

'Hi, can I help you?' she says.

'Hi, yes. I'd like to see Olly Corrigan. It's about a business matter. It won't take long,' I tell her, feigning confidence, even though I'm beginning to wonder what the hell I'm doing.

She raises an eyebrow, clearly not quite sure what to make of me. I may be acting like I know what I'm doing, but I don't think she's buying it. I don't exactly look business-like. Today I'm rocking jeans and a slightly ratty grey sweater that I found in a charity shop. It definitely doesn't scream businesswoman, but there must be something about my firm, forthright manner that makes the receptionist decide to assist me.

'What's your name?'

'Polly Wood,' I tell her.

'And which company are you from?'

'To the Moon & Back,' I admit.

'Right….' The receptionist raises an eyebrow, nodding slowly, as she reaches for her phone. Her face doesn't give much away, but I can tell she's a little taken aback.

'Hi Olly. I have a lady in reception here to see you. Polly Wood from To the Moon & Back.'

She cups the receiver to her ear as Olly says something. For a moment, I have a strong urge to turn around and slip back through the revolving doors. What am I doing? Heading up to that swanky office to confront Olly Corrigan? This was probably a really bad idea.

'Okay, yes. I'll send her up.' She hangs up the phone and meets my gaze, her eyes stony.

'He can see you now. If you could just head to the tenth floor, Olly will meet you there,' she says, with that polished, well-practised smile.

I thank her and head to the lift.

As I step inside, I glance over my shoulder wondering if it's too late to turn around and dash out. But then, I really want to know what Olly's playing at. Derek's right, he is a bit of a cad. He shouldn't be poaching clients from To the Moon &

Back and spying on us and being so competitive. He's so annoying, with his swanky office and cool young team who all want to crush us under the heels of their shiny stilettos. No. Some people actually want to earn an honest living, take care of their families and live a comfortable life. Why can't Olly just co-exist with Derek? Why does he have to try to crush his competition like this? By the time the lift reaches Olly's floor, I feel really pumped and all of my nervousness and misgivings have gone.

The lift doors open and there Olly is, standing by a plant in the foyer of his open plan office, waiting for me, his arms folded across his chest. He looks gorgeous. Disarmingly handsome and for a moment, my stomach does a little flip and butterflies replace the frustration burning inside.

'Polly,' he says, stepping forward to shake my hand. A wry smile plays on his lips. He doesn't seem at all surprised or taken aback that I'm here.

'Hi Olly,' I reply, clasping his hand.

'Taking a break from chartered surveying?' Olly jokes, his eyes sparkling mischievously.

I roll my eyes and try to give him a stern stare, but his handsome, playful expression is difficult to contend with. I forgot how good-looking he is. I forgot how much his presence just *radiates*. His sparkling brown eyes, natural charisma and his wide bright smile are making this whole thing a little difficult.

'Can we speak in private please?' I ask, glancing over at his watchful team, a few of whom immediately avert their gaze when they catch me looking over. Do they have to be so nosy?

'Sure. Come to my office,' Olly says, beckoning me to follow him.

I can feel his staff watching us as we walk to Olly's office, but I ignore their curious looks and take in Olly's outfit instead. Today he's rocking a pair of ridiculously over-the-top embroidered beaded trousers and a Gucci T-shirt.

'Take a seat,' he says, gesturing at the chair opposite his desk. I sit down on the edge of the seat, careful not to make myself too comfortable. I'm not planning to stick around.

'So, has Derek send you back to snoop around again.'

'No, he hasn't,' I tut, feeling irritated.

'Then, erm, why are you here?' Olly asks, raising an eyebrow.

'I'm here because of Elliot,' I tell him.

Olly frowns. 'Elliot?'

'Yes, your business development manager. I just saw him outside. I take it you sent him to visit To the Moon & Back?'

'Oh, that…' Olly murmurs, leaning back in his chair.

'I guess you figured out Derek was up to something and decided to send someone to spy on his agency. Was it a retaliation or something?' I ask.

'No,' Olly laughs, shaking his head. 'I didn't even know Elliot had visited your offices, but I can figure out why.'

'Why?' I stress.

'Derek has a great location there – right on the top floor of that financial advisory firm. It's a perfect place to get clients. All those single finance guys with money… Elliot's been talking about buying Derek's premises for a while, so I guess he just went to have a look around,' Olly explains.

'What? Seriously?' I balk.

'Yeah.' Olly shrugs. 'He's responsible for expanding my business and he thinks buying up Derek's office would be a good move. He's been talking about it for ages.'

'Derek's office isn't for sale,' I point out, exasperated.

'Oh, I know, but we know the property manager. Derek's only renting. If we wanted to buy, he'd just give Derek notice on his tenancy,' Olly explains, before picking up his phone and calling his assistant to bring us two glasses of sparkling water. He places the phone back down on the receiver and leans back in his chair, crossing his hands over his stomach.

'What's up?' he asks, as I stare at him in disbelief.

174

'Do you really think it's okay to just trample over everyone?' I ask.

'I'm not!' Olly insists, looking affronted, although his indignance doesn't quite ring true.

His assistant comes in carrying a tray with two glasses of sparkling water, which she lays down discreetly on the table, clearly sensing the tension in the room. Olly and I quietly thank her and she slips back out.

Olly takes a sip of his water. 'Look, I didn't know Elliot had gone to check out Derek's premises, but I knew he was interested in the office. It's a good location and we are a business, after all. I haven't taken offence over you coming to spy on my agency. I get why Derek did it. It's just business, Polly!' Olly shrugs.

I sigh, giving him a withering look. Here he is, sitting in his fancy office with his state-of-the-art giant Mac computer and original artwork on the walls and team of cool trendy staff next door. I get that he's running a business, but he already has it all. Why can't he just let Derek be? He'd still be thriving. And it's not like Olly has a wife to worry about. He probably splurges his money at designer boutiques and yet Derek has genuine worries and real financial needs.

'I only came to see you because you were taking business from Derek and he wanted to find out what your secret is. He's just trying to save his business. He really needs to,' I emphasise.

'Well, I really need my business too,' Olly huffs.

'Sure…' I mutter.

'I do!' Olly insists, but he has no idea. He spends his money on Gucci tops, not medical bills.

'Derek's wife's unwell you know,' I blurt out. I know I shouldn't be divulging Derek's personal information, but I can't help it. Olly's frustrating me too much. 'Can't you just leave him be? I know it's the New York way to clamber over everyone until you get to the top, but could you maybe have some humility and just

175

let To the Moon & Back exist too? There's room for both agencies in New York, you know?'

Olly raises an eyebrow sceptically, but I stare back, not willing to let him get to me with his cynical dog-eat-dog corporate attitude. Gradually his expression changes and becomes softer.

'I've worked hard to build up this business,' he says eventually. 'I'm good at it.'

'I know, but so's Derek,' I insist. 'It's his passion. He really lives for it.' I think back to how Derek was today after having seen Brandon enthusing about Eve. 'He lights up when one of his clients finds love. It's because of his wife. He really loves her. He said she saved him, and now she's unwell and he wants to help her.'

'She's unwell?' Olly asks, a hint of concern in his eyes.

'Yes, she's got an issue with her knee,' I tell him.

'Oh…' Olly mutters, reaching for his glass of sparkling water.

'She's seeing doctors and needs surgery. Derek has all these medical bills to pay and yet you're making his life difficult just to make a bit of extra money. Money you probably don't even need.'

Olly frowns, but he looks pensive and I can tell my words have struck a chord. He looks away, avoiding my gaze. His jaw's gone tense and a muscle twitches in his neck. He takes another sip of his sparkling water and places it down, not saying a word. For a moment, I wonder whether I've said too much, perhaps I've gone too far.

'I'm sorry…' I move to get up. 'I'll go.'

'No, don't.' Olly gestures for me to sit back down. 'You're right.' He lets out a raggedy breath and throws his hands up in mock surrender.

'Maybe I have been too competitive. It's just how I do business.' He scratches his head. 'I wasn't thinking about Derek's personal life. Of course, I wasn't. I was just thinking about…' He pauses, searching for the right word. '… Money.'

I smile sympathetically. Olly meets my gaze and he really does look quite contrite. Behind his fancy designer glasses, his eyes are concerned and tender. Guilty. And I can see that there is something to him. He's not just a fancy label-obsessed corporate asshole, he has depth. It's obscured behind a lot of layers of vanity, distracting clothing, dazzlingly bright teeth and swanky surroundings, but it's there. A raw, tender person with emotional depth is definitely there. It's just been buried deep.

'It's understandable,' I comment.

Olly nods. 'Maybe. But maybe I have been taking it too far. I'll tell Elliot to leave Derek alone. We'll back off,' he says, fixing me with that penetrating look. His eyes are deep and rich and full of thoughts and feeling and without realising it, I've edged my seat closer to his desk. I suddenly realise I've tilted my head to the side a little and I'm just gazing. Gazing into his eyes. He's looking back into mine and neither of us are actually saying anything. But it's as though we're communicating anyway. He's telling me he's sorry and he's telling me it's okay that I've spoken to him about this. And I'm telling him that it's okay that he's been ruthless and competitive. And underpinning the mutual understanding is this raw magnetism, this intense attraction pulling us together. It's like we're just bonded by the look passing between us, creating our own energy field, a pull. If I ever tried to convince myself I wasn't attracted to Olly Corrigan, I was wrong. He may dress like a bit of an idiot. He may be twenty years older than me. He may have the whitest teeth of all the insta-famous people I've ever seen but he's also got a soul. An open, vulnerable and sensitive soul. I can see it in his eyes. I can feel it.

His phone suddenly rings, and he looks away to answer it, switching back into corporate mode. I pick up a paperweight from his desk and pass it between my hands as Olly takes the call. It seems to be a journalist calling about a story – something to do with Olly's PR firm.

'Sorry, one moment,' Olly says, cupping his hand over the receiver. He turns his attention back to me. 'Sorry, Polly. It's the *Washington Post* calling about setting up an interview with one of my PR clients. I can't ask them to call back. Journalists hate that kind of thing.'

'That's okay.' I place the paperweight back on the desk. I'm not sure what I was hanging about for. Aside from the simmering unresolved tension between me and Olly, there's nothing really left to say. I stand up and hitch my bag back onto my shoulder. 'I need to get back to work anyway.'

Olly smiles. 'Okay, well don't worry, I'll back off. I'll give Derek some breathing room,' he says kindly, but there's tension around his brow now and I can tell he's eager to get back to the phone call.

'Thanks Olly, I really appreciate it,' I reply.

He nods, smiling a little tightly, before raising the receiver back to his ear. I cross the office and wave distractedly over my shoulder as I leave. Olly waves back before swivelling his chair away so I'm no longer in his eyeline.

I slip out of his office, gently closing the door behind me, before walking towards the lift. I ignore the curious stares of his staff as I wait for the lift to arrive and step inside. As the lift sinks down to the ground floor, I feel strange and torn. I fancy Olly. I really fancy him. I'm drawn to him. I want to know more about what's going on in those deep mysterious eyes. We saw eye to eye in that office – literally and metaphorically – and I could have sworn something occurred between us. We formed a connection. And yet unfortunately, it sort of feels like we're done. He's handling his call, he's dealt with me. He's agreed to stop trying to crush To the Moon & Back. We won't need to be interfering with each other's businesses anymore and there's no reason for us to ever deal with each other again.

The receptionist catches my eye as I arrive back down in reception.

'Did you have a good meeting?' she asks, with her polished smile.

'Yes, thanks,' I reply.

'Great. Well, have a good day,' she comments.

'You too.'

'Bye,' she adds.

'Bye,' I echo sadly as I leave.

Chapter 19

'Hang on a minute.' Gabe raises his hand to stop me talking. As usual, our little argument on Saturday was completely forgotten and instead of going over it, I told him all about my encounter with Olly.

'You just popped in to see Olly Corrigan and asked him to stop being so competitive in business?' Gabe asks, his lips twitching.

'Umm, yeah. Basically,' I admit.

Gabe's lips twist into a smile, his cheeks growing red until he bursts into laughter. He laughs so hard that he reaches for a nearby cushion and buries his face in it. I giggle along but I'm not quite sure what the big deal is.

'What?'

Gabe keeps laughing. When he eventually pulls the cushion away from his face, his eyes are wet with tears he's been laughing so hard.

'Oh my God, sorry Polly,' he wheezes, shaking his head as he recovers himself.

'Why's it so funny?'

'You're just…' He pauses and looks me up and down as he searches for the right words. '… The least corporate person in the whole of Manhattan! You don't just walk into your rival's office and say, "Hey, would you mind not competing with us? That would be fab, thanks", Gabe teases, laughing to himself.

I shrug. 'Well, it worked.'

'Seriously?' Gabe doesn't seem convinced.

'Well yeah, Olly promised to back off and give Derek a break. He literally promised. Anyway, I'm not bothered about Derek anymore! I'm worried about me!'

'You?' Gabe raises an eyebrow. 'What's up?'

I glance down at my lap and take a deep breath. 'I fancy Olly Corrigan,' I confess, my eyes still fixed on the hem of my shirt. 'I really fancy him.'

It's unnerving hearing the words leave my own mouth when so far, they've just been rattling around my head. I can't believe I've said it. I haven't fancied anyone for ages. In the whole two and a half years I've known Gabe, I've never properly been into anyone. Sure, I've had little crushes, like with that Greek guy Demetrius who I sent the embarrassing peach and aubergine emojis to but nothing significant. Nothing that's shaken me up or gotten to me in the way Olly has.

'Oh yeah.' Gabe nods. 'I know you fancy him.'

'What?' I gawp. 'What do you mean you know?' I sneer.

Gabe rolls his eyes. 'It was pretty obvious, Poll.'

'How was it obvious?' I scoff.

'I could just tell from the way you were looking at him and talking to him at Milano's,' Gabe insists.

'Oh really? I didn't even fancy him back then!'

'Sure,' Gabe jokes. 'Of course, you fancied him. He's hot. He's got that cool, charismatic, rich thing going on. He's super sexy.'

I think back to his eyes today, the enigmatic depths and tenderness I saw in them. He is sexy. His cool attitude coupled with his sensitive eyes and charming smile: it's an intoxicating combination.

'Yeah, he is sexy. So sexy…' I murmur wistfully.

'So are you gonna hit it?' Gabe asks with a cheeky smile.

'*Hit it?*' I scoff. 'I can't hit it. He's Olly Corrigan. Super cool businessman. Dating Entrepreneur of the Year. PR boss. I can't just hit him up on Tinder and invite him over for some Netflix and chill.'

Gabe smirks. 'Yeah, I guess not. But if he agreed to stop going after your business, I'd imagine he didn't just do that from the kindness of his heart.' Gabe winks.

'What do you mean?'

Gabe rolls his eyes exasperatedly. 'What do you think I mean?! He probably wants to bang you! I know you don't really under-stand the corporate world, but people don't just stop being competitive because someone asks them nicely. He fancies you or he wouldn't have agreed to back off,' Gabe states firmly.

Gabe's conviction is quite compelling, but I can't help thinking back to the way Olly answered his phone and swivelled his chair away from me, as though we were just done. As though our busi-ness was finished. Surely if he fancied me, he would have at least said goodbye properly?

'Maybe he was just being nice,' I suggest. 'Derek's wife is unwell after all. I just really don't think he's interested. Why would he be? He's, like, twenty years older than me and he's incredibly cool! He could take his pick of all the fashionable cute girls in the city. There are at least a dozen in his office alone. I doubt he wants a scruffy broke wannabe photographer.'

Gabe rolls his eyes. 'Seriously? Is that how you see yourself? As a scruffy broke wannabe?'

'Yes,' I admit, with a sad smile.

Gabe looks at me sympathetically. 'Babe…'

I force myself to meet his gaze. 'I know it sounds self-hating, but it's true. I am a scruffy broke wannabe. I've been broke for ages. I haven't got any nice clothes. I haven't had a decent haircut for years. I do feel scruffy.'

'Oh, hun.' Gabe shuffles closer to me and wraps his arm around my shoulders. 'When do you get paid? Or if you want, I'll treat you! We'll go shopping! We'll go to a nice salon and get your bangs cut if they're bothering you that much.'

'It's okay, you don't have to treat me. I might be able to cover it,' I say, thinking of the Alicia payment. I don't want to tell Gabe about it until the money arrives in my account, in case I jinx the whole thing.

'You know you're beautiful, right? With or without expensive clothes or a fancy haircut,' Gabe reassures me, rubbing my back.

'I wouldn't go that far.'

'Babe, stop putting yourself down. You know the only thing those sassy girls in Olly's office have that you don't?'

I look up. 'What?'

'Confidence. You just need to believe in yourself a bit more.'

I nod, thinking back to Eve's mantra, which seems to ring true for so many situations in my life right now: *you set the standard for your worth.*

'Yeah, you're right. But perhaps I could do with a makeover. Particularly since Derek's party's coming up.'

'Ah yes, Cupid's bash.' Gabe grins. 'There'll be plenty of single guys there.'

'Yeah, tons. But I shouldn't really mix business with pleasure,' I comment, although the truth is, I doubt Derek would care if I coupled up with one of the clients. As long as they end up with someone, his obligation is fulfilled, even if that someone is me. In fact, I'd be doing him a favour if I dated one of our clients. The real reason I don't want to date anyone from the party is because I'm into Olly. Really into him. And even if nothing's going to come of it, I at least want to give myself time to get over these feelings before I find someone new. The last thing the business needs is for me to date one of the clients to distract myself from a crush I have on someone else, only to ditch them later when I get bored. No, that would definitely not be good for our reputation.

'Well, even if you don't mix business with pleasure, a good night out, a new haircut and a bit of TLC is in order.'

'Yeah, you're right.'

'Course I am. I can't have my best friend feeling like she's not cool because of a scruffy hair do, now can I?' Gabe says, ruffling my hair with his knuckles.

I giggle. I'm still not sure a haircut, a makeover and a bit of sass is going to get Olly's attention, but even if it's not, it's still a fun way to pass the time.

Chapter 20

'So, how do you want your hair?' The hairdresser asks.

Gabe's brought me to the swanky salon in Tribeca where he and Adam get their hair cut. It's located in a converted warehouse with exposed brick walls and tall ceilings covered with industrial-looking pipes. The staff are all impossibly thin, several of the women are wearing fedoras indoors and the men have artfully groomed facial hair. It's a far cry from the place I usually get my hair cut: a small salon tucked away on a backstreet around the corner from mine and Gabe's flat ran by a Polish woman. It's called Paulina's, after her. It has a peeling paint sign and the haircuts are pretty basic – they're certainly not fashionable or cutting edge – but they're thirty dollars and you can't complain for thirty dollars. Gabe's always taken the piss out of me for going there, but I just ignore him. I've grown quite fond of Paulina and her no-nonsense approach to hair cutting. But the payment from Alicia came through and I couldn't resist the opportunity to treat myself. With the money in my account, I finally told Gabe about it and he was more than happy to accompany me.

'Erm...' I hesitate, remembering that the hair stylist, Malcolm, is waiting for an answer. How *do* I want my hair? I take in my reflection. My hair is just... hair. It hangs at the sides of my face in two frizzy curtains. It has no shape or style. Or shade for that matter. It's just a godgiven mousy brown. If I'm feeling fancy, I occasionally curl tendrils and let them fall around my face, but most of the time, I just bung it into a scruffy bun and get on with my day.

'What about a bob or something?' Gabe suggests. He stands next to me, his hand to his chin as though he's about to start stroking an imaginary beard. He looks like he's appraising an artefact in a museum as he takes in my reflection.

'No.' Malcolm shakes his head. He pulls my hair back from my face. 'It wouldn't work. Her face is too round.'

'How about darker? With bangs? An edgy block fringe?' Gabe suggests.

'I'm not so sure.' Malcolm pulls a face. 'With wavy hair, fringes can be a nightmare.' He plucks at my hair while silently appraising it. Eventually, he lets go of my hair and takes a step back, assessing me.

'Um, how about something short?' I suggest. 'I've always quite liked short hair. Pixie cuts.'

'Oh, I don't know.' Malcolm looks reluctant. 'That's a bold move.'

I shrug.

'Yeah Polly, a pixie cut?' Gabe raises an eyebrow.

'I feel like a change.'

'Well, once you do that, there's no going back. There's no quick fix. It takes a long time to grow back,' Malcolm warns. 'You have to be sure.'

'I know, but I'm willing to risk it,' I say, with an air of confidence that belies the tremor of anxiety in my stomach. My hair has always been troublesome. Maybe Malcolm's right, this could be a big mistake that I'll end up having to patiently endure for months until my hair finally grows out. But the thing is, I don't want to look how I always look. I want to try something bold and different, even if it does end up being a mistake. I'm willing to risk it.

'Yeah, just cut it. I'm ready,' I insist, taking Malcolm's nervous expression head on and fixing him with a confident look.

'Seriously?' Gabe raises an eyebrow. 'I don't know if you should, Polly.'

'I want to. I'm ready for a change,' I insist. Gabe eyes me uneasily and Malcolm is still looking on edge. It's quite fun watching them squirm. Maybe I should ask for a mohawk.

'If you want to go short, are you sure you don't want something shoulder-length or maybe around here?' Malcolm asks, placing his hands by my jawline.

'I thought you said my face was too round for a bob?' I remind him, taking in his nervous expression. For a cutting-edge salon, he certainly seems timid. 'Honestly,' I say, in a firm voice, 'I'm sure.'

He meets my gaze and I can see he realises that I'm not messing around.

'Okay!' he says, forcing a wide, slightly tense, smile. 'Pixie cut it is.'

'Thank you!'

'Oh my God, Polly. If this isn't a quarter-life crisis, I don't know what is,' Gabe sighs exasperatedly.

'It's not a quarter-life crisis,' I tut. 'It's just a new look. Why do people get so over dramatic about cutting hair? It's not like I'm splashing out forty grand on a Mercedes? It's just a haircut.'

'Yeah, but if it looks awful, there's no going back. You'd have to wear a wig or something,' Gabe points out, looking stricken, as though wearing a wig is the worst possible fate that could befall me.

'Coming from the man who wears wigs every Friday night,' I remind him.

'Well, yeah.' Gabe rolls his eyes. 'But it's not like I'd be seen dead in any of those wigs at work or in daily life.'

187

Malcolm shoots Gabe a curious look.

'I'm a drag queen,' Gabe explains matter-of-factly. 'Only on Friday nights though,' he adds. 'The rest of the week, I work in HR.'

Malcolm seems fascinated by this nugget of information and he and Gabe launch into a detailed conversation on everything from the best and worst gay clubs to the highest quality wigs offering both breathability and secure fastening. I interject every now and then to be polite, but I'm more interested in what I'm seeing in the mirror. Malcolm is gradually snipping away at my hair, taking it from just below the shoulders to ear-length. As they talk about wig caps, he begins snipping even higher, and with a few clean cuts, he's taken my hair up to ear length. It's not been shaped yet, but there's definitely no going back at this point. My hair is short. And the weird thing is that I can already tell that I like it. It's like I can suddenly see my face. My eyes pop. My lips are there. There's no crappy frizzy hair distracting from my features.

'You're really doing this,' Gabe says, suddenly focusing on me as Malcolm chops away at my hair.

'Yep. No going back now.' I grin.

My eyes look twice their usual size without being flanked by waves of hair and even though it's still just a shabby mess, I can already tell I'm going to like it.

Malcolm's eyes laser in on my reflection in the mirror and I can tell he's beginning to warm to the idea of the pixie cut. Gabe makes another comment about some gay club in Brooklyn but Malcolm mumbles a half-hearted answer. It's clear he's focusing on me now. He leans close to my head and makes delicate snips around my hairline. Gabe plucks a magazine left on the seat next to mine.

'I'm just gonna…' He gestures with the magazine to a bench in reception.

Malcolm nods distractedly.

Gabe gives my shoulder a squeeze. 'Good luck,' he says.

'Thanks,' I reply, making eye contact with him in the mirror. I smile, but I make a deliberate effort not to move my head in case it screws up Malcolm's handiwork.

'Right, see you in a bit,' Gabe says. He wanders off and from the corner of my eye, I can just about make out him sitting in a corner in reception, flicking through the magazine on his lap.

Malcolm and I lapse into a companionable silence as he snips away. He's frowning and leaning close, his face etched with concentration. The more he snips away, the more confident I feel that I've made the right decision. A pixie cut may have seemed like a bold move, but bold is good. Fortune favours the bold, doesn't it? That's the kind of sentiment I'd imagine Eve would agree with. I almost wish I could just take a picture of my hair now and send it to her. Although of course, I can't. I'm a random woman who she doesn't even know.

'This is going to look great on you,' Malcolm says, in a deeper tone, and I can tell he means it. He's getting serious. He genuinely likes my hair. Maybe for once I can have a *look*. Cool hair that gives an edgy finish to my outfits. The kind of trendy hair that people in Olly Corrigan's office have. Maybe I can be that type of person.

Malcolm keeps snipping with that intense concentration and I can't believe how with every chunk of hair that's falling to the floor, that I'm actually looking better. Long hair is generally considered to be covetable and glamourous, yet, the more hair I lose, the more polished I'm feeling.

'Right...' Malcolm makes a couple more snips. 'I'm pretty much done here. I'll blow dry it and then I might make a few more adjustments.'

'Great,' I reply as he reaches for a hairdryer and round comb and begins blow-drying and sculpting my hair into shape.

'Oh my God, I love it,' I say, over the sound of the hairdryer, as I drink in my reflection. It's cute and young-looking. It looks trendy.

189

Malcolm turns off the hairdryer.

'I can't believe it! It's so cool!' I turn my head, taking my reflection in from all angles.

'Yeah, it really suits you,' Malcolm notes, with a hint of surprise in his voice. 'It's really good on you.'

I turn and call Gabe over. He's engrossed in a celeb gossip magazine and looks up with a dazed air, before his eyes land on me. His eyes widen and his mouth drops open as he tosses the magazine aside and gets up to come over.

'Wow!' he gawps. 'Who are you and what have you done with Polly?'

I grin. 'Do you like it?'

'It looks amazing!' Gabe enthuses and I can tell he means it. I haven't seen him look this excited since he saw Lady Gaga opening a new Topshop store in Time Square.

'It's so cool, right?' I say.

Gabe walks around my chair, taking in a 360-degree view of my new look.

'It's incredible. You look amazing. Like a model!' Gabe insists. He might be pushing it with the model comment, but it does look nice. 'It really lights up your eyes.'

'Thanks. Malcolm's done an amazing job.' I meet Malcolm's gaze in the mirror.

'I'm so glad you like it. It was a good idea,' he says, squirting some serum onto his hand, which he proceeds to run through my hair, giving it a final gloss.

Gabe praises Malcolm's handiwork too. I can tell Malcolm likes the final result, but it's clear that even though this new cut might be transformative for me, it's all in a day's work for him. Paulina's might have been cheap and cheerful and got rid of my split ends, but I can see now why Gabe's a regular here.

'So, you're all done,' Malcolm says, placing his hands on my shoulders and looking at me in the mirror.

'Thank you! I absolutely love it!' I grin at him. This may be a cool swanky salon where people skulk around in fedoras, but I have no chill and I'm not even going to attempt to hide my glee.

'Awesome.' Malcolm grins back. I get up and he helps me out of my hairdresser robe, before directing me to reception, where one of the fedora-wearing girls is waiting with a card machine and a whopping bill. After paying – and trying not to think about how much I'm paying – Gabe and I head back out onto the street and breathe in the New York air, which smells refreshingly unlike hairspray.

'So, sexy, what now?' Gabe asks.

'Sexy? Is that my new nickname?' I joke.

'Yep.'

'Cool, I'll take it.'

Gabe smiles. 'Come on, let's get you a fabulous dress to go with that fabulous hair.' He steps out into the street and hails down a cab, sticking his arm out until one of them slows down and signals that it's coming over.

'What are you doing?' I look between him and the cab which is drawing to a halt.

'Oh come on, today is not the day for subway travel and penny pinching. You just splashed out $320 on your hair.'

'Shhh!' I hiss, trying to live by the principle that if I don't say it out loud, it didn't really happen.

Gabe rolls his eyes. 'Just relax. Have a bit of fun today. It's on Alicia. Let your hair down,' Gabe comments, before cracking up with laughter. 'Oh wait, you can't!'

We get into the cab, giggling away, high on the rush of spending money and living it up. I know Gabe's had disposable income for a while, and even though he'll happily take me out for the odd meal here and there, it doesn't feel quite as fun and relaxed as it does today. It's always been a treat, and even though it's sweet and I appreciate it, it still highlights the disparity between us, creating a certain awkwardness. But today, we're on the same level. We can both blow a bit of cash, we can have fun without me feeling guilty over the fact's that Gabe's the one picking up the bill. It's freeing to just be having a carefree day. I know Alicia's payment won't last forever and I'm certainly not going to blow the whole lot, but I can at least afford one good day and a new look.

Even the cab driver admires my new hair as he weaves through the traffic and takes us to Macy's.

'You look great. Like a movie star,' he says, no doubt vying for a tip.

'Haha, hardly,' I laugh. I know he's just being nice, but I can't help but feel complimented. It's not often you get told you look like a model and a movie star in one day.

I take out my pressed powder from my handbag and study my reflection in the small mirror, drinking it in. I love my new look, but more than that, I love that I was bold enough to go for it. I feel excited, thinking of what other previously unchartered territories might be in my grasp.

We arrive at Barneys and pay our driver, tipping him generously, before dashing into the store and heading to the nearest display of dresses. Dresses aren't my usual thing, but I can't exactly rock up to Derek's party to end all parties in jeans and a shirt. I flick through the display, and grab half a dozen pretty dresses, from stylish slips and vintage numbers to sleek sleeveless skater dresses.

Gabe glances over and takes one of the vintage dresses draped over my arm. He looks it up and down. 'This looks like a vintage school uniform, not a party frock.'

I roll my eyes. 'Well, my school uniform certainly wasn't that cool.'

'Okay, fine. Maybe it's a bit better than a school uniform but not by much. It hardly screams glamourous New York matchmaker.'

I laugh. 'Firstly, is there such a thing? And secondly, I don't exactly need to be glamourous. Like I said, I'm not really interested in dating the clients.'

'Not even Brandon?' Gabe asks, giving me a knowing look as he rifles through the dresses on a nearby rack.

'Nope, not even Brandon,' I insist.

'Seriously? But he's Brandon Fox,' Gabe reminds me pleadingly.

'Yeah I know. He's brilliant. He's such a brilliant man but he's really into the woman I set him up with, Eve. Plus. he's just too perfect, you know.' I put the vintage school uniform dress back on the rail and rummage through to find something different.

'What do you mean too perfect?' Gabe checks out a wholly inappropriate patent leather strappy dress and then places it back on the rail. He eyes me curiously.

'He's just so handsome and clever and successful and efficient that it's almost off-putting,' I explain, and as I say the words out loud, I realise they're true. They're not just some line I'm telling myself in order to feel better about the fact that I'm clearly not Brandon's type. They're genuine. I do find Brandon's efficiency a bit off-putting. He's just a bit too slick. He's charming, kind, and the work he did with Alicia was incredible, and yet I just don't fancy him anymore.

'It's a bit like God,' I announce as I flick past another uniform-style dress. Gabe looks over quizzically. 'You admire him, but you don't exactly want to tap him.'

Gabe bursts into laughter and I can't help joining in, until a snooty-looking sales assistant gives us a stern look and we pipe down.

'So, what about Olly then? Is he not too God-like for you?' Gabe says as he reaches for a flimsy black dress.

I think of Olly the last time I saw him, chatting in his office, his eyes swimming with depth. 'No. Olly's different. Olly's definitely tappable.'

'I'd second that,' Gabe says. 'How about this?' He holds up the flimsy black dress. It's a tiny bum-skimming length with spaghetti straps and dark gold glittery fringing. It's very Twenties flapper. It's not something I'd ever have chosen, and yet I can totally see why Gabe went for it. It has the slightly theatrical dress-up vibe that he loves.

'Umm…' I take it from him and hold it up against my body. 'It's a bit short,' I say, observing the hem which rests on my upper thighs.

'Yeah, and you're going to a party!' Gabe reminds me. 'Look babe, I know you like to live in jeans and slouchy shirts and stuff and to be fair, you do kind of rock that laid-back grungy look, but why don't you just dress up a bit? Buy a fabulous dress to go with your fabulous hair?' Gabe suggests.

'Umm…' I hold the dress out and take it in. 'It's a bit glitzy.'

'Yeah, no shit!' Gabe cries. 'That's the point. It's a party.'

'Alright. I'll try it on, but no promises.'

'Cool,' Gabe relents.

I find a couple more dresses – the kind that actually cover your body parts – and then we head to the changing room. I try on a couple of the skater dresses I chose, but surprisingly, they don't actually look that great. I never thought my hairstyle would shape the kind of clothes I wear, but with the short hair, the less feminine dresses look kind of butch. I put on the flapper dress Gabe chose and the moment it settles into place around my body, I just know, it's the dress for me. It goes perfectly with my new haircut, providing a soft girlish counterbalance. I check myself out in the mirror, admiring my reflection from all angles. I really do look like a different person to the woman I was this morning. I stand on my tiptoes, imagining a pair of strappy sandals on my feet and I have to admit, I love the look. If I was excited about the party before, I'm even more excited now. I can't wait to rock my new look, even though there isn't really anyone I'm trying to impress.

I pull open the changing room curtain to show off the dress to Gabe. I do a little twirl, making that fringed edges of the dress swish and flutter.

'You look sensational!' Gabe says, his eyes lighting up. 'Oh, Polly… that dress!'

and each is adorned with a grand flower display bursting with roses in pink, red, yellow and white shades. There's an entire table dedicated to cupcakes, arranged prettily on a tall tiered display. Even the wooden floor is covered with tiny pieces of heart-shaped confetti. It couldn't be any more romantic, it's stunning.

I head over to Derek, who is standing by the bar, sipping a glass of champagne and looking slightly smug and amused at my awe-struck, dazed state as I take it all in. Even Derek's looking good, having swapped his usual lurid shirts for a smart well-fitted tuxedo with a pink bow tie.

'Impressive, Derek,' I comment, appraising the venue once more. 'When you said you were going to throw the most romantic party in the city, you really meant it, didn't you?'

Derek smiles. 'I don't say things I don't mean, Polly,' he says with a wink, handing me a glass of champagne from an arrangement of bubbling glasses laid out on the bar. 'But it's not all down to me. You chose the venue. And it's thanks to you that several of our star clients are coming here tonight with dates. That's what it's all about.'

He clinks his glass against mine. 'To teamwork then,' I suggest.

'To teamwork,' Derek concurs.

I look at him over the rim of my glass as I sip my champagne, and I don't know if it's the incredible dream-come-true party, the delicious bubbles spreading across my tongue or what, but I feel a warm rush of affection for Derek. I may have joked about his diabolical fashion sense, his shady past or his love of Oreos. I may have poked fun at him being a cuddly Cupid, but he's also been a bit of an angel too, coming into my life and giving me a job when I really needed it. And not just giving me a job, but giving me encouragement and kindness too. He's treated me well. I'm about to say something sentimental when a guy who looks distinctly like Andy Graham walks in.

'Andy!' Derek calls out. He grabs a glass of champagne and strides towards him, beckoning for me to follow.

Andy looks exactly like his pictures. Derek introduces me as his matchmaker and Andy blushes, as though a little embarrassed by the whole thing. He reaches hungrily for the glass of champagne Derek offers and practically necks it.

'So, are you excited to meet Heather?' I ask, since the last message I exchanged with him involved me telling him how brilliant Heather is, filling him in on the conversation we'd had so far and giving him his Match.com account login details so he could pick up the conversation where I left off and arrange a date. Conversation between Heather and I had descended into niche museum trivia and I wasn't sure I could pull it off convincingly. It felt like time Andy stepped in and a few days later he messaged to say he'd established a 'promising' connection.'

'Oh yeah…' Andy pulls a face. 'No, that didn't work out.'

'Oh no, what happened?' I ask, feeling a prickle of irritation. How could it not work out with Heather? I searched high and low for her. She was a great fit for Andy.

'I got talking to someone else,' Andy says, taking a sip of his drink.

'What? Who?' I blurt out, with a little too much incredulity. Derek shoots me a look.

'Another woman from Match. Katarina,' Andy says.

'Katarina?' I gawp, recalling the stunning model/actress from Midtown who seemed completely out of Andy's league.

'We just got chatting one Friday night and we couldn't stop. We were up all night messaging. It was crazy!' Andy enthuses with a far-away look in his eyes at the memory.

'Oh… right,' I reply flatly. So, there's absolutely no chance with Heather then?'

'No! Sorry, she's just not my type.'

Not his type!? Urghh. Heather was lovely. She was so ideal for Andy.

'That's a shame, I thought you'd get on.'

'She was perfectly pleasant,' Andy says, holding out his glass to a passing waiter who refills it. 'But we just didn't click. Not like I did with Katarina, anyway.' Andy thanks the waiter and takes a sip of his drink. He nods thanks.

'Okay... Well, congratulations!' I say, clinking my glass against his, although I'm completely taken aback. How could Andy have hit it off with Katarina? How could he possibly have got along better with her than Heather, who had all the same interests. It makes no sense.

'She's brilliant. She's an absolutely fascinating woman,' Andy gushes.

A few more men in suits arrive and Derek waves at them over Andy's shoulder. Both Andy and I look over with a complete lack of recognition. Derek excuses himself and goes over to greet the new guests, leaving me and Andy alone.

'So, are you and Katarina going to meet?' I ask a little hesitantly. I can't help worrying that Katarina might have wound up chatting to Andy one night to pass the time, not realising he'd end up falling for her.

'Oh yeah.' Andy nods. 'She's coming along tonight.'

'Tonight?' I echo. 'Wow, great!'

Andy grins. 'I can't wait.'

'That's fantastic!' I beam back at him, trying to get my head around it. Katarina and Andy. Andy and Katarina. They seem like such an odd match. I'd never have imagined them getting on in a million years and yet she's coming to the party. Maybe I still have a few things to learn about the matchmaking game.

Andy and I make small talk as the venue suddenly fills up in the way that always seems to happen at parties, with everyone arriving at once. After dropping their things off at the cloakroom, the guests take glasses of champagne from the bar and stand around chatting and mingling, while admiring the incredible venue. Everyone seems to be in high spirits. It's hard not to be in such a beautiful place. Andy starts talking to another of the agency's clients and I wander off to gather my thoughts and get another drink. I get a refill of my champagne and take a sip. I look across the throng of people until I spot Derek chatting with a couple I vaguely recognise as one of the success stories profiled on the website – a couple who met at another of Derek's singles mixers. I'm wondering whether I should introduce myself when I'm suddenly distracted by a fashionably late arrival: Brandon. Dressed in an exquisite designer tux walking hand-in-hand into the party with an absolutely stunning blonde. None other than Eve. I thought she was beautiful before from simply swiping through her pictures, but she looks like she belongs on the red carpet. I don't think I've ever even seen someone so glamourous in real life before. Tall and slender, with the body of a Victoria's Secret model and long sweeping golden hair that falls over her plunging red silk gown. A hush spreads through the venue as everyone turns to look. I've never seen a couple look so good together. Eve's stunning – truly stunning – but Brandon looks incredible too.

Derek catches my eye and raises his glass of champagne. He's clearly really impressed that I managed to find Brandon someone so utterly gorgeous. I smile back, before returning my attention to Eve and Brandon. They're captivating. They move effortlessly through the room, dipping into conversations, greeting people, engaging them, whilst still maintaining a sense of intimacy and closeness with one another. Eve will touch Brandon's arm, or he'll let his hand graze her back. They're outgoing and extroverted while also being intimate and insular. It's hard to believe that they only met a couple of weeks ago because they look like they've been together for years. They're the ideal couple. I glance over at Andy, who's standing chatting to another guy who I vaguely recognise as an agency client, someone Derek's been looking after. Andy keeps glancing anxiously over towards the entrance, obviously wondering when Katarina's going to arrive. I feel nervous for him. What if she stands him up? It would be awful. Katarina may be a bit out of his league, but she should at least show up if she said she's going to be here. Andy could really do with a date. It's not fair that people like Brandon – high-flying entrepreneurial lawyers blessed with good looks and natural charm – should get all the luck. Nice, unassuming, hardworking, hopeful guys like Andy deserve a break too.

I sigh and take another sip of my champagne, before heading over to say hi to Brandon and Eve.

'Polly!' Brandon's eyes light up the moment I approach them. 'You look absolutely fantastic,' he enthuses, taking in my hair and dress.

'Oh, thank you! I thought I'd get a new look,' I comment, glancing shyly at Eve. She smiles back. She's even more gorgeous up close. Her skin is absolutely flawless and her eyes sparkle, even though she's looking at me with a blank curiosity. She glances at Brandon, clearly expecting an introduction. It's weird to think that I already know her. I already know about her thoughts and feelings, her life philosophies, the tough times she's been through, her hopes and dreams and yet here she is, regarding me like a total stranger. I feel a twinge of guilt. Brandon and I exchange a look, which doesn't last more than a second, but it's clear we're both feeling a little awkward.

'Polly, this is Eve,' he says, introducing us. 'Eve, Polly.'

Eve and I shake hands. 'Lovely to meet you,' she says. Even her voice is nice: gentle, smooth and lilting.

'Polly's a friend of mine. She works at the agency,' Brandon explains.

I nod weakly, trying to suppress the awkwardness.

'Oh, great!' Eve says, with a big friendly smile.

'And what do you do?' I ask, even though of course, I already know.

'I work in the city,' Eve says. 'As a fund manager. It's great.'

'Oh, impressive,' I reply moronically. Brandon and I exchange another guilty look.

'Thanks!' Eve says.

A silence passes between us. I take a sip of my drink.

'So, have you two been dating long?' I ask, avoiding Brandon's gaze.

'Oh no, not long, just a few weeks,' Eve tells me, giving Brandon a sweet affectionate smile.

'Oh, lovely. You two seem like a good match.'

'Thanks. Yes, it's been great,' Eve says, giving Brandon an affectionate look. He gazes back at her with a look of total adoration.

'I'm so happy for you!' I enthuse. 'It's lovely to see two people really falling for each other.'

'Yes, Brandon's a great guy,' Eve says.

I nod. She really seems to love the word 'great'.

'You old romantic, Polly,' Brandon says, nudging me. 'Fabulous party by the way. When you said it would be unmissable, I thought you were just trying to hype it up, but it really is. You and Derek really went to town.'

'Yeah, it's a great party,' Eve adds.

'Thanks, we did our best!' I enthuse, trying not to wince at Eve's use of the word 'great' yet again. Is it like a nervous twitch or something? To just describe everything as great? She doesn't look nervous though. She regards me with a calm smiling expression; she seems totally relaxed. If anything, a little vacant. She's not at all how I imagined her to be. I thought she'd be sparky and interesting and edgy, and yet here she is, echoing everything Brandon says and describing everything as 'great'.

'What do you think of the venue, amazing isn't it?' I ask her.

'Oh, it's great,' she says.

I laugh awkwardly. *Great?* Again!? Does Eve have any other words in her vocabulary? I glance at Brandon, but he doesn't seem to notice. He looks completely content. He smiles affectionately at Eve. I try to think of something else to say, when suddenly a whispery hush sweeps through the room and everyone turns once more to look at the entrance. I glace over my shoulder to see a six-foot-tall familiar-looking striking beauty in a floor length shimmering sequined gown walk into the party. She pauses on the steps, almost like a model striking a pose at the end of the runway. She slowly surveys the room, and as her head turns towards me, Brandon and Eve, I suddenly realise why she looks so familiar.

'No way,' I utter, thinking out loud. It's Katarina. It's actually Katarina. I recognise her long flowing blonde hair, her large blue eyes, and striking looks.

'Katarina!' A male voice cries out and everyone in the room turns to look at Andy, who's waving maniacally, flashing his sweaty underarm.

'Katarina! Over here!' he shouts, a massive delighted grin plastered over his face. He has absolutely no chill whatsoever and I can't help cringing a little, except when I look back to Katarina, she's also grinning widely and waving back, suddenly appearing to have tunnel vision only for Andy as she walks down the stairs, before weaving through the guests towards him. I'm glad I'm wearing high heels as I can just about see across the room as she and Andy embrace. And when I say embrace, I mean *embrace*. They literally clutch each other hungrily like they've been waiting for days. Katarina can't stop smiling.

'Who are they?' Brandon asks, looking over.

'He's a client,' I tell him, still feeling a bit bemused.

'Did you set him up with his date?' Brandon asks. 'They look so happy to see each other.'

'Umm… yes, I guess I did set them up. Inadvertently,' I add. Brandon gives me a puzzled look, but I don't elaborate.

'They look great together,' Eve observes.

'They do,' I agree, even though I feel like I might need to start a drinking game soon, knocking back a shot every time Eve says 'great'.

Derek suddenly interrupts. He greets Brandon with a big hug and gets introduced to Eve. While Brandon compliments Derek on the party, a waiter comes over with a plate of canapes – tiny blinis piled with smoked salmon, caviar and a sprig of thyme. They look mouth-watering and we all take one.

I pop mine in my mouth and watch Eve as she does the same. I'm bracing myself for her to describe them as 'great'.

'Delicious,' she opts for instead.

'Really delicious,' I echo, meaning it. Not only has Derek gone all out with the décor, but he's gone all out with the canapes too. They're so tasty and I can't help looking through the crowd to see where the waiter has got to, in the hope of having another.

'This really is a good party,' Eve says.

'Thanks. Derek wanted to shake things up and make a bit of a comeback so he decided to pull it out of the bag. I think he's trying to show everyone what the agency's capable of. Setting the standard for his worth,' I add, blurting out the last line without any thought.

Damn it, I'm echoing Eve's mantra, even though I'm not supposed to know anything about Brandon's conversation with Eve. That was meant to be a private text chat between them. I'm not meant to know about it, let alone have had anything to do with it. Oh God. I take another sip of my drink, although I've probably already had too much. I regard Eve over the rim of my glass.

'Sounds great,' she says blankly.

'Hmm, yeah, really great,' I echo, frowning. It's like she doesn't have a clue. My comment hasn't jarred her at all. I smile politely, wondering what happened to the cool, interesting, vibrant person I'd been messaging. That woman had a ton to say and I expected her to be just as interesting in person, but Eve seems totally different in real life. Brandon places his hand on Eve's waist and gives her another one of those smitten looks. He seems completely taken with her. She must have some kind of social anxiety or something or be overwhelmed by the party. It's the only reason I can think of as to why she'd be behaving in this way. But if she is feeling awkward, she's covering it well. Apart from her verbal stuntedness, she looks completely at ease. She stands tall, looking poised and beautiful with a gorgeous smile on her fine-featured face. My mind is reeling. I turn to look at Andy and Katarina and for a second, I can't spot them, until I realise they've moved off to sit at a table in the corner of the venue together. They're huddled close, talking animatedly, their eyes fixed on one another as though they're the only people in the room.

On the surface, both Katarina and Andy, and Eve and Brandon, appear like winning matches. And yet something's not sitting right with me about either of the couplings. I can't get my head around Andy and Katarina and there's something odd about Eve too.

'Are you okay, Polly?' Brandon asks, and all of a sudden, I realise I've been watching Katarina and Andy with a deep frown. I must look like the most miserable matchmaker. I quickly correct my expression.

'Yes! Fine!' I insist, forcing a smile. 'I think I'm just going to get some air,' I add.

'Ah okay, see you in a bit,' Brandon says.

'See you, Polly,' Eve echoes, with a charming smile.

'Yep, see you.' I dash off before she has a chance to tell me how great it was to meet me.

I slip through the crowd and head out onto the street. The hum of conversation is replaced by the hum of New York traffic, the rumble of engines, the honk of a horn and the sound of a cool breeze rushing through the branches of a nearby tree. I know I shouldn't really sit down on the stone steps, particularly in my nice new dress, but I can't resist. I'm not used to wearing heels and I need a break. I need to relax while I try to fathom what's going on.

I lower myself down and absently watch the passers-by when all of a sudden, my phone beeps. I take it out of my handbag. It's a notification from Tinder. Urghh. Just what I need while I'm

205

trying to make sense of all this dating stuff. But nevertheless, I enter the security code of my phone and open the message up. It's from Eve. What the hell?! I never got round to logging out of Brandon's account on there, or deleting it entirely. Why is Eve messaging him on there? They've got each other's numbers. And anyway, they're side by side at the party right now!

I open the message.

Eve: *Hey.*

'Hey'?! Just 'Hey'? What's that meant to mean? If I was confused before, I'm even more confused now. I get up and look back through the glass door to the party. I can see Eve and Brandon. He's leaning in close to say something and she's listening intently. She's holding a glass of champagne in one perfectly manicured hand and the other hand is resting on Brandon's arm. There's not a mobile phone in sight.

My phone buzzes again. It's another message from Eve. I'm so confused. She's not even touching her phone. I open the message.

Eve: *I miss chatting to you.*

She's still not touching her phone. What on earth is going on? Another message comes through.

Eve: *You look stunning tonight. I love your new hair.*

Okay, now I'm freaking out. I stand up and do a quick scan of the street and the park, but I can't see anyone I recognise. My skin prickles and I have a horrible creepy feeling as though I'm being watched.

I bash out a message.

Brandon: *Who is this??*

I glance about as I hold my phone, waiting for it to buzz with a reply. A stooped homeless man draped in a ratty old blanket wanders past and asks for change. I'm so unnerved that I hand him the first dollar bill I can find: a twenty dollar note. Possibly a bit generous but who cares. Here I am at a beautiful party, it's the least I can do. He looks delighted and shakes my hand. He tries to strike up a conversation, asking me about my night and for a moment, I look at him and wonder if it's him. Could *he* have been messaging me? He starts asking me what I'm doing later.

'Got any plans? How long's this party going on for then?' he asks.

I smile awkwardly. Does this guy actually want to hang out with me or something?

'Umm… I'm not sure,' I comment. I look back towards the party and I'm just about to make an excuse and head back in, when a movement catches my eye. A figure emerges from behind one of the pillars of the New York Public Library and passes down the stairs. It's a man in a long dark coat with a familiar walk. I can't quite make out his face, until he turns his head and the lamplight falls across his features, revealing a pair of round glasses, angular cheekbones and slicked back brown hair. It's Olly. Olly Corrigan.

'Olly,' I utter, taking him in. He looks at me with a wry expression as he approaches, laced with something deeper: affection.

'Is this your boyfriend?' The homeless guy asks.

I'm about to answer when Olly slips his arm around my shoulders. 'Yes. Sorry, I'm going to have to steal her from you,' he says, in a jokey but firm way.

'Can't blame a guy for trying.' The homeless guy grumbles, before wandering off.

Olly and I stare at each other for a moment. His deep brown eyes are just as entrancing as always, and I feel my insides turn to mush.

'Eve…' I utter.

'Hi Brandon,' Olly says, the corner of his mouth curling up.

I open the message.

Chapter 22

I gawp at Olly, unable to believe it's him. 'What's going on? What are you doing here?'

'I gave Eve a lift,' Olly explains, looking a little deflated. 'She's one of my clients.' He clears his throat and glances to the ground. 'Sorry, I didn't mean to startle you.'

I laugh, with a mixture of relief and disbelief. I still can't believe he's here. Olly Corrigan is standing in front of me, looking ridiculously hot, and not only is it weird to see him since he's been on my mind so much the past few days, but for some reason, he's now following me, lingering behind pillars and messaging me as Eve.

'Hiding behind pillars and sending people weird cryptic messages tends to have a startling effect,' I point out.

'Oh God, I'm so sorry,' Olly says, rolling his eyes at his own idiocy. He glances after the homeless guy stumbling along the pavement and takes in the darkened street with fresh eyes. 'Yeah, I can see why you freaked out. I didn't mean to scare you.'

'That's okay,' I mumble. I can feel the tension passing, but I'm still totally flummoxed by this whole thing. 'So, it was you? The whole time, when I was pretending to be Brandon, I was really messaging you and you were pretending to be Eve.'

Olly nods. 'Yep, I'm afraid so. I was trying to find Eve a date, the same way you were trying to fix up Brandon,' Olly explains, regarding me with his sultry yet playful eyes.

'Right…' I murmur. 'But why were *you* trying to set up Eve? Surely your assistant would be handling stuff like that? All the swiping and messaging.'

'Normally, yes, but Eve's been near impossible to find a match for. I decided to take matters into my own hands,' Olly says.

'Just like Brandon,' I mutter, averting my gaze towards a deserted park bench. It all makes perfect sense now, from the way Eve was messaging at times of the day I'd have imagined a high-flying banker to be busy, to her chatty, reflective character, which just didn't fit with the person I just met. Of course, it wasn't her that I was messaging. No wonder she looked blank when I inadvertently referenced our conversation. It should have occurred to me that she might be using a dating agency too.

'You really do look stunning by the way. I love your new hair.' Olly glances down at my dress, distracting me from my thoughts. 'You look spectacular,' he says in such a serious tone that I can't help but laugh, even though my insides are turning to mush. Did he really just say I look spectacular? I can feel myself beginning to blush and so I look away from him, glancing down at my toes which are peeking out from my strappy sandals. They're painted a blood red colour which is hopefully not reflected on my cheeks.

'You really do. The hair's great on you. It shows off your pretty face,' Olly says, making my insides dissolve and my cheeks burn. I pray that the weak street light is too dim to reveal how much I'm blushing, but somehow, I doubt it.

'Thank you,' I croak, looking shyly towards him. He looks back at me with a cute, affectionate smile and takes a step forward, placing his hand on my arm. His touch feels electric. I look down at his fingers, which are tracing along my wrist. He's wearing several chunky gold signet rings that catch the light, and his tattoos peek out from under the sleeves of his coat. I trace my gaze up, past his long, checked scarf, which I'm sure is by some up-and-coming edgy New York designer, back to his face. I drink it in. He looks even more handsome than usual in the glow of the fairy lights. His animated enigmatic eyes glimmer like his signet rings and his features look bright. He really is incredibly good-looking. He's not like the other fashionistas in New York, who edit their photos to look better online; Olly truly is handsome. He's naturally gorgeous. I can feel the blood pulsing through my veins as I gaze into his eyes. My hearts beat hard.

'Wait.' A thought hits me. 'I still don't get this whole thing. How did you know it was me pretending to be Brandon? How did you figure it out?'

'Brandon came to see me when he was looking to sign with an agency,' Olly explains. 'When I followed up, he told me he'd signed with To the Moon & Back instead, so when I saw his profile on Tinder, I assumed you guys were running it. I didn't realise it was you I was messaging at first and I was impressed by Derek's messaging style, but then when I ran into you in that café and realised you were working for him, it all made sense. That's when I realised it must be you I was messaging. Derek's not that witty.'

'Right…' I mutter, taking it all in.

'He's not as interesting either,' Olly adds with a wry smile.

I laugh weakly, as I do a mental re-run of all the things I said. None of it was too embarrassing – after all, I was trying to impress Eve into going on a date – but our conversations were still pretty intimate.

'So, all those things you said, about believing in yourself and asserting your worth and everything, that was all you?'

'Yeah.' Olly smiles, a little bashfully. 'I knew I should have stuck to the hey-how-are-you-fancy-a-drink script, but I got totally carried away.'

'Same,' I admit, thinking back to all the messages I sent, at any spare moment, while on the subway to work to late at night in bed.

'Do you remember when we were messaging until 3 a.m.? I was absolutely exhausted at work the next day,' Olly laughs.

'Me too! I think Derek thought I'd been out the night before,' I say.

'Yeah, my colleagues thought I'd been out too.' Olly smiles mischievously.

For a moment, we just look at each other again, and it's a look of both recognition and re-assessment as we morph into the new Olly and Polly. The Olly and Polly who are also Eve and Brandon, and everything else in between. It's a strange feeling, to see Olly in this new light and yet everything is beginning to make total sense.

'It's so funny,' I think aloud.

'What?' Olly asks.

'I spoke to Eve inside the party and she was nothing like the person I was chatting to online,' I explain.

'Oh yeah. She's super dull,' Olly says dryly.

I poke him, and he flinches. 'Ouch,' he grumbles, laughing.

'She isn't what I expected,' I whisper, even though she's deep inside the party and couldn't possibly overhear. 'She describes everything as "great". And I mean *everything*.'

'I know!' Olly grins mischievously. 'When I first met her, I couldn't believe it. Single life was great. But finding someone would be great. And what was she looking for?'

'Someone great?' I suggest, giggling.

'Too right!' Olly laughs.

We both chuckle naughtily.

'It's surprising,' I comment. 'Brandon doesn't seem to mind.'

'Why's that surprising?' Olly asks, narrowing his eyes and tilting his head slightly.

'Because Brandon's…' I pause, trying to think of a way to describe Brandon that doesn't make it seem like I'm into him. I think Brandon's a brilliant man and I don't have anything other than glowing adjectives to use about him, but I'm definitely not

211

into him anymore. 'Brandon's a high-flyer,' I state. 'He's done so much, I thought he'd be looking for someone as vibrant as him.'

Olly scoffs. 'I can tell you're new to this.'

'What do you mean?' I ask, meeting his sardonic gaze.

'Guys like Brandon don't tend to want someone stimulating,' Olly insists.

'Why not?' I ask.

'He's stimulated enough as it is, with his career and his businesses,' Olly says. 'A lot of guys like him view women as a way of letting off steam. They don't care whether she's interesting or not. In fact, the less interesting, the better. They just want someone who looks good on their arm, doesn't cause too much drama and knows how to satisfy them in bed.'

In bed. The words rolling off Olly's tongue are oddly distracting, and I can't help thinking back to Gabe ribbing me for how long it's been since I had any action. It doesn't help that Olly's still tracing his fingers over my wrist. I will my cheeks not to burn up again. I really don't need Olly to see me turn into a flushed wreck at the mere mention of the bedroom.

'Hmm…' I murmur, trying to focus on the content of what he just said and not just the images of satisfying him in bed that are running through my mind. Brandon. Back to Brandon. I'm not sure if I buy into Olly's theory about him. Sure, he's a busy guy, but he doesn't view women as Stepford-wife-style accessories. Eve may not have come across as the boldest, most interesting person around, but I don't believe Brandon would be interested in her if she didn't have some substance. He's not that superficial.

'Trust me. I've met a lot of men like Brandon,' Olly continues. 'They do so well because they compartmentalise and delegate so efficiently. They have their cleaners, their accountants, their personal trainers, and then they have their girlfriends.'

'Oh, come on.' I roll my eyes. 'Surely it's not that soulless?'

'You'd be surprised,' Olly insists, giving me a knowing look. I roll my eyes but I don't bother to dispute him. I don't know if it's male competitiveness or what, but I can tell he's pretty convinced about this theory he has on Brandon.

'And you're different then?' I ask. Our eyes lock.

'I'd like to think so.' Olly takes a step closer. 'I'm not perfect. I'm a far cry from perfect,' he sighs. 'I've made a lot of mistakes, but I definitely don't want a girl who's just going to laugh at my jokes and look pretty.'

I nod.

'Although, I'm not saying you can't laugh at my jokes,' Olly adds. 'They are pretty funny.'

I laugh, although underneath the amusement is the realisation that he just referred to me directly in a conversation about the kind of girl he wants. This isn't just some late-night flirtation, he's acting like he wants to be with me, as though he's been toying with the idea of us being a couple. I gulp. This is unnerving. First, he turns out to be Eve and now this? Can this really be happening? Olly gazes at me with that intense penetrating look. I need to say something to break the tension that's simmering in the air between us.

'I really liked talking to Eve,' I blurt out, a little nervously. 'Like, really liked her! I was beginning to question my sexuality, I thought she was so cool. I was really sad when I had to let go.'

Olly grins. 'Same.'

'You could have carried on speaking to me if you'd fessed up earlier,' I point out.

'I could,' Olly admits shyly, 'and I probably should have. I suppose I was using Eve as a shield.'

'A shield?' I question.

'Yeah.' Olly glances sideways. Now it's him who's looking a little flushed and embarrassed. 'A shield against rejection.'

'Rejection?' I scoff, frowning at him to see if he's really being serious. Olly Corrigan was worried about rejection?!

'Yeah, you're pretty and young,' he answers in a matter-of-fact way. 'I'm twenty years older than you. I didn't think you'd want to get to know me.'

He looks genuinely humble. Modest. Like he really doesn't believe he's a catch.

'You're Olly Corrigan. Surely, you're inundated with girls wanting to get to know you,' I comment. And it's true. He's smoking hot. He may be older, but it's certainly not an issue for all the girls I've seen leaving flirty messages under every photo he posts online.

'You'd be surprised. I get attention but it's not always the right kind of attention,' Olly says.

'What do you mean?'

He looks into the middle distance as he thinks. 'Let's put it this way. I get attention from girls who want to be around me, not from girls who want to get to know me.'

'Right…'

'They know who I am. They know about my businesses. The parties I go to and the fancy bars. They want to get to know all of that, but they don't want to get to know me. I could tell you weren't that kind of girl. I was curious about you, and then when I realised it was you behind Brandon's profile, I couldn't resist getting to know you better.' He scratches his head. 'Well, as much as you can get to know someone when you're pretending to be a 28-year-old woman.'

I laugh. 'This is so ridiculous. For two matchmakers, we couldn't even matchmake ourselves.'

'Hey, we kind of did…' He reaches down and laces his fingers through mine, taking my hands, holding them gently. 'In a round-about way,' he says, stroking my fingers with his thumbs.

Every cell in my body springs alive at his touch. I hold his gaze. It feels like time is slowing down as he gazes into my eyes and lowers his lips towards mine. I close my eyes. My insides have turned to mush, and I can't remember ever having wanted to kiss someone so badly.

'Olly!' A man's voice interrupts.

We both look over to see Derek bursting through the venue doors, with a sweaty and slightly red-faced Andy Graham in tow. Olly immediately let's go of my hands and we spring apart.

'What are you doing here?' Derek's eyes roam between us. 'I though you said he was going to be leaving us alone from now on?' he asks me, looking aggrieved.

I did promise Derek that while filling him in a few days ago on what happened with Elliot Brown and my conversation with Olly in his office. It's no wonder he's not exactly pleased to see Olly lingering outside his party.

'I was just… Sorry, Derek. I was just passing by,' Olly says with a sheepish air.

'Right. Well, this is a private party,' Derek informs him snootily. I resist the urge to roll my eyes. The catty competitiveness between these two is just silly.

'It's okay, I'll be off,' Olly says.

I look at him imploringly. Does he really need to head off?

'It's Derek's party,' he says in a resigned tone. 'I don't want to step on his toes. I've already done enough of that the past few months,' he says in a voice quiet enough that Derek won't hear.

'Okay,' I sigh.

Our eyes lock and I desperately want to lean forward and kiss him as we were just about to before Derek interrupted, but I can feel Derek watching me. Olly glances over my shoulder towards Derek, confirming my suspicions that his eyes are lasering into my back. He's no doubt wondering what the hell I'm doing standing out here with Olly Corrigan.

'I'll message you,' Olly says in a low voice.

'Okay.' I take a step closer and whisper into his ear, 'Bye Eve.' I lightly squeeze his hand, subtly enough so that Derek probably can't see, as my cheek brushes against his. It feels like our bodies are electrodes and a current is passing through us. Our eyes meet, our lips only inches apart.

'Bye Brandon,' he says with a wink.

I smile and let go of his hand as we pull away.

'See you later, Derek,' Olly calls over my shoulder. 'Looks like a great party,' he adds with what sounds like genuine warmth but I can't quite tell. I can't quite understand the vibe between these two.

'Hmmpph... Bye,' Derek grumbles.

Olly gives me one final look – intimate, affectionate and yet self-conscious – before saying goodbye one last time, walking away and hopping into a nearby cab.

I really wish I could go with him. There are so many things I want to talk about. I want to continue the conversations I had with him as Brandon, but be able to engage with them properly, to fully be myself and to truly find out about him. But he's slipping away into the night, probably back to whatever swanky apartment he owns. I watch as he opens the cab door and looks over his shoulder at me as he gets in. We smile at each other and then he gets inside, the cab pulls away from the kerb and disappears down the street, its rear lights shimmering in the darkness.

'Polly, what's going on?' Derek asks, bringing me back to reality.

'Oh...' I turn around to see him and Andy staring at me. 'Err, I'm not sure.'

'Oh no.' Derek rolls his eyes. 'Please don't tell me you have a crush on Olly?'

'No!' I squawk with an awkward laugh.

'How has he managed that?' Derek huffs. 'Poaching my clients, dating my staff.'

'We're not dating,' I point out, although I can't help wishing that we were. 'And he's not poaching your clients anymore. He's backed off.'

'Hmm... Well, we'll see. But don't go there. He's a player. You don't want to end up falling for someone like that,' Derek advises.

I try to shrug off what he's saying as just another element of his professional disdain for Olly, but the look of sincere concern in his eyes is a little unnerving.

'I need to get back inside,' Andy pipes up. I'd almost forgotten he was there, lingering behind Derek. He wipes sweat from his brow with the back of his palm. He looks flushed – hot and bothered.

'No, give me a second,' Derek says. 'Look, I don't mean to be rude or anything.' He claps his hand on Andy's shoulder in a matey way. 'But cool it with the PDAs, buddy.'

I raise an eyebrow. *PDAs?*

'I get that you and Katarina are excited to meet and can't keep your hands off each other and that's great, but I don't want people getting the wrong idea about this party.'

The wrong idea? What has Andy been up to, the dirty dog? Now I see why he looks so hot and bothered.

'Sorry Derek. I guess we were just so excited to meet that we got carried away.'

I raise an eyebrow.

'It's understandable, but tone it down a bit, buddy,' Derek suggests.

'Maybe it's time for us to go somewhere a little more private,' Andy comments, with a slightly lewd look in his eyes.

I can't help balking at him. Here's me being too afraid to kiss Olly or even hold hands with him in front of Derek, while Andy's clearly been brazenly getting it on with Katarina.

'Well, that's up to you, but you know, maybe just tone down the fondling in corners,' Derek says with a stern tone to his voice. I can't help giggling. *Fondling?*

Derek shoots me a look and I immediately cup my hand over my mouth and pretend to cough, avoiding eye contact.

'Got it,' Andy says, smiling. 'We'll tone it down.'

'Great. Thanks mate,' Derek says, clapping his hand on Andy's back as he turns to head back into the party.

We all go back inside. The party's in full swing now, most of the guests are a couple of drinks down and the conversation's flowing. Everyone seems to be having a good time, mingling and chatting, while enjoying the canapes and drinks. Derek and I stand on the steps and take it in. I watch as Andy heads back to Katarina who's sitting in a booth delicately sipping champagne and grinning excitedly at Andy.

'I can't believe those two,' Derek says. 'They were all over each other. Thought we were going to have a live sex show on our hands. I had to practically tear them apart.'

I burst into laughter as a waiter comes along with a tray of champagne flutes. Both Derek and I reach for a glass.

Derek takes a sip and lets out a weak laugh. 'I can see why it's funny to you, but it was such an ordeal tearing Andy away from her. I was really worried about what people might start saying about the party, particularly as Katarina doesn't exactly look like the kind of woman who'd be all over Andy. At least not for free.'

'Oh, right.' I take a sip of champagne. So, Derek was worried Katarina might look like paid company. 'What do you think her deal is?' I ask. 'I saw her on Match. We chatted a bit, but I thought she was far too glamourous for Andy. I found him this lovely girl called Heather who was into museums and Harry Potter but apparently she wasn't his type. I never thought he'd get on with Katarina.'

'Well, it's interesting,' Derek says, watching with a look of trepidation as Katarina and Andy slip their arms around each other's waists, cosying up. 'She's a model, but apparently it's just something she does on the side to support herself. It turns out she's studying for a PhD on eugenics in Nazi Germany and apparently the two hit it off discussing the Second World War. They both have a passion for history.'

'Seriously?'

'Yeah!' Derek laughs, shaking his head. 'That's how they bonded. Katarina's incredibly bright. I looked her up on my phone, her work's been cited in hundreds of academic journals.

218

She and Andy have really hit it off intellectually, and romantically too it seems! It's sweet, isn't it?'

'Yeah, it is,' I admit, as I watch her cuddling up to Andy. They look like the most unlikely match and yet they're clearly getting along like a house on fire. I feel a little ashamed of myself as I take them in. I'm the superficial one, not Katarina. Here she is, connecting with someone because of their shared interests, while I've been hung up on looks. I think about Brandon and how I fancied him because he looks like something out of a high-end fashion magazine, and yet it took me ages to see that beyond Olly's tattoos and wacky clothes, there might be more to him.

'We try our best to match clients with people we think are right for them, but sometimes there's no rhyme or reason to attraction, it just happens between the people you'd least expect,' Derek comments thoughtfully, taking a sip of his champagne.

'You're right,' I say, thinking of Brandon and Eve. Eve might seem different in person to how I imagined her, but there must be something there – some connection draws her in and Brandon together and I might never fully understand it, because love isn't a checklist. It's not about criteria; it's a weird alchemy that's almost impossible to understand. People like Olly might try to write off guys like Brandon and claim they know why they go for certain women, but you can never really tell what draws one person to another.

'Are you okay?' Derek asks, eyeing me as he takes a sip of his drink.

I blink, coming back out of my thoughts. 'It's just this job, it's teaching me more about romance than I expected,' I admit.

Derek smiles. 'Yeah, it has that affect. I've been married to my wife for twenty years, but I'm still learning new things about love and relationships every day thanks to this job.'

'You're good at it though, Derek. Genuinely.' Derek may not have the flashiest of offices or slickest of websites, but he does understand romance. He understands people and he's patient

219

and kind with them. He's warm and welcoming and that trickles down to everyone around him. I only need to look at the party-goers, having a brilliant time, all loved up and happy and content, to see that Derek knows what he's doing. This isn't some desperate singles party or some sort of superficial meat market, this is a celebration of love, just like Derek said it would be.

'Thanks Polly, that's sweet of you,' Derek says just before another one of his former clients, an attractive dark-haired woman called Leila who I recognise from one of the website's success stories, comes over to say hello and sweeps him up into a hug.

'Leila, meet Polly, my star matchmaker,' Derek says, turning to me and bringing me into the fold. I grin and reach to shake Leila's hand, which is now adorned with a wedding ring.

Chapter 23

I hobble into the kitchen the following morning in a hungover daze and flick on the kettle. I need coffee. Gabe is asleep on the sofa, still in last night's make-up and dress. It's one I've seen before – a particularly garish pink number covered in sequins. He's teamed it with a blonde wig that's sliding off his head. I spoon some coffee granules into the mug and listen to the kettle boiling before pouring in the steaming water. Coffee in hand, I make my way over to the armchair and snuggle into it. Gabe's snoring lightly. The curtains are closed even though it's daylight outside and the sunlight filters through the green fabric, giving the room a muted hue, which suits my still half-asleep mood. I place my steaming mug down on the coffee table and retrieve my phone from my dressing gown pocket. There's already a message alert from Tinder.

Eve: Hey gorgeous. Forgot to get your number last night so it looks like I'm still Eve for now ;)

I smile to myself. Being called gorgeous by Olly is such a thrill.

Brandon: Hey you. Yes, let's switch to our real numbers. This whole Brandon-Eve thing is probably not healthy :p

Eve: No, probably not. Who knows where we could end up?

Brandon: **Cries out 'Eve' in bed**
I type mischievously.

Eve: **Eve – I mean Olly – gets too excited by the thought of Olly and Polly in bed together to think of a witty response**

'Why are you smiling like that?' Gabe grumbles. I glance up to see him watching me from under his huge false lashes, his eyes sleepy but curious.

'Like what?'

'Are you sexting or something?' Gabe asks, reaching for a glass of something clear on the table, which I'm really hoping is water and not last night's vodka and tonic.

'No!' I scoff. Gabe gives me a knowing look.

'Okay, maybe. Kind of. But was it really that obvious?!'

Gabe takes a sip of his drink. 'Umm, yeah!' he says, placing the glass back down. 'You had that naughty look about you.'

'Oh God,' I groan. 'Remind me never to sext in public!'

Gabe laughs. 'Please tell me it's Olly Corrigan you're messaging and not just some random girl on Tinder,' he pleads.

I grin. 'Yeah, it's Olly! Definitely not a random girl.'

'Oh my God!' Gabe's eyes light up. 'Wow! Tell me everything!' He sits up, suddenly bright and alert.

I reach for my coffee. 'Okay, so…' I launch into the whole story of messaging Olly as Brandon and thinking he was Eve, before explaining everything about how the truth emerged at the party last night.

'That is so incredibly cute! And weird!' Gabe enthuses. 'No wonder you were putting in so much overtime. Messaging Eve all evening even after work. I thought you were taking the whole matchmaker thing a bit too seriously, but if it was Olly the whole time, then it makes perfect sense!'

'Well, kind of. Except, I didn't know it was Olly. I just thought Eve was super interesting.'

'Right.' Gabe nods, frowning a little. I can tell he still finds the matchmaking world a bit strange. 'So, Olly has it all. The looks, the personality, the businesses, the success…'

'Yep, so far so good!'

'Wow!' Gabe gushes. 'Can you imagine if you were his girl-friend?! It would be the coolest thing! Olly knows everyone, doesn't he? And he goes to all the coolest places. Doesn't he have like half a million followers on Instagram?'

'Erm…' I hesitate. 'Yeah, he has quite a lot.'

I think back to last night when Olly made that comment about women being interested in him for his lifestyle rather than being into him simply for him. No wonder he feels like that when people like Gabe's first reaction is to get excited over his wealth and status.

'What's up?' Gabe narrows his eyes at me.

'Oh, nothing.' I bat the thought away. 'Let me just quickly text him back.'

'Alright. I'm going to make a coffee,' Gabe says, dragging himself up.

Brandon: *Sorry, just got interrupted by my hungover flatmate. Anyway, here's my number.*

I add my number, before adding a second message.

Brandon: *Looking forward to chatting more, Eve. Oops, I mean Olly ;)*

I send the message and then flick through the pictures of Eve, looking so polished and pretty. The whole time we were messaging, I'd imagined her in some pencil skirt suit in a corporate office or relaxing at home with her tousled side plait. It's funny to rethink all those moments and picture Olly in his trendy office, his signet rings glinting as he typed messages.

'Still day dreaming about sexy time with Olly?' Gabe jokes as he returns to the sofa.

'Maybe…' I comment cheekily.

Gabe places his coffee cup down on the table, making room by moving a flyer from The Eagle advertising last night's show, billed as a 'pop extravaganza'.

A silence passes between us.

'So, how was last night?' I ask.

'It was good,' Gabe says, hesitantly. I can tell he's holding something back.

'Just good?'

'Yeah, it was fun. I did a few Madonna covers, it was cool, but they've hired this new guy. That George Michael impersonator Jim mentioned. He's Cypriot and honestly, he's the spitting image of George Michael – a young sexy George Michael that is. Everyone was going absolutely wild for him. It's like everyone's favourite sex symbol has come back from the dead.'

'Uh-huh…' I take a sip of coffee. Gabe reaches for the flyer.

'But the thing is, he can't sing. He's not versatile at all. He only sings George Michael songs because he's got the look and he can just about get through the big hits. Just about. I guess he's had a lot of practice so he manages not to hit too many bum notes, but he's got such a bad voice and the annoying thing is that no one seems to mind. Everyone loves him,' Gabe says sadly, absently fidgeting with the corner of the flyer. He folds it over and then flattens it back out. 'It just got me thinking that you were right. I am too good for that place. I'm more than just a pop star lookalike.'

'Of course, you are. You can actually sing,' I point out.

'Exactly. And the sad thing about the people at The Eagle is they don't care if you can sing or not. They just want a hot guy to look at and pop songs to dance to when they're drunk. They're not really bothered about quality,' Gabe says sadly and although he looks down, I can't help but feel happy for him. Finally, the penny's dropped. Finally, he realises he can do better than The Eagle.

'You need to perform somewhere where people actually appreciate what a brilliant singer you are,' I insist.

'Yeah, I do,' Gabe agrees, fiddling more with the flyer. He seems nervous. 'But I think I might start writing my own music again. Quit The Eagle, take a break from all the gigging and drinking and, if I'm perfectly honest, attention-seeking. I need to stop performing other people's music just to get an audience and have a good night out. It's just an ego thing – a short-term thrill – but it's at the expense of my longer-term potential. I can do better than this.'

He looks up at me with a shy expression, as though he feels awkward even admitting to believing in himself. Gabe's become so stuck in a rut at The Eagle that he's almost forgotten what he's capable of. That place is like a toxic friend. They might make you feel great in the moment, but they don't encourage you or support you in your goals. You might have a good night out with them, but essentially they won't appreciate you staying at home to work on your projects. Essentially, they're holding you back. Gabe has an almost traitorous air about him as he says this stuff. The Eagle has been part of his life for so long that I can see why he feels a bit uncomfortable finally admitting to himself and others that it may not be the best place for him.

I move to sit closer to him.

'Gabe, you don't know how glad I am that you're doing this,' I tell him, draping his legs over my lap.

He smiles shyly. 'Really?'

'Yeah. You're a fantastic singer. Like, truly fantastic. I know this is a big change, but it was really beginning to bother me that you wouldn't quit. You were just wasted on that place.'

'Yeah.' Gabe nods. 'I got too comfortable there. When I was really trying hard to be a singer back when I first came to New York, I actually had to put myself out there. I had the creative struggles, the hard work, the rejection, but at The Eagle, I just got into this bubble where I was still singing and performing and getting to express myself to a degree, and there was no rejection. People liked me. I got free drinks and I always had a good time. It was easy, but easy can be a cop out.'

'Totally. It was like a hamster wheel,' I note.

'What?!' Gabe blows on his steaming coffee before taking a sip.

'You were just going round and round and not getting anywhere.'

'Yeah,' Gabe sighs. 'Exactly. I was just like a little drag queen hamster.'

I giggle. 'At least you've finally realised,' I joke.

'Finally.'

'So, what are you going to do? Are you going to quit your job?' I ask.

'Don't be silly!' Gabe scoffs. 'I may be abandoning my hamster ways, but I'm not ready to leave the rat race.'

'Fair enough.'

'I have bills to pay,' Gabe sighs. 'Quitting The Eagle is one thing, but giving up regular work, I don't think I could face that again.'

'Nah, you're too used to your comforts these days. Organic almond milk lattes and cashmere V-necks,' I tease.

'Exactly,' Gabe laughs. 'But hey, I still live in a tiny flat in Brooklyn so I can't be that middle-class.'

'No, you're still keeping it real.'

'Totally,' Gabe jokes, taking another sip of his coffee. 'Not too middle-class to drink instant coffee.'

'True. You're ghetto.'

Gabe grins. 'So ghetto.'

'But really, jokes aside, I'm happy for you, Gabe. I know you loved The Eagle, but I feel like this George Michael lookalike has been a blessing in disguise, coming along to get you out of your rut and make you realise your potential again. People like him belong in The Eagle. But you have something special and I'm so glad that you're not going to waste it.'

'Thanks babe, who knows what'll happen, but at least I won't be consciously wasting my talent anymore. I know I gave you a hard time about always pushing forward with your photography and not just enjoying it for what it is, but your tenacity is inspiring. I guess it struck a chord, which is probably why I got so weird about it the other day. I knew deep down that I needed some of your focus,' Gabe admits ruefully.

'I needed some of your enjoyment though. You were right. I was getting too obsessed with trying to get ahead. I'd forgotten about simply enjoying photography for photography's sake.'

'Well, I guess we both got a bit side-tracked,' Gabe says.

'We can't be perfect all the time,' I reason.

'Most of the time though.' Gabe winks.

'Of course,' I reply, snuggling up next to him.

My phone buzzes. It's a text from Olly.

Olly: Hey Polly, it's Olly (for once) ;)

I smile.

'Is it him?' Gabe asks, looking over my shoulder at my phone screen.

'Yep!' I enthuse.

Polly: Hey Olly x

Chapter 24

Olly: *I'll take you on a date to remember. Meet me at The Fifth at 7.x*

That was the last message Olly sent me and now I'm sitting opposite him in The Fifth – one of the most exclusive restaurants in New York nestled among the designer boutiques and high-end hotels on Fifth Avenue. I may keep an eye on the city's fine dining scene, but I never thought I'd get a chance to go to The Fifth. It's on the top of a high-rise hotel, opposite the Empire State building, with a spectacular view across the whole of the city. Not only is it incredibly expensive but it's notoriously hard to get into, frequented by celebrities and the super-rich. It's the last place I thought I'd be having dinner on a Saturday night and yet here I am, sitting opposite Olly, his face golden in the warm light of the low-hanging lamps, our fingers interlaced across the table as we wait for our food to arrive. Conversation has been so non-stop between us that the waiter had to come back three times to take our order as we kept on chatting instead of looking at the menu. It almost feels like we're two long-lost friends, catching up on everything.

Olly wants to know all about my life before I moved to New York.

'It was quiet,' I recall, wrinkling my nose. 'We lived in this little ramshackle, higgledy-piggledy cottage in a little village. I went to—'

'Hang on a minute,' Olly interrupts. 'You lived where?'

'In a cottage,' I tell him, feeling a bit bemused. I get that he grew up in a fancy New York town house, but we don't really have those in the tiny village where I'm from.

'Yeah, a cottage, but what did you call it?'

'A ramshackle, higgledy-piggledy cottage,' I repeat hesitantly.

Olly sniggers. 'Ramshackle? Higgledy-piggledy? Are you speaking English? What the hell is that?'

'What do you mean?'

'We don't have those words!' Olly insists.

'Fine!' I laugh. 'Ramshackle means something that's kind of run-down. And higgledy-piggledy is sort of cluttered and messy, jumbled,' I tell him, as though it's obvious.

'Oh my God, you Brits. Ramshackle? Higgledy-piggledy? I'm going to have to hire a translator,' Olly teases.

'Hey! Stop taking the mickey!' I protest, taking a sip of my wine. It's a wine that a critic I followed recommended getting at The Fifth. It's just like she said – 'rich and full-bodied with a flavour of juicy red fruits and a hint of pepperiness'.

'Who the hell is Mickey?' Olly laughs.

'It's just a phrase! Come on, everyone says that!' I sigh.

'No, we don't.'

'Hmpphh…' I huff. 'I'm pretty sure you do.' I get out my phone and Google the phrase and it turns out that 'taking the mickey' was originally cockney rhyming slang for 'take the Mickey Bliss', aka 'piss'.

'Okay, fine, I feel extremely English right now.'

'It's okay.' Olly laughs. 'I love it. I want to hear all about your ramshackle, higgledy-piggledy cottage.' He smiles.

'Okay, as long as you don't take the mickey anymore,' I warn Olly.

'I won't, I promise,' he insists, his lips twitching.

Our food arrives – crispy duck with chanterelle mushrooms and spiced plums for Olly and mushroom Wellington for me. As we tuck in, I tell him about my childhood in Cornwall, from my parents' love of gardening to our annual village folk festival. I explain how cream teas should be served, emphasising how important it is that jam is spread on the scone first with the cream added on top, and that anything else (such as the Devonshire way) is sacrilege. I describe the quirky shops along the coast that sell crystals and magic potions and wands carved from tree branches. I even describe the local druids and the fortune tellers.

'It sounds like another world,' Olly comments dreamily, as he takes a bite of his meal. I feel like I've been talking about Cornwall for ages, but Olly hasn't seemed to mind. In fact, he seems fascinated, as though he genuinely wants to know everything about me and understand my life.

'It really is,' I agree, taking a bite of my mushroom Wellington, which is one of the restaurant's star dishes that reviewers consistently rave about. With truffled mushrooms and a rich bordelaise sauce, it truly is as good as the reviews claimed.

'So why did you leave?' Olly asks, looking up at me.

'Cornwall's amazing. It's beautiful, but it just felt a bit…' I hesitate, looking for the right word. '… Small. I was only going to have one kind of life there. My mum wanted me to get a job as a receptionist at the local GP surgery. I'd probably have bought my own little cottage one day—'

'A cute little ramshackle, higgledy-piggledy cottage,' Olly cuts in.

'Exactly,' I smirk. 'And I'd have married a nice Cornish boy and we'd have gone to the beach at the weekends. It would have been a nice relaxed kind of life, but it's just a bit predictable. I suppose I wanted a more exciting, surprising lifestyle, I wanted more adventure,' I muse, reaching for my wine.

'Do you feel like you're having adventure now?' Olly asks, his eyes flickering in the soft light.

'Yeah, I do,' I reply, tracing the toe of my heel along his ankle under the table. We hold each other's gaze for a moment, before the waiter interrupts, stopping by our table to ask if everything's okay with our meals.

Olly looks a little irritated to have been interrupted, but it was probably a good thing the waiter came to our table at that moment. The tension between us was getting a bit high for a first date.

I turn the conversation to Olly, asking him the opposite question: if he ever felt the urge to leave his hometown. His hometown being New York.

'No,' Olly replies without a second's hesitation. 'I was lucky enough to be born in the greatest city in the world, why would I leave?'

I smile; I'd probably feel exactly the same if I were him.

'Don't get me wrong,' Olly says, brandishing his fork, 'I've travelled. I've travelled the world. I've been all over Europe. Paris, Milan, Amsterdam, Hamburg, London... although I haven't been to Cornwall.' He winks. 'I've been to Asia, Australia, even New Zealand, but New York is home. I always end up back here, it's my base. I think it always will be.'

Olly takes another bite of his meal. I watch him, observing how assured and relaxed he looks, despite eating in one of the fanciest restaurants in the city. If I were with anyone other than Olly right now, I'd probably be totally giddy and over-excited to be here. I'd probably be a bit awkward in such an incredibly exclusive environment and I'd probably end up taking a million pictures on my phone of everything, from the food to the views. But Olly isn't like that. He looks at home. It's so obvious that this city is his stomping ground, his base.

We finish our meals, chatting about our mutual love of New York.

After having desert and an aperitif, we leave the restaurant, descending the seventy-story building in the lift.

'What do you want to do know?' Olly asks. 'We could go to a bar for another drink? Or we could go back to my place and have a drink there?'

I smile, noting how he didn't even consider the possibility that I might go straight home like a good girl. It's obvious I'm not going to. The conversation is just flowing too well, we're both having too much of a good time. The last thing I'd want to do is hurry back to my flat, even if it might leave him wanting more or whatever else dating guides advise. They probably also advise against going back to a guy's place on the first date too, even if it is apparently just for a drink, and yet that's exactly what I want to do. As much as I've enjoyed the atmosphere of The Fifth, I feel like being somewhere a bit more relaxed – a little less high-end and self-conscious.

'Let's go to yours, just for a drink,' I say, as the lift reaches the ground floor.

We take a cab across town to Tribeca, where Olly lives.

'Only two blocks away from Harry Styles' apartment,' Olly tells me, as the cab weaves through the traffic on Fifth Avenue.

'Seriously?' I balk. It was splashed all over the papers when Harry Styles bought a twelve-million-dollar apartment in Tribeca, in the same exclusive building where Jennifer Lawrence, Blake Lively and Ryan Reynolds also live. I saw pictures at the time and it looked incredible – tall expansive rooms, private pools, impeccable décor. If Olly lives around the corner from a star-studded building like that, he must be truly loaded.

'Yeah, seriously! I've been there for twenty years. The area's become really fashionable lately,' Olly says.

'Do you see Harry around?' I ask.

'Sometimes,' Olly replies. 'I once saw him at my local café. He bought tomato soup and then left. He wore sunglasses inside.'

'Wow…' I utter.

I've seen quite a few celebrities in Manhattan, but to live around the corner from Harry Styles is something else. I knew Olly was successful, but I didn't realise quite how successful he must be if he can afford to live in a multimillion-dollar area good enough for world-famous celebrities.

We compare celebrity sightings as we cross the city. Mine are mostly glimpses on the street or sightings in Central Park, whereas Olly's are conversations at parties or anecdotes from VIP sections in clubs. It's strange how different our lives are and I almost begin to feel a little unnerved, wondering why someone as wealthy and connected as Olly would go for a regular girl like me.

'Everything okay?' Olly asks as I gaze out of the window as we drive along a wide residential street in Tribeca.

'Yeah, everything's fine,' I reply, forcing a smile as I try to put the distracting thoughts out of my mind.

We pull up outside Olly's building, which is, to my relief, nothing like the images I've seen of Harry's pad. It's impressive – a well-maintained apartment block – but it's not too intimidating either. It's a fairly normal-looking three-story apartment complex with a zig-zagging white fire escape above an old-fashioned tailor's shop.

Olly pays the driver and we cross the pavement to the entrance.

'I'm on the top floor,' Olly says as he twists his key in the lock and holds the door open for me.

The lobby is warm and inviting inside. We head up the winding staircase to Olly's apartment. He twists his key in the lock and opens the door for me. I expected his décor to be as swanky and minimalistic as his office, but his personal aesthetic is completely different. The flat is filled with a jumble of stuff: piles of books on everything from art history to philosophy stacked in towering piles against the walls, old records displayed on shelves, ratty-looking patterned rugs and an electronic keyboard leaning against the wall. He has a few antiques too: a tall sculpted lamp, a grandfather clock and a gramophone. Vintage posters of old Hollywood movies sit alongside abstract oil paintings on the walls. It's characterful, chaotic and yet so cosy.

'Take a seat,' Olly says, gesturing towards the huge comfy looking sofa.

I sit down while Olly heads to the open plan kitchen.

'What are you drinking? I have wine, whisky, vodka, coffee, tea…?'

'I'll have wine,' I reply.

Olly pours two glasses of red wine and brings them over, handing one to me.

'I love your apartment,' I say, glancing around at all the kooky items. 'It feels so homely.'

'Thanks. I've collected bits and pieces over the years. My ex-wife was really into antiques so we used to go to markets and auctions. That's where I got this lamp. It's original Art Deco, from the Thirties,' Olly says, flicking the switch of a decadent lamp featuring a nude woman standing on tip-toes holding a shining orb.

'Oh right,' I reply, admiring the lamp even though a feel a tiny twinge of concern at the mention of his ex-wife. The wife that he founded his PR company with, according to articles online. Is he still into her? Is that why he keeps the antiques they shopped for together in his home? As reminders of the good times they shared, or does he just genuinely like his finds?

'How long were you married?' I ask, taking a sip of my wine. It tastes delicious – rich and smooth.

'Ten years. We got married when we were twenty-five,' Olly replies matter-of-factly. He doesn't look nostalgic or heartbroken.

'Take off your shoes if you like,' he says, glancing down at my feet, which are still encased in the pointy boots I wore to the restaurant. His sofa is so big and comfy that I would quite like to tuck my legs up under me. It's like Olly's reading my mind.

I unzip my boots and get comfortable. Olly kicks off his brogues and does the same.

'Twenty-five is pretty young to get married,' I comment, taking another sip of wine. 'At least, it is these days.'

'I guess,' Olly replies. 'We started off as just being really good friends. We met on an entrepreneurship course and we immediately clicked. We were both really ambitious and the more we got to know each other, the more we realised we had totally complementary skillsets. I was good at sales and numbers, whereas Olivia was more of a creative, ideas person. We decided to go into business together and we set up our PR company, Impact PR. I had a ton of contacts in the music industry from all the years before the course that I'd been trying to make it as a rock star—'

'You were trying to make it as a rock star?' I raise an eyebrow, although the records on display around the room, keyboard and box of sheet music are now making sense.

'Oh yeah! I wanted to be the next Jim Morrison. I spent years trying to make it with my band,' Olly reminisces, with a look that's more wistful than bitter or resentful at having never made it.

'Oh, what happened?' I asked.

'We were no good,' Olly admits bluntly. 'We were all style and no substance. I wanted the lifestyle of a rock star, but sadly didn't quite have the talent.'

I can't help laughing. Fortunately, Olly joins in.

'It's a bit tragic, isn't it?' he jokes.

'A bit! Is that where the tattoos came from?' I gesture at his arms.

'Yeah, exactly. I considered getting them lasered off at one point, but I've grown to accept them. There'll always be a part of me that's a wannabe rock star,' he laughs.

'So, you went from rock star to businessman?'

'Exactly,' Olly replies, taking a sip of his wine.

'And your wife? Is she still in business?' I ask, hoping I don't sound too nosy.

'No, she got tired of it after a while. She wanted a different life – the country life. A big garden. A nice peaceful community. She wanted to have kids and leave Manhattan,' Olly says, smiling sadly.

'And you didn't?'

'Not really. But by the time she got to that point, we were already done. We'd gone from being friends, to lovers, to business partners, and for a while, we managed to be all three to one another, but as the years went on, we were just business partners. We just totally grew apart,' Olly admits.

I take a sip of wine as I let Olly's words sink in. Suddenly his tick-box approach to dating is beginning to make a bit more sense. If Olly's marriage was more of a business partnership then perhaps his prescriptive approach to running a dating agency is an extension of that.

'What's she doing now?' I ask.

'Oh, she got the life she wanted. She remarried. She lives in a big house with a sprawling garden in Idaho. Two kids. Rosie and Jake,' Olly says, smiling fondly. 'We've stayed in touch. She still has a stake in the business, so we catch up from time to time, but now it's strictly business!'

'You sound fine with it,' I observe.

'I am,' Olly insists. 'We had a good marriage. We were always good to each other, but you can't build a long-term marriage on just mutual business interests.' Olly smiles.

'I guess. What about a mutual love of antiques?' I joke, glancing towards the lamp.

'Even that couldn't sustain us.' Olly laughs.

We sit there, chatting about everything, from my relationship history, which Olly asks about (not a lot to tell), to our hopes and dreams. We even end up debating which band was better: The Doors or Pink Floyd. Eventually, we go from the sofa to Olly's bedroom, but even though there's tension between us, I know that he's not going to try anything. Instead, we just lie in bed, under Olly's soft duvet, and continue our conversation. Sex would be nice, but for now, the only intimacy I crave with him is the intimacy of getting to know him and allowing myself to open up to him. I've met tons of cool people in New York, but it's been a long time since I connected with a guy like I'm connecting with Olly, and I don't feel the need to instantly have sex with him. I'd rather build up to it and savour the connection we seem to have.

At some point, we fall asleep and I'm woken hours later by light streaming in through Olly's tall bedroom windows. Late last night, I draped my clothes over a chair by Olly's bed, but I'm still wearing my underwear and a camisole. Olly's still fast asleep and for a moment, I watch him, taking in his eyelashes, resting delicately on his cheeks, the crow's feet emerging from the corners of his eyes and his lips, which are wide and soft-looking, a muted pink. Even after an incredible date and staying up all night talking, we still haven't kissed. Just as I'm having that thought, Olly opens his eyes, blinking sleepily and squinting as the sunlight streaming through the window hits his eyes. I quickly look away, as though I haven't been staring.

'Morning!' I say chirpily.

'Morning,' Olly grumbles through his sleepy fog. He yawns loudly and I suddenly get the feeling that maybe I should go. What if he's not a morning person and I'm overstaying my welcome?

'I should probably head off,' I say, sitting up.

'What?' Olly looks taken aback. He's only wearing his boxers and in the light of day, the sight of his naked chest is oddly distracting. 'Why? How come? Are you busy?'

'Umm, no. I just thought you might want some space.'

'No!' Olly insists. 'I thought we could hang out today, if you want?'

I look at him, taking in his upbeat, cheerful expression. He clearly doesn't want me to leave.

'Sure!' I lie back down next to him. 'What shall we do?'

'Let's go to Central Park and take one of those ridiculous horse-drawn carriages?' Olly suggest, with a twinkle in his eye.

I laugh, thinking of the horse-drawn carriages that tourists take through central park. They're like something from a fairy tale and they're totally over-the-top. I see them all the time, but I've never considered going on one. The idea of taking one with Olly is ridiculously romantic and totally cheesy, but I kind of love it.

'Let's do it!' I reply cosying up to Olly and wrapping my arm around his warm chest.

'Have you seen 'Starry Night' by Van Gogh?' Olly asks, referring to the iconic painting, which is on display in the Museum of Modern Art.

'No, I haven't,' I admit, having never gotten around to it.

'Let's go see that too!' Olly suggests, smiling sweetly at me.

'You're such a romantic, aren't you?' I tease, although underneath my jokey bravado, I'm actually incredibly touched. Not only does Olly want to spend the day with me, but he seems to want to turn it into the most lovely, romantic day imaginable.

'Well, I am a matchmaker, after all,' Olly jokes.

Chapter 25

'Hi Derek,' I say, breezing into the office.

Derek is sitting at his desk with a steaming mug of black coffee, crunching through an Oreo.

'Hi Polly,' he says, his voice muffled by the biscuit. He takes a sip of coffee and sits up a little straighter.

'Great party on Friday!' I say as I pull off my jacket and sit down at my desk. Strangely enough, Friday feels like a lifetime ago. It was a brilliant party, but so much has happened since. My date with Olly still hasn't properly sunk in. It was the perfect night, having a romantic dinner, getting to know each other at The Fifth, followed by staying up late talking at his place. Not to mention the day after, which was just incredible. I felt like I was starring in my own Hollywood rom com sitting in the back of a horse-drawn carriage in Central Park, snuggled close to Olly. And then if that wasn't enough, we saw 'Starry Night', taking in Van Gogh's swaying trees and swirling ocean-like sky full of bright stars. It was the perfect, most majestic way to round off what was without doubt, the best date of my life.

'Yes, it was a great party, wasn't it?' Derek says, eyeing me curiously as though he can sense something's different. And the truth is, I feel different. I feel brighter and more alive than I've felt in weeks. It feels a bit strange to be back at work.

'Really great! It was such fun. Everyone seemed to be having a brilliant time,' I say. By the time Derek and I went home, we were both pretty wasted. My last memory of the night is of Derek hugging each of the waiters to say thanks, before drunkenly stuffing a load of dollar bills into the palm of a cab driver and telling him to get me home safe.

'Oh yes, what a night!' Derek says with a laugh. 'So, you had a good time then, Polly?'

'Yes, I had an amazing time!' I reply, with an awkward laugh. I can tell Derek's getting at something. I turn on my computer and try to ignore his piercing gaze.

'Okay, look. I'm just going to come out and say it,' Derek says, after popping his last piece of Oreo into his mouth. He wipes the crumbs from his shirt. He clears his throat. 'Are you dating Olly Corrigan?' he asks.

Oh God, he went there. He really went there. Right for the jugular. I swallow hard.

'Erm… I wasn't, before Friday, but umm…' Derek's looking at me with a piercing look and I can feel my cheeks burning up. 'We, umm, went on a date this weekend though,' I admit sheepishly.

Derek smiles tightly. 'Look, it's none of my business and I don't mean to pry or pass judgement, I'm sure you know what you're getting involved in, but I just needed to know. If you two are going to get serious, all I ask is that you're discreet about the business.'

'Of course, Derek. I get it. Of course, I'd be discreet,' I insist, but I can't help feeling a twinge of unease. What does he mean pass judgement? Why's he making dating Olly seem so ominous?

'Derek, what was that about me knowing what I'm getting involved in? I'm just dating a guy. It's not that big a deal, as far as I'm aware.'

'Oh…' Derek frowns and scratches his head. 'It's just, you know, his reputation,' Derek grumbles, glancing at an incoming email popping up on his screen.

My stomach sinks. *His reputation?* Derek reaches for his mouse. He edges his chair closer to his screen as though the conversation is over, and he needs to get on with work.

'What reputation?' I ask. Derek's eyes are fixed on his monitor and he's clearly pretending to be engaged. He no doubt wants me to crack on with work now too, but I need to know what his issue with Olly is first.

'Derek? What are you talking about? What reputation?'

Derek turns to look at me.

'Do you not know?' he sighs.

'No! Know what?' I groan. I'm getting exasperated now. I really need to know what the hell he's on about.

'Olly's a bit of a ladies' man,' Derek explains.

'Well yeah, he's gorgeous. Most gorgeous, successful men have had their fair share of female attention. I wasn't planning on holding that against him,' I insist, a little defensively.

'Well, fine. That's not quite what I meant about his reputation, but never mind. If you're happy, I'm happy.' Derek turns his attention back to his computer screen.

'Derek!' I snap. 'Can you stop being so vague. What do you mean about his reputation then? If you're going to say something, say it. Stop mincing your words.'

Derek's eyes widen. He looks a little taken aback at my outspokenness and for a moment, I wonder whether I should have just suppressed my irritation and not said anything. Perhaps having cosy intimates chats with Olly all weekend has made me too vocal.

'Okay fine,' Derek sighs. 'I honestly thought you'd have heard about him on the grapevine or something. I assumed if was common knowledge. If I tell you about Olly's past and you don't like what you hear, he's going to hold it against me. He could really stir things up. It could be bad for business.'

'Oh, for God's sake!' I yelp. 'I get that you care about your business, but could you stop thinking just about the business for five minutes? If there's something dodgy about Olly, then I need to know about it. Please just tell me,' I huff, feeling quite exasperated.

'Okay, look...' Derek says. 'I'll tell you but just don't tell him it came from me, okay?'

'Okay fine, I won't,' I insist.

'I know a few of Olly's former clients – you remember Leila from the party?'

I nod, thinking back to the dark-haired woman he introduced me to at the party who features on the website as one of the agency's success stories.

'Well, she originally signed up with Elite Love Match. She was in her late thirties. All her friends were married, and she'd really got to her wit's end. She'd tried all the dating sites. Dated high and low. Outside her type. Older, younger, richer, poorer. Nothing was clicking, and the biological clock was ticking. Loudly. She wanted to settle down and have kids, so she decided to try out a dating agency.'

'Understandable,' I comment.

'Exactly,' Derek agrees. 'Well anyway, she originally signed up with Elite Love Match. She even sold stuff to pay the fees. She sold jewellery, furniture. It was her last hope.'

'Uh-huh...'

'Well, things started off professionally enough. Olly set her up on dates with a few guys who on paper met her criteria, but she didn't feel a spark. Then he set her up with this guy she really liked – a super successful banker, family focused, a good catch – and Leila was really into him, but he wasn't into her. She was devastated. Apparently, they'd had a few dates, a few kisses, she really thought it was going somewhere and then he just changed his mind, decided he wasn't into her and told her it wasn't going to work. She broke down in Olly's office and he comforted her.'

'Right,' I say, struggling to see why any of this is so bad for Olly's reputation. So far, it seems like he did exactly what was expected of him as a matchmaker. He arranged dates for his client and he comforted her when they didn't work out.

'It was the end of the day, so he offered to take her out for dinner. They went to a fancy restaurant. Somewhere super impressive, apparently. Low lighting. A sexy vibe. Opposite the Empire State Building.'

I gulp. 'It wasn't The Fifth, was it?'

'Yeah, I think that's what it was called,' Derek muses. 'Yeah, that's the one.'

'Okay...' I murmur.

'Read about it, have you?' Derek asks.

'Yeah,' I reply weakly, leaving out the fact that I was there on Saturday night with Olly. Is The Fifth just where he takes all his conquests?

'So they had this romantic meal and apparently they went back to his and spent the whole night talking. She poured her heart out to him, naturally. She was in a vulnerable place. And then one thing led to another and they were in bed together.'

I look down at my lap, trying to breathe evenly. This is all too familiar. All too bloody familiar.

'They had a passionate night together, then the next day he took her on a horse-drawn carriage in Central Park and they went to see Van Gogh's 'Starry Night' at the MOMA. She said it was the best date she'd ever had.

'Oh God,' I utter, feeling my stomach flip. No. This cannot be happening.

'What?' Derek asks, taking in my aghast expression.

'No, it's just...' I trail off, unable to meet his gaze. I swallow, embarrassed. 'Never mind, just carry on.'

'Okay, well that's it really. They had a brilliant weekend. She thought she was onto something. Leila thought in a funny twist of fate, she might actually end up with her dating coach.'

I nod. Not only was the date routine exactly the same but to add salt to the wound, the funny twist of fate element was there too. Maybe Olly likes that – dating someone in the context of an unconventional twist. Maybe that's why he wanted to date me after chatting to me as Eve for so long.

'What's wrong?' Derek asks, interrupting my thoughts.

'Nothing,' I insist, even though everything is wrong. 'I just want to hear the rest.' My heart is sinking, but I need to hear it. I need to know the truth, however painful, before I get sucked any deeper into this thing I have with Olly.

'Well, there isn't much more. At least not where Olly's concerned. He never called her. He just cut Leila off. She was absolutely devastated. Two rejections in a week. The first one had been bad enough but then she was left high and dry by a so-called relationship expert. And to make matters worse, he terminated her contract with the agency.'

'What? Seriously?' I utter.

'Yes,' Derek says sadly.

'Isn't that against the rules?'

'He refunded her, but that wasn't the point. He behaved terribly. He just cut her off. He used her and then never spoke to her again. He got his assistant to handle her termination from the agency. It was just brutal.'

'That's awful.'

'It is. She was still fuming when she came to see us a few months later. She'd pretty much sworn off men but her sister-in-law's colleague, Jess, insisted we were different, so she figured she'd come in for a chat. I couldn't believe her story. I felt so sorry for her that I gave her a month free,' Derek says.

'Wow,' I utter, in total shock. I cannot believe Olly could have behaved in such a cold, callous way, and yet I'm forced to believe it's true. All the other details of the story are spot on, it clearly isn't just made up. And to be fair, I don't really know Olly. I mean, most of the time I've been speaking to him, I thought he was someone else entirely. I thought he was Eve. I didn't even know him properly back then. And I've only spent about twenty-four hours with him in the flesh. That's not enough to truly know someone.

'It was pretty messed up,' Derek continues. 'Trust me, I had my work cut out for me trying to rebuild Leila's trust in men. She was really hurt after Olly.'

'Is this why you hate him so much?'

'Kind of. Yeah, it's part of it.' Derek reaches for another Oreo. 'Olly just goes after everything with such ruthless determination – women, clients, money. He has the charm, but essentially, he only really cares about himself,' Derek sighs. 'I like you, Polly. We've spent a lot of time together the past month or so and I know you're still finding your feet in New York. I just don't want to see you being taken advantage of. I don't want Olly to mess you around and leave you as bitter and hurt as Leila was.'

'Oh God. I understand.' I turn away and stare blankly at my keyboard. 'Are you sure there isn't more to the story?' I ask, in a last-ditch attempt to salvage something – a morsel of doubt – over what Derek's told me.

'What do you mean?' Derek asks.

'Are you sure Leila told you the whole truth? Like maybe there was a reason Olly didn't call or something?' I ask, but even as I say it out loud it seems weak and desperate, as though I just don't want to hear the truth.

'Look, if you want to speak to her yourself, I'm sure she'll tell you all about it. Or I can put you in touch with the others.'

'The others?' I gawp.

'There were a few other former clients that seemed to have similar stories. At least that's what I've heard.'

'Oh my God.'

I feel deflated. Five minutes ago, I was strutting into the office, feeling on top of the world, and now I feel like a complete fool. I wasn't finally getting lucky in love, I was being played by a callous scumbag who uses his dating agency to prey on desperate women. It's no wonder he went for me. He probably saw me for the lonely, confused girl I so evidently am. I feel my palms prickle with sweat.

'I think I need to take five minutes. Is that okay, Derek?'

'Of course,' Derek replies. 'Sorry Polly, I didn't mean to upset you. I just thought you should know what he's like.'

'That's okay,' I grumble as I scurry out of the room.

I close the office door and perch on the edge of the sofa in the client lounge as I try to wrap my head around what Derek has just told me. I knew there had to be a catch with Olly. He was just too handsome and cool and charming. The whole thing was too much like a fairy tale to be real. I hadn't met my Prince Charming, I just met Prince Player: Prince Charming to every girl. It's like my mum always used to say, if something seems too good to be true, it usually is. Olly isn't some eligible, cool, exciting guy, he's just yet another tragic bachelor who refuses to settle down.

I get up and wander over to the window. I watch a few builders in orange hard hats smoking in front of a construction site opposite. A few girls, who look like tourists with SLR cameras slung around their necks wander into an Italian café down the street. A pigeon flies off the road and onto the pavement to avoid a passing cab. I look on, feeling rotten. I should have known what I was doing. I shouldn't have allowed myself to get so carried away over Olly. I sigh as I try to let the fantasy go. I thought our date had been so special, but the idea of it being a routine that he's gone through with tons of other girls is unbelievably depressing. I feel ashamed and embarrassed at having been duped into caring, like so many others. Olly may have got all the other girls he wined and dined and took back to his place to become obsessed with him, but if he thinks that's going to be me, he has another think coming. I am not going to flatter his ego. I'm going to be strong and resolute. Guys like him need a cold hard dose of reality. They need to realise that they can't just wheedle their way into everyone's hearts. I get my phone out of my jeans pocket and find his number. The last message he sent me was a cute 'Feeling sad to be waking up without you this morning x' message sent only a few hours ago. I erase our chat history and go to delete his number. My finger hovers over block, but I can't quite bring myself to block him. Instead, I re-save his contact details, delete his name and rename him 'Ignore', just in case I feel weak and get tempted to pick up if he tries to call me later.

I take a deep breath and watch a plane swoop across the sky before heading back into the office.

'Sorry about that, Derek,' I mutter as I sit back down at my desk.

'You okay? I didn't mean to upset you,' Derek says, looking genuinely guilty.

'I'm fine. Honestly, Derek. I'm really glad you told me,' I insist, as I scan my inbox.

'Okay. I'm glad you think so. I was beginning to regret saying anything, but I wanted to warn you.'

'I totally understand. You did the right thing.'

'Okay, good.' Derek reaches into his desk drawer and retrieves his pack of Oreos. He offers one to me. 'Cookie?'

I laugh. Oreos are Derek's solution to everything.

'No, it's okay, Derek,' I say, and then instantly, I reconsider. Maybe biscuit consumption isn't the most sophisticated solution to every problem, but it's a start. I reach for an Oreo, thank him, and then crack on with work.

Following the party, a few new clients have signed up and Derek's already forwarded me their details. One of them, a 37-year-old accountant called Lionel, reminds me of Andy Graham. He has the same sort of non-descript look. He's reasonably tall – five-foot-eleven apparently – but his slightly overweight, middle-aged sprawl is beginning to catch up with him. And his face is unremarkable – his hairline is receding and he has a slightly weak chin – but he's not exactly ugly. Like Andy, he's just *there*. And like Andy, the selection of pictures on his Facebook account is just dire. They're all either crappy selfies taken at the world's worst angles or pictures of him standing in front of monuments in which he's so small that you can barely make out that it's a man, let alone see his features. I click through the pictures, feeling despondent.

'Derek,' I pipe up.

Derek looks over. 'Yeah?'

'Have you seen Lionel's pictures?' I ask.

'Err… One or two.'

'They're awful,' I comment. 'Like, truly bad. No one would want to date him based on these pictures.'

'Really?' Derek looks sceptical.

'Really.' I turn to my screen and click onto what's probably the least flattering photo of Lionel. I really don't know what he was thinking. It's as though he was just holding his phone, put it into selfie mode and then took a picture without lifting the phone up at all. The picture makes him look like he has an enormous double chin, it shows his nose hair and the sloping shadows across his cheeks from his glasses. It's a dreadful picture. There's no denying it. It looks like found footage from a low budget horror film. Derek grimaces.

'Yeesh. That's not the best. Surely there are some better shots than that?' Derek asks.

'Not really. All of his selfies are like this. I don't know what he was thinking.'

'A lot of our male clients aren't the best selfie takers,' Derek notes.

'Tell me about it.' I sigh.

'Doesn't he have any other photos that aren't selfies?' Derek asks.

'Well, yeah, but they're not much better.' I select a picture of

Lionel standing in front of the Eiffel Tower in which he resembles a speck.

Derek narrows his eyes, trying to make Lionel out. 'Are they all like that?'

'Yeah, pretty much.'

'Hmm... I can see this is going to be a problem then,' Derek says. 'I'll email him and ask him to send some more pictures over.' He turns back to his computer screen.

An idea hits me as I watch Derek click into his inbox. He opens a new message window. I feel a tremor of nervousness about suggesting what I'm about to suggest, but I force myself to say it anyway.

'Wait a second, Derek. How about I take some pictures of Lionel? He clearly has no idea what he's doing, and I am a photographer after all. I may as well help him out.'

Derek turns to me and I can see the idea resonating with him. He looks pensive, but his eyes have become brighter.

'That's not a bad idea, you know,' he says. 'Why didn't I think of that? Do you have portrait photography experience?'

The question is music to my ears. It's been ages since anyone asked me about my photography in a serious way.

'Yes! I completed modules in it at university. I've done a few freelance portrait jobs too. I took staff pictures for a marketing company and for some social workers in Queens,' I tell him, recalling a few freelance jobs I've done.

'So, you're actually pretty well-qualified for this then,' Derek muses.

'Yeah! Definitely! Well, I'd like to think so!'

'And all this time, we've been missing out on this opportunity.'

'What do you mean?'

'I should have been getting you to take photos of clients ever since you started. It could have been great for their dating profiles, but it didn't occur to me. We could have offered it as part of our package, rather than just trying to get by on the photos the clients

249

provide. Professional pictures might have saved us a lot of bother when it comes to messaging people. They could have sold our clients better and done half the work for us. They say a picture speaks a thousand words after all. If our clients have better pictures and are getting better matches, that frees up our time to take on more clients,' Derek says. I can tell he's thinking aloud, but it makes perfect sense. Business is clearly his passion. It lights him up the way photography lights me up.

'Sounds good. So, I'd be taking photos of all our clients?' I ask, unable to mask the hopeful inflection in my voice.

'Well, we should definitely trial it and see how it goes,' Derek says.

'Okay, great!' I clap my hands together with glee. It may only be a trial, but I can't contain my excitement. I'll get to take photos as part of my job. How cool is that? I can't wait.

'This is brilliant, Derek! I'm sure we can sell the clients so much better! I'm sure it'll pay off. How about I trial it with someone today?' I suggest, feeling excited. My mood has already transformed, considering that not long ago I was feeling awful over Olly. What a rollercoaster today is turning out to be.

'Yes, let's do a trial today. Good idea.' Derek smiles.

'Cool! Who shall I photograph?'

'Me!' Derek points out like it's obvious.

'You?'

'Yeah!' Derek grins. There are still quite a few Oreo crumbs caught between his teeth. 'I'll be your guinea pig. If you can make me look dateable then you can make anyone look dateable.'

I can't help laughing at his self-deprecating humour. He has a point. With his giant pot belly, terrible shirts and awful glasses, Derek isn't exactly handsome. He's the kind of guy who, if you were trying to set them up with your friend, you'd probably describe them as having a 'great personality', omitting the looks part.

'Having doubts?' Derek jests.

250

I grin. 'No, I'm game if you are!' I insist, although I'm already trying to figure out how the hell I'm going to do this. There is no camera angle I can use or pose I can put Derek in that will make him look slim. There's no filter that can hide his jowly neck or indelicate features. I'm already mentally abandoning all thoughts of making Derek look handsome. That's clearly going to be a non-starter. My best bet is to focus on his personality and strive to bring out his kind eyes, the exuberance of his smile and his natural warmth. If I can get that across, then I'm onto a winner.

'Great, let's do it!' Derek says.

Chapter 26

As I expected, it's not exactly easy to take dating profile pictures of an eighteen-stone man with the look of an ageing porn director, which is of course what Derek is. But I do my best. At first, Derek and I try an office shoot. I get him to don a smart blazer. Well, I say smart. It's been dangling on a peg on the back of the office door ever since I started working at the agency and I had to spend quite a while brushing dust off it. Nevertheless, Derek puts it on, and then I ask him to stand by the office window with his arms folded across his chest in an executive *Apprentice* style pose. The light from the window is falling onto his face and I'd hoped the image would capture Derek's passion for business and make him look ambitious and intelligent. In reality, he just comes across as stiff and vaguely creepy.

'Hmm, okay, let's try something different,' I suggest as I scroll through the pictures on the back of my camera.

'Like what?' Derek asks.

'How about Central Park?'

I tell Derek to abandon the blazer. It clearly isn't having the right affect; it just makes him look stern and Derek is not stern. He's a softy and that's what I want to get across in the pictures. Derek's kind and warm; those are his selling points and that should be the reason anyone would want to date him. That's what I need to capture. Not give him the look of a disgruntled scary office worker.

So, we head to Central Park and I get Derek to sit on a park bench. Bad idea. I take a few snaps, but within seconds, a giant bedraggled-looking pigeon lands on Derek's belly and begins pecking at some leftover Oreo crumbs. He loses his shit and immediately jumps off the bench. The pigeon flaps around and Derek swears. I watch the whole thing through my camera lens, and in some kind of photographer's trance, I continue to take photos, despite the commotion. Derek gets increasingly red-faced as he calls the pigeon an 'annoying pest'. The photos are not the best.

'Stop taking pictures!' Derek shouts as the pigeon finally launches off in search of someone new to harass.

'Sorry.' I get up from my squatting position, turning my camera off. I may have stopped taking pictures, but I'm not planning on deleting the ones I've taken just yet. I'm pretty sure Gabe and I can have a giggle over them later.

'We need a different setting. The park isn't cutting it,' I declare.

'*Another* setting?!' Derek sighs. His brow is already glistening with sweat from his altercation with the pigeon and he has a rather unbecoming pair of sweaty half-moons under his arms.

'Just one more,' I assure him.

'Where?' Derek asks with a look of dread in his eyes.

Where? I haven't quite got to that yet. I rack my brains while Derek's unimpressed eyes bore into me and then suddenly it hits me: we could go to Brooklyn and take pictures next to the murals and street art where Scarlett and I took pictures a few weeks ago. It might be a little bit too hip and urban for Derek, but in the moment, I can't think of anywhere else.

We take a cab to Brooklyn and I get increasingly worried on the way. Why am I taking a 50-year-old balding man to one of the youngest and coolest parts of New York for a photoshoot? If

I thought Derek looked bad in front of an office window and in a park, why do I think he's going to look great in front of the weird graffiti artwork covering the walls in Brooklyn? It's the kind of place that cool young Instagrammers clamour towards to do amateur photoshoots – I know, I'm guilty of it myself (even if I'm not that cool) – but it's hardly appropriate for a dating photoshoot for an ageing pretend bachelor.

'What's up?' Derek asks as I fret, fiddling with my camera strap and gazing despondently out of the window.

'Oh, nothing!' I reply, plastering an optimistic smile on my face.

I'm beginning to worry that I'm going to totally screw up this experiment and that all my photos of Derek will be be a bust, meaning that I'll have to go back to sitting in the office all day messaging random people on dating sites instead of getting to take pictures. I might be starting to enjoy life at the agency, but the prospect of getting to take pictures as part of my job is just too alluring. It would make a fairly enjoyable job a really enjoyable job and it would actually be relevant to my career. I'd go from waking up feeling relatively content to probably waking up with a spring in my step and I want that so much. So much that I decide then and there as the cab crosses Brooklyn Bridge that I'm not going to let a slightly unusual location choice ruin this shoot. I'm going to smash it. I'll find some way of making Derek look brilliant, weird graffiti or not.

The cab pulls up on a side street and I immediately spot the first mural – a reggae-inspired tribute to Bob Marley. Derek takes it in with a raised eyebrow. Okay, maybe not quite the right backdrop.

'This way!' I say with a false air of confidence as I lead him to one of my favourite streets, where Scarlett and I hung out a few weeks ago. I'm worried it will be full of amateur models who'd sneer at me and Derek, but fortunately, it's pretty empty, aside from a woman walking her dog and a cool-looking mum playing with her kid on a chalk hopscotch etching on the pavement. Perfect.

I usher Derek towards a wall painted black with giant butterfly wings.

'There. Stand in front of the wings.'

Derek shuffles awkwardly into position. I'm not quite sure how I'm going to pull this off, particularly since posing in front of these giant wings is something hipsters tend to do, not guys like Derek, but whatever, I figure I'll give it a shot.

'What should I do?' Derek asks as he stands with his arms limp against his sides.

'Umm…' I lift the camera towards my face. 'Smile, hold your arms out and, erm, pretend to fly?' I suggest.

'Pretend to fly?' Derek laughs and the second his face relaxes and a big familiar smile spreads across it, I take a picture. The moment I press the shutter, I know I've got a good shot. Okay, so Derek's arms are still hanging limply at his sides, but his face is Derek-like. He looks good-natured, amused and a little wry.

'That's great, Derek,' I say. 'Give me a few more poses. Hold your arms out.'

Derek rolls his eyes indulgently and holds his hands out as though he's Rose in *Titanic*. He turns his eyes towards the sky with an ironically 'deep' expression on his face. I giggle a little behind my camera as I take another few pictures. I'd really begun to have serious doubts about how successful a backdrop of hipster murals was going to be, but actually, it's working out surprisingly well. It comes across as idiosyncratic and ironic, and surprisingly, it's bringing out Derek's light-hearted playful spirit in a way I totally hadn't anticipated. We move onto the next mural and the effect is the same.

Derek is totally vibing off the creative atmosphere and the lively scenery. He seems happy and carefree and younger. Taking the pictures and larking about with him in Brooklyn, I can almost imagine what he must have been like as a student back at art college. He probably was as fun and popular as he makes out. Even though I thought his anecdotes seemed a little fantastical when he first dropped in a few back at my interview, I can believe them now. I bet he was one of those guys that everyone gets on with. The kind of bloke who may not be the most handsome but who will go along to a party and everyone will slap them on the back and say hi.

I get so carried away with the shoot that Derek has to interject as I try to get him to stand in front of the tenth or eleventh mural.

'Surely you've got enough?' he asks.

'Oh!' He's snapped me out of my bubble. I definitely have enough photos. I probably have at least a dozen really good pictures that would definitely work for a fictional dating profile. Not that an average profile even needs twelve photos.

'I can tell photography's your thing!' Derek comments with a wink.

'Haha, yep! Told you!' I glance behind Derek at the street art of an apple tree. 'Just one more shot. Pretend you're picking an apple,' I suggest.

'Fine!' Derek sighs as he strikes a silly girlish pose, kicking one foot back and pretending to reach for an apple.

Again, I giggle to myself as I take six or seven snaps. Eventually, I lower my camera.

'Okay, Derek. That's a wrap!'

'Great, because it's not easy being this pretty,' he jokes.

I scroll though the pictures in the back of the cab on the way back to the office. Derek tries to get a look over my shoulder, but I won't let him. I want him to see them once I've brightened them up on Photoshop and made a few tiny improvements, but they're great. They're so fun and warm, so quirky, so Derek. I can't believe it. Despite the rocky start, I've done it! I've taken portrait shots that fit the brief perfectly for a dating site: they show the person's personality, they make them look as physically good as possible and they don't look too cold, fake or posed, like a magazine editorial. I can't wait to get back to the office, edit the pictures and show them off to Derek. I don't mean to blow my own trumpet, but I'm fairly sure he's going to love them.

And I'm right. Derek is so impressed when I scroll through the edited images on my computer screen a few hours later.

'Wow!' He utters, coming over to my computer to take them in. 'Great shots! Even I'd date me.'

I laugh.

'Okay, not quite. I'm the kind of guy who punches above my beltline. But still, you've actually made me look mildly dateable. You can't polish a turd, but you've had a damn good go.'

'Stop it, Derek!' I laugh some more.

'No really, Polly. Jokes aside, these are great shots. You're really talented. I suspected that already, but I can see it. You've actually made me look good! These are really fun pics. My wife is going to absolutely love them. She'll want to frame them. Can you email them to me?' he asks.

'Of course.' I turn back to my screen and open up an email. 'And thanks, Derek. I'm so glad you like them,' I comment, as I select a few pictures and add them to the email. I know I have to ask whether the trial has been a success. I strongly suspect it has been, but there's a small insecure part of me that is still worried that Derek will back off the idea and that all that will be left of our day will be a series of fun pictures stuck to his fridge door at home, or possibly honoured with a frame. I try to pluck up the courage to ask but I keep losing my nerve.

'So, a new client – Amanda Bragnell, a vet from the Upper East Side, is coming in tomorrow. You can take a few photos of her,' Derek suggests, as he sits back down at his desk.

'Really?' I turn to look at him wide eyed.

'Yes.' Derek's face breaks into a smile. 'Really. This is going to be a fantastic addition to our service. I'll get Lionel booked in

257

for next week as well. My only regret is that we didn't start doing this sooner,' Derek says.

I laugh with relief. 'I can't wait to get started!' I enthuse.

But I don't just file the idea away until the following day, when I'm set to take pictures of Amanda Bragnell. Oh no, as the day goes on, I start wondering whether this could be something I could do on the side too, taking dating shots for regular daters, not just clients of To the Moon & Back. After all, not everyone wants to sign up to a dating agency, but most single people could probably benefit from some decent dating profile shots. Maybe it's all the time I've spent around Derek, absorbing his entrepreneurial spirit, or maybe it's the weekend I shared with the slutty self-starter Olly, or maybe it's just me, but I begin to wonder whether I could combine my background working in a dating agency with my pretty respectable degree and offer a legit-sounding dating shots photography service. I could start my own business, setting up a nice website using some of the money from Alicia. I decide to walk part of the way home, crossing Brooklyn Bridge, and as I do so, I imagine what my website would look like. I start picturing myself networking at dating events, mingling on behalf of my own business and To the Moon & Back. And the more I think about it, the more perfect the idea seems. I could finally be a portrait photographer, like I've always dreamed, and maybe I wouldn't be photographing the leading artists and actors and celebrities of my generation, but I'd be meeting interesting people from all walks of life.

As I'm thinking this, my phone buzzes. A text from 'Ignore' – formally known as Olly Corrigan.

Ignore: *Hey Polly, What's happened? Are you okay? Please text back x*

I hit delete and stride across the bridge with a newfound sense of purpose in my step.

Chapter 27

You'd think it might be difficult to create a website for a business that only just popped into your head, but it's surprisingly easy. I've spent every evening since Monday working on my new project. I've spoken to friends about it, testing the idea out on them to make sure I've not gone completely crazy, but they all thought it was great. I've had a look at local competitors; there are a few but their photos are a bit naff and I'm pretty sure I can do better. I've browsed a ton of portrait photography websites to see what I like about them and what I dislike. I even made a list. I did the same for dating business websites, adding to the list of likes and dislikes. Eventually, I studied my lists and started trying to envision a website that would not only sell my services as a professional photographer but would also appeal to people who are single and keen to find love. Then I created a website using one of those sites that enables you to tweak templates. It was a bit fiddly at first and it wasn't the flashiest site imaginable, but after a while, I managed to get it close to how I wanted it.

I uploaded a few pictures of Derek, a couple of portrait shots of obliging friends from my university days who said they didn't mind me using them. Finally, I added the images from my shoot with Amanda Bragnell – the vet who's recently signed up with

To the Moon & Back. We had our shoot the other day. She's a slim, wholesome-looking blonde and I took some gorgeous photos of her in Central Park. Unlike Derek, she didn't look like a creepy dude on the bench swamped by pigeons. She was completely at ease and even stopped to pet someone's dog. I snapped away, capturing her affinity with animals, reflected in her profession as a vet. I managed to get some lovely pictures that really made her shine. It was such a great shoot. Amanda loved the photos. She said she's been single for seven years and I think she's been out of the dating game so long that she stopped believing she was pretty. It was good to present her with some images which showed that wasn't the case. She even offered to give me a client testimonial for my site.

Once I uploaded the pictures, I wrote some biography text, and tried to sell myself as much as possible while also sounding modest and approachable. I even got Gabe to check it over from a HR point of view to make sure I sounded professional, and then without further ado, I clicked publish. With a twinge of anticipation, I watched the site's stats, waiting with bated breath to see my first visitors arrive. I waited for twenty minutes and I didn't get a single visitor apart from myself – not even a bot – so I called it a night and went to bed. I expected I'd wake up to more activity, after all, I'd clicked publish at half past midnight and who browses portrait photography websites at that time? Surely by lunch time the following day, I'd have some visitors. But no. Nothing. Despite me integrating some SEO key words into the template. Hmmpph. That evening, I decided to set up an Instagram account with some of the pictures and the link to the website in the bio details. I followed a ton of dating accounts, and the people who followed those dating accounts (most likely singletons and hopefully potential clients) and then I set about liking posts, commenting, and generally engaging with people, until I got some followers and people started to engage with my feed. By 1.30 a.m. (I got a bit carried away), my Instagram account had 32 followers, my photos had a collective 67 likes (not exactly smashing it but a start) and my site had had nine hits! It was working.

It's now Friday night and I'm still Instagramming. I know I should probably be out socialising but I've just somehow become a bit obsessed with this project. It's invigorating. It's like suddenly all the pieces have come together, as though everything that's happened to me over the past few months has fallen into place to create a brilliant opportunity. The stars have aligned and I'm finally going to have my own little business. I sit on my bed and gaze for a moment at the Mario Testino poster I stuck on the wall as a reminder not to give up on my photography dreams; it feels like it's actually helped and I might be finally getting somewhere. My phone buzzes. It's a text from Derek. I raise an eyebrow. Derek and I are friendly but not exactly text-each-other-at-10.35-on-a-Friday-night friendly. I open the message.

Derek: *Hi Polly, quick message. Amanda asked me to give you the number of her friend, Becky. She's not interested in using the agency but wants some pics for dating and personal/professional use. Can you help? Maybe discuss it with her. I'll send over her contact details. Have a good weekend. See you Monday.*

Without realising it, a squeal escapes my lips. A moment later, Gabe pops his head around the door.

'What's up?' he asks. Unlike Friday nights for the past few years, he's wearing pyjamas instead of a frock and he's at home instead of belting out Eighties pop anthems at The Eagle. In fact, he's been sitting in his bedroom strumming along to his guitar and working on a new song. The sound's been trickling through the bedroom wall for the past week. It's been nice. I've heard it develop from a few notes, to a melody, to a melody woven into a chorus, with a couple of verses added in. I can't quite make out all the lyrics but from what I can gather it's inspired by his love for Adam and it's really good. I've even found myself humming it in the office. It's catchy and it's so good to hear Gabe playing his own music again.

'Guess what?!'

'What?' Gabe comes over and sits on my bed.

'I think I may have just got my first paying client for Polly's Pics!' I gush. Oh yeah, I decided to call the business 'Polly's Pics'. It's a bit silly but it's catchy and simple, and it has that personal touch. After all, they are pics and they are taken by me.

'Seriously?' Gabe's face lights up.

'Yeah! A friend of the woman whose photos I took the other day,' I tell him.

'That's amazing, Polly!' Gabe grins and pulls me into a hug. I squeeze him back.

'I know! I can't believe it! It's so soon!'

'You must have tapped into a need. I bet this is going to be huge!' Gabe says.

I shrug. 'I don't know about huge, but a bit of money on the side would definitely not go amiss!'

'For sure.' Gabe glances at one of the magazines on my bedside table where I've circled a review of a new restaurant in Chelsea called Per Se. It's a chic French bistro with two Michelin stars and critics across the board have been singing its praises. 'Maybe we could go there?' Gabe suggests, gesturing at the article.

'Ha! Maybe!' I laugh, feeling a little bit embarrassed. My weird obsession with top restaurants is something I indulge in away from prying eyes. I have a stack of magazines by my bed with all the best restaurant reviews bookmarked with post-it notes. It's not exactly normal. Just like it's not exactly normal to circle reviews of restaurants you could never afford, but Gabe's right. Maybe – just maybe – I might get to be able to experience such places if my business takes off.

'I'm so happy for you,' Gabe says in a serious tone, his eyes twinkling, and I can tell he really means it. It may just be one client but it's a start.

'Thanks Gabe,' I reply. I'm just about to ask him about his new song when my phone buzzes again. I quickly check it, expecting it might be another message from Derek about the client, but it's not. It's from someone else entirely. Someone I've been ignoring all week. Actually, ignoring is too strong a word, I've just been too busy to register this person's existence.

Ignore: Hey Polly. Not sure what's going on. You haven't replied to my messages all week. I've tried to just let it go but I can't. We had such a good time at the weekend and I really thought it was going somewhere. Never in a million years did I think you'd end up ghosting me. I've had a think and I'm pretty sure something else is going on here. I know Derek's not my biggest fan. Has he said something to you? Please talk to me and let's discuss this. I'm thinking about making some big changes, let me explain. Olly. X

'Urghh…' I groan.

'Who was it?' Gabe asks.

'Oh nothing. Just work stuff,' I lie. I can't be bothered to even have a conversation about Olly Corrigan right now.

'Oh okay,' Gabe demurs, although he looks a little perplexed.

'So—' I drop my phone onto the covers '—isn't it about time you played me your new song?'

Chapter 28

'I don't know what's going on in the city at the moment, but there seems to be a huge number of single people who've suddenly decided they're desperate to find love. We're inundated.' Derek sighs, as he hits send on an email.

'Wasn't that the idea of the party?' I remind him as I log out of Match and close my browser. 'Get some new business? Raise the profile of the agency.'

'Yes, of course,' Derek replies. 'But I didn't expect *this* many enquiries!'

Derek's phone has been ringing all morning with calls from potential clients, but he can hardly complain. That's exactly what he wanted.

'What else is up, Derek? Is your wallet too small for your fifties too?' I laugh as I get up from my desk and pull on my coat. I managed to arrange the photoshoot with Amanda's friend, Becky, for today. We got chatting by text over the weekend and figured out that we work only a couple of blocks away from each other. Becky lives over an hour away and commutes in, so we decided it would be easier to meet up on a weekday. She had evening plans all week, so we arranged to meet during our lunch break. Derek's been nice about it and let me have a long lunch as long as I stay a bit later this evening. I think he's just really happy to see my business idea take off and as a fellow entrepreneur, he wants to support me as much as possible.

'What the...' Derek mutters as he frowns at a new email that's popped up on his screen.

'I'm sorry, Derek, but I have no sympathy. You can't complain that you don't have enough clients and then whinge when you get them!' I say as I wind my scarf around my neck, before reaching for my camera bag.

'No, it's not that,' Derek says ominously. 'It's Olly.'

'Olly?!' I echo. 'What do you mean?'

'He's quitting,' Derek utters, while scanning at a document on his screen.

'What do you mean "quitting"?' I walk closer to his desk to get a better look.

'He's closing up shop,' Derek says with a tone of disbelief. 'He's closing Elite Love Match.'

'Seriously?' I balk.

'Yeah, look.' Derek moves his chair to the side to give me a better look of his screen. I take in the press release.

Elite Love Match, one of New York's leading dating agencies, has today announced that it is closing.

The agency was founded by entrepreneur and PR specialist, Olly Corrigan. Elite Love Match has experienced considerable success, going from a small start-up to a well-respected agency. It has been the proud recipient of the 'Dating Agency of the Year' award at the New York Dating Awards in recognition of its impressive track record in creating loving relationships, marriages and thriving families.

However, a business that specialises in matters of the heart must come from the heart and unfortunately, due to personal reasons, founder Olly Corrigan is no longer able to give the business the full attention it requires. He will now be focusing

265

his full efforts on his PR company Impact PR, which operates from the same premises as Elite Love Match.

Elite Love Match will continue to fulfil obligations to its current clients, providing the high level of service they signed up for and have experienced so far. However, the business will no longer be taking on any new clients.

Olly Corrigan said: 'I started Elite Love Match with the goal of bringing New Yorkers together and I'm proud to say that ambition has been achieved. It's been incredibly rewarding to have helped clients enter into strong loving relationships and to have witnessed marriages between people who, without Elite Love Match, may never have met.

'Running a dating agency is a uniquely fulfilling endeavour and one which requires a strong and whole-hearted sense of leadership. Due to changes in my personal circumstances, I am no longer able to give the agency the love and attention it deserves and will be dedicating my business interests towards my company, Impact PR. I'd like to thank everyone who has supported Elite Love Match along the way. It's been a pleasure.'

'Oh my God,' I utter. 'What the hell?'

'I know. I can't believe it!' Derek shakes his head in a state of complete shock.

'What are these "personal circumstances"?' I ask, although I'm really just thinking aloud. Derek's hardly going to know about Olly's private life.

'No idea. Have you spoken to him lately?' Derek asks, giving me a curious look. I know he's not Olly's biggest fan, but he looks concerned, almost worried, about Olly's well-being. And his worry is making me worry too.

'No. Not at all,' I reply guiltily, thinking of all the text messages I've ignored from Olly over the past week. Come to think of it, he did mention wanting to make some 'big changes' to his life in one of the messages. Was shutting down his dating agency what he meant? He'd wanted to talk to me at the time, but I simply ignored him.

'I stopped talking to him after you warned me about him,' I admit.

'Oh… right…' Derek utters, glancing away. 'So, you don't know what he means?'

'No.' I shrug, although I don't feel blasé. In fact, my stomach has started to fizz with a vague sense of anxiety. I may have been a bit pissed off with Olly after I found out that our date was simply his cookie-cutter idea of romance, but I don't like the idea of something bad having happened to him, and the fact that he's chosen to shut down his agency feels weirdly out of character. Only a few weeks ago, he was trying to poach clients from To the Moon & Back.

'I have absolutely no idea what's up with him,' I reply, feeling a bit lost and helpless.

'Odd,' Derek adds and we both slip into a pensive reverie, while staring at the press release, as though by re-reading it, we might somehow deduce a hidden meaning in its text. After a minute or so, my phone buzzes. It's a message from Scarlett saying that she's waiting outside the building and wondering where I am. I managed to rope her into coming along to my first proper shoot. She's bringing her reflector screen to make the pictures a little bit more professional.

'I'd better go, Derek,' I say.

'Yes, of course,' Derek answers, a little distractedly. He's clearly still in shock from the press release and I can see why. He's been in competition with Olly Corrigan for so long that Olly taking himself out of the game is going to completely change the business landscape for him. No wonder he's been getting so many enquiries from new clients.

'Let's catch up later,' I say, grabbing my camera and edging towards the door, leaving Derek still staring at his computer screen.

'Sure,' he mumbles, still totally perplexed. My long lunch is probably a good thing; it'll give Derek time to wrap his head around this new development.

As I slip out of the office, I can't help wishing I had the same luxury. As grateful as I am to have my first proper client for Polly's Pics, I feel like I need to take this new information in, rather than head to the shoot feeling oddly distracted and disconcerted. I get into the lift and glance at my watch as it slides down the shaft. I'm meant to be meeting my new client Becky in ten minutes and I really need to come across as professional as possible, which means putting Olly and his 'personal circumstances' out of my mind.

Scarlett is lingering outside the building, looking a little out of place in her ratty old jumper and jeans in the middle of Wall Street. She eyes the suited office workers with a slightly wary, fearful look as they stride purposefully past her. This is most definitely not her domain. She is every inch the photographer, from the giant camera slung over her shoulder to the massive bag of supplies and the collapsed reflector screen tucked under her arm.

'Hey,' I greet her as I approach.

She turns to me, her face transforming from unnerved to her usual self. We hug.

'So, are you excited?' she asks, giving my arm a squeeze.

'Yeah, kind of,' I reply vaguely as I wonder whether to tell her about the whole Olly thing that's detracting from my excitement levels but then I think better of it. Now is not the time to get that off my chest, it'll only screw up my focus even more ahead of the shoot.

'Kind of?' Scarlett raises an eyebrow.

'Yeah. I mean yeah, I'm excited,' I insist with a smile. 'Really excited.'

We walk a few blocks towards the café where we've agreed to do the shoot. Becky's an avid reader and dreams of becoming a published author, so we agreed some bookish café shots would be good. Plus, the café is just down the road from where she works and she needed to fit the shoot into her busy day. I called the café yesterday to ask if it would be okay to shoot there and they helpfully promised to clear a table at the back. Scarlett and I arrive to find Becky having a cappuccino at a window seat. Her hands are shaking a little and she seems on edge about the shoot, even though she's clearly gone to a lot of effort to prepare for it. At least, it seems that way. She's heavily made-up, which I suspect is for the benefit of the pictures although it could be her standard everyday look. And she's very well dressed in clothes that look crisp and brand new. She looks brilliant, but I expect it'll take a fair few shots to get her to relax and start to feel comfortable.

I decide to start the shoot with a couple of pictures of her reading in the café, so she can get used to having her photo taken without having to engage much with the camera. She's brought along a book she's reading, so she pretends to read it while Scarlett holds up a spotlight to brighten her face. I snap away. In the first few pictures, she's a little stiff. There's some tension around her eyes but the more I snap away, the more she starts to relax. I think she actually starts to read the book and a few pictures later, I get a perfect shot.

We then take a few shots of her enjoying a cappuccino. She's still a little stiff so I decide to try something out. She's into romance novels so I suggest a little technique, getting her to imagine a romantic scenario. I ask her if she could be on a date with anyone, who it would be. Without skipping a beat, she responds, 'Ryan Gosling'. I then get her to pretend she's sitting across from Ryan Gosling.

'Okay, so Ryan's just bought you a cappuccino,' I say, glancing at the cappuccino that Scarlett fetched a few minutes ago. 'Give him your best thank-you-Ryan-you're-the-best smile.'

Becky cracks up and then starts smiling playfully.

'Ryan just suggested the best date ever. He wants to go for a candlelit meal.'

She smiles into the camera and raises an eyebrow suggestively. It's working! My weird plan is working. She no longer seems awkward!

I take a few more pictures and then we head outside and take some really nice headshots against a wall. It's a bright, clear day and with Scarlett holding up the reflector screen, the fresh February sunshine lights up Becky's face, giving her a beautiful glow. By this point, she's relaxed and got into it, and she smiles effortlessly. I take a few more in front of some trees in a nearby park. We manage to get some great shots. Becky dons a blazer and we take a few more full body slightly corporate looking shots, which she also hopes to use professionally. Becky's phone starts buzzing.

'Urgghh, sorry,' she groans. 'My boss needs me back in the office. We're working on a really demanding project and apparently the client's already arrived for our afternoon meeting.' She rolls her eyes.

'No problem!' I insist. 'We've got plenty of photos.'

'Oh great.' Becky stashes her phone back in her handbag. 'Thank you,' she says.

'No, thank you!' I insist. 'It's been fun!'

'Excellent!' Becky grins. 'You know…' she ventures, looking a little pensive. 'I was a bit nervous about this. If I'm totally honest, I was kind of dreading it, but I just knew I needed some decent photos, and actually, it's been surprisingly fun. I've really enjoyed it.'

I smile broadly. Her words are music to my ears. 'I'm so glad!'

Becky beams back, hesitates for a second and then pulls me into a hug. I have to pull my camera out of the way, but she hugs me tightly and gives Scarlett a hug too. I get the feeling the shoot has meant something to her, perhaps it's helped with confidence-building since she seems a lot more relaxed now compared to how nervous she was when we first met up.

'Thanks guys!' she says, waving over her shoulder as she turns to head back to her office.

Becky and I wave goodbye.

'Well, that went well,' Scarlett says as she collapses her reflector screen.

'Yeah, really well!' I echo, and I mean it. The shoot really did go incredibly well. Despite finding out about Olly's press release just beforehand, I somehow managed to completely put it out of my mind. What started as a deliberate effort not to think about him quickly became natural. While I was taking pictures, Olly was the furthest thing from my mind. All that mattered was the shots. But that's what happens when I'm in the zone and doing what I love: real life just somehow ceases to exist and all I care about are the pictures.

Scarlett finishes collapsing her reflector screen and zips it up inside its bag. I place my camera in its case. I can't help feeling a twinge of pride and anticipation as I think about all the images on the sim card; I'm already itching to get home this evening and edit them. As I sling my camera bag over my shoulder and Scarlett and begin walking down the street, my thoughts return to Olly. After we've chatted a little bit about the shoot, I decide to fill her in.

'Do you remember that guy I told you about? The dating agency one?'

'Derek?' Scarlett asks.

'No! Not Derek! The hot one – Olly Corrigan. The one with the tattoos?'

'Oh yeah!' Scarlett nods. 'What about him?'

'Well, he's…' I pause, not quite knowing where to start. Do I tell her about the messages we sent each other when he was masquerading as Eve? Or start with an account of our incredible date? Or do I simply tell her that I started to have feelings for him? I need to fill her in on why I began ignoring his texts, not to mention the recent news about how he's shutting down his business. And I still don't even know quite why that's bothering me so much or how I feel about it. So much has happened since I last saw Scarlett and I should probably be heading back to work, not filling her in on everything.

'What?' she presses me.

I glance at my watch. I still have half an hour until I said I'd be back at the office; not a hell of a lot of time, but I doubt – given the news he's just received – that Derek's going to be watching the clock.

'Let's go for a coffee,' I say, gesturing back towards the café.

'Okay, cool, let's do it,' Scarlett agrees.

We head back inside the café, grab coffees and sandwiches and then we sit at a table and I tell her everything. Scarlett listens patiently to the whole story while eating a cheese toastie and sipping on a mocha latte.

'So, hang on a minute,' she says, once I've got it all out. 'You got pissed off with this guy because he took other girls to the same restaurant and museum as he took you.'

'Oh, come on,' I scoff, 'when you put it like that, it sounds terrible, but it was more about the way he treated Leila. She was his client and he preyed on her. He exploited her desire to fall in love, led her on, and then never called her again. Then he had the audacity to kick her off his agency's books!'

Scarlett holds up her hands in mock surrender. 'Okay, okay, that is pretty bad, but don't you think you're being a bit hard on him? You haven't even heard his side of the story and anyway, none of us are perfect. It's not like you've never done anything bad in relationships, just luckily for you, Olly doesn't know anyone who knows you and so he can't gossip like Derek's doing.'

'Derek wasn't gossiping, he was just trying to warn me,' I insist, taking a bite of my sandwich.

'I'm not saying he wasn't well-intentioned. Derek probably did just want to warn you, but I feel like maybe you shouldn't have just cut Olly out without talking to him. You clearly care about him or you wouldn't be bothered about why he's shut his business down,' Scarlett points out.

'Suppose,' I admit, a little reluctantly.

Scarlett takes a sip of her drink.

'I guess I'd better message him,' I say eventually.

'Yep, I think you'd better,' Scarlett agrees.

I get my phone out of my bag and draft a message.

Chapter 29

When I messaged Olly at lunch, I didn't expect him to reply straight away. After all, I have been ghosting him, but he replied instantly and suggested we meet somewhere private to talk. I ventured that we go to a bar, but Olly said it 'might not be quiet enough' and suggested we meet at his office instead. So here I am, standing outside the slick offices of Elite Love Match, taking a deep breath in an effort to calm my nerves before slipping through the revolving doors and striding in. The receptionist greets me with recognition.

'Hi Polly,' she says with a friendly smile. 'Olly's waiting for you upstairs. Just head up.'

'Thanks,' I reply, smiling politely back before heading over to the lift.

I get inside and press the button for Olly's floor. I quickly check my make-up, dabbing my nose with powder as the lift shoots up the shaft. For someone who's been trying to distance herself mentally from Olly, I'm certainly not acting like I'm over him. My head is all over the pace and I don't know what to feel. I'm torn between concern and yearning, and annoyance and hurt, and all the feelings are jostling for prime position in my mind. The lift doors open and even though it's the evening, the office is still bustling. In fact, Olly's staff look so busy and pre-occupied that they don't even give me their usual once over and instead just busy themselves with work as I head to Olly's office. I knock gently on the door even though I can see him inside through the glass. He looks over from behind his monitor and gestures for me to come in.

I push the door open and there I am. Back to Olly. His office smells of his aftershave and the warm musky scent makes my heart flutter, immediately taking me back to the night we spend together, cuddled up in his bed, talking late into the night, wrapped in each other's arms.

'Hi,' I mutter, shuffling over to his desk

'Hi Polly,' Olly replies, his expression still blank and unreadable. He's sitting stiffly at his desk, looking ridiculously handsome as usual, and he's dressed in a typically outlandish outfit of a yellow argyle jumper teamed with black and white striped trousers, but something doesn't feel right. His jaw looks tense.

I sit down in the seat opposite him. Our eyes lock. His are sad and uneasy, and immediately, I feel that magnetic draw to him. I want – need – to find out whether everything's okay with him. All the feelings I've been suppressing all week begin flooding back. Regardless of everything Derek said, and despite me convincing myself that Olly's probably just another player, I have to know that he's okay, because I care about him. In spite of everything, I really do care.

'What's happened Olly? Why are you closing down? Are you okay? Has something happened?' I blurt out.

Olly laughs. He just seems amused.

'What?' I ask as I watch his lips twisting into a smile.

'That's one of your things,' he says, as though making a mental note. 'You don't just ask one question, you ask a series, like a torrent of questions. I noticed it at the weekend too.'

'Oh, haha! Right...' I smile awkwardly. 'Well, can you answer them please?!' I ask, mirroring his playful tone.

'Okay. What happened? Nothing. I just did a lot of thinking. Why am I closing down? Because I'm a fake. Am I okay? Yes, I guess I'm okay. Has something happened? Yes, I've made a decision that I want to be less of a phoney, I want to change.'

'Wait, what?' I frown as I try to wrap my head around his answers.

'See why people usually ask just one question at a time?' Olly jokes. 'Don't change though. I like it.' He smiles affectionately and it's as though I haven't been ignoring him for the past week. Despite my coldness, he seems warm and happy to see me.

'Yeah, I can see that. So, what do you mean, you've "done a lot of thinking and you've made a decision to change"?' I ask, doing air quotes.

'Well...' Olly glances away and a pained look replaces his playfulness. All of a sudden, it occurs to me that maybe I'm prying. Maybe this is none of my business at all. As long as Olly's healthy and nothing terrible has happened to him, then is it really appropriate for me to pry into his personal life, especially since I've ignored him for a week?

'Erm...' Olly hesitates as though he can't quite find the right words.

'It's okay,' I say. 'You don't have to tell me.'

Olly raises an eyebrow, looking perplexed.

'I mean, I haven't spoken to you for a week, I don't really have any right to just rock up at your workplace and ask you to tell me all about your deepest darkest thoughts.'

Olly laughs. 'What if I like sharing my deepest darkest thoughts with you?' he asks, holding my gaze.

Instantly, I feel a surge of chemistry flood through me. That undeniable spark. Why is he so irresistible? Despite everything Derek's said and despite a week of resolutely ignoring him, how is it that all I need to do is gaze into his gorgeous brown eyes to be reduced to mush?

I look away, breaking eye contact. 'I'm sorry I ignored your messages,' I say. 'I started to have doubts because—'

'Because of Derek,' Olly finishes my sentence.

'Yep, basically,' I admit. I may be dropping Derek in it, but it doesn't really matter anymore since they're no longer business competitors.

'I knew that was why.' Olly sighs. Derek's not my biggest fan, and to be honest, with good reason.' Olly smiles sadly.

'What do you mean?' I ask.

Olly leans back in his chair, looking deflated. 'I haven't always been as respectful as I should have been towards women,' he admits, reluctantly meeting my gaze. His expression seems truly contrite and I can tell he's been doing some serious soul-searching. 'I've dated some people I probably shouldn't have and maybe I didn't treat them quite as well as I should have done.'

'You mean Leila,' I suggest.

'Exactly. I knew Derek would have told you about her,' Olly says sheepishly.

'Yeah, I was a bit disappointed,' I confess. As I say the words out loud, I realise – with a pang of emotion – just how true they are. I was really, truly, disappointed in Olly, and instead of acknowledging those feelings, I've spent the whole week pushing them down by ignoring all of Olly's messages and throwing myself into building my new business. And until now, it's worked a treat. I force myself to look at Olly and as silly as it seems – considering we've only had one proper date – my eyes have gone glassy with tears.

'I'm so sorry, Polly,' Olly says, his eyes full of sincerity. 'I didn't behave well. I shouldn't have just kicked Leila out of the agency, that was cowardly. I could have got one of my colleagues to look after her as a client, but she was freaking me out. I couldn't handle her behaviour, so I took the easiest option.' Olly sighs.

'What do you mean she was "freaking you out"?' I ask. As far as Derek's story went, it was only Olly who was behaving badly.

'We spent the weekend together and the next day, she messaged me a hundred times. Literally. I was at work, so I couldn't reply. She tried to call over and over and left a ton of voicemails. I mean a ton. Thirty. I knew then why she was single. I'd found it baffling before. She was pretty, she seemed to have a good personality. Perhaps she was a bit picky, but I couldn't see why she hadn't found a boyfriend, particularly considering how hard she'd been trying, but then I realised that she was the kind of obsessive who stalks all her dates. I was busy with work so I ignored her. I turned my mobile off and finally got some peace. The next day, I turned it on and a tsunami of messages flooded in again. I ignored them all and then you'll never guess what she did…' Olly sighs, shaking his head.

'What?' I ask a little apprehensively.

'She called the office and convinced one of the interns she was my mother and that she was sick and urgently needed to speak to me. The intern pulled me out of an important meeting, told me there was a family emergency and naturally, I started freaking out. My mum has a heart murmur, I was worried something really serious might have happened. Then I answered the phone and it was Leila. She was ranting at me with a barrage of angry accusations and insisting that I'd used her, that I was a terrible person, all sorts. I was in the middle of the office. I couldn't have that kind of conversation – and I didn't even *want* to have that conversation. As far as I was concerned, I didn't owe her anything. We'd spent less than twenty-four hours in each other's company and yet she was demanding all this attention from me. I flipped out. The mother thing really wound me up so I told the intern there and then to terminate her contract and refund her, then I called my mobile provider and blocked her number.'

'Wow. Derek definitely didn't tell me that part,' I utter, in shock.

'No, I didn't think he would have. I don't think he even knows. I may not have behaved particularly well but I didn't go around trashing Leila across town. Unfortunately, she didn't spare me the same courtesy,' Olly comments bitterly.

'I would never have thought she was like that. I met her at the Valentine's Day party and she seemed really nice.'

'Yeah.' Olly nods. 'She seems a lot better now. I know I whinge about Derek, but I think he helped her out. Derek's a good guy.'

I stare at Olly, trying to take all of this in. He's complimenting Derek. Not long ago, these two were arch nemeses.

'Derek treated Leila with a lot more kindness than I did,' Olly says sadly, and I can tell he really does feel remorseful.

'She sounded crazy. And what she did with pretending to be your mum – that's just nuts.'

'Yeah, but she needed support. Probably professional support and all I did was treat her like a nuisance. I didn't try to help her. That's the difference between Derek and me. He's patient. He treats people like people. He doesn't just try to create efficient business-like love matches like I do, eliminating people when they no longer fit the right requirements.'

Olly's right. Derek does have a remarkably personal approach. He cares about everyone, and not just in a broad meaningless way but in a personal sensitive way. Even I've been affected by it. I'd been lost in New York before I met him and he's helped me find a sense of belonging. He's been caring and sweet, despite his shady past. He's become something of a father figure to me.

'Derek is pretty cool,' I comment.

'Yeah, he's a good guy,' Olly agrees.

'But I still don't understand. How come you suddenly closed down the business? How come you've suddenly had all these revelations? What caused it all?'

'Another question avalanche,' Olly jokes. 'I know you're probably not going to believe this, but last weekend genuinely meant something to me and when you stopped talking to me, it got me thinking. I started reflecting on everything. I figured you'd been talking to Derek. I could see why you wouldn't want to talk to me. I spend all my time focusing on my clients and trying to set them up with people, but I have no luck in romance myself. My love life has been a mess for years, ever since my divorce. Actually, it was a mess while I was married too!' Olly laughs, rolling his eyes.

'The thing is,' he continues, 'I'm good at finding matches for other people but I can't seem to find anyone for myself. I felt like a hypocrite. When I realised you didn't want to date me, it forced me to take a long hard look in the mirror. I realised my approach to love has been all wrong. All this time, I've been going for people I thought would be right for me: women around my age, high-flying career women with a certain look and then you came along. You weren't the kind of person I'd expected to fall for and yet I haven't been able to stop thinking about you. You made me realise that finding someone you like isn't about ticking off a mental checklist of criteria; it just happens sometimes. I started to realise that my approach to love has been wrong all this time. I felt unqualified to run a dating agency given that I'm still figuring all this stuff out.'

Olly sighs, before continuing. 'It pains the businessman in me to admit it, but I got thinking about what you told me about Derek and his wife's medical bills. Someone like Derek *is* better suited to running a dating agency than me. He's actually found love, he's a caring guy. I've just been this dog-eat-dog idiot thinking only about myself. I have my PR agency to worry about, we're already doing well. It occurred to me that maybe I should step down and leave the dating side of things to Derek.' He smiles awkwardly, looking sheepish.

'Okay, wow…' I murmur, taking it in. I think back to the message he sent me the other night when he mentioned that he wanted to make some 'big changes' to his life.

'Is this what you meant in that message when you said you wanted to make big changes?' I ask.

'Yes,' Olly admits.

I can't help feeling bad that while he was reflecting and striving to make changes to his life, I was just ignoring him completely. I guess I just thought I was yet another one of his girls; it never occurred to me that Olly might actually care, really care. And it had never occurred to me that deep down, he might respect Derek.

'I can't believe I was the trigger,' I comment, feeling almost guilty. Meeting me seems to have completely shaken Olly up.

'Yes.' Olly looks deep into my eyes and my stomach does that twisty nervous excited thing again. 'Why do you find that so hard to believe, Polly?' Olly asks, holding my gaze. 'Our date was good, wasn't it? We had a good time, didn't we?'

I think of how it felt to be lying in Olly's bedroom – the smell of his sheets, the cosy feeling, the late-night confessions, the sense of intimacy and belonging, of feeling like I had a safe warm cocoon in this big crazy city. It's an understatement to say we had a good time; it was bloody brilliant. It was perfect. Except, while it may have felt unique and novel for me to be lying in his arms chatting late into the night, it wasn't novel for Olly.

'It was amazing. But it wasn't unique to me, was it? You took Leila to The Fifth as well! She came back to your place and you stayed up late chatting to her too. I guess when you find a date idea that works, why deviate from it?' I say bitterly.

Olly visibly winces. 'You hit the nail on the head,' he says. 'I found a date routine that worked, and I kept using it.'

I sink my head into my hands. 'Great,' I grumble, looking over my shoulder towards the door. I almost want to get up and go.

'Hear me out,' Olly says, sensing my discomfort. 'You know that thing I was saying about reducing people to a checklist of qualities and trying to make efficient matches, well, I applied that same no-nonsense approach to my own dating life. I got a date routine down and I just kept using it. I'll admit, it was soulless. I somehow became a bit soulless. It wasn't deliberate, but I'm a businessman. In PR, I run a smooth efficient ship. We hit targets week in, week out. We're ruthlessly efficient and our clients love us, but you can't run a dating agency like that. A dating agency needs heart and that's where I was lacking.'

'I see.' I can't bring myself to look at him.

'I developed a good date routine, but all I was having were good dates. And yes, I had fun, but I wasn't truly connecting with anyone,' Olly says.

I steal a glance at him. He looks embarrassed, but his eyes are sincere and vulnerable. He picks up a pen from his desk and spins it around nervously between his fingers.

'Things were different when you and I had our date. I'll admit, I rolled out the usual date routine, but I truly enjoyed it with you. With you, it wasn't just a good date, it was a fantastic date. I felt the spark and I know that sounds a bit lame coming from someone like me, but I did. I'd truly begun to wonder if I'd ever feel that again. I've dated amazing women since my wife and I split up, but I didn't connect with any of them like I connected with you.'

'Really?' I ask.

'Yes, really,' Olly says, his eyes unmoving from mine. 'I know on paper, we're probably not a conventional match. I'm twenty years older than you. I've grown a bit cold and cynical, whereas you're still heartfelt and open and optimistic. But for some reason, I feel like we work well together. It's like some strange alchemy happens when we're together. We click. And sparks fly.'

Olly looks into my eyes with such affection and tenderness, and I want to say something, but I feel overwhelmed and lost for words.

Olly smiles to himself. 'I always thought that was just a lame phrase from romance novels or movies but I feel it when I'm around you. I literally feel it.' Olly looks into my eyes. 'Okay, well not literally, flying sparks might be kind of painful, but you know what I mean, don't you?'

I nod, smiling. 'I totally know what you mean,' I say, my eyes soaking him up. When I'm around him, I feel like I'm drinking him in, absorbing him, uninterested in anything else. It doesn't matter whether we're wrapped in each other's arms in Olly's bed, cocooned in the sheets, when we're around each other, nothing else matters. It's like the real world just disintegrates, everything beyond a small radius of each other just falls away. Remembering about the real world, I suddenly look over my shoulder to catch several of Olly's colleagues watching us through the glass panels of the office. They quickly look away. Olly sees me looking and gets up to pull a blind across the window.

'Nosy assholes,' he tuts.

I laugh as he sits back down. All the way on the opposite side of the desk. He feels too far away. I get up and walk around towards him and instantly, our bodies connect like magnets seizing upon each other. Olly slips his arms around my waist and I wrap mine around his shoulders. I sit on his lap and he pulls me close. We kiss. Hungrily and yet gently. I brush his hair from his forehead and gaze into his eyes. They're so rich and full of emotion and even though he may be a bit of a player with quite a few notches on his bed posts, I know he's being genuine when it comes to me. I can feel it. He isn't faking this. Our date may have been formulaic, but the look in his eyes is most definitely not a routine.

'Oh God,' I sigh. 'I missed you, Olly. I'm so sorry for ignoring you. I was just hurt. I didn't want to get close to you and then to end up as just another girl tossed onto the scrap heap.'

Olly laughs. 'Bit harsh!' He wraps his arms tighter around my waist. 'I'd never throw you onto the scrap heap. You've changed everything for me.'

'Everything?' I ask.

'Yeah. I didn't think I'd fall in love but then you made me realise I might be wrong. You made me realise I'm a total phoney. I go around matching people, creating relationships, when I can't even have a relationship myself. I can't even have original dates, let alone relationships!'

I laugh as I play with his hair, cup my hand on his jaw, soak him in.

'You made me realise that I need to experience love properly before I can go about being a matchmaker,' Olly says.

'I know the feeling,' I sigh. 'So that was the "change to your personal circumstances" on the press release then?'

'Yes,' Olly admits.

I can't help smiling, thinking of that official-sounding press release having such a personal and vulnerable side to it.

'I don't want to run a dating agency anymore. I just want to date. I want to figure love out for myself. And if you're up for it, I'd like to date you, from scratch this time,' Olly says with a warm wide smile. He reaches up to my face and strokes his finger along my cheek, adoringly.

'Okay, I think that could be arranged,' I say, leaning in for another kiss.

Chapter 30

I'm not really sure that Olly or I knew what to do for our first proper unscripted date, so like most couples in the early stages of dating, we decided to go to a nice restaurant for lunch. Olly said we could go anywhere, and I knew he genuinely meant anywhere, and so I suggested Per Se – the new French bistro with the review I circled in *Time* magazine a few weeks ago. It felt too tempting. After all, I've been dreaming of going to nice restaurants like that ever since I arrived in New York and what better opportunity than to go with a guy I'm really into.

We meet at Grand Central Station and have a drink at Campbell Bar to catch up before heading to the restaurant. Campbell Bar is another place I've always wanted to go. The converted office of a Jazz Age financier, it's like something from *The Great Gatsby* with low lighting, and leather, wood and brash furnishings. Olly and I order bourbon cocktails and sit in the corner, chatting away as we sip our drinks. He's dressed up for our date, having donned a white shirt and cable knit sweater, and with his tortoiseshell glasses and classic handsomeness, he looks almost like he could belong in the Twenties, except for his signet rings and the tattoos poking out from under his sleeves. I lace my fingers through his, the butterflies on his arms like the ones in my stomach.

We finish our drinks and walk through Grand Central Station. Its marble walls and floor give the light a buttery sepia hue. A saxophonist busks, playing bluesy melodies, with an upturned hat on the ground to collect change from passers-by. Olly drops in a few dollars and we walk arm-in-arm, the sound growing quieter as we leave the station. I feel like I'm starring in a Twenties movie and I couldn't be happier. But for once, I feel like the lead character and not just someone on the sidelines. It's magical.

We walk a few blocks towards Per Se and join a small queue of people waiting to get in. Clearly, everyone's been reading the rave reviews the restaurant's been getting as it's already bustling even though it's only been open a few weeks. I glance down the queue and spot a woman dressed in an expensive-looking long lace maxi dress standing a few places in front of me and Olly with long luscious blonde hair. Her laugh is familiar and it's only when she tosses her hair over her shoulder and glances over that I realise who it is: it's Alicia. She's dyed her hair from brown to blonde but it's her alright. She clocks me too, after a second's pause, no doubt taken aback by my new haircut. She then quickly looks away, glancing at Olly instead. From the quirk of her eyebrow I can tell she recognises him. She frowns in puzzlement as she turns back to her companion; she's clearly wondering what the hell Olly and I are doing together.

'Why are you cowering?' Olly asks, and it's only then that I realise I've shrunk behind him a little bit.

'Oh. That girl.' I nod my head in Alicia's direction. 'She's just someone I know. We had a bit of a fall out,' I tell Olly.

He looks at me, curiously, as though expecting more.

'I took pictures for her wanky cookbook, she didn't credit me, so Brandon sued her.'

Olly snorts with laughter so loudly that Alicia turns around, looking a little irritated. 'Are you serious?' Olly whispers.

'Yep!'

'Brandon worked his legal wonders! Wow.'

286

'I look after my clients, they look after me,' I reply.

Olly laughs. 'You sound like the mafia.'

As the queue nudges slowly forward, I fill Olly in on the whole story. He gets his phone out and looks Alicia up on Instagram.

'Olly!' I hiss. 'Not here. What if she sees?'

Olly rolls his eyes indulgently. 'She's not going to see,' he says, holding his phone close as he scrolls through her feed.

'Fine,' I sigh, cupping my hand behind his phone to make sure it's tilted away from her.

'Big fan of bananas, isn't she?' Olly comments, scanning a few pictures Alicia posted about a banana smoothie recipe. 'They really shouldn't be a health food, do you know how packed they are with sugar?' Olly says, before launching into a story about a friend of his who had some kind of issue with diarrhoea while following a banana smoothie diet. I'm half-listening but I can't help glancing over at Alicia. The last time I saw her, I found her kind of intimidating with her bossy attitude and army of cool friends, but now I don't feel any of that. I feel confident and happy, content in my own skin. I feel like a different person. It's strange to look at her with completely different eyes and realise that she's not intimidating to me now at all.

The maître d' ushers the people in front of Alicia into the restaurant and then with a strained bright look, Alicia plasters a smile onto her face and asks for a table for two.

'Do you have a reservation?' The maître d' asks, regarding her blankly.

'Oh, no, sorry…' Alicia replies with a tactical flutter of her lashes.

'I'm sorry, but if you don't have a reservation, we can't let you in,' the maître d' says firmly, already looking over Alicia's shoulder at the next people in line.

'But, the people in front didn't have a reservation,' Alicia comments, her cheeks flushing.

'I'm sorry, there's nothing I can do,' the maître d' replies in

287

a clipped, disinterested tone. Alicia's cheeks grow redder. Her discomfort is palpable. She's clearly dying to get into this restaurant, but here she is, dressed to the nines and being turned away.

The maître d' looks down the line and clocks Olly.

'Olly!' he says, his eyes lighting up. Olly looks up from his phone and a big smile spreads across his face – that winning smile that everyone loves and that just makes him naturally charismatic. Even watching him smile makes me smile. He steps forward and greets the maître d', clapping his arms around him. Then he turns and introduces me. The maître d' leans in for a hug, kissing me on both cheeks, his eyes sparkling charmingly. I hug him, smiling politely, but I can feel Alicia watching me and I can't help thinking of the cool hard way he spoke to her, only to turn on the charm five seconds later with me. He clearly only wants to let in friends, or friends of friends.

Olly and the maître d' catch up, chatting a bit about business, before the maître d' remembers about the queue behind us.

'Table for two, guys?' he says. 'Did you make a reservation?'

'Oh no, we didn't…' Olly says, a little awkwardly.

'No problem,' the maître d' declares with a charming smile. 'I'll show you to your table.'

'Great, thanks,' Olly says, as the maître d' ushers us into the restaurant.

'Hang on a minute,' Alicia pipes up. The maître d' turns to her, looking faintly irritated.

'Yes?' he answers with a faint eye roll, and I have to admit, even though he's being nice to us, he's clearly a bit of a dick.

'I thought you said you had no tables for people without reservations?' Alicia says.

Oh God. I glance down at the ground, wishing it would swallow me up. This is so cringe-worthy.

'Uhhh…' The maître d' stammers, glancing uncomfortably at me and Olly.

We all stand in silence for a few seconds, although it feels like ages.

'Look, why don't you just give our table to Alicia?' I suggest.

Olly shoots me a stunned look. The maître d' looks completely taken aback and Alicia's eyes widen with hope. She doesn't even attempt to object, she clearly just wants to get inside the restaurant and start posting photos on Instagram. As long as she gets in, she doesn't care how cringe-worthy and awkward it is to get inside. She's so desperate that I almost feel sorry for her. I may have wanted to come to Per Se, but she needs it more than me. She lives for this fancy vapid Insta-worthy life, whereas I have Olly by my side and we could eat in McDonald's and still have a perfect evening.

'Come on Olly,' I say in a low voice, 'we can come back another day.'

I squeeze his hand and he looks into my eyes, and an understanding passes between us. Even though technically, it's only our second date, it's like we've already mastered non-verbal communication.

The maître d' looks at Olly, expecting an answer.

'Yeah, let her have our table. We'll come back next weekend,' Olly says.

'Right, okay,' the maître d' grumbles, clearly not particularly pleased. 'If you're sure?'

'Yeah, we're sure,' Olly insists.

'Okay, well in that case, you can come through,' the maître d' replies in a terse tone to Alicia.

She grins and links her arm under her friend's before following the maître d' into the restaurant. He and Olly say goodbye.

'Oh, thanks Polly,' she throws over her shoulder as she heads inside. You'd think after everything that's happened between us, that she might be a little uncomfortable or awkward, but all she cares about is having got into the restaurant. Brandon was right: the money was nothing to her and neither was the legal notice.

I smile to myself, knowing that that chapter is closed and our paths will probably never cross again.

'It's okay,' I reply, but she's already turned her back to me as she disappears into the restaurant. I roll my eyes indulgently.

'I don't get why you'd want to be nice to her,' Olly comments. 'After what she did to you.'

I shrug. 'She's Alicia. All she has is Instagrammable restaurants. I have you,' I tell him as I link my arm through his and snuggle close.

Olly smiles indulgently back. 'Come on you,' he says, linking his fingers through mine as we turn and walk away from the queue.

After wandering around for a bit, we find ourselves inside a pizza place, sitting in a booth, enjoying two big greasy slices of pizza from striped paper trays.

'This is hardly the romantic dinner I'd envisaged,' Olly teases, before taking a bite.

'It's perfect,' I insist, and it is. We're sitting opposite each other, so close in the small booth that our legs are overlapping under the table. Grainy Italian pop songs are spilling out from speakers behind the counter and a waiter places a flickering tea light in a glass cup in between our plates. It's cosy and actually, it couldn't be any better.

'It is perfect,' Olly agrees.

We exchange another meaningful glance before tucking into our pizza, while chatting away about everything and anything, from whether anchovies are delicious (Olly's opinion) or so disgusting that they shouldn't even be considered edible (my view), to our work goals and my new business venture.

'Do you know what you should do? The dating profile pictures thing is a good USP but it's a bit limiting. You should offer general portrait photography. Think about it, every single person you take photos for will have friends they could recommend you to, but if you only do dating photos, then they'll only mention you to their single friends. You're limiting your market. Change your tag line to 'Photographer specialising in dating profile pictures that capture your personality and make you look great, as well as portrait photography for professional or personal use.' Boom. Double the market.'

'You memorised my Instagram bio?' I joke, noting that he recalled the first part word for word.

'Of course!' Olly smiles before taking a bite of his pizza, having effortlessly made an incredibly insightful analysis of my business, as though it were no more of a big deal than asking the chef for extra anchovies. I watch him eating and I'm struck with yet another wave of admiration. Not only is he incredibly sexy, smart, sensitive and cool, but he's also savvy and entrepreneurial. He'd be the kind of boyfriend who would support me in everything, from being myself, to giving up a table in an exclusive restaurant for an annoying Instagrammer to helping me grow my business. This is the kind of relationship that will nourish my heart, soul, body and mind. All the reservations I've had before over settling down with a guy don't feel relevant to Olly. I don't feel like he's going to be a distraction. Unlike all the other guys, who I feared would hold me back from achieving my goals, from moving to New York to doing well at university, I feel like having Olly in my life will help, rather than hinder me. I feel comfortable about the prospect of being with him. He's right, there is a weird alchemy that just makes us work.

'Why are you looking at me like that?' Olly says, giving me a wry look.

'Sorry!' I glance away, a little embarrassed. 'I was just thinking that you're so right about my business description. That's exactly what I'll do!'

I take a bite of my pizza.

We finish lunch and head back out onto the street.

'So, what do you want to do now?' Olly asks, clapping his hands together. 'New York is our oyster.'

'Do you know what I've always wanted to do...?'

'What's that?'

'It's a bit touristy...' I hesitate, feeling a bit embarrassed.

Olly smiles. 'Hit me.'

'I've always wanted to go to the Statue of Liberty. Like actually visit it, go inside it.'

'Hmm... that's a first.'

'Not on the date script, eh?'

'No, definitely not!' Olly replies. 'I don't know anyone who's done that. Aren't you meant to just look at it from afar, not actually visit it?'

I laugh. 'I want to visit it. I've always looked at it from afar, but I want to see it up close. I've just been waiting for the right moment,' I admit, thinking back to the fantasy I've had since childhood, of standing right inside the statue's crown. I think of the little stick figure I drew in biro in the statue's crown. I want to be that stick figure; I want to do my 12-year-old self proud and fulfil her dream.

'But why?' Olly asks, bemused.

'Because it's cool! It's iconic. Anyway, don't forget, you're a New Yorker, you take this stuff for granted,' I remind Olly. 'I grew up in Cornwall, I'm still a New York fan girl at heart.'

'The ultimate country bumpkin tourist,' Olly teases, pinching my side.

'Ouch!' I grin, pulling away. 'So, are you game?'

'Yeah, I'm game,' Olly laughs. 'Even though I can't believe we're actually going to do this.'

We jump in a cab and head across Manhattan down to Battery Park, where the ferry that takes groups of tourists to the Statue of Liberty departs. We buy our tickets from the kiosk and board the ferry, which sways heavily on the water. It's a bright day and we climb up to the top deck, where we manage to find a space to sit on a bench at the back. The ferry is full of tourists, including a middle-aged couple wearing matching 'I love New

York' T-shirts and cheesy green visors shaped like Statue of Liberty crowns. They enthusiastically take photos of everything, from the inside the ferry to the view of the dock. For a moment, they stop taking photos to buy a bottle of water from a drinks machine.

'How much do you bet they'll take a picture of the water?' Olly jokes in a low whisper.

I giggle. 'Shhh…' I hiss, but then sure enough the woman comes back with the water, unscrews the cap and then nudges her husband to take a picture of her drinking it.

'Told you,' Olly sniggers and I can't help laughing.

An ocean breeze blows through our hair.

'Well, you know what they say,' I comment, giving Olly a side-long look.

'What's that?' He raises an eyebrow.

'If you can't beat 'em, join 'em.' I hold out my phone to take a selfie of us.

Olly rolls his eyes indulgently. We snuggle up and grin into the camera as I take a picture, the wind making our hair blow over our shoulders. I turn my camera around and take a look at the picture. It's adorable. We look stupidly happy.

'That's cute,' Olly says, glancing at the picture before planting a kiss on my forehead.

We cuddle up, fending off the cool sea breeze as the ferry crosses the water towards the statue. Manhattan retreats into the distance, the sharp winter sunlight glints off its skyscrapers. It feels a little strange to be seeing it from a distance after spending years in the thick of it. The only time I've ever seen Manhattan from the water was during a holiday visit when I was 15. I fell in love with New York back then and seeing the city from afar now still fills me with the same sense of awe, yet the longing I had as a teenager desperate to move to the Big Apple as soon as I could is replaced by a feeling of gratitude that living here is now my reality. Just before I sink too deep into reflection, the ferry arrives and the Statue of Liberty stands tall and proud, her blueish green surface bright and almost glowing up close.

'Wow,' Olly says, taking her in.

'Impressive, isn't she?' I add.

'Incredible,' Olly utters.

We stop at an information stand and read about how the statue came to be, from being conceptualised by French sculptor Frédéric Auguste Bartholdi to having its structure designed by the engineer Gustave Eiffel, who later went on to create the eponymous Eiffel tower. We read about all the obstacles the statue faced in its creation, from encountering financing challenges which led to a funding campaign launched in newspapers across the city urging residents to donate, to the structure itself being transported from France in 350 pieces that had to be assembled upon arrival in the States, like the world's biggest jigsaw puzzle. The more I read, the more the statue starts to feel like more than just a symbol of the American dream, but evidence of it in itself: the statue's creation shows that with hard work and determination, you can achieve the seemingly impossible.

We head over to the entrance and present our tickets, before making our way up the narrow winding staircases leading up to the crown, getting breathless as we climb the 354 steps to the top. But once we're inside the crown, it pays off. The ceiling is domed, reinforced with Eiffel's heavy steel frame and it feels strange to be looking out of windows that are the gaps in the statue's iconic crown.

'We're here!' Olly wraps his arms around my waist from behind, holding me close as we take in the views.

'We're here,' I echo, feeling a little emotional as I think of the 12-year-old me who stuck the poster of the Statue of Liberty on her bedroom wall and vowed to go there, to get to New York. I've become the stick figure; it feels like my dreams are now truly a reality.

'What's up?' Olly asks, looking at me with concern as my eyes well up. I decide not to tell him. That stick figure was a private fantasy – a girl making a secret wish – and it still feels private. It's precious, like a talisman I kept close to my chest that helped materialise my dreams over time.

'Nothing, I'm just so happy to be here with you,' I tell him.

'Aww, me too Polly,' Olly says, giving me a squeeze.

As I look out over the city, taking it in, my nostalgia changes into something else: a calm but resolute sense of determination and hope. For the first time, I truly feel like I might actually make it here. My photography dreams might come true. Success doesn't feel like some vague, desperate dream – a fraught sense of longing like the feeling I've had I've had in recent months wrought with frustration and self-pity. Instead, it feels achievable, a graspable reality. My business may only be in its infancy and I may still be working as a matchmaker at a dating agency, but it's a start. I feel happy. I may not be quite where I want to be yet, but I've found a good place to launch myself from. I'm on my way. And I feel it – that distinct New York spirit of freedom, optimism and ambition that's drawn people here for years.

Olly pulls me closer and I sink back into him, feeling his warmth through his thick jumper. I look up at him and see that he's smiling.

'This wasn't such a terrible idea, was it?' I comment, nudging him.

'No, it wasn't. Hopefully it will be the first of many not-so-terrible ideas and not-so-terrible things we get to do together,' he says, his eyes soft and tender.

'Definitely.' I smile.

Neither Olly or myself may be particularly great at relationships – especially not for people who call themselves matchmakers – but it's clear that we both want to get better. We're both committed to doing our best to make this work, and despite our questionable track records, that's good enough for me. There may be a small part of me that still feels daunted by the idea of opening up and giving my heart to him, but a larger part just feels incredibly grateful to have found my match and excited about what's to come.

'Come here,' Olly says softly.

I turn around to face him, smiling up at him as I slip my hands under his jacket and wrap them around his body, taking in his warmth. He smiles back at me.

I close my eyes and we kiss.

Acknowledgements

A massive thanks to my brilliant editor, Charlotte Mursell, for her incredibly insightful suggestions and feedback. It's a real privilege to work with such a talented and supportive editor.

Thanks to the team at HQ Digital for turning my dreams into reality by publishing my books. It means so much to me.

Thanks to my mum and trusted friends for all the encouagement. And last but definitely not least, thank you to all the readers, bloggers and reviewers for buying my books and cheering me on.

**Please read on for an extract from
Zoe May's *How (Not) To Date A Prince***

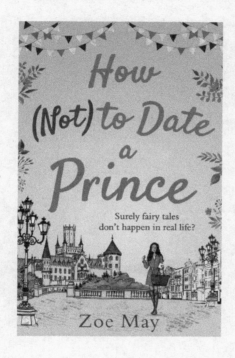

Chapter One

'What on earth is this?' I thrust the news agenda onto my boss's desk.

Phil reluctantly tears his gaze away from an article he's reading and casts a withering glance at the agenda, which assigns reporters to the key news items of the day. Normally, I look forward to getting my hands on it, to see what I'm working on, but today, it's a different story.

'What about it?' He shrugs, turning his attention back to his screen. He pushes his glasses up the ridge of his nose to continue reading the article, as if I'm not actually there.

I push the news agenda closer to him, dragging his attention back to it.

'The royal wedding?' I tap my fingernail against the part of the agenda which shows my name next to coverage of the latest royal engagement.

'Is this a typo?' I ask, even though I know it's not. If there's one thing Phil refuses to tolerate, it's typos.

'Yes, the royal wedding,' Phil states simply. 'Is there an issue?'

I narrow my eyes at him, trying to figure out what he's playing at, but he looks back at me with bored disinterest. If it wasn't for the fact that he's been my boss for the past ten years, sometimes

I'd genuinely think Phil hates me, but his off-hand manner is part of the package that comes with being a news editor at a national tabloid newspaper. The tougher you appear, the more revered you become. I used to live in fear of Phil as a junior reporter, until a few years passed and I began to realise that underneath his gruff no-nonsense exterior lurks a secret softy who's more likely to be worrying about how much revision his fifteen-year-old daughter Abby's been putting in for her GCSEs than about what's happening in the news.

'The *royal wedding*? Since when do I cover the royals?' I scoff. 'Let alone weddings!'

'One second.' Phil's phone rings and he takes the call.

I sigh. You see, royal weddings are not my thing. I'm a politics reporter. I cover Westminster, not weddings! My last piece was an interview with the Chancellor of the Exchequer on the latest budget reform. And before that, I was covering a vote on welfare cuts in the House of Commons. I write about the kind of policies that shape the country. I don't cover weddings! Weddings aren't news. Weddings are just lace and flowers and cake and silliness. Even royal ones.

'Sorry, not interested.' Phil slams the phone down into its cradle. 'Bloody freelancer with some batshit story. How do these people get my number?'

'Dunno,' I mutter. 'Anyway …' I tap my fingernail against the agenda.

'Needs must, Sam. Ella's on maternity leave, so I'm leaving it with you,' Phil sighs.

Ella is the *Daily Post*'s royal editor. Obsessed with marriage, family life and patriotism, she's far better cut out for the gig than I am. When the shock engagement between reality TV star Holly Greene and Prince Isaac of Norway was announced, Ella squealed so loudly that she silenced the newsroom. This story was absolutely made for a romantic like her, but she left work last week at six months' pregnant. If she wasn't already ecstatic to be having a baby, she'd be kicking herself for missing out on covering Holly and Prince Isaac's wedding.

To be fair, it has everything. A rags-to-riches tale of a sweet girl-next-door type from Leeds – Holly – who rose to fame on a cheesy island survival reality TV show, with the nation embracing her down-to-earth character and surprisingly quick one-liners. She took on various presenting jobs until she ended up fronting *The Morning People* – the nation's most-watched breakfast show. Holly's dated a couple of other celebrities, but she's always been coy about her love life in the press and never seemed to have a long-term boyfriend. Then bam, it emerged that she'd been swept off her feet by Prince Isaac – a gorgeous strapping Norwegian prince first in line to the throne, who she'd interviewed on TV when he'd been visiting the UK to promote his charity work. According to reports, it was pretty much love at first sight. If Holly hadn't already had the nation hooked with her dramatic rise to fame, her engagement to a dashing prince was the perfect fairy-tale ending – giving hope to every normal girl in the country that she too could come from nothing and have a happily-ever-after. Even I can admit that it's a sweet story, but it's not exactly political by any stretch of the imagination and politics is what I do. It's my job! Plus, I'm not exactly the biggest fan of weddings. Not after mine ended three years ago when my fiancé stood me up at the altar.

'But I don't cover weddings,' I whine. 'This is just—'

'Look, Sam,' Phil interrupts, fixing me with a pointed look. 'I know you like your nitty-gritty Westminster stories but why not lighten up for once? Do you realise how many reporters would kill for the chance to cover the royal wedding for a national newspaper? This is the biggest story of the year. You're one in a million right now. You should be thanking me.'

'But …'

Phil rolls his eyes, when the assistant news editor, Jeremy, who's sitting next to him, butts in.

'Earthquake in Mexico. Seven point two on the Richter scale. Five dead,' he says, quoting a Reuters report open on his computer screen.

'Get the TV on,' Phil barks and, before I know it, they're turning up the volume on the enormous TV screens that dangle from the ceiling of the newsroom and tuning in to the coverage.

'Get on that, Matt,' Phil orders one of the news reporters who begins scrolling through coverage on Twitter, one eye on the news broadcast.

I stand there for a moment, lingering by Phil's desk, half watching the crumbling wreckage on TV.

'Still here?' Phil asks, raising an eyebrow in my direction. 'Go and do a feature on the happy couple. Where they met. How they fell in love. A real heart-warmer.'

'A real *heart-warmer*?!'

Phil shoots me a look, before glancing up at the live footage of a town being reduced to rubble.

'How close are you from getting that online, Matt?' he says over his shoulder. 'We don't need much. Just a couple of pars.'

Matt's sweating at his desk as he bashes out a few sentences in a mad rush to get the story onto our website before our rivals publish it.

'Five minutes,' he mutters, over a flurry of typing.

Reluctantly, Phil turns his attention back to me. I'm well aware that I've outstayed my welcome. I'm old news, but I don't care. Yes, journalism is fast-paced, but that doesn't mean my boss can just change my role to royal reporter overnight and inform me on a sheet of paper the next day.

'Sam, just go and do it, okay?' Phil groans.

'I'm not happy about this. You know how I feel about weddings,' I add in a lower voice, hoping none of our other colleagues catch my words.

Even saying them out loud gives me that shiver-down-the-spine sinking feeling of dread and it's been years since my fiancé

304

– my boyfriend of five whole years – ditched me on our wedding day to run off with a bouncy American girl with the name – I kid you not – Candy Moore. That's her actual name, even though it sounds like the kind of thing a stupid spoilt baby would cry out to its parents. Candy! More! If Ajay had gone for someone slightly less annoying, I might have been able to forgive him, but Candy Moore? I mean, seriously? Actually, who am I trying to kid, there isn't a woman in the world he could have wrecked our wedding day for that would have made me not hate his guts or, for that matter, anything and everything associated with *weddings*.

'Sam?' Phil interrupts my thoughts and I realise my eyes have gone glassy with sadness and frustration at the mere memory. See? The slightest mention of the word 'wedding' and I'm a wreck.

'If I wanted a desk ornament, I'd have gone to IKEA,' Phil quips. 'Now are you going to write up that feature or not?'

'No, actually, I'm not,' I reply, raising an eyebrow. 'I think you'll find that I'm a news reporter, not a royal one! You can't just change my job description overnight simply because Ella had to take time off.'

Phil rolls his eyes. 'Are you really doing this? Anyone in your shoes would be over the moon to be asked,' he tells me.

I shrug. 'Well, I'm not.'

Phil sighs loudly. 'Wait a minute.'

He swivels his chair over to Matt's desk so he can read the article on his monitor, editing it line by line at super-fast speed and barking corrections at him, which Matt rapidly fixes, his fingers darting over the keyboard. Matt's cheeks are flushed, his mind working at razor-sharp speed as the adrenalin of breaking the story surges through him. I know that feeling. It's the feeling I chased when I went into journalism; the rush of breaking a story is one of best natural highs. The eagerness to be first, to beat the competition, and deliver your story straight to the public.

It's thrilling. It happened to me a few weeks ago when I published a piece on a gritty political investigation I'd spent weeks working on.

'Right, that'll do,' Phil says, scanning Matt's article one last time. 'Now put it on the site. Just one image. No links. You can add them later.'

Matt nods, his brow glistening with sweat, as he starts pasting the article into the content management system.

'Right.' Phil turns his attention back to me, frowning with irritation. 'Come on, let's discuss this situation in the boardroom,' he sighs, before getting up and striding across the office, not even bothering to look over his shoulder to see if I'm following.

But of course, I am. I hurry after him, struggling to keep up in my pointy heels. I try not to stumble as we cross the newsroom.

Finally, Phil pushes open the door to the boardroom and I manage to grasp it, just before it slams shut in my face.

I push it open and take a seat at the huge mahogany table. Phil is already sitting in one of the plush high-backed seats, leaning back and watching me gather myself. Unlike the newsroom, which is a clutter of Mac computers, stacks of old papers, abandoned press releases and gimmicky products sent in by companies desperate for coverage – from novelty baseball caps to pizza boxes left over from when a high street chain sent us samples of their latest vegan range – the boardroom is slick and minimalistic. It's where the editors meet advertisers, lawyers and senior executives, it's where the mechanics of the paper are determined and its vibe is way more serious than the chaos outside. It's flooded with crisp natural light, unlike the artificial glare of the strip lights in the newsroom, and has tall windows overlooking city office blocks reflecting the crisp morning sunlight off their shining glass exteriors.

'So, what's this all about then?' Phil asks, looking unimpressed.

'You tell me,' I retort, crossing my legs.

'I need someone to cover the royal wedding and you know your stuff, so I chose you. Simple.'

I raise an eyebrow. 'But why me, Phil? Why didn't you line someone else up? There are plenty of other people you could have chosen who also know their stuff. What about Jessica? She'd kill for this gig. Give it to her.'

Aside from Ella, Jessica is the office's resident Royal Family fanatic. She's obsessed, to the point that she drinks her tea from a Royal Coronation mug and her boyfriend proposed with a replica of Princess Diana's engagement ring. Technically, she's an editorial assistant, which means she spends most of her time fact checking, dealing with PRs and handling day-to-day office admin, but I'm sure she could step up to the plate if she were given the chance.

'Jessica?!' Phil frowns. 'We both know she's not ready for this. You, on the other hand, are.'

Phil fixes me with one of his intense looks – a serious, penetrating gaze that cuts right to my core as though he's recognizing my talent. It's one of the looks he used to give me sometimes when I'd done a particularly good piece of work that would drown out the chaos of the newsroom and make me feel like I was important, smart and going places. It's a look I cherished. But now, that look feels all wrong.

I uncross and recross my legs, looking down at the table.

'The problem is ...' I gulp, hating everything about this moment. I'm meant to be a tough go-getting journalist. Vulnerability is not something that comes naturally.

'The problem is I don't think I am up to it,' I admit in a small voice, dragging my eyes up to meet Phil's.

His brow is furrowed. 'You are, Sam. I have every faith in you. It's a big story but you're more than capable. You've been working for me for years, I know you can do this.'

'It's not the work side of it,' I sigh. 'It's the ...'

Phil leans a little closer, resting his forearms on the table. 'It's the...?' He nods encouragingly.

'It's the *wedding* aspect of it all,' I admit, shuddering at the thought of writing wedding stories day in day out.

It's been three years since my car crash of a wedding day, and even now, I'll still cross the road to avoid walking past bridal boutiques. Every time a wedding show comes on TV, you can guarantee I'll be changing the channel quicker than you can say 'divorce'. I have no time for weddings. Not only was my wedding day the worst day of my life, but I no longer see the point of weddings in general. You see, my fiancé Ajay was my dream guy. If I had to write down a list of all the qualities my perfect guy would have, Ajay had them all, and then some. He was clever, handsome, charming, funny, well dressed, cool and successful. He was kind and sweet too, or at least I thought so, before he ditched me overnight for Candy and left me questioning everything, from my own self-worth to my belief in love. After all, if Ajay had ever loved me, how could he have mercilessly stood me up like that, in front of all my friends and family? He could have at least had the decency to end things beforehand, not via a stream of cowardly text messages sent while I was on my way to the church decked out in my wedding regalia. If it wasn't for my best friends picking up the pieces and supporting me back then, I don't know where I'd be.

A few weeks after my wedding day, which we ended up referring to as 'The Day That Shall Not Be Named', we went to a pawnbroker in town, sold the ring (which fetched a surprisingly decent amount for a guy who didn't really love me) and used the money to go on a girls' holiday to Spain, where we lay in the sun, drank cocktails and spent an extremely therapeutic week bitching about men, whilst simultaneously checking out hot Spanish waiters. I came back to London, still a little bruised, but I got back on my feet. I cracked on with work and I moved in with my best friend Collette. Things picked up, but the experience did mark a turning point in my life. Until then, I'd always wanted to settle down, but after The Day That Shall

Not Be Named, I decided that other things were more important, like careers, like having your own home and being
independent. Men come and go, but your career and your
achievements, they stick by you. For example, I was shortlisted
for an Investigative Reporter of the Year award at the National
Press Agency Awards last year and the year before. Being on
that shortlist and knowing I'd worked really hard to get there
was far more fulfilling than any date I've been on recently. Not
that I've been on many.

'Come on, Sam. Think of it as a scoop,' Phil advises.

I sigh. 'I already have plenty of scoops. If it's just a scoop, then
give it to someone else.'

'I don't want to give it to someone else,' Phil insists. 'I want
to give it to you.'

'But why me?' I whine. 'You know how I feel about this.'

Now it's my turn to give Phil one of those pointed looks,
reminding him what the fallout from my wedding was actually
like. There was one afternoon shortly after The Day That Shall
Not Be Named, when I burst into tears at work, and to lift my
spirits, Phil invited me for dinner at his place with his lovely
wife Jill, who cooked up a huge meal with three courses: home-
made bean soup, spaghetti Bolognese and apple pie with ice
cream, served with red wine and a heart-to-heart. Phil saw into
my world that day and I got a glimpse into his: his home life
was so far removed from what I'd expected based on his
no-nonsense exterior. His house was a small but cosy book-lined
terrace with Persian rugs spread over ratty old carpets, rooms
shimmering with Indian wall-hangings and a musty clothes
horse sagging with laundry in the hall. A shaggy dog called
Bruce bounced around and Phil's bookish daughters hugged
him so tight when he got home from work that his eyes sparkled.
It was that day I realised that, despite his bravado, Phil is a
really good egg, and essentially, he's on my side. Sometimes,
even in the midst of the tersest work conversation, I'll catch a

whiff of his musty-smelling shirt and I'll be sent right back to that evening, and the clothes horse, and I'll remember what a softy he is.

'Yes, I do know how you feel about this, and that's another reason you're the right person for the job,' Phil states.

I narrow my eyes at him. 'How does that work?'

'Remember when you first started working here and I made you step in as assistant news editor that time Jeremy went on holiday?' Phil says, reminding me of the two-week holiday cover I took on only a couple months after I started working at the *Daily Post*. It was an opportunity I'd never imagined I'd get as a junior reporter still cutting my teeth and I was a bit out of my depth, but I did my best, and it was those few weeks that gave Phil the confidence to promote me to my current role of politics reporter.

'Yeah...?'

'You freaked out then too. You thought I was throwing you in at the deep end, and yet once you got into it, you excelled.'

'Uh-huh, but how's that the same? I'm not afraid of the professional challenge, I'm afraid of the wedding aspect!'

'Exactly, which is why I'm throwing you in at the deep end. You can't spend your whole life pretending relationships don't exist, Sam. Turning a blind eye to men and marriage isn't healthy,' Phil explains.

I let out a disbelieving laugh. 'Hang on a minute. You're giving me this job so I can confront my fear of weddings?'

'Yes,' Phil admits a little sheepishly. 'Basically.'

'That's not exactly professional,' I point out.

Phil's lips twist and I can tell he's trying not to smile. He clears his throat and corrects his expression.

'It's a professional opportunity that I think would also benefit you in a personal capacity,' he comments, sensing I might be backing him into a corner.

'So, it's professional advancement, you'd say?' I query him.

'Yes.' Phil nods affirmatively.

'More responsibility?'

'Yes, exactly,' Phil remarks.

'Right, well in that case, if you want me to cover the royal wedding, then don't you think I should get a raise?' I ask, trying to act confident even though my stomach is quivering a little.

Ever since I decided to focus on my career since The Day That Shall Not Be Named, I began saving up for a flat: a bricks and mortar home all of my own. I even know the perfect place – it's in this cool converted warehouse by the river. I stumbled upon it on a riverside stroll one day after work. There's a communal garden where you can sit on a bench and watch the boats go by on the Thames; it's peaceful and idyllic yet modern and trendy, and it's only a fifteen-minute walk to work. I cut out a picture of it from an estate agent's brochure and stuck it to a motivational pin board in my bedroom to keep me focused.

'Honestly!' Phil tuts. 'Most people in your shoes would be falling over themselves for this opportunity and you're demanding a raise?' He stares at me incredulously.

'Umm…yes. Like you said, it's more responsibility.'

'If I hadn't already worked with you for years, I'd tell you where to go.'

'Same,' I retort cheekily.

'Fine,' Phil sighs. 'We can work something out, but this wedding coverage better be royal-tastic, Sam. No cutting corners! I want the works.'

He meets my gaze.

'Sure!' I gulp.

'Okay.'

We talk numbers and Phil suggests a reasonably good pay increase that will definitely help me get one step closer to buying my dream home.

'So, are you happy now?' he asks.

'Yes, thanks Phil.'

'Good,' he replies. 'I'll get a new contract drawn up. And, in the meantime, I want that slushy wedding feature. And I want you to make it extra romantic after all of this.'

'No problem,' I trill. 'An extra slushy feature coming right up.'

Phil smiles. 'Finally.'

DIGITAL
HQ

If you enjoyed *When Polly Met Olly*, then why not try another delightfully uplifting romance from HQ Digital?

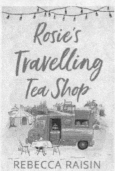

Dear Reader,

Thank you so much for taking the time to read this book – we hope you enjoyed it! If you did, we'd be so appreciative if you left a review.

Here at HQ Digital we are dedicated to publishing fiction that will keep you turning the pages into the early hours. We publish a variety of genres, from heartwarming romance, to thrilling crime and sweeping historical fiction.

To find out more about our books, enter competitions and discover exclusive content, please join our community of readers by following us at:

🐦 @HQDigitalUK

📘 facebook.com/HQDigitalUK

Are you a budding writer? We're also looking for authors to join the HQ Digital family! Please submit your manuscript to:

HQDigital@harpercollins.co.uk.

Hope to hear from you soon!

The next book from Zoe May, *As Luck Would Have It*, is coming later this year!